Perfect
PROPOSALS

MARRY ME

D0306172

Perfect
PROPOSALS
COLLECTION

Perfect
PROPOSALS
WEAR MY RING

Ally
BLARE

Lindsay
ARMSTRONG

Kate
HARDY

March 2016

Perfect
PROPOSALS
BE MY BRIDE

Natalie
ANDERSON

Jessica
STEELE

Kathie
DeNOSKY

April 2016

Perfect
PROPOSALS
MARRY ME

Charlotte
PHILLIPS

Lynne
MARSHALL

Catherine
MANN

May 2016

Perfect
PROPOSALS
JUST SAY YES

Mara Lyn
KELLY

Marion
LENNOX

Ann
MAJOR

June 2016

Perfect
PROPOSALS
MARRY ME

Charlotte   Lynne   Catherine
PHILLIPS MARSHALL MANN

First Published in Great Britain 2016
By Mills & Boon, an imprint of HarperCollins*Publishers*
1 London Bridge Street, London, SE1 9GF

MARRY ME © 2016 Harlequin Books S.A.

The Proposal Plan © 2013 Charlotte Phillips
Single Dad, Nurse Bride © 2007 Lynne Marshall
Millionaire in Command © 2009 Catherine Mann

ISBN: 978-0-263-92154-0

09-0516

THE PROPOSAL PLAN

CHARLOTTE PHILLIPS

Charlotte Phillips has been reading romantic fiction since her teens, and she adores upbeat stories with happy endings. Writing them for Mills & Boon is her dream job. She combines writing with looking after her fabulous husband, two teenagers, a four-year-old and a dachshund. When something has to give, it's usually housework. She lives in Wiltshire.

This book is for Nick, who made me finish it.
With all my love always.

CHAPTER ONE

'WILL YOU…?'

Lucy Telford leaned forward expectantly, mouth slightly open, sea-green eyes wide. So certain was she of how this sentence would end that for a moment she actually thought she'd heard the words 'marry me'. But by the time her brain caught up and performed a reality check, Ed had moved on to describing the cottage for sale on the outskirts of Bath—on which he hoped she would supply the deposit. And it dawned on her to her utter disbelief: it had happened again.

She drove grimly through the quiet streets of the city early the following morning. Apparently the strength of cliché and female experience on her side meant nothing in the face of the male inability to take a hint. It was Valentine's Day, *check*. She was out with her boyfriend of two years, relationship good, *check*. He'd booked her favourite restaurant, bought her favourite flowers and told her he had something special to ask her that evening. *Check, check, check.* What girl wouldn't have expected a marriage proposal given a situation like that? Add in the heavy hints she'd been dropping for at least the last six months. Surely the odds were somewhere approaching dead cert?

She tightened her grip on the steering wheel, her face set, her dark curls even more defiantly springy than usual, reflecting the way she felt. The rest of the evening had passed in an angry red blur. The night hadn't been much better. She'd tossed and turned, alternately hot and throwing the covers off, then freezing cold. Then somewhere around two a solution of sorts had come to her. A way of taking control.

She pulled the car into a roadside space in one of Bath's lovely streets, the golden stone of the Georgian terrace picked out by the winter sunshine. It was a perfect February morning, icy cold but bright. Running her own bakery business had made her accustomed to extremely early starts and she adored the way the city looked when it was still half asleep. It did nothing to distract her today.

Killing the engine, she stalked, as well as she could in trainers, across the pavement and up the stone steps to the three-storey town house of the one person she could moan at unreservedly. The one person who would let her vent her anger, calm her down and give her an objective opinion on what she should do. Childhood friend, adult protector, confidant and big-brother figure, Gabriel Blake was about to kiss his Sunday morning lie-in goodbye.

Gabriel tried mashing one of the pillows over his head and holding it against both ears but the ringing simply faded to a more annoying level. Opening one eye to glance at the bedside clock, he groaned. Seven-thirty.

He only knew one person who got up this early on a Sunday. The ringing continued and he eventually crawled from the bed and staggered half asleep down the stairs, gripping the banister for support. His thick dark hair stood up in crazy sleep spikes and a shadow of stubble defined his strong jaw. He rubbed at his scratchy eyes. By now she had obviously tired of intermittent ringing and was simply keeping the button depressed, resulting in a constant noise that challenged his impending hangover like an ice pick.

He opened the door a crack and, closing his aching eyes against the morning sun, he snarled through the gap. 'Lucy, it's seven-thirty on a Sunday morning. What the hell do you think you're doing?'

'You've got your eyes shut. How did you know it was me?'

'Nobody else I know would dare disturb me at this time of the morning.' He opened one eye and squinted at her. 'Especially on a Sunday.'

She made a move to lean around the front door and see past him into the house, glancing indifferently as she did so at his toned torso and the muscular broad shoulders that were set off by the remains of a tan from his last trip abroad. She'd stayed with him in this house for a while a year or so ago and as a result she had developed a unique immunity to the fact that with no shirt on he looked like a god. Unlike the rest of the female race, to her he just looked like Gabriel. Best friend of some twenty-three years. No romantic attraction involved.

'Is there someone with you?' she asked him bossily. 'Because if there is, get rid of them. This is an emergency.'

He ran a hand through his hair, mussing it more than ever, and tried to think straight. 'There's no one here—it's just me. What do you mean an emergency? Are you OK?'

'I can't discuss it on the doorstep. Let me in!'

He leaned wearily back against the wall and she lost no time in pushing past him like a tornado into the hall. He looked longingly back up the curving stairway in the direction of his bedroom and waved a mental white flag. Now he'd let her in the house there was no way sleep was going to be on the cards. He closed the front door and followed her resignedly to the kitchen to put coffee on.

She turned as he entered the room and he felt a fresh stab of exasperation as he noticed for the first time she was wearing jogging gear. Three-quarter-length running shorts hugged her lean frame, giving away for once the fact that she was fit and toned. She was so tiny that ordinary loose clothes gave her the impression of fragility. Ironic, he sometimes thought, that someone whose life revolved around cake should be so slender. Her dark curls were caught up in a band, but tendrils escaped as usual around her face. The clothes could only mean one thing. She intended to persuade him to go running with her when he still had at least three hours' sleep to catch up on.

On the brink of losing his already frayed temper, he saw just in the nick of time the dark smudges under her green eyes, starkly contrasting with the creamy complexion, and the troubled expression on her face. Unable to feel anything but protective towards her when she was unhappy ever since she was six years old and he was eight, he abandoned his mission to fill the kettle and gave her a hug instead. He couldn't help noticing the stiffness in the muscles of her shoulders even through her clothes, and her hands against his bare skin as they slid around his waist were cold enough to make him jump. Everything about her exuded tension.

'What's up?' He spoke gently over her head, which nestled perfectly just under his chin, coils of her caught-up hair brushing his jaw lightly. Her hair had a lovely lemony scent, making him dimly aware that he could do with a shower. She didn't seem to notice, though, as she made no move to pull away from his chest, and she would normally be the first person to point out if he smelled of last night's curry. 'Tell me it's something serious to justify waking me up before eleven on a Sunday.'

She looked up at him in obvious anguish.

'Oh, God, it's not one of your parents, is it? Are they ill?'

Now she pulled back to arm's length, an expression of incredulity on her face. 'Something happening to either of my nightmare parents doesn't come very high on the serious metre—you of all people should know that.'

'OK, then,' he conceded. 'It obviously *isn't* to do with your wonderful parents.' He ignored Lucy as she made a face. 'But I'm not up to playing guessing games. Come and sit down and tell me what's up.'

Abandoning the coffee, he pulled her by the hand into the sitting room, shoved aside a pile of newspapers and dragged her down next to him on one of the squashy white sofas. She gazed down at her tiny hands, the nails always short and never varnished because that interfered with her baking.

'It's Ed.' One of her hands crept up to her mouth and she chewed on one of the thumbnails distractedly.

'I knew it! What's the idiot done now?' He had no real opinion of Ed. There seemed nothing about him to provoke strong feelings one way or the other. He seemed to treat Lucy well enough and he didn't interfere with their friendship. That was all Gabriel really cared about. She always seemed too focused on building up her bakery business to be serious about anyone.

'It's not what he's done.' She looked at him miserably. 'It's what he hasn't done.'

'I'm not following.'

She sighed. 'We've been together now for, what, two years. It's all going fine, ticking along, you know.' He nodded encouragingly. 'And at Christmas, I thought that was going to be it…'

'What was going to be it?' His head had begun to ache. He wished she'd get to the point.

'When he gave me the necklace. You know, the moon-shaped silver one?' She searched his face. Gabriel had no idea what she was talking about but nodded anyway. 'He handed the box over with this big grand gesture and I thought for sure that was it. I would open it and there would be the ring.' She held a hand out, palm upturned, as if expecting the non-existent ring to materialise there in front of her eyes.

So this was it.

'You mean you thought he was going to propose and it turned out he'd bought you a necklace?' He laughed, feeling an unexpected flash of passing sympathy for

Ed. Women. Sometimes there was no pleasing them. 'Hey, at least he bought you a necklace!'

She threw her hands up in exasperation. 'You're missing the point. What was last night?'

He scratched his head. 'You've got me. Saturday night?'

She shoved him. 'No, you idiot. It was Valentine's Day, wasn't it? Surely you must remember that—the postman probably got a hernia heaving your sackload of cards up the steps.' She looked away and muttered disgustedly almost to herself, 'I can't *believe* you don't remember.'

'Of course, of course, Valentine's Day. I did get a few cards as it happens.' He glanced at the waste-paper bin in the corner, into which he'd dropped all the love-related correspondence of the previous day.

'I don't care about your cards! It was Valentine's Day, and Ed had booked a table at our favourite restaurant, that Italian one, you know. And he'd told me he had something special to discuss with me. And I thought, well…'

Gabriel sighed. He could see where this was heading. 'You thought he was going to propose.'

'Yes.'

'And did he?'

'No! He started going on about this investment opportunity and wondering if I might consider putting some money in. The bakery has been doing pretty well lately…' She trailed off miserably.

Gabriel looked at her, torn between concern for her and amusement. He'd known, of course, that she had a bit of a dream of ending up with the perfect happily ever after. Marriage, two-point-four children and a dog. How could he not know that when they'd been friends for so long? After the insecurities of her childhood it made perfect sense that she would want to build her own secure family in later life. But he'd never seriously considered it would happen in the foreseeable future; she was far too ambitious and engrossed in her growing business. And he'd never for a moment considered Ed as…

As what? Competition? His stomach did a slow and unexpected flip, adding to the hangover symptoms he was gradually developing. Where the hell had that thought come from? *As permanent fixture material,* he corrected himself. He must really need some sleep; he wasn't thinking straight. He put a hand to his head and massaged his temples with his thumb and forefinger. 'Lu, it's just one of those things. He hasn't done this to upset you—he probably hasn't got a clue you feel like this. Did you tell him?'

She shook her head.

'You know what Ed's like. It probably doesn't occur to him that you might like him to propose marriage.' Gabriel didn't particularly consider Ed to be the sharpest knife in the drawer, but, even if he was, mind-reading was likely to be beyond him. 'It doesn't mean he isn't happy, does it?'

She shrugged. He decided to try a more brutal tack. He felt an unexpected compulsion to talk her out of the marriage dream. Nothing to do with disliking Ed. If anything he was completely neutral on that subject. But Lucy was only just approaching thirty. She was far too ambitious to settle down; this would turn out to be one of her temporary crazes. Occasionally she got a mad idea into her head and threw her heart and soul into it, only to tire of it ten minutes later. The only thing she'd ever been totally committed to was creative cookery.

Straight talking was what was needed here. He took a deep breath. 'Look, Lucy, you really need to get over this sudden obsession with settling down, with marriage. Marriage isn't the be-all and end-all of everything these days, you know. Loads of people are happy just dating long term, or maybe moving in together. And don't forget your business has just taken off. Ed probably just thinks there's no rush.' As an afterthought he added, 'And he's right.'

She shook her head vigorously. 'You're not getting it. I know loads of people don't go for marriage these days and that's up to them. But this is about me. And for me moving in together is a cop out. Not enough.'

She looked up at him, her green eyes wide and clear. He felt as if he could see every fleck of colour in them. 'My parents just lived together and one or other of them was always either about to leave, leaving, or left. Maybe if they'd been married they might have taken it all a bit more seriously. Moving in is not enough of a commitment. Not for me. Not deep down.' She made a fist and pressed it against her flat stomach. 'Ed has no excuse. He's more than up for getting married when we discuss it in principle, which we have done *loads* of times.'

Gabriel stood up and started back to the kitchen. He needed coffee and painkillers. Not necessarily in that order. The hangover was kicking in with a vengeance.

She called after him. 'He's quite happy to say of course he wants to get married one day. But when it comes to actually stepping up to the plate and making

it official? Nothing! I've had it up to here!' She indi-
cated a level somewhere above her head. 'I obviously
attract commitment-phobic men. And so that's why I've
come to get your help.'

He stopped in his tracks halfway to the door and
looked back at her dubiously. 'What do you mean, *my*
help? What the hell can I do?'

'You have loads of girlfriends, right? And you're the
most commitment-shy person I know.'

'Well, yes…I mean no.' He tried to work out if there
was a compliment or insult in there and decided there
was probably both. 'How is this relevant?'

'Well, I've decided to take matters into my own
hands,' she said firmly. 'There's no point hanging
around waiting for Ed to get his act together. I'll be
ninety before that happens and my clock is ticking.'

Gabriel pulled a revolted face. 'OK, can we not
talk about the clock-ticking thing? Men don't want to
know about that biological time-bomb stuff. In fact, if
you've mentioned that to Ed, it could be your reason
right there.'

She held up a hand to shut him up. 'Exactly my point.
You can advise me on all this kind of thing.'

He raised his eyebrows at her quizzically.

'Where I'm going wrong, of course. Why he isn't
falling over himself to get a ring on my finger.' She
warmed to her subject. 'You must have a *wealth* of experience just waiting to be tapped. You can show me how
to be totally irresistible to him. And then…' she swept
past him into the kitchen and crashing sounds began
as she started to make the coffee herself '…I'm going
to ask him to marry me. On February twenty-ninth.'

He thought for a moment she might actually be going mad.

'It's a leap year,' she supplied helpfully, as if she had read his mind. 'Women have a chance, no, a *right* to propose to their man on this day, once every four years. And you are going to help me do it in a way which means he will have to say yes!'

Hangover forgotten, he barged into the kitchen behind her. She'd had some crazy ideas in her time, but this...

'No. Absolutely no way.'

'Why not?' She looked up from scrabbling about in the cutlery drawer to give him a petulant frown.

'Because I don't have time to provide you with an insight into the male mind, and, even if I did, it's not right, Lucy. You have to go home, tell Ed how unhappy you are and force the issue.'

'Do you think I haven't tried that?' Her voice began to take on an angry pitch. 'I did all of that at Christmas, he was totally clear on my feelings and gave me the same old rubbish about it "happening one day soon". It's made absolutely zero difference.' She slammed two cups down on the counter so hard he was amazed they didn't break. 'He bought me perfume for my birthday— another missed opportunity right there—and now Valentine's Day. The most romantic day of the year and we spent the evening discussing cash flow for his property development business.'

Gabriel shook a generous mound of instant coffee directly from the jar into his cup. If he was going to survive this conversation he needed all the caffeine he could get. 'Have you considered that maybe he just isn't the right guy?'

Her face twisted and the anger gave way to frustration. 'He *is* the right guy, Gabe. We get on great. He's supportive, he makes me laugh and I love him. He's got his own business like me, so he understands when I disappear on evenings and weekends to finish off wedding cakes...'

None of these things particularly struck Gabriel as evidence of true love—more like plenty of free time to watch football on the weekend and free evenings to go out with his mates.

'Please, Gabe. I'll do the same for you one day.'

'I have absolutely no need of help on how to propose to women, thanks very much.'

'I wasn't suggesting that. I just meant I'd owe you a favour. I know you've denounced commitment since Alison died.' She looked at him uncertainly, and well she might. She knew perfectly well this would touch a nerve.

He felt the usual stab in his chest, where his heart was, he supposed. It was a low blow mentioning Alison. He devoted most of his waking hours to keeping all memory of her locked in a corner of his mind that he never visited. He certainly had no intention of talking about her now. He fixed a neutral expression on his face and grappled for a subject change. Thinking on his feet being one of his strengths, he very quickly found one.

'Now that you mention owing me a favour...' He spun away from her suddenly and grabbed a gilt-edged piece of stiff cream card from beneath a magnet on the fridge. 'Will you come to my law firm dinner with me?' He passed her the card and she scrutinised it.

'You want me to be your date for some work do?' she asked. 'I thought you had them queuing up? Can't that Tabitha go with you? Or is it Agatha? God, I lose track.'

'Tabitha was months ago, keep up. I think you must mean Susan.'

'Who the hell is Susan?'

'It doesn't matter, to be honest. We broke up last week. She was getting a bit full-on.' Unable to find a clean teaspoon in his bombsite of a kitchen, he began to stir his coffee with a fork handle.

'Well, in that case, you should be due to meet someone new…' she consulted her watch with a flourish '…any time right about now. The dinner's in a couple of weeks, so she should be at the perfect point in your relationship. Falling for you, but not yet far enough to scare you into dropping her like a hot potato. Problem solved—you really don't need me. And anyway…' she passed the invitation back to him and picked up her cup '…we're talking about *my* problem, not your logistical dating rubbish.'

He shook his head. 'You don't understand. This is serious. I can't be taking just anyone. It's a big deal, this dinner, all our major clients will be there, and all the partners in the firm. I need a date who isn't too showy and who won't be draped all over me or hanging on my every word. In short, someone who will act the way I ask them to. That's where you come in. Tabitha will be there, too, since she works for us, and things didn't really end well with her.'

She raised her eyebrows. 'Are you for real? You're so

arrogant. Have you ever thought it might be the type of woman you go for that causes the problem? Or maybe, shock-horror, the way you treat them? You never show any interest beyond a couple of dates.'

He shrugged. 'I'm always honest with them. I never give the impression that I want anything serious. It's not normally an issue, but the thing is I've dated a couple of the women at work, women who'll be at the dance. You're well known as just a friend of mine. So no chance of any jealous scenes. No one will feel remotely threatened by you. Problem solved.'

Lucy gave a cynical laugh. 'I wouldn't be convinced of that. Your girlfriends are never my biggest fans. Women are eternally suspicious of the female best friend. You automatically wonder what he's getting from her that he can't get from you.'

Gabriel was mystified. 'No, no. They always say they like you. And they know you're with Ed.'

'They would say that. They're trying to please you. You really could do with my insight, you know.' She sighed. 'But look, I'll make a bargain with you. I will go to the dinner with you and solve your dating problems.'

He grinned triumphantly, but she held up a hand. 'Please, let me finish. On condition that you help me with my proposal plan. I need the male point of view.' She looked at him expectantly. 'Do we have a deal? I thought we could start right away. We could go for a run by the river and discuss some details.' She stood up and did a couple of sample stretches, lunging forward on her slightly built legs.

He watched her in horrified amazement. 'You're insane if you think I'm up to running anywhere. I only got to bed at three.'

Was it just that? He felt an irrational negativity towards the idea of helping her propose to Ed, and crushed it. It must be the hangover. Why should he care if she got married, as long as she was happy? That was all he ever wanted for her, after all. Based on past experience she would be bored with the idea in a couple of weeks, and if he got her to look closely enough at Ed's faults he might even be able to speed it up and everything would get back to normal. Best to just go with the flow for now.

'Let me go back to bed and I'll come round to your place tomorrow night,' he said. 'I'll even bring a bottle of wine. And, though I say it with a measure of dread, *then* you've got a deal.'

CHAPTER TWO

DESPITE Gabriel's protestations that he needed sleep, after Lucy left to go running and he fell gratefully back into bed it totally eluded him. *Lucy getting married.* His mind worried at it like a dog at a bone. It was a given that if she were to propose, Ed would accept. He didn't question that for a second. Any man would be a fool to refuse her. Knowing her as he did, she would storm ahead with the arrangements and be married by the end of the year. Her life would revolve around someone else then. His mind picked at this one thing. Where was the space for their friendship in that?

When she wanted help with anything Gabriel was the one she came to. It had been the same since they were kids. Hell, it had been him who'd found the property that was now her first shop, and persuaded her to move to Bath and expand her successful cake business, which up until then had operated through word of mouth from her own kitchen. He'd even let her live with him rent free for six months while she got the shop off the ground. If something really great or really bad happened to him she was the first person he wanted to tell about it. The great things because he knew she'd get a kick out of them just as he did. The bad things because her effervescent personality always made him feel better, no matter what kind of day he'd had. How did he feel about having someone else step into that role? If he were totally, brutally honest he hated the thought. Sleep was a long time coming.

Three hours later, Lucy was peeling potatoes in her cosy little kitchen when the front door slammed and Ed came into the flat. He gave her a smacking kiss and looked over her shoulder at the pans of vegetables.

'Hi, baby. Smells great.'

'Thanks.'

He was wearing a T-shirt and tracksuit bottoms, hair still slightly damp from the shower. Ed played for a local football team and trained most Sunday mornings. He opened the fridge and took out two beers, holding one out to her. She shook her head.

'No, thanks, I'm fine. How was training?' She didn't mind him playing. It was the one day of the week when she had a relaxed morning to herself. Except for this morning, of course. She felt exasperated still with Ed's insensitivity the night before, but she was doing something about it now, wasn't she? In a couple of weeks' time they would be engaged. She smiled inwardly at the thought.

'OK. Knee's been giving me a bit of grief. Think I'll go and put it up for a bit. Anything I can do?'

'No, no. You go and sit down. I'll just get the potatoes on and then I'll be in.'

When she entered the lounge ten minutes later Ed was sprawled in the armchair, sports channel on the TV, foot resting on the coffee table.

She sat down on the arm of his chair and ruffled his blond hair affectionately. It fell over his forehead and the sideburns were grown long in homage to Ed's music hero Elvis Presley. 'I saw Gabriel this morning. I was going to drag him out jogging but he was hung way over. In the end I went on my own.'

'Hmm.' He didn't avert his gaze from the TV screen.

'He's asked me if I'll go to a dinner dance thing with him. It's a work do.'

Ed glanced up at her.

'Can't he take one of his women? God knows there's enough of them.'

She smiled. 'That's exactly what I said. Apparently he's offended one of his ex-girlfriends and she's going to be there. He needs a neutral date to avoid any grief. It's the weekend after next—you don't mind, do you?'

He took a swig from the bottle of beer. 'No. I'll go out with the lads probably. You go and enjoy yourself. Keep him in check.'

'He's coming round tomorrow night, too. Got a few work issues to discuss, but you'll be out anyway.'

He simply nodded, clearly more attuned to the television than to her. She watched him. There had been a time, once, when they'd first got together, that they would have had a stand-up row at her suggestion she have a night out with Gabriel. The few boyfriends she'd had before Ed had been the same. She didn't blame them. It normally took a good few months before they realised her relationship with Gabriel really was totally platonic and then they quit protesting and questioning her about him. Even so, Ed still couldn't resist the occasional dig, and liked to amuse himself by promoting the view that Gabe took advantage of her friendship when it suited him. But he didn't try to stop her seeing him, and that was all that really mattered to her. She simply rose above the masculine posturing.

After lunch, she watched Ed as he stacked dishes in the dishwasher. This was exactly what she liked so much about being with him. Domesticity. Her mind wandered before she could stop it towards her own childhood home. She had lived with her parents in the tied cottage on Gabriel's family estate. The cottage went with her father's job of groundsman. Anything to do with the upkeep of the manor house and its gardens and outhouses had been his responsibility. And to his credit, she thought, he did a good job for almost the entire time they were there. Until the end when his drinking had more charge of his life than he did himself.

Dragged down with him was her mother, who developed her own drinking problem alongside him, almost in sympathy with him. The rows had become more and more frequent, verbal at first, then at times physical. By the time Lucy was sixteen her mother had left and she was running the house herself as well as managing her own schoolwork. She had kept everything perfectly as if she could somehow bring order to the rest of her life by making the house run smoothly.

Watching Ed now in her tiny kitchen, helping her clear up after eating the meal she had cooked for them both, she felt a warmth deep inside her. She felt totally at ease, relaxed, secure. She wanted that feeling to last and to envelop every aspect of her life. She wanted to start thinking about having children now, a family of her own to look after. It was the logical next step for them, and getting married was the way she wanted to start that journey. She felt excited at the thought of it—a proper family at last.

The following evening, Gabriel was late as usual. *Only in his private life, though,* Lucy thought fondly as she tidied up. He was always impeccably presented, perfectly prepared and absolutely on time when he was working. In fact he was the most professional person she knew, totally reliable and with absolute integrity when he had his lawyer hat on. A rising star in legal circles, he had attained partnership before the age of thirty and his career was going from strength to strength. Unfortunately it never seemed to wrap over to his personal life. He always late and his beautiful house was always a pigsty.

She let him in and he kissed her on the cheek. She caught a whiff of his aftershave, something woody that made her want to breathe in deeply. He marched straight through into her neat little kitchen, grabbed a couple of glasses and rummaged in the drawer for a bottle opener. She followed him in and leaned against the doorway, watching him with amused interest.

'Make yourself at home,' she said teasingly.

He grinned without looking up. 'You're such a creature of habit, Lu. After living with you for six months I could probably find any given kitchen utensil or crockery item in this room without even looking.'

'Steak knife?'

He opened the drawer below the hob and pulled the knife out with a flourish. She liked all sharp items to be close to hob and chopping board.

'Luck!' she protested. 'Olive oil?'

He pointed at the high cupboard on the left. 'In the ingredients and condiments cupboard, of course.'

She didn't have to open the cupboard to know he was right. Everything in her kitchen had order to it. She liked it that way. 'Salad spinner?'

'What the hell is one of those?'

She laughed and he grinned back at her as he uncorked the bottle of wine.

'OK, let's get started.' She took one of the glasses and led the way into her little sitting room. It was neat and tidy. The scented candles she'd lit earlier gave off a delicious warm winter scent of orange and cloves. He followed with the bottle and took the armchair. She settled herself close by on the sofa.

'So, where do you think we should start, then?' she asked him as soon as she was comfortable.

He glanced up at her as he poured the wine.

'Should I ask him on his own, or with all our friends and family there?' She put her head on one side and screwed her nose up, considering. 'Do you think it would be too weird if I bought myself a ring?'

He held up a hand for her to be quiet and she waited impatiently while he took a slug from his glass. 'Firstly, for the record, I want you to know I think this is possibly the most crackpot idea you've ever had. I'm including in that the time when we were kids and you convinced me my mother would be pleased if we repainted the sitting-room door yellow with my finger-paints.'

She laughed and he smiled back at her. He had a heart-melting smile that gradually crept up to his eyes, creasing the corners and giving him a look of intensity.

She always felt he kept that smile just for her. No doubt many other women felt the same, she thought wryly.

'But since you've agreed to watch my back at this wretched work dinner dance,' he went on, 'I will help you.'

She clapped her hands together excitedly.

'But if we do this, we're going to take it seriously and we're going to do it my way. OK?' He looked at her sternly for agreement.

'OK.' She sat on her hands to keep herself from fidgeting, and made herself wait for him to carry on. Once Gabriel had committed to something she knew he would take it totally seriously and wouldn't allow her to sidetrack him with her enthusiasm. It was one of the things she adored about him.

In all the years she'd known him, he'd never let her down. Unlike most of the other main players in her life, she thought, with a pang of regret. The finger-painting memory reminded her of how much she'd loved spending time with him as a child. Gabriel was an only child, just like her, except that his parents were very loving and very wealthy. She hadn't cared about the wealthy part, but she had envied him for the happy, unworried and loving life he had. His family were warm and kind and had always welcomed her. For her the 'big house', as she'd thought of it, had been a refuge from the constant escalating fights in her own home.

Gabriel dragged her back to the present by making an enthusiastic start on his plans. 'OK, there's only two weeks until the twenty-ninth so we need to get our skates on. That means radical plans to make him sit up and take notice of you.' He leaned back a little and looked at her critically. 'I know you, Lucy. You'll be wanting to jump in and plan a massive party culminating with you getting down on one knee. But it's not enough to plan a speech and a big sweeping gesture of a proposal.' He paused for effect. 'For true success you need to get to the bottom of why he doesn't feel he needs to propose to you himself. If we can do that we can change the way he thinks of you and we'll be guaranteed a positive outcome.' He grinned at her across the coffee table.

'How do we do that?' She marvelled at how well he knew her. It was almost spooky. One of the options she'd been secretly considering was a party ending in a firework display. Another was hiring a barbershop quartet to sing the proposal to Ed while she looked smugly on awaiting his resounding 'yes'. Her own enthusiasm could easily overshadow her common sense, which was why Gabriel's calm perspective was exactly what was needed.

'We're going to scrutinise every area of your life,' he said. 'Find out why he needs a rocket lit under him to get him to commit. We'll look at your home life, your social life, your wardrobe, your appearance...' He sat back again for a moment and looked her up and down appraisingly from the extra distance. His slate-grey eyes looked puffy and sleep-starved, but nothing could detract from the strong jawline and determined mouth. *Even when he's tired he looks gorgeous,* she thought. *How unfair. And now he's going to criticise the way I look.*

She pushed her fingers through her curls defensively. 'What's the matter with my appearance?' she demanded.

He leaned forward again to pick up his glass. 'Nothing, sweetie, except that Ed is used to you looking like that. We need to make him see you through fresh eyes and the easiest way to do that is by working on your appearance. I know someone who runs the personal shopping service at Jolly's in town. Leave it to me.'

'Right,' she said dubiously. 'Because if your intention is to boost my ego, let me tell you you're falling way short.'

He ignored her. 'Tell me about your average day.'

'Weekday or weekend?' His businesslike attitude was beginning to tug at the edges of her temper. This was her life they were talking about after all, not some legal transaction.

'Weekday. What do you both do? When do you see each other? How often do you get together?'

'Wow, twenty questions.'

He simply looked at her expectantly, eyebrows raised as if she were a misbehaving toddler, and she spoke quickly before he could admonish her for not taking it seriously. 'Well, I get up early, of course. Usually about five so I can get to the bakery and sort out the stock for the day. So he rarely stays over on a weeknight.'

'So you don't see him during the week except in the evening?'

'Well, no, but he usually rings me every day midmorning,' she said brightly. 'That's if he's not in the middle of something at one of the houses.'

Ed was a property developer. Fed up with his job in IT, he'd given it all up three years ago, just before they'd met in fact, and now spent his time buying run-down shacks and doing them up, then selling them on for profit. It wasn't yet turning out to be the giant money-spinner he always talked it up to be.

Still, early days, she told herself. Give the guy a chance. She liked the fact that he'd thrown himself into building up a business, being his own boss. Taking responsibility for his own success or failure. It was something she could relate to. After all, it had taken her years of hard graft to build up her cake business. They had a lot in common, and that always made for a good, strong relationship, in her opinion.

Gabriel pressed on. 'And how much does he actually do around the house?'

'Plenty.'

'Not good enough. What's his house like? Imagine you're married and living together in this lovely flat.'

She glanced around the perfectly tidy room with satisfaction. She loved her little flat, filled with unusual bits and pieces of furniture that she'd picked up in markets and antique shops. Gabriel had always teased her about it, telling her she was 'nesting'.

'Imagine you go away on holiday or business for a week,' he went on. 'You leave him alone here. Based on what you know of him, what would the place be like when you got back?'

She pulled a face. 'Well, he's not that good on his own, to be honest. He's not really a cook, so he'd probably have lived on pizza and takeaways. The place would most likely look just like his house. A hovel. You'd feel at home in it!' She dodged as he threw a cushion at her.

'I'm not that bad!'

'Your flat is a pigsty, Gabe. Face facts. The only time there's been any semblance of order was when I stayed with you and that's only because I can't live in your kind of squalor.'

'You're not doing yourself any favours here, you know.' He put on a hurt expression. 'Anyway, we're talking about Ed, not me. What else?'

She pursed her mouth, considering. 'There'd be an overload of washing. I'm not sure he knows how to work the machine.'

'Pathetic!'

'And the plants would probably be dead. He never remembers to water them.'

He held up a hand to stop her. 'I think I've heard enough. Basically, Lu, and I'm going to be brutal here…' She looked at him expectantly. He paused dramatically then announced loudly, 'You have become Ed's mother.'

Silence for a moment while this sank in and then she exploded. 'Don't be so ridiculous! You're twisting everything. You make it sound like he's some layabout slob who doesn't lift a finger while I do everything!'

'Sounds about right.'

She stood up, feeling irrationally that it might somehow give her the advantage to be taller than him. 'You're wrong, Gabriel. We're just very different people with different priorities. There must be millions, zillions of couples just like us.'

'I'm sure there are,' he said with calm amusement. 'But what you *think* you have is the traditional "he hunts it, she cooks it" model of relationship. Only trouble is, unless he changes his ways *you* will hunt it *and* cook it because, face it, if you get married to Ed, you are going to be the main breadwinner.'

'That has nothing to do with it!'

'It has everything to do with it!'

Hands on hips, she glared at him angrily.

He held his hands up in a calm-down gesture. 'OK, let's take a different approach. Have you told him about going to the dinner as my date yet?'

'Yes,' she said, relaxing a little at the change of tack. She sat down again. Ed had been more than reasonable when she'd asked him. *Let's see you pick holes in that, Gabriel.*

'And what did he say?'

'He was totally fine about it, as a matter of fact. Didn't bat an eyelid. Even told me to have a good time,' she said triumphantly.

'Oh, dear.' He looked at her sympathetically.

'What now?'

'Well, it's good for me, of course, problem solved for the dinner and dance. But for you…you are being taken for granted! Big time.'

She felt her temper strain madly at its leash. This was rapidly becoming a character assassination of Ed and she wasn't going to take it lying down. 'I don't see that,' she countered coldly. 'Surely it's a positive thing that he's being so reasonable.'

'Aha! That's where you're wrong.' He leaned in close to her suddenly, grabbed her wrist and looked into her eyes. Her stomach made a sudden unexpected flutter and she felt her pulse increase. She ignored it, assuming it must be part of the effort required to keep her temper from flaring. 'Lucy, if I was in a relationship with you, lovely you, I would not let you go on a date with any other guy but me. I wouldn't care whether he was your friend, if he was gay, whatever.'

She looked into his eyes. Clear slate grey filled with nothing but genuine love and concern for her. The pit of her stomach felt warm and soft suddenly, like melting chocolate. She felt the tiny spark of a long-forgotten memory, almost there and then gone again. Her mind felt adrift, as if sand had suddenly shifted below her and she was no longer standing firm. *What the hell is this?* Grappling for self-control, she focused hard on her train of thought.

'He used to be like that when we first met,' she protested in a small voice. 'He couldn't stand the sight of you.'

'There you go.' He released her hand and sat back with a triumphant nod, grabbing his wine glass as he went. She felt an odd sensation of loss and put her hand in her lap to compensate. 'He's got used to the fact that you will always be here, you'll never look at anyone else, no one else will ever look at you...'

'Hey!'

'I'm not criticising you, Lu, I'm just telling you that he's got complacent. He's taking you for granted. No need to make an effort because he counts on you always being here. Stopped working at it, hasn't he? That's the key.' He was nodding his head emphatically.

'What is?' She was rapidly losing the point of this conversation. Hadn't it been to focus on the positives of her relationship? Instead he seemed to be implying that Ed was coasting along and taking her for granted. Just what was going on here?

'He thinks he's got it all sewn up. He doesn't need to propose to you because he's already got you. What we need to do is shake that perception up a bit. Make the ground shake a little bit underneath him. Make him realise how fabulous and gorgeous you are and that he has to work to keep you.'

That sounded a bit more like it. 'OK, so how do we do that, Sherlock?'

'You need to move the goalposts,' he said firmly. 'One of the things you can do is see a bit more of me. Get him to miss you a bit. I'm the winner then, too, because I get to spend a bit more time with you. I've missed you since you moved out.'

The warmth in her stomach bubbled back up again and she took a hefty slug of wine to stop it. That strange sense pervaded her again, of falling backwards in time. She shook her head as if to clear it. Of course, she assured herself firmly, it was perfectly normal to feel nervous and emotional. She was sitting here planning her future, after all.

'Have you?' She'd missed him at first, too, after she'd moved out of his house. It had been lovely seeing him every day for those few months after her arrival in Bath.

'Yes.' He grinned mischievously. 'The house has a more relaxed look about it without your obsessive tidying and I get to keep the remote control to myself. But I kind of miss having a fridge full of proper food and coming home to someone. I liked talking to you every day.'

She took another glug of wine and reminded herself that this was Gabe she was talking to. Her best friend with her best interests at heart. He wouldn't be trying

to assassinate her relationship; he really was only trying to help, which, after all, was what she'd asked him
to do. 'Aww, that's sweet. Bit of a backhanded compliment though. And "relaxed" isn't a word I'd use to describe your hovel. You've got a nerve criticising Ed's
domesticity.'

'This isn't about me, though, is it? And anyway,
backhanded compliments are the best kind. I'm saying I wish you still lived with me despite all your faults.
Not the same as wanting you to change.'

'Hmm, I suppose so,' she said grudgingly.

He refilled her glass, then his own. 'So you agree
on how to proceed? Excellent. Why don't you come to
lunch with my parents this Sunday? They'd love to see
you. They're always asking about you.'

'You mean go back to Gloucestershire?' She felt a
vague sense of unease and squashed it. She generally
avoided going back to her home county, as if the new
life she'd built since leaving would somehow be challenged by revisiting her old one. Her parents were long
gone from there, of course, but the memories wouldn't
be.

'Of course. Sunday roast. Not cooked by you. Sound
tempting?' He grinned at her expectantly.

She debated to herself. She knew she should put an
end to the avoidance of anything relating to her childhood. She was an adult now and could recognise it
for what it was. Maybe going back to Gloucestershire
would do her good—she could lay a few ghosts, and
she had to admit he had a point about Ed. Wasn't absence meant to make the heart grow fonder? They had

fallen into a bit of a rut recently, doing the same things on the same days.

She gave in. 'It does sound tempting. And I suppose you could be right—perhaps Ed needs to miss me a bit.'

'He definitely does. He needs to appreciate you a bit more and feel like he's lucky to have you and he ought to snap you up officially just to make sure. He feels too sure of you, that's the root of the whole thing. And in the meantime, we'll have a look at your appearance and see what we can do with that. And I need to observe you out together socially.'

Lucy looked doubtfully down at her plain T-shirt and jeans with a vague but undeniable feeling of dread at the idea of Gabriel analysing her wardrobe. In an attempt to divert him she latched onto his second suggestion. 'No problem. We're all meeting up tomorrow night at that new wine bar on George Street. You could come along if you like. Do all the observing you want to.'

'Who's we?'

'Ed's friends,' she said. 'Well, mine, too, of course. There's Digger and Yabba, and their other halves, Suzy and Kate. Probably one or two others—it varies depending on who's free.'

'Digger and Yabba,' Gabriel repeated. 'They sound like rejects from some kids' TV show.'

Lucy laughed. 'That's their nicknames. No one in Ed's friendship group is called by their proper name. It's a man thing. Even Ed isn't his real name.'

'You're kidding,' Gabriel said with sudden interest. 'What is his real name?'

'Roland,' she said, expertly ignoring Gabriel as he almost choked on his wine with a sudden snort of laughter. 'Ed is some schoolboy name to do with heading a football or something. I've never questioned it because frankly Roland is awful and Ed suits him far better.'

Gabriel shook his head in mock wonder. 'There's a whole laddish culture going on that seems to have passed me by.'

'You haven't missed much,' she said. 'It might have been vaguely funny once when they were in their teens but there's something a bit sad about having the nickname Yabba when you're pushing thirty and working as a fireman.'

She leaned back on the sofa and looked at him expectantly. 'So what do you think, then?' she asked. 'Do you want to drop in and join us for a drink?'

'Sure,' he said. 'Should be interesting. Are there any single women going?'

She threw her hands up in exasperation. 'For heaven's sake, Gabriel, can't you forget about your next conquest just for one night? Is it too much to ask? You're meant to be concentrating on me and Ed, not chatting up the nearest single woman.'

'I know, I know.' A pause. 'But are there? Any single women going?'

She sighed wearily. 'Well, there's Joanna, I suppose. She's Kate's sister. She's been single for a bit and she's started hanging out with us. But she's been through a horrible break up and the last thing she needs is a three-week dalliance with the likes of you!'

'That hurt!' he protested. 'I just meant it would be nice if I wasn't the only single person there, that's all.'

'Hmm,' she said dubiously. 'I'll believe you. Thousands wouldn't. I take it that means you're coming, then? Eight o'clock at Hardings. I'd tell you not to be late but there would be no point, would there?'

CHAPTER THREE

LUCY glanced at her watch for the third time. Quarter to nine now and still no sign of Gabriel. His habitual lateness never usually bothered her and she was annoyed with herself for letting it get to her this evening. Despite the fact that she'd asked him for help, his negative comments about her relationship with Ed had been getting on her nerves. She'd been looking forward to proving him wrong by showing just how great a time she and Ed had together. Not that tonight seemed to be going that way so far, she admitted to herself. Ed's day hadn't gone well—a structural problem had been picked up at the house he was currently working on and it was going to be costly to have it sorted out. She noticed he'd moved on to whisky from his usual beer and it wasn't even nine yet. Great. Maybe it would be for the best if Gabe didn't turn up after all. The last thing she needed was him to see Ed slowly getting drunk at the opposite end of the table from her. Just how the hell would *that* look?

As if he had somehow read her mind, the door suddenly swung open at the end of the bar and Gabriel sauntered in, absently looking at his mobile phone as he walked, in no rush whatsoever. He glanced up, quickly searched the room and, seeing her, made his way over to their table. She saw out of the corner of her eye Joanna, the only single girl there, sit up imperceptibly as he approached and viewed him herself for a moment with objectivity. He was wearing a dark shirt, open at the neck, quite snug-fitting, which showed off the heavily muscled shoulders and brought out the depth in his grey eyes. Outside the weather was cold with a tinge of fog in the air and the moisture had tousled his dark hair a little. She gave herself a little shake to clear her head and pasted a smile on her face as she got quickly to her feet.

'You came,' she said through slightly gritted teeth. 'Finally.'

'Am I late?' he whispered in her ear as he leaned in to kiss her cheek, and his breath felt warm against her neck. She felt the shivery sensation of goosebumps beginning and moved away from him as quickly as she could.

'No more than usual,' she said, and mustered a more genuine smile before turning to the table. 'Everybody, this is my friend Gabriel. Gabriel, this is Digger and Kate, and Yabba and Suzy. Digger and Yabba play football with Ed.' Nods were exchanged around the table. 'And this is Joanna.' Lucy gestured towards the blonde at the end of the table, who was apparently unable to tear her gaze away from Gabriel. 'And you know Ed, of course.' Ed raised his whisky glass in a perfunctory hello gesture from the other end of the table.

She sat down as Gabriel hooked a spare chair from a nearby table. Fully expecting him to sit next to her, she felt a little piqued as he dragged it two spaces away and sat down between Joanna and Yabba. She was left to continue the conversation with Kate, who was sitting on her left, about the plans she was making for the summer holidays later in the year.

Gabriel lost no time in buying a round of drinks and then quickly immersed himself in quiet conversation with Joanna. Ed was steadily getting drunker at the other end of the table and Lucy sipped her own glass of orange juice defiantly. If this was the way the evening was going to go, with her boyfriend and her best friend both apparently having no need of her to have a good time, she would damn well make the most of her own company.

Time and again her eyes strayed to Gabriel. She found she was able to largely tune out the ongoing conversation with Kate and Suzy, who were planning a shopping trip in the next few weeks, and who invited her along with no real conviction because they were both fully aware that Saturdays were one of the busiest days of the week for the cake shop. The occasional yes or no seemed to maintain her part in the discussion perfectly well. Joanna's curtain of blonde hair swung glossily as she leaned in towards Gabriel. She seemed oblivious to the rest of the table. Lucy felt a stab of annoyance. And she had every right to feel annoyed, she told herself. She'd invited him out after all, to watch her interact with Ed, and yet he'd barely glanced her way even once. Lucy found she was able to make out the occasional snatch of conversation between them.

'…go out for dinner some time…nothing heavy, just a relaxing evening…' she heard Gabriel saying. She picked up her orange juice, trying to keep the smug smile from her face. Same old Gabriel. Get the caveat in up front. No chance of the relationship being any more than a couple of dates, so make it clear from the outset. She noticed the firm set of his jaw at this angle and the way his dark hair curled a little over his collar. He was truly gorgeous. No wonder Joanna was mesmerised. And he certainly seemed to have the gift of making her feel as if she was the only woman in the room for him. Because it didn't appear to matter how often Lucy glanced his way, she might as well have been invisible for all the notice he took of her. She stood up and went to the bar to get another drink, deliberately ignoring them as she passed. Why should she care if Gabriel chatted up yet another woman? It wasn't as if it were anything she hadn't seen before, after all. She picked up the menu at the bar and looked through the fat-laden snack list. If this was going to be a long and extremely dull evening, she'd need something to get her through.

Lucy checked her watch. Six forty-five. They'd only been jogging for five minutes and already she was flagging. She'd had hardly any sleep, tossing and turning half the night, unable to switch off. When she'd eventually dropped off at about three it had felt as if her alarm had gone off ten minutes later. Her head ached horribly. Gabriel seemed as fresh as a daisy however, despite the fact it was so early in the morning. She wondered if he'd be seeing Joanna again and mentally slapped herself down. It was nothing to do with her and she absolutely didn't care.

'So what conclusions did you get from last night, Relationship Guru?' she panted, more to bring her mind back on task than because she really wanted to speak.

Gabriel glanced sideways at her and then slowed to a stop. There was a bench a short way off and he slowed her down too by grabbing her arm, then pointed at the bench as they approached it. 'Let's sit down for a bit, shall we? You look beat.'

She was too out of breath to argue, and frankly the idea of sitting down for a few minutes sounded wonderful. She followed him to the bench and they sat down and gazed out across the still river. The early morning was fresh and cold and she could see her breath, the clouds from her mouth diminishing slowly as her breathing recovered from the run. Gabriel opened a bottle of water and handed it to her.

'It was an interesting evening,' he began.

'I'm surprised you noticed anything that went on between Ed and me,' she grumbled. 'You spent the entire time trying to prise Joanna's phone number out of her.'

'Just setting up my cover,' he protested with a grin. 'Don't want Ed to work out there's something going on, do you? Don't you think he would have wondered what the hell was going on if I'd spent the entire evening watching the two of you interact? Not that you really did,' he added pointedly.

'Hmm,' she said, unconvinced. 'What are your conclusions, then? Tell me there was a point to it all.'

'Of course there was a point to it. I spent a couple of very useful hours observing you and Ed, and what I saw confirmed what I already thought.'

'Which was…?'

'The reason it doesn't occur to Ed to propose to you

is because it won't give him anything more than he already has. Except perhaps a large bill for wedding costs.'

Lucy groaned. 'Frankly I was expecting something a bit more insightful than that.'

'I can give you insights. That was just the concise version.' He took a swig from his bottle of water and glanced at his watch.

'Go on, then.'

'OK…' He stood back up and began stretching to keep warm. Lucy made no move to join him. The way her muscles felt this morning a few stretches were going to make no difference. She might as well give up right now and walk home. But not before she'd heard him out.

'First of all, just look at the people you are hanging out with,' he said.

She frowned. 'What about them? I didn't see you moaning last night when you were chatting to Joanna over drinks and nibbles.'

He shook his head at her. 'You're missing the point. They're all settled, aren't they? Well, except for Joanna, but just from a quick conversation with her I can tell she wants to be settled, too. They're all married or about to be married.'

'I see where you're going with this, but you're wrong. Digger and Kate aren't married, they live together—'

'That's only while Kate pushes Digger towards marriage. You can see the pattern with them—it's the same as you and Ed. The only difference is that Digger has actually moved in with her while Ed's hanging on for dear life to his bachelor pad. What I'm trying to say is that marriage is essentially a girl thing. Your average guy has no real drive to get tied down like that. He's quite happy to live with his girl without all the trappings.'

'Marriage isn't just about trappings,' she protested. 'It's a commitment. It gives proper, constant stability.'

'Only if you choose to see it that way,' he countered. 'Living together is a commitment, too, you know. You just don't have to spend a fortune on a wedding in order to do it. But that doesn't make it any less significant.'

She shook her head to try and clear it. He always did this—confused the issue so she ended up questioning her own certainties. 'Get to the point!' she snapped.

He took a deep breath, the way he always did when he was going to say something that he knew would provoke her. 'Part of the reason for you wanting to get married is a subconscious desire to fit in with your social group. And Ed will never ask you unless he's painted into a corner, because when you pare it right down, he has nothing to gain over and above what he's already getting from you. He has the freedom to keep his own social life; he has you looking after him from every angle. And the pair of you already fit in with all his mates. Why go and spend a fortune making it official? Eventually he probably thinks he'll ask you to move in with him, but, hey, there's no rush.'

His sideway glance to measure her reaction told her he knew perfectly well that he was making her angry. Her head ached and her brain felt as if it were swathed in cotton wool. She didn't have the energy to explode at him as she normally would. Instead she settled for sharpening her tone.

'To be perfectly honest, Gabe, this amateur psychology rubbish is starting to get on my nerves. All I want is a few pointers. I don't want or need my whole life deconstructed.' She stood up, wincing at the throb in her head at the sudden movement. 'I'm starting to wish I'd never told you about any of this.'

He shrugged. 'No problem, Lu. I thought you wanted my help, and I'm not going to just tell you stuff you want to hear. That's not how I work. I'll give you my opinion and then it's up to you how you act on it. But what I'm saying is, if you change nothing about your relationship, if you carry on playing the part of a wife before you actually *are* one, then don't expect Ed to propose to you any time soon.'

'I don't expect him to propose any time soon. I'm going to propose to him. Isn't that the whole point of this?'

'Of course. But don't you think it makes sense to work out why he hasn't taken the bull by the horns himself? Then you can make changes that keep him on his toes and stop him taking you for granted. You have to admit that would be a good thing for your relationship. He doesn't seem to feel like he has to make any effort with you at the moment, does he? I mean, just look at him last night, sulking into his whisky glass at the end of the table. I'd be surprised if he said more than ten sentences to you all night. Why does he think it's OK to treat you like that? He might have had a bad day, but that's no excuse. I'll tell you why—it's because you let him think it's OK.'

She looked at his serious expression. The problem with her friendship with Gabriel was that their usual sparring was self-perpetuating. She heard herself talk to him sometimes and thought she really was just arguing for argument's sake because she never wanted to be the one that gave in. She couldn't fail to see that he had a point and she would be an idiot not to accept it. Too tired to keep bickering, she sighed. 'OK, OK, I'll admit I can see where you're coming from.'

To his credit Gabriel obviously knew her well enough to restrain himself from making any gesture or sound of triumph, simply nodding in agreement, and so she felt able to continue calmly rather than taking the plunge back into the row that any crowing on his part would have provoked. 'Where do we go from here, then?' she asked. 'I'm putting myself in your hands.'

He began jogging lightly on the spot. 'Well, the next logical step is your appearance, of course. We've covered your social life, we've looked at the way you react and respond around Ed. Now, you need to make him sit up and take notice. We start with how you look and then we move on to the way you behave. Right?'

'Right,' she repeated, with more conviction than she felt.

'Good,' he said in a businesslike tone. 'Then as you're obviously desperate to quit running you can go home now. Meet me on Thursday night in the city centre.'

Her heart sank.

Lucy locked the door of the cake shop behind her and listened until the alarm system finished beeping and set itself before heading to her battered yellow Mini car. It was already dark outside and she cursed the car's next-to-useless heater, which roasted her right foot but left the rest of her freezing cold as she made her way through the steady traffic into the main city centre. Towards the shops. The knot in her stomach wouldn't go away. She didn't like clothes shopping and applauded the ascent of the Internet, where she could buy what she wanted online in the comfort of her own sitting room, a cup of coffee to hand, and send back anything she didn't like. She had aspirations to extend her cake business one day to encompass online shopping.

Sighing to herself as she parked, she realised that if she wanted to keep expanding her business then the cash investment that seemed so important to Ed wasn't likely to be a reality any time soon. Still, Ed would understand that, she was sure. He was as steady as a rock, one of the things that attracted her to him. Not unpredictable or headstrong. *Not like Gabriel at all,* she thought unexpectedly, and frowned. She had no place thinking that, she admonished herself. It was of no consequence to her how Gabriel differed from Ed; she wasn't one of his endless stream of girlfriends, thank goodness. She had no idea how they put up with him, not knowing if he would be there for the next date or not. She easily silenced the small voice at the back of her mind that protested that unpredictable was a million times more interesting and exciting than steady. It was also a million times less safe.

It was Thursday night, late-night shopping in Bath, and Gabriel had 'called in a favour', as he described it, and organised a personal shopping session for Lucy. Not necessarily to buy anything, he had placated her when she'd raised a frugal eyebrow—Gabriel had expensive tastes and she really didn't need that kind of encouragement. But to try on a few new things and look at the kind of thing men apparently liked their women to wear. According to Gabriel this was a world apart from what women *thought* men liked them to wear.

'A subtle distinction, but by the end of today I think you will agree an important one,' he said confidently as he led the way into the heart of the city on foot, having parked the Aston Martin close enough to her Mini to make it look shabbier than ever. Bath looked beautiful in the dark, lights from the shops brightening the cobbled side streets. 'A few changes and it could kick-start your relationship. Ed won't know what's hit him.'

'I've never had any complaints before,' Lucy pointed out. 'In fact, Ed's really good about complimenting me on my appearance. He always notices when I get my hair cut. He likes the way I look.'

Gabriel nodded admiringly. 'He's got his head screwed on, I'll give him that. Always stick to the rule.'

'What rule?'

'You know, if you can't say anything good, then don't say anything. She always looks beautiful, especially in the morning, and if she ever asks you if something makes her look big the answer is always no.'

'Even if it does?'

'Especially if it does.'

Lucy stared at him. 'Is there really this underlying theme of men playing some kind of game with us or are you just messing about?'

She sounded shocked and he slowed his pace to a stroll and looked at her with a grin. 'Maybe I'm overstating it a bit,' he said. Then he raised an eyebrow as he apparently debated the question to himself. 'Though not that much. There *is* something of an unwritten rule for men.'

She looked at him quizzically.

'You learn about it as you go along. It's not worth the grief sometimes to be brutally honest so you tell her what she wants to hear and then enjoy your quiet life. Men don't notice what women wear half as much as other women do.'

'In that case what the hell is the point of us being here?' God, he could be exasperating at times.

'Because we want Ed to sit up and take notice, don't we? Look at you through fresh eyes. And the easiest way to make a man do a double take is with your appearance, right?'

Gabriel dragged her by the arm into the beautiful old building that housed Jolly's department store. Designer and high street in one vast place, with chandeliers and lots of steps up and down to different departments. As they stepped out of the lift and walked into the lusciously carpeted personal shopping suite Lucy was surprised to see him kiss the cheek of the impeccably dressed assistant who greeted them. Surely that was a bit overfamiliar, wasn't it?

'Lucy, this is Amanda,' Gabriel said.

Lucy nodded uncertainly at the perfectly groomed blonde woman in her understated suit and heels.

'Amanda, thanks so much for fitting us in,' he said warmly, and led the way into the suite, walking next to the woman as Lucy lagged a few paces behind them feeling drab in her jeans and sweater. 'Getting married soon, could do with a makeover...' she heard him say and her eyes widened. What a cheek!

Amanda showed them both to a huge squashy leather sofa, and then disappeared through a side door. The moment they were sitting down and she was out of earshot, Lucy elbowed Gabriel hard in the ribs.

'Ow!'

'Serves you right!' she said in an angry stage whisper. 'Could do with a makeover? There's nothing wrong with the way I look!'

'Calm down, Lu.' He held his hands up in mock surrender. 'I'm just keeping her sweet. Just making sure she realises we're not, you know, *together.* Do you have any idea how booked up this place gets? Told you I'd call in a favour. I knew Amanda would squeeze us in, time being of the essence and everything.' He winked at her.

She rolled her eyes skyward in exasperation. 'You mean I'll be getting dress tips from one of your conquests? You must be joking!'

He made an urgent shushing gesture, which infuriated her all the more. 'Keep your voice down! She's not a conquest, since you ask, but she is a friend of a friend and—'

'Oh, great. She just isn't a conquest *yet,* then. Big difference.'

'Will you just chill out? She's excellent at her job and you want to try on some new stuff. Where's the problem?'

She shook her head impatiently at him and then pasted a polite smile on her face as Amanda reappeared with an armful of clothes and began hanging them on a rail at the side of the room.

She threw a glance Lucy's way and smiled. 'Size

eight,' she said. 'Possibly a ten in jeans and definitely petite.' It was a statement, not a question.

Lucy nodded in admiration. 'You're good,' she had to admit.

Amanda came over to the sofa and smiled at them. 'That's what I'm paid for,' she said. 'Follow me, Lucy. I'll pull some things together for you to try and we can get an idea of what suits your body type best and what colours work well for you, that kind of thing.' She shifted her gaze to Gabriel. 'Make yourself comfortable, Gabriel. There'll be some drinks along in a minute.' She flashed him a brilliant smile. Gabriel smiled back at her and stretched out in the corner of the sofa, his arms behind his head.

Lucy followed Amanda into the curtained fitting-room section of the suite. None of the horror of the communal changing room here, thankfully. No desperate shrugging into clothes and deliberately avoiding eye contact with everyone else, all of them doing exactly the same thing. Instead a large, private square room with a clothing rail down one side and a mirror down the other. A much larger bank of mirrors was placed outside, of course, by the sofas, where you could have a three-hundred-sixty-degree view of yourself as you walked around, and where your guest could watch and give you feedback. In her case that meant Gabriel. She felt absurdly shy. It was ridiculous, she told herself. She'd known Gabe all her life practically. And anyway, it shouldn't matter what he thought about how she looked; this was all aimed at Ed, after all. She shrugged out of her plain T-shirt and took the first item off the hanger.

Gabriel surreptitiously got out his smartphone. Not

entirely to check his emails, but also to avoid conversing with Amanda, who drifted back to him on a cloud of her own perfume every time she left Lucy to change into some new item. Attractive as she was, he had no time for a fling right now. Another assistant had briefly appeared and deposited a tray of sparkling wine and nibbles to one side of him.

He looked up at the swish of the curtain as Lucy walked self-consciously out into the centre of the mirrors. She was wearing a long black skirt and a flowing blouse over it with a busy floral print. He could tell just by looking at her that she liked it. Of course she did. It could have been from her own wardrobe.

Amanda was shaking her head. 'Pretty, but it totally drowns your figure, there's no definition there.' She deftly grabbed a handful of blouse and held it against the small of Lucy's back. 'See how much better it would look if it was nipped in at the waist? I'd like to see you in something a bit more eye-catching, too.'

'Amanda's totally right,' Gabriel piped up, and the stylist flushed with pleasure. Two birds with one stone, he congratulated himself. Look interested and keep Amanda on side at the same time.

There was a ratcheting sound as Amanda expertly flipped through the clothes on the rail. 'Something a bit more tailored,' she was saying. 'You're so tiny you just look swamped in these floaty designs.'

Lucy disappeared back behind the curtain. Gabriel absently flipped through an email about a case he'd just taken on. It looked as if it might be more complicated than he'd first thought, he'd better request some more information. Then, glancing briefly back up, he froze, the phone held aloft. When had Lucy got legs like that?

Lucy had a fragile silhouette, making a mockery of the fact that her life revolved around the creation of cakes and pastries. But rather than make her look skinny as loose clothes often did, the scarlet shirt she wore now clung in all the right places. The nipped-in cut showed off her tiny waist and with it she was wearing a pair of figure-hugging black cigarette pants. His mouth felt suddenly dry, as if it were full of sawdust, and he automatically took a swig of the very inferior sparkling wine.

'Those trousers aren't really Lucy's style,' he heard himself say. 'Tell her, Lu, you run a bakery. That kind of thing isn't practical.'

Both women totally ignored him. 'Try them with these, Lucy,' Amanda said. 'More definition and height.'

Lucy stepped into the nude platform heels and he inadvertently pressed 'Send' on the email he'd only half written. The extra height from the shoes made her legs go on for ever. She was looking at him for approval and he floundered to get the words out.

'Very nice,' was the best he could manage.

'Perhaps some evening wear next…' Amanda said and held a gold satin dress up against Lucy. Even on its hanger he could see it fell a good three inches above the knee and his heart lurched involuntarily in his chest.

'That'll never work,' he remarked.

Amanda turned to him in exasperation. 'A bit more positive input wouldn't go amiss, Gabriel. Know a lot about styling someone, do you?'

'It's all because he likes to go out with stereotypes,

Amanda,' Lucy said loudly, making sure Gabriel could hear her. '"Arm candy" is the phrase, I think. He likes his women to wear killer heels and fitted tops and skinny jeans, don't you, Gabe?' she teased him. 'I'm the polar opposite of your type, aren't I? How could I ever look good in something your exes would wear?'

She turned to Amanda. 'I'm not really a woman in Gabriel's eyes,' she said. 'More of a female-yet-one-of-the-lads hybrid.'

'A ladette?' Amanda grinned, glancing smugly at her own very satisfactory feminine reflection in the mirror behind Lucy's.

'Yes, a ladette! Exactly!' Lucy laughed at him from across the room. 'You'd no sooner put me in that dress than you would one of your rugby mates, eh, Gabe?'

'Don't be ridiculous. I just meant it's…well…it's different from the kind of thing you usually wear, that's all.' He struggled to justify himself.

'That's the whole point of a styling session—to push boundaries and try new things so you can emphasise your good points,' Amanda pointed out knowledgably. He was beginning to actively dislike the woman. He couldn't remember the last time he'd felt this uncomfortable in female company.

He was glad when the pair of them disappeared behind the curtain. He hadn't counted on this. He'd expected Lucy to have a fun hour or so trying things on while he did a bit of work. He hadn't banked on Amanda pushing clothes on her that his own girlfriends might wear. His Lucy most certainly did not look like girlfriend material in his head and she shouldn't be looking like it in reality.

The curtain swished back again and she sashayed out towards him, her confidence growing before his eyes. The gold dress flowed against her skin and clung to her every contour. The mirrors made it worse—he could see her from every angle. He tugged at his collar, which suddenly felt unbearably tight, and beads of sweat broke out on his brow. Lucy had curves. She had a tiny waist and long, long legs, and skin that was the colour of double cream. She smiled at him, waiting for an opinion, and all he could feel was shock that she could look so grown-up, so…sexy. He felt a sudden rush of longing deep inside and his face must have given it away because a puzzled expression crossed her face.

'What's wrong? Don't you like it?'

He looked at her face, her eyes wide. His mind whirled. He recognised this feeling of course; he had it all the time. Pretty much whenever an attractive woman came into his field of vision. He just wasn't used to having it about Lucy. In his mind he had her very comfortably pigeonholed as Best Friend, and he'd known her for so long he realised he never even usually noticed how she looked. It seemed the wake-up call planned for Ed was working on him, too.

You're jealous! The thought came from nowhere with the force of a sledgehammer, making him feel dizzy. This was just about Lucy getting married ruining their friendship, wasn't it? *Was it really?* He mentally shook himself, noticing her crestfallen expression, and forced himself to speak.

'You look beautiful, Lu. I love it.'

'You had a weird look on your face.'

'I guess I'm more used to seeing you in T-shirts and jeans.'

'I think it would benefit from some good lingerie,' Amanda interjected, holding up a beautiful black bra and knickers set, adorned with delicate silk and lace. 'What size are you, Lucy?'

Gabriel almost choked on the foul sparkling wine. He had to get out of here. Now.

'I have to, er, make a move,' he blurted out suddenly, holding up his phone like an idiot. 'Urgent. Work thing. Can't be helped. Sorry.' Aware he was now gabbling, he snatched up his jacket to create a diversion.

Lucy looked momentarily surprised, but, delighted as she was with her transformation, her attention was quickly diverted by the clothes Amanda was holding. She walked briefly over to him, the heels emphasising her legs even more. He fought to keep his eyes off them. 'No problem, Gabe, I'll call you later,' she said. She flashed him an excited smile. 'Thanks for organising this—you're such a good mate!' She looked up into his face for a moment and her smile faltered. 'You know, you work too hard. You have dark shadows under your eyes.' She ran a fingertip across his left cheekbone and he felt his skin prickle deliciously as if it might burst into flames at her touch. Her scent, something light and floral, enveloped him. He felt as if his senses were sharpened to a needle point, as if every nerve in his body were standing on end.

Amanda saw him to the lift, leaning in close enough to whisper in his ear. 'Call me,' she said, giving him an inviting smile. He was glad when the metal doors slid shut between them.

He left the store as fast as he could, relishing the fresh air on his burning face as he walked to the car. As he drove home he barely saw the road, barely noticed the other cars or people. One person filled his head. This was a whole different ball game. And he had no idea how he was supposed to play it.

CHAPTER FOUR

'So you went clothes shopping with a woman, what, have you lost your mind?'

Gabriel slung a towel round his neck and took a swig from his water bottle. Playing a couple of games of squash with Joe, a work colleague, he intended to beat the tension out of himself with physical exertion. So far it wasn't working.

He hadn't been able to focus now for two days. Whenever he tried, his mind was invaded by Lucy: how she'd looked, how she smelled, how her skin felt when she held his arm. He couldn't remember a woman making him feel like this since Alison, and even she was now beginning to become a blur. To his dismay it was beginning to dawn on him that the reason he didn't want Lucy to get married had less to do with the impact on their friendship and more to do with the fact she was marrying someone else.

You want her for yourself, his mind whispered, and it seemed he was powerless to crush that thought. When he remembered Alison now his mind seemed to have sideslipped into comparison mode, where her smile was lovely but Lucy's smile made every cell in his body tingle. Alison's blonde hair had been silky and pretty but

Lucy's insane curls made him want to tangle his hands in them and never let go.

'Not in the sense you think,' he panted in reply. He leaned against the wall and towelled the sweat from his face. 'She's going to propose to her boyfriend. There's some kind of leap year thing where women are supposed to be allowed to propose marriage instead of men. I was helping her pick some clothes out.'

To his surprise, Joe nodded. 'My sister did it. She asked her husband to marry her eight years ago on February twenty-ninth. Poor guy didn't stand a chance.'

Gabriel ran his hands distractedly through his hair. 'Thing is, Lucy's a friend. More of a sister really—we grew up together. But watching her showing off in these clothes... I never really noticed before just how stunning she is. Now I can't stop thinking about her. And I'm meant to be helping her plan this proposal to the guy in less than two weeks' time. Right now I feel like I want to knock his head off if he goes anywhere near her.'

Joe stared at him as if he were mad. 'You are kidding me, right? You need to see the new girl in the office. That'll soon get your mind back on track.'

Gabriel buried his face for a moment in the towel. He felt no spark of interest whatsoever in the new girl in the typing pool. But two weeks ago he would have already been dating her. He felt as if his life had been turned upside down.

'Maybe you're right,' he said, more to placate Joe than anything. 'I haven't dated for a few weeks. Every waking moment's been taken up with the Pryor case and this thing with Lucy.'

'Course I am.' Joe clapped him encouragingly on the shoulder as they walked back onto the court. 'Get the proposal out of the way and things will get back to normal. She'll have a wedding to plan and, trust me, you don't want to get within a hundred miles of a woman doing that.'

Gabriel picked up his racket and smacked the squash ball with every ounce of strength he had. The thought of Lucy marrying Ed was beginning to make him feel ill.

'Lucy, darling, you look as beautiful as ever. It's so good to see you.' Gabriel's mother Elizabeth swept Lucy into a tight warm hug, and Lucy momentarily closed her eyes so as to soak up every drop of love in it. She thought for the hundredth time what a lovely person Elizabeth was and felt that age-old pang of childhood jealousy against Gabriel for having such a supportive close family when her own home life had been such a shambles.

'These are for you.' Lucy handed over the white cardboard box she had brought with her. Elizabeth lifted the lid and exclaimed delightedly at the sight of the cake selection inside. Billowing swirls of jewel-coloured meringue nestled alongside delicately decorated cupcakes.

'Lucy, they're marvellous. Although just one of them is more pudding than I normally eat in a week! You are kind. Gabriel's told me all about how well you are doing. We love hearing about the shop—I'm so pleased it's such a success.'

Lucy followed her as she led the way through the cool hallway to the large kitchen at the back of the manor. She met Gabriel's eyes behind his mother's back.

He shrugged apologetically but she shook her head at him and smiled. She adored Elizabeth, and thought it was wonderful to have a mother to whom you could entrust all the tiny details of your life. Her own mother had been totally preoccupied by her own life and problems and Lucy had never been able to confide in her. The kitchen was warm from the Aga with a huge scrubbed wooden table and a kind-faced woman of about fifty preparing the lunch.

'This is Angela,' Elizabeth said. The woman turned from peeling vegetables at the sink and smiled at them. 'Angela's an absolute treasure,' she confided to Lucy as they returned to the sitting room, having deposited the cakes in the kitchen. 'Keeps the house perfect and cooks for us when we need her to. Like today. I'm more than capable of rustling up scrambled eggs for Gordon and myself, but it's such a joy to have someone else cook the more demanding meals now.'

The lunch proved to be delicious, the multitasking Angela serving them all as effortlessly as she had apparently cooked the meal. Lucy realised she was having a wonderful time; she really did feel as if she'd come home. She supposed Gabe must feel like this every time he came—how lucky he was.

'How are your parents, Lucy dear? Do you see much of them?' Lucy felt a stab of embarrassment that Elizabeth knew what a nightmare her mother and father were.

'Not really. Christmas and birthday cards, you know. The occasional phone call.' Exactly the way she wanted it. She had total control now over her own life, the polar opposite to her awful childhood years. 'My mother's in Las Vegas now with her latest husband. Number three.

And my father's up in Birmingham. A friend of his offered him a job. Nothing like the work he did for you,
of course.'

Elizabeth nodded politely.

'Hospital porter, I think he is now,' Lucy added
vaguely. 'It suits me, to be honest, that they've both
moved away. I have my own life now and that's the way
I want it.' She smiled at Elizabeth. 'It's lovely coming
here, though. Reminds me of the fun Gabriel and I had
as kids.' She'd changed the subject swiftly and effortlessly. God knew she'd had enough practice at avoiding
discussing her parents.

After lunch, Gabriel and his father had coffee in the
drawing room, and Elizabeth asked Lucy to accompany
her on a walk in the gardens. They strolled arm in arm.

'It's looking lovely.' Lucy admired the beds and the
well-kept lawn. She could almost see herself and Gabriel kicking the old football around here when they
were little. There were some fantastic trees to climb
on the estate too. She smiled to herself. She'd been
such a tomboy.

'How kind of you to say so, dear. I don't do so much
of it myself these days, of course. Gordon has a man
come in a few times a week in the spring and summer.
Keeps it up together. Less to do in the winter of course.'

They walked on in silence for a moment. Elizabeth
seemed faintly tense and Lucy couldn't help thinking
she'd asked her to come for a walk deliberately so that
they could talk privately. She had no idea why that
might be.

'Is something wrong?' she asked curiously.

Elizabeth smiled at her. 'Not especially, dear. I just

wondered how Gabriel is. I know he tells us he's fine but I can never really get any information out of him. I was hoping you could give me some insight. Do you think he's happy?' She sighed. 'We don't see as much of him as we'd like these days.'

Lucy looked at her in surprise. She'd always thought of Gabriel as very close to his parents.

'Yes, of course he is. He's done so brilliantly at work, you know. He's ahead of his time. He's quite well known in legal circles, I think. And he has an incredibly busy social life.'

Elizabeth didn't miss the implication. 'Still no one special, then.' She sighed again. 'I do worry about him so. When he lost Alison he was still very young. Young enough to start again. She was such a lovely girl, I knew it would take him some time to get over it. But he's never even once brought a girlfriend to meet us since.'

Lucy patted her hand reassuringly, thinking that the word 'lost' just didn't really cover it. It was Elizabeth's shorthand for the fact that Gabriel's first love, his college sweetheart, had died in a car accident the year after they left university. She knew he'd been devastated at the time. But as the years had passed he had never opened up about it beyond the bare facts, not even to her. Eventually he had stopped talking about it altogether and Lucy had taken her cue from him and avoided the subject like the plague for fear of upsetting him. Gabriel behaved as though Alison had never existed at all. Until you took a closer look and realised that he'd simply spent every relationship since making sure nothing like it could ever happen to him again. None of his girlfriends were ever allowed to get close enough for them to mean anything to him. Elizabeth was right: after ten years he really hadn't moved on.

She did her best to be reassuring. 'He'll settle down one day, Elizabeth. I'm sure of it. He just seems…I don't know…happy with the way things are at the moment.'

'You know, Gordon and I always hoped you and he might end up…' Elizabeth spoke wistfully, then quickly pulled herself up short.

Lucy jumped a little, as if she'd taken a whiff of smelling salts. She felt the heat of an unexpected blush creep slowly upwards from her collar and was momentarily flustered. A long-buried memory surfaced and she tried her best to push it back to the depths of her mind from where it had come. The very idea of her having a relationship with Gabriel should be laughable. She was sure Gabe would laugh out loud at the suggestion. She certainly shouldn't be having this reaction. Heart rate increasing, temperature rising. She felt embarrassed and hoped fervently that Elizabeth wouldn't pick up on how agitated she was.

The truth was there had been a time, long ago, when her feelings of friendship for Gabriel had become something more. Only in her mind, of course, never his. She pondered for a moment that you never realised the true value of something until it had gone. She had learned that when Gabriel left for university all those years ago. Up until then he'd been hers. Two years older. Protector. Brother. His mother had a dislike of boarding school, instead sending Gabe to a nearby prep school. Lucy, of course, had gone to the local primary school. Their education was a world apart, just like their houses, their parents, their backgrounds, but none of it had mattered to them. They had remained close despite and, she thought now, perhaps because of their differences. Each was everything the other needed. She had been an antidote to his stuffy school atmosphere and her sense of fun had brought him respite from the intense studying it had demanded. He had been her port in a storm. The rows and upheaval at home had gradually worsened through her teens and she'd found herself relying on him more and more. His reasoned thinking had encouraged her to consider the long term, to believe that it wouldn't be like this for ever, stuck in a village in the middle of nowhere with her warring parents and no means of escape. One day she would have her own life and she would be free.

Gabriel had never been taken away from her until he'd accepted a place to study law at Oxford. Her initial delight for him had given way to a growing, gnawing dread as the day had approached when he would start his first term. She hadn't realised how heavily she'd come to depend on him. She was used to barely a day going by without speaking to him.

She'd missed him painfully, dreadfully, and she'd imagined he must be feeling the same way. Her sense of embarrassment now was rooted in the memory of how in his absence he'd begun to take on more than just the role of friend in her mind. She'd begun to fantasise about them being together as a couple, falling in love, having a future together. On his brief weekend visits home his touch had begun to make her skin tingle and her heart had begun to race when he entered a room. Greedy for his time and attention, she'd hung on his every word.

'I'm sorry, dear.' Elizabeth spoke apologetically, bringing Lucy sharply back to the present. 'It's nothing to do with us, of course. It's simply that, well, I remember the first time he met you, knocking on the front door, only about six you were, looking for your lost kitten. Gabriel must have been about nine. It was that really hot summer.'

She was relieved at the change of subject. This part of memory lane she could cope with. 'Sooty,' she remembered. 'I was beside myself. We'd only just moved in and my mother had let him out before he'd had a chance to get used to the house.'

'Gabriel spent the entire afternoon searching with you, until you found him, remember?'

'He'd just got shut inside one of the outbuildings.' She smiled at the memory. 'I was frantic.'

'All Gabriel wanted to do from that moment on was look after you and make you happy. I've watched him over the years and he's never changed. You've always been so close, I suppose I hoped it might one day become more than just a friendship.'

'We're more like brother and sister really,' Lucy said, firmly, for her own benefit as much as Elizabeth's. She cuddled closer to the old lady. 'I was always so jealous of him when I was little. I wanted to be part of your family, too. I was so happy up here at the big house. And he's always been there for me. He's never once let me down.'

Elizabeth smiled at her. 'How is your young man, dear?' she asked politely. Lucy felt a rush of sudden guilt. Her mind had been full of Gabriel and talking about their shared past had made her feel happy and nostalgic, but also unsettled. She could kick herself for feeling so girly and flustered at the suggestion of them ever being a couple. She hadn't spared a thought for Ed all day. But that didn't necessarily mean she was betraying him, did it? It was just this place, nothing more. Being here was bound to stir up her feelings. Her past here had been so turbulent, it would surely be strange if it didn't evoke strong emotions.

'Ed? He's well, thank you.' She felt a sudden desire to confide in Elizabeth, to affirm to her, and perhaps also to herself, that romantic thoughts in her head were linked only to him and not for a second to Gabriel. 'Between you and me I was hoping we might settle down and get married, but he doesn't seem to take the hint. Gabriel thinks he's lazy and doesn't do enough to look after me, but you know how overprotective he can be.'

Elizabeth sighed. She was quiet for a moment before saying, 'Relationships, Lucy, *good* relationships, don't come along by accident in my experience. You have to work at them. Both of you. One of you doing everything just isn't enough—it has to be a partnership. Gordon and I have had our ups and downs—goodness, we've been married a long time now. But we've always pulled together. He's a pain sometimes but I wouldn't be without him, not for anything.'

Lucy grinned.

'Only you can say if this Ed puts enough effort in. You make sure he's the right one for you. You deserve nothing less.'

Shortly afterwards they returned to the house and Lucy was glad when she and Gabriel left for Bath. Talking to Elizabeth had stirred her mind up far too much for her to relax on the journey home. She sat in silence in the car next to Gabriel, the memory coming unbidden to her in all its clarity of the first time she'd met Alison, and her face flushed with mortification as she remembered the circumstances of that meeting.

If Gabriel had guessed how she was feeling after he left for uni, he never let on, just behaving the way he always did, full of news about his course, his new life and his new friends. Yet her delusions had grown until she'd believed herself to be in love with him. The brotherly hugs he gave her and the occasional holding of her hand she'd begun to construe as reciprocation of her fledgling feelings, and she would lay awake at night thinking about him.

She blushed as she remembered her behaviour. A typical stupid teenage crush, that was what it had been. And she'd come so close to Gabe finding out about it that the memory alone still made her heart hammer and her cheeks burn.

Shortly into Gabriel's second term, his visits home began to dwindle and he was useless at keeping in touch. Lucy phoned him so often that she later realised she must have been becoming a pest. She recalled now that there were many occasions when his housemates had told her he was out. With the benefit of age and maturity she now saw that he was probably fed up with her constant contact and was trying, albeit gently, to avoid her.

Convinced Gabriel would feel the same about her if she could just see him and declare her feelings, she'd decided on impulse to visit him one day, when missing him had all become too much. She remembered gazing out of the window of the bus from the train station and thinking to herself how busy and vibrant Oxford seemed compared to the Cotswold villages she was used to. She remembered the butterflies in her stomach on the bus to his digs as the miles between them fell away…

She grinned as she climbed the steps to his front door, thinking how pleased he would be to see her. She was wearing a new sea-green top, which she knew brought out the colour of her eyes, and she'd spent ages trying to get her hair to behave itself. But the broad smile she'd been unable to keep off her face dwindled as the door opened. Not Gabriel but a slender and impossibly pretty blonde girl.

The girl smiled kindly at Lucy. 'Can I help you?'

Lucy craned to see behind her into the hallway. Maybe she'd got the wrong house. But before she had time to say anything Gabriel himself appeared. He came to the door and suddenly she felt light-headed. She didn't look up into the gorgeous slate-grey eyes and walk into his embrace, the way she'd planned to all the way here. She couldn't tear her eyes away from his arm, which slid easily around the blonde girl's waist as he nestled close enough to her to enable him to see around the door.

'Lucy!' he exclaimed, in obvious surprise. She noticed he didn't let go of the girl as he opened the door wider. Instead he slipped his hand into hers and they surveyed her together. Lucy felt her heart twist in her chest and she swallowed hard to stop the burning sen-

sation that began at the back of her throat. She had to find a way out of this.

　'Surprise!' she said on impulse, weakly shrugging her shoulders. She was agonisingly aware suddenly of how idiotic she must seem to Gabriel just turning up like this unannounced, like some runaway.

　'Lucy, this is a lovely surprise, but does your dad know you're here?' His unintended patronising concern made her face flame with humiliation. She was sixteen after all, not a child.

　Before she could speak, he addressed the blonde girl. 'Ali, this is Lucy.' Lucy couldn't seem to look away from the entwined hands. 'I told you about her. Kind of like my baby sister from back home.'

　Alison smiled at her. 'Hi, Lucy,' she said warmly. 'It's good to meet you. Gabriel's mentioned you a few times. It's nice to put a face to a name.'

　A few times. Gabriel hadn't been out of her thoughts for longer than a few minutes these past weeks, but he clearly hadn't been dwelling on her in the same way.

She was snatched back from her thoughts of the past when Gabriel touched her hand briefly before replacing his on the steering wheel. 'You're quiet, Lu. Everything all right?'

　'Fine. I'm just tired.' Her hand tingled at his touch and she stared down at it. *Oh, what is happening here?* She felt the blush creep up her face, as if Oxford had happened yesterday, and she was grateful that his attention was focused on the road so he wouldn't notice. She remembered that she only managed to stomach an hour or so of seeing the two of them together. Alison was studying medicine and they both had rooms in the shared house. She could see they were besotted with each other. Lucy had been so full of excitement at seeing him, believing him to be unknowingly in love with her, expecting to fall into his arms as it all became clear to him. Well, she'd certainly found him in love, just not with her.

She'd managed to hold it together at the house but she'd sobbed her heart out all the way back to Gloucestershire on the bus and then the train. The only comfort she'd had was that she'd stopped short of making a fool of herself by exposing her feelings to him. *His baby sister.* It stung. She was so hurt and humiliated that her first instinct had been to avoid him completely. She stopped calling him after that. But she quickly realised how stupid she was to think she could cut him from her life. She needed him far too much for that.

So when he'd brought Alison back to the manor she hadn't stayed away. It had crushed her to see how happy he was. It became clear that their relationship was not going to be over quickly. That it was a proper, adult relationship. Alison completed him in a way Lucy never had. They'd been all things to each other for so long and now she wasn't enough for him any more. And she began to see with growing, frightening clarity that there could very easily be no place for her at all in all this. She was totally dispensable in the face of his perfect future with Alison. And under threat of losing him altogether, she'd made a decision. Better to keep him as a friend than to lose him completely from her life because of her own stupid pride.

And so it was that she had played the part of childhood best friend until it became no longer an act and was second nature to her. In the years since she had managed to convince herself that her behaviour had been nothing more than a ridiculous teenage crush, brought on by the sudden gap he had left in her life when he went to university, combined with the worsening hell that was her inescapable home life.

Since that awful moment at sixteen she'd never again allowed herself to consider Gabriel as more than a friend, a brother, but that apparently hadn't stopped his parents doing just that. Thinking about it now made her feel suddenly hot, as if she'd walked into a sauna. Before she could stop herself she was trying the idea for size in her head. Her stomach fluttered and she covered it angrily with her hands. It had been a *crush*. Nothing more.

Then why did you blush when his mother mentioned it? She fought that thought with all her might. She couldn't imagine a circumstance in which she would lay their friendship on the line. Gabriel was useless at relationships; they rarely lasted longer than a month. He just didn't seem to have it in him since Alison died. Lucy's talk today with his mother had highlighted that more strongly than ever. What if they got together and it didn't work out? For the first time since she was sixteen she considered what it would be like to have a life without Gabe in it, and it shocked her to the core now as it had then. She would never allow that to happen.

'Come on up.'

The moment the buzzer sounded as Lucy unlocked the outer door of her building, Gabriel shoved the door open and leapt up the stairs two at a time. The door of her flat was shut, which struck him as a little unusual because she usually left it ajar for him when she buzzed him up. The reason became clear when he gave it a brief double tap.

'You can't come in!' a determined but high voice called out. It was followed by fumbling sounds as the door was opened and Lucy appeared in the gap with an apologetic expression.

'Sorry, Gabe. This one thinks he's Spiderman. I had to keep the door shut in case he wandered out looking for Dr Octopus.'

Opening the door wider, Gabriel saw a small figure dressed in a Spiderman costume standing behind Lucy, who was looking red and flustered. Her unruly hair was even more uncontrollably curly than ever. Unable to stop himself grinning, Gabriel knelt down to one knee so his eyes were level with the mask on the child's face. A pair of alert brown eyes blinked at him through the eyeholes.

'Hello, Spiderman,' he said. 'I'm Lucy's friend, Gabriel.' He held out his hand and the child shook it solemnly.

'Shall we go into the living room?' Lucy said impatiently from above them, and led the way without waiting for a response. 'Steven, I'll put your Fireman Sam DVD on.' As Gabriel caught up with her she added over her shoulder, 'Thank goodness you've arrived. Backup at last!'

It was Monday night. The day after their lunch in Gloucestershire. Gabriel had taken advantage of the car journey home to organise yet another opportunity to spend time with Lucy. At this rate she and Ed would grow apart through lack of contact without his having to do or say anything at all. When Steven was settled in front of the television with a cup of milk, Gabriel joined Lucy in the kitchen. She made them each a mug of coffee and they watched Steven through the open door as he sat perfectly still, his attention focused on the TV screen.

'He's Sophie's boy,' Lucy said. 'You know, she works part-time in the shop?'

Gabriel nodded, continuing to watch the child. 'What's he doing here?'

'Sophie's mum was rushed to hospital this afternoon with chest pains. I think there's some kind of history of heart problems. Sophie is her only family, so I said I'd have Steven overnight while she's at the hospital. He's been here since six.'

'Where's Ed?'

She made an impatient noise and Gabriel glanced at her in surprise. 'He made an early exit to go for extra football training. To be honest he looked pleased to be going. I don't think the prospect of entertaining Steven was his idea of a good time.' She ran a flustered hand through her hair. 'It doesn't matter what I say, he refuses to take the Spiderman suit off. He's going to have to sleep in it at this rate.'

As they watched Steven lifted the mask off his face just enough to fit the rim of his cup of milk underneath it.

'I mean, he's only four,' Lucy said, almost to herself. 'How hard can it be?'

Gabriel burst out laughing. 'For goodness' sake, Lu,

lighten up. Remember when we were kids and you practically lived in that tutu one summer? All kids like dressing up. Just let him get on with it.'

She looked at him crossly. 'I don't mean that, you idiot. I admit it's a bit weird not seeing his face but I actually think the superhero outfit is quite cute. I mean he keeps asking me about his gran and I don't know what to tell him.' She lowered her voice. 'I got the impression it was touch and go and I don't want to give Steven false hope.'

She looked up at him worriedly and he put an arm around her and gave her a reassuring squeeze.

'Don't worry. It'll be OK. We can sit with him together and I'll distract him until bedtime. Then tomorrow Sophie can take over and talk to him.'

She smiled up at him, relieved, and he realised how happy it made him just to help her out with the slightest thing. It always had done, no matter how old they were. He felt protective of her in a way he never had about anyone else.

An hour later Lucy watched from the doorway, her empty coffee mug held against her chest unnoticed. She was totally absorbed by the sight of Gabriel playing with Steven and she couldn't stop herself comparing it with Ed's sharp disappearance when she'd told him Steven would be staying. It hadn't occurred to him that she might need a hand, had it? But Gabriel hadn't batted an eyelid. She realised, in all the years she'd known Gabe, she'd never watched him interact with children before. Not so surprising, she supposed. He was an only child like her, so there were no nieces or nephews to get involved with, and his friends were very much like him. Generally they were single sports-obsessed professionals with no fixed girlfriend. Yet to see him now you'd think Gabriel came into contact with four-year-olds every day of the week. She felt a tug at her heart and shook herself. She had deliberately banished those ridiculous feelings from yesterday's lunch. It was just cold feet about making things permanent with Ed, that was all.

'I'm not really just Lucy's friend, Gabriel, you know,' she heard him telling the child. 'I just let Lucy think that—it's part of my cover. I'm really Sonic Man. I can hear things that happen miles and miles away. That's my super power, just like you can climb walls and spin webs.'

Lucy watched the small dark head looking up at Gabriel. 'My nana's in the hospital,' she heard Steven say in a small voice. 'She got taken away in an ambulance.'

'I know she did,' Gabriel said. 'Lucy told me. Your nana's very ill, Steven, but they're going to do the best they can to make her better. And she's in the best place she possibly could be. There are lots of brilliant doctors there. I'm sure your mum will call soon, so try not to worry, OK?' He smiled at Steven. 'Shall we ask Lucy for a biscuit before you go up to bed?'

Lucy stepped back from the door in the nick of time as Steven pelted through to the kitchen looking less agitated than he had done since he'd arrived. Gabriel followed him and she shot him a grateful smile over Steven's head. He'd made more progress with the child in ten minutes than she'd made in three hours. Steven had refused to say anything to her about his grandmother, however hard she'd tried. She itched to talk to Gabriel about it but made herself wait until Steven was settled in bed. Steven insisted on Gabriel tucking him in, and she made more coffee while she waited for him.

She held one of the mugs out as Gabriel re-entered the room. 'Here you go, Sonic Man. I think you've earned it.'

Gabriel looked mildly embarrassed. He took the mug from her and sat down on the sofa. 'You were listening,' he said.

'It was sweet,' she insisted, smiling at him. 'He's a million times happier now. I know it might be bad news tomorrow but at least he'll get a good night's sleep.' She took a sip of her drink, watching him over the rim of the mug. 'I had no idea you were such a natural with kids.'

A pause. 'Am I?' he said lightly. 'I really hadn't given it a thought.' He seemed to be avoiding meeting her eyes but she wasn't going to be put off that easily. Their recent discussions about her own relationship had made her realise that they never discussed his. Well, she corrected herself, only in terms of her ribbing him about being a playboy and teasing him that he couldn't remember the name of his latest conquest. He never ever talked about how he felt in relation to any of them. She couldn't believe she'd been wondering whether she and Gabe could ever be a couple. Especially when she already had her relationship for life all worked out. Perhaps she should try and encourage him to find someone more permanent, too. As she was his best friend that should be her role, not this mad daydreaming about something that could never and should never happen.

'Yes,' she said pointedly. 'You are. You'd make a

great dad. Don't you ever think about that? About settling down and having a family?' She watched him closely for his reaction.

He stood up and made a move towards the kitchen. 'Got any biscuits or cakes, Lu? I'm starving.'

'In the cupboard behind the door,' she called after him, and waited determinedly until he returned with a handful of biscuits.

He sat down again and ran a hand distractedly through his thick dark hair. 'So, have you given any more thought to how you're going to propose to Ed?' He offered her one of his biscuits with a smile.

She flapped a dismissive hand at him. 'Don't change the subject,' she said purposefully.

'I'm not!' he protested. 'Wasn't your proposal the whole reason for me coming over?'

'Technically, yes, but since you've been relishing pulling my lovelife apart and sticking it under a microscope, I think I deserve to be allowed to question you for a change.' She ignored his frown and carried on. 'I want an answer. Where do you see your future? Do you want a family one day, or do you plan to just cruise on through life rudderless?'

Gabriel gave a cold little laugh. 'I don't want to talk about it, Lucy, so let's just get back on task, shall we?' His grey eyes, normally full of warmth for her, flashed dark and dangerous.

Lucy pretended not to notice how agitated he was becoming. His reluctance to talk only spurred her on. She knew, of course, why he was so on edge. She was skirting around the issue of Alison. But after talking to his mother she couldn't help thinking it would be for his own good if Gabriel did open up about Alison and how he felt. After the embarrassment of that day in Oxford, she hadn't permitted herself the easy luxury of disliking Alison. She couldn't let herself feel jealous because that would be to admit that she cared. Alison had been a sweet and kind person and Lucy had genuinely liked her.

'Don't brush me off like that, Gabe.' She leaned forward in her chair and grabbed his hand impulsively. He looked down at it, concealing his face from her so she couldn't read any emotion. 'Don't you think it's time you let go?' she said gently.

He didn't look up and his voice was mechanically neutral. 'I don't know what you're talking about.' He pulled his hand away from hers and she was suddenly left clutching fresh air. She looked down at her empty fingers and shook her head. No way was she letting this slide now.

'Yes, you do,' she said, firmly and deliberately.

He still didn't look up.

'You forget, Gabriel, that I knew Alison, too,' she said softly, as much to herself as to him. 'She was lovely, Gabe. Women can be really gossipy, you know, really catty sometimes. But not her. And she was never once bothered by me—do you remember that? All your new conquests can't stand you having a female best mate, but Alison just saw me as someone to go shopping with, who she could moan to about your rugby obsession. I can understand why you were so devastated when she died, but do you really think she'd want this? You, the eternal bachelor, never moving on? The Alison I knew would have wanted more for you.'

She paused, wondering if she'd gone too far. *God, Lucy, you never ask him about the girl for nigh on ten years and then put him on the spot. You'll be lucky if he ever speaks to you again. Is that really what you wanted?* For a moment there was silence in the room, and still Gabriel didn't look up at her. He simply stared down at his glass of wine. But then, just as she was wondering if she really should let the subject drop after all, he spoke.

'We talked sometimes about having kids,' he said quietly, almost to himself. She had to strain to pick up on what he was saying because she couldn't see his lips move. 'She always used to say she wanted six. A tribe, she called it.' He uttered a strangled laugh. 'It sounded a good plan to me. I'd always wanted a big family.'

'I never knew that,' Lucy said gently, marvelling that she'd known him most of her life and yet he'd never mentioned it. And worse, she'd never thought to ask him. How shameful that was. 'You never told me.'

'Yeah, well, I didn't want to do any of it without her so there wasn't much point telling you, was there?' he said quietly and glanced up at her for the first time since he'd started talking. His eyes were dry and his voice showed no sign of emotion. Lucy tried to put a finger on how he sounded. *Empty.* He sounded empty.

There was a long pause. Lucy forced herself not to speak, hoping that he would continue. He was looking down at his hands.

'I didn't want to do any of it without Alison,' he said eventually. 'Without her I'd rather not do it at all. I didn't even want to think of having a family, being a husband or a dad, because she was always meant to be part of the deal.'

'And do you still feel like that?' Lucy asked him, biting her lip. For some reason the question seemed incredibly important to her. Out of concern for him, of course, she told herself. Certainly not for her own information. It had no real impact on *her,* after all. She was Gabe's friend, nothing more.

'I don't let myself think about it, so I really wouldn't know.' He glanced up at her for the briefest moment and his expression was one of such suppressed sorrow that she felt her heart constrict inside her chest. Poor Gabriel. So strong and full of life but never really addressing the feelings at the centre of his soul. He'd put his grief in a box ten years ago and thrown away the key. What an absolute tragedy that after all this time he was no closer to moving on and putting what happened to Alison behind him than he had been at the time.

Lucy couldn't bring herself to press him any harder. She decided to ease up, change the subject. *But this is a breakthrough,* she told herself. *Just getting him to discuss it.* She resolved to find a way to help him get over the past and be the complete person she knew he should be. That was what she should be doing, as his friend. That was where her role was in his life. She stood up.

'Tell you what, I'll put some more coffee on.' She smiled at him supportively. 'And then I'll tell you the latest news from Planet Ed. Did I tell you he's bought me Elvis Presley's film collection? As if bombarding me with his music isn't enough, he's decided we can watch them back to back!' She felt the tension in the room lift as Gabriel laughed. She could see he was relieved at the shift in subject. That was enough soul-searching for one night. *But I'm going to bring it up again soon,* she thought. This burial of emotion just wasn't what she wanted for him.

Gabriel let himself into his house on autopilot three hours later. His mind swam. It was the first time he'd discussed Alison with anyone in at least eight years. During that time he'd built a new normality, he'd become so used to sidestepping conversations about her, to avoiding even *thinking* about her, that it had become second nature.

This evening all that had changed. He felt…he struggled to find the correct word…*exposed* was the closest he could get to it. Laid bare. And the person who'd enabled that to happen was the person he was already confused about beyond all reason.

Turning on the lights, he walked purposefully through his sitting room, straight to the desk in the far corner. Opening one of the deep drawers, he rummaged inside it until he found what he was after. He drew out a small book, its slightly rough burgundy cover interrupted by a single word embossed in cream. 'Photos.'

Not allowing himself to pause, he sat down on the nearest chair and rested his fingertips against the cover for a few moments, steeling himself. It had to be six years at least since he'd opened this book. He knew so well what was inside it but he'd deliberately cut those images from his mind. That was why he'd hidden the book away. He didn't want or need tangible reminders of the past; he had enough of a battle keeping the memories inside his head at bay. He gripped the book tighter for a moment, forcing himself to recognise that hiding these reminders from himself was not a healthy way to live.

With a small intake of breath he opened the book and stared down at the first picture before him. A smile touched his lips. Alison with her pale blonde hair smiled back. No tears came to his eyes, no lump constricted his throat. He'd shed all his tears the first year or two after she'd gone. Night after night when sleep refused to give him respite and he was totally immersed in his grief. Now, looking down at the picture, he realised that he *had* moved on in a sense. *Not that Lucy would agree,* he thought wryly. She seemed to believe that serial dating was symptomatic of long-term grief, but she was wrong. He wasn't stuck grieving; he knew that. He'd chosen not to get involved with anyone since because he didn't want to go back to that period of dreadful loss. Not ever again. But the touch of Lucy's hand tonight, the rush of excitement he'd felt when she'd curled her arms around him and kissed him goodbye on the cheek, made him consider for the first time that maybe in denying that closeness with someone he was only living half a life.

For the last ten years his main thought when he met an attractive woman was how many dates it would take to get her into bed. Now perhaps he could begin to contemplate that there could be more to it than that. The only problem was that his inclination to get any closer than that seemed to be conditional on the particular woman he was thinking of. And ever since he'd taken Lucy shopping there had been no one else for him.

He closed the photo album. Was it possible that he'd

had feelings for Lucy even before her recent talk of marriage plans? Perhaps. He just hadn't had any reason to give them any credence before. Why should he, when he already had her friendship without having to take the scary step forward to make it into anything more? Why try to fix something that wasn't broken? But now... Now he wasn't sure if her friendship was enough. And that one thing, he supposed, was the strongest indication that he was ready to move on and put the past behind him. Properly behind him, this time. As a gesture to himself, he deliberately didn't rebury the book in the drawer he never looked inside. Instead he left it on top of the desk, where he could see it any time. Where he would see it, often.

He lay awake into the night knowing that Lucy belonged to someone else. All those things she'd said to him, about moving on, finding someone new and having the family he'd chosen to forget he wanted. She meant finding some other girl. Not her. She already had her happy ever after sorted. And after all this time, was he capable of sustaining a proper long-term relationship? Was it a skill that you had to relearn or did it just come back to you, like swimming or driving? His mind swam with confused feelings. He wasn't about to chance his friendship with Lucy by telling her how he felt. Not when he wasn't even sure himself. And definitely not when their friendship might be the biggest casualty if it all went wrong. Turning over in bed, he resolved to keep his feelings well and truly to himself. Maybe if he did that and kept Lucy at arm's length, these new feelings for her would pass. If he could keep some distance between them until her betrothal to Ed was a done deal, he knew he would never compromise her future and maybe then he could finally move forward properly.

CHAPTER FIVE

GABRIEL did a very efficient job of avoiding Lucy for the next couple of days. This was no mean feat based on the fact that Ed seemed to be paying her more attention. Determined to bury her growing feelings for Gabriel and spurred on by the fact that their plan seemed to be working, she was eager to talk to him about the proposal night and in her usual impatient way bombarded him with phone calls trying to arrange just that.

Eventually, with every moment he spent away from her making him more determined to keep out of her way, he'd even begun to convince himself that his new attraction to her was no more than the result of an off-day. It was the shopping trip, he told himself. He'd just been wrong-footed by being forced to focus on her appearance when he'd never had reason to do that before. Hell, as a kid he'd seen her eating mud, hair all over the place, and as an adult staying with him he'd seen her at her worst. That time she'd drunk too much red wine and had spent the night on the bathroom floor throwing up. She'd looked like death the next morning. No, he told himself, he could brush any mad feelings aside. She was still the same old Lucy, no regard for what time of day it was or whether she was disturbing him, simply ringing him when it suited her.

He picked up the phone one morning at eight, believing she would be too tied up at the bakery to call then, so he would be safe. His heart gave an involuntary lurch as he heard her voice.

'Gabe, anyone would think you've been trying to avoid me. Either that or you should sack your secretary. I've left getting on for half a dozen messages for you.'

He covered the receiver with his hand and took a deep breath. 'Yeah, yeah.' He made a huge effort to sound normal. 'I'm sorry. I've been wrapped up in a case, some major hitches, been in constant meetings. I *have* meant to ring.' Plausible vague lies, exactly what the situation needed. It seemed to work because she didn't appear to have heard him, instead sweeping on with her own stream of consciousness in her usual impatient way.

'Well, never mind. I've got hold of you now. It's Ed!' She couldn't keep the excitement out of her voice.

'What about Ed?' *Walked out? Decided to become a monk? Sadly no.*

'The clothes are working! He noticed my new heels right away.'

He grinned ruefully into the phone. 'Told you.'

'And I keep catching him stealing sneaky glances at me when he thinks I'm not looking. He's much more touchy-feely than usual, too. You're a genius! I should market you to women everywhere!'

Gabe felt a stabbing pain somewhere deep in his gut, not unlike a punch. Miserably he realised this was what jealousy must feel like. It wasn't an emotion he was used to. The women he dated never evoked enough interest for him to be bothered if another man came along. His mind spun. It wasn't just a blip, then. Something he could talk himself out of by using willpower. There really had been a shift in his feelings for her. He rubbed his temples with his thumb and forefinger. Problem was, how the hell did he shift them back to where they were supposed to be? Because it was obvious that Lucy didn't feel the same way. And why should she? He was just good old Gabriel, brother-figure, who was currently masterminding her happy ever after with another guy and who'd apparently just kick-started her relationship.

Wanting to get the conversation over with as quickly as he could, he was uncharacteristically abrupt with her. 'Lucy, I've really got to be somewhere, so can we do this later?'

'I'm sorry! I always forget how busy you are. I think of you as my personal property.'

He felt a surge of happiness at this remark followed swiftly by despair. What the hell was he going to do?

'I just wanted to organise getting together,' she said. 'You know, to talk through my proposal. I've got loads of ideas. Maybe we could make it a lunchtime, though, because Ed's been talking about taking me out to dinner.'

What, every night? he wanted to snarl at her. He shook his head briefly to try and clear it. 'Are you sure you really need me, Lucy? I mean, you sound like you're doing great on your own.'

'Of course I need you.' She sounded puzzled and hurt and he experienced a jolt of guilt. 'I need your views, Gabe. You've helped loads already. I know I haven't been exactly positive about some of your observations, but you know that's just my way. I've taken everything you've said on board.' Then she added cynically, 'Or are you just too busy for friends? Is that it?'

He pulled himself together with a stupendous effort. He was used to his emotions being pretty constant, not this swinging between jealousy, anger and misery. If love was this much grief, he decided he had been thoroughly justified in choosing to give it a miss all this time.

'Don't be silly,' he said, as lightly as he could. 'Like I said, it's just been busy.' He realised he couldn't avoid seeing her. His only hope was to carry on as normal and hope these feelings would just wear off. In fact seeing her might help. Maybe he was building the whole thing up in his mind. 'How about tomorrow?' he suggested. 'I'll meet you at Smith's for a sandwich.'

'Great. Can you make it about two?'

He gritted his teeth in exasperation. 'Do you always have to eat so late? Can't you have lunch at twelve or one like normal people?'

'I can't help it,' she countered. 'Twelve until one is our busiest time at the shop. We need more than one person to make it run properly. If we make it two, I can leave Sophie in charge and not have to rush back.'

'OK, OK, two it is.' There was no point arguing with her.

He replaced the receiver with a feeling of trepidation.

Lucy put the phone down feeling reassured. Her feelings were focused exactly where they should be. It was just a simple matter of keeping your mind in the right place. She'd made a stand to herself by telling Gabriel in no uncertain terms how wonderfully her relationship plans were going. After all, she reasoned, if she focused enough on Ed there wouldn't be time for feelings for anyone else to develop, especially stupid feelings for Gabriel, which could never come to anything. Things with Ed really *did* seem to have been boosted. Surely that was a good sign. She could make Ed sit up and take notice after two years and that had to stand them in good stead for the future. She could even look at these irrational feelings for Gabriel as a test of her love for Ed. If she could get over this then nothing could shake them once they were committed.

She ignored the small voice inside that told her she was just scared of change. Understandable really after the shifting sand of her childhood. Scared of losing Ed and the secure life she'd built with them both in it, where she knew when she went to sleep what would happen when she woke up again. If she wasn't deliriously in love with him, she certainly loved him for the life and stability they had together. Her mother had loved her father with desperate passion and look where it had got her. No, she was certain. Love that lasted was built on a lot more than lust. And she needed Gabriel as a friend to talk to and lean on in times of trouble. *Mess with that, Lucy,* the voice said, *and everything teeters on the precipice. Follow these mad feelings and end up losing Ed, and then after three weeks, or maybe a month if you're lucky, commitment phobic Gabe will be just about ready to quit, and you can lose him, too.* Because it would never be the same between her and

Gabriel again—that was the one thing she knew beyond question. That kind of elephant never left the room.

Plus the fact, she reassured herself, Gabe showed no more sign of reciprocating her feelings now than he had when he was eighteen, so she would most likely make a fool of herself as well. He obviously hadn't given her a second thought this week—she'd had to practically stalk him to get a phone conversation. The best way to put this whole mess behind her would be to direct all her energy at Ed, who she knew loved her and wanted to be with her and who was showing loads more enthusiasm for their relationship than he had in months. She should be making the most of that. Once he'd said yes and they were engaged, everything would be fine, she was sure of it.

It was a perfect winter's day as she walked through the streets from her shop to meet Gabriel at Smith's. This was a quaint little coffee shop in one of the side streets just off the main city centre. She and Gabriel met there often because it was roughly halfway between his office and her shop. The cakes and pastries were always delicious, and Lucy always enjoyed comparing them to those she made in her own bakery. She always judged coffee shops and restaurants by their food; she couldn't seem to stop herself. A dry Danish pastry or a soggy eclair had the instant ability to turn her off an establishment for good. The sun was shining as she walked and the air was crisp and clear. It reminded Lucy of the last day like that, when she'd had lunch at Gabriel's parents' house. She thought of them fondly. Any nostalgia she might have about her childhood had them and their home wrapped up in it.

She wondered sometimes how much further and how much more she might have achieved in life if she'd had an upbringing that hadn't demanded she dive headlong into adult responsibility while she was still in reality just a child. But then on the other hand she was so proud of how far she had come. The fact she'd done it in spite of all that her parents had thrown at her made her achievements all the sweeter.

She allowed herself to think of her parents for a moment. She'd found them creeping into her thoughts more and more frequently these past few days. They had never married, despite the fact it was still really the done thing when she was a child. When things were good and they were getting on sometimes they would talk about it. She remembered her mother even looking at booking the ceremony once and she had been beside herself with excitement. But it never came to anything. It was just forgotten about, never mentioned again. All her schoolfriends had married parents and she had longed to be the same as them. In her child's mind she had built it up to be the answer to all their problems. If only her parents were married they would get along properly and be happy. The fights would stop. Of course as an adult now she knew that wasn't the way things worked. But she still saw marriage as a magical, wonderful thing, a way of cementing a stable relationship. In her mind she knew this wasn't rational, but all the same she had always known she wanted to be married and have a family of her own one day.

She checked her watch and grinned to herself. Late

again. Luckily for her she knew Gabriel well enough by now to simply factor in his lousy timekeeping. She didn't expect him for half an hour after the time agreed. As it was, today he arrived only twenty minutes late, looking tired and a little harassed, she thought, but impeccably dressed as ever in a beautifully cut dark blue suit that made his grey-blue eyes seem more intense than ever. He pulled up a chair next to her.

'Do you want anything to eat?' She picked up the menu and scanned it.

He shook his head. 'I've already eaten, like the rest of the human race. Lunchtime for me was an hour and a half ago.' She wasn't used to him being short with her and she looked at him, puzzled. Had she done something to upset him? As she looked he checked his watch.

'Are you in a rush, Gabe?'

He looked up at her distractedly. 'No, why?'

'No reason,' she said, with a hint of irritation. 'Except that you've only just arrived for our lunch date, but you aren't actually planning to eat anything and now you're acting like you need to leave again.'

As she watched him he seemed to shake himself out of his mood and he smiled at her apologetically. 'Sorry. It's been a bit of a manic week.'

She smiled a little. 'It's OK. You don't seem yourself at the moment. I guess this case is taking it out of you.'

He nodded and that feeling of confusion increased. Her conversations with Gabe were never normally stilted like this. Their usual affectionate bickering was a world away from this distracted style of talking. They were interrupted by the waitress, who took their order, Gabriel pointedly asking only for coffee as she defiantly chose a sandwich with side salad. Silence ensued again when the girl left.

'Right, then,' she said, a little uncertainly, when he didn't speak. 'Let me tell you my plans for proposing to Ed. I need you to be totally honest. Don't spare my feelings.'

He gave an odd little half-smile. 'Are you sure you want my total honesty?'

'Of course.'

'Go on, then.'

He was behaving really strangely. She wondered whether she should just scrap the planned discussion and pester him into talking about whatever was bothering him. After the way he had opened up the other night about Alison, she was tempted to try. But in a public place like this she didn't think he would thank her for digging into his thoughts again. If he didn't want to talk he had a stubborn streak that meant he would first clam up and then get angry. Plus the fact she was determined to keep the whole conversation centred on Ed and lock Gabriel well and truly into the role of supportive friend. She had her own agenda here and the best thing to do was surely press on and not to be diverted.

'OK.' She fished a notebook out of her handbag and ignored his raised eyebrows. Before he had the chance to mock the fact that she had actually put something in writing she began skimming her notes. 'Here's what I'm thinking. Book out our favourite restaurant—you know, the Italian place on the square?'

She glanced up at him. He pulled a dubious face but didn't comment.

'Ask all our best friends to come along and get there

before us. You'd be invited of course—I'd need you there as moral support.' She tapped him pointedly on the arm with her pen. 'Then we arrive at the prearranged time.' Her voice got louder as she warmed to her subject and several people in the café glanced over. She ignored them. 'Of course, he'll realise all his mates are there and wonder what's going on, and I'll get down on one knee and ask him to marry me. Then we can all have a big celebratory meal and have a fantastic evening! What do you think? Does that work from a male point of view? I thought including our friends would be a good move.'

As she spoke his facial expression had become more and more sceptical, but she refused to be silenced and rushed on with her usual enthusiasm. Still, by the end of her description she had to admit she'd been hoping for a bit more encouragement than this, and to be honest it was taking the wind out of her sails a bit.

'OK, you said you wanted me to be honest and I'll tell you what I think,' he told her. 'Just about everything that could be wrong in that scenario, is.'

She looked at him with barely concealed annoyance. 'Why?'

Gabriel sat back and folded his arms. 'Firstly, inviting all his mates along is the worst thing you could do. Basically what you're doing is embarrassing him. No guy wants to be put on the spot like that. You have to realise you're taking over his role by doing this. Taking over the *male* role. He will for ever be ribbed by his mates about being under the thumb. *Your* thumb, to be specific. Trust me, even if your girlfriend is in charge, you want the world to think that *you* are. It's an unwritten rule.'

There seemed to be a whole book of unwritten rules by which the average man lived, according to Gabriel.

'So go on, then, enlighten me,' she said sarcastically. 'What does your average guy want?'

'Well, he wants to feel like he's the one in charge. He chooses when he makes you his wife and he chooses how he does that.' He leaned in conspiratorially as if imparting a great secret, as if he might suddenly be lynched by a gang of average men if he were overheard handing over this information to the other side. 'You're messing with the natural order of things here, Lucy, and you need to tread carefully.'

She bit her tongue as the waitress appeared with their order. As soon as they were alone again she leaned in towards him. 'The natural order of things? I'm talking about proposing to my boyfriend, not time travel, for goodness' sake.'

'I just meant you need to do it in such a way as it makes him feel like he's got the upper hand.'

'You mean, make him think it was his idea all along.'

'Exactly.'

'Well, how the hell is that possible when the words "will you marry me?" are going to be coming out of my mouth and not his?'

'Your approach needs to be different. Submissive. As if you're asking him an enormous favour. You could include that in the words you choose. Maybe say something like, "I would be honoured if you would consider being my husband" or "I feel my life is worth nothing without you."'

Lucy stuck two fingers in her mouth and made vomiting sounds.

Gabriel raised an impatient eyebrow and looked at her as if she were a naughty toddler. 'A little class would be good,' he remarked. 'I don't suggest you take this attitude with him or all you'll end up with is a resounding *"no"*.'

She sighed and rubbed the corners of her eyes wearily with a thumb and forefinger. 'I don't know, Gabe. I'm not sure I want to be his doormat just to get him to agree to marry me. I was thinking he would be delighted to be asked and see it as a massive compliment, not some challenge to his manhood.'

'That's because you're a woman and that's how you'd feel if he proposed to you. Men don't think like you do. How many times do I have to tell you?'

She decided to shift the subject a little. 'OK, well, let's come back to the exact wording of the thing. What about the location? Are you saying it's fine to invite everyone who knows us as long as I portray myself in the subservient role, caveman style, or am I just better off asking him when it's just the two of us?'

'Much as I would be sorry not to witness you playing the role of submissive cavewoman to Ed's captain caveman, you'll have far more chance of success if you ask him on his own. If you invite along those Neanderthal football mates that I met, you'll definitely shoot yourself in the foot. All you'll achieve is to make him feel pushed into a corner. He can't say no to you because a) he can't be seen to be so cruel in public and b) he won't want to scupper what you've set up to be a massive party.'

She shook her head. 'But that's good, isn't it? He will be forced to say yes.'

'But for all the wrong reasons. If you push him into it you are just as likely for him to backpedal the moment the party's over. At best he might resent you for putting him on the spot and that's hardly the best start for a marriage made in heaven, is it?'

She sighed. 'I suppose not.' She sipped her coffee moodily. 'Give me the perfect scenario, then, Einstein, and I'll try and work with that.'

A frown crossed his face and she saw him rearrange his features to hide it. It was so brief that she almost missed it. She couldn't place what it meant, but then apparently it meant nothing because he carried on as before.

'To maximise your chances of a yes, if you're asking the average man to marry you, you need to look hot as hell and you need to do it somewhere quiet without friends or family present, and last but not least you need to do it before you have sex. Definitely not afterwards.'

Lucy almost choked on her coffee. At the mention of sex from Gabe when she felt so mixed up about him she felt a blush creep up slowly from her neck and fought it with all her might. She took a bite of her sandwich to buy time and steady herself, looking down in the hope that the blush would subside and he wouldn't notice. When she felt able she spoke in what she hoped was her normal voice.

'Just as a matter of interest, why not afterwards?' she ventured. 'I would have thought that was the perfect time to do it. When you're all loved up and everything's wonderful.'

Gabriel patted her hand sympathetically and she felt as if electric shocks raced through her fingers at his touch. The thought struck her abruptly that she wasn't sure she could remember a time when she'd jumped like that at Ed's touch, even when they'd first met. She tried to concentrate hard on the conversation.

'Like I keep saying, Lu, you need to start thinking like a man. Before you've had sex you hold all the cards, you have the power, he'll hang on your every word. Afterwards, if you manage to get him to stay awake, anything you say will seem less important to him than going to sleep. It's basic biology.'

Lucy made a disgusted face. 'You lot are emotionally backward,' she complained.

Gabriel laughed out loud. 'We're just different, that's all. If men thought the same way as women Ed would have asked you to marry him months ago. Don't you think that makes life seem dull?'

'No! I think it makes perfect sense!'

Gabriel looked at his watch again and she felt her temper slip a notch.

'Gabe, what is your problem? You seem to be desperate to avoid me at the moment and it's getting on my nerves. Is it too much to ask for you to focus for half an hour on one conversation with me?'

He didn't quite meet her eyes. 'Just busy, you know,' he said vaguely. 'I need to make a move.' He made as if to stand up, then for some reason he clearly thought better of it and sat back down. He looked flustered and uncomfortable and she was on the brink of asking him why when he leaned in unexpectedly and covered her hand with his. Her heart leapt involuntarily inside her chest and her pulse increased.

'Lucy, I really think you should reconsider all this, you know,' he said urgently. Her mouth felt suddenly as dry as sandpaper. Just what was he going to say?

'What do you mean?' She tried her best to keep her voice calm, although she felt oddly as if she might start shaking at any moment.

'I'm your friend, Lucy. I'm going to be totally honest with you. You might not like it but I can't help that.'

Her heartbeat seemed to be getting louder. She could hear it inside her head.

He looked into her eyes. 'I think you want to get married and settle down because you didn't have a settled childhood. You want to build your own little happy ever after. The fact that you're surrounded by Ed's mates in a social circle all playing happy families makes you want it even more. I can understand that, but I think you need to be sure it's what you really want, for the right reasons.'

She looked at him, puzzled. Whatever she'd expected him to say, it wasn't this. 'What exactly are you suggesting?'

He took a deep breath. 'I think you should talk to your parents.'

The words fell on her like rocks. She stood up before she even knew that was what she was going to do. Her chair fell backwards with a clatter at the force of her movement. *How could he?* How hard it had been to start again without them. After the years she'd spent cutting them painfully out of her life. Managing by herself. And he'd been there through all that. All the times he'd backed her up, given her strength in her conviction that it was the right thing to do, that they would hold her back and drag her back down and that she could make a life for herself, she really could. She was suffused by confusion and cold anger.

She wiped her lips with a trembling hand. 'I can't believe you are suggesting I actually talk to them about this. My mother the three-times-wed, most irresponsible, self-centred woman in the universe. My father the lush. Just what the hell makes you think either of them is qualified to advise me on how to successfully live my life?'

'I'm not saying they are. It just seems to me you're so hung up on this dream of two-point-four kids and a dog that you're losing sight of the fact that that doesn't automatically make you happy. This is because of your parents—any amateur psychologist could see that.'

'Even if it is, why is that so wrong? With a childhood like mine I certainly know what I'm *not* going to do and that's pretty much everything they did!' Her temper was completely out of control now and she was distantly aware that she was shouting.

Gabriel kept his voice calm and soothing, but to her it just sounded patronising. 'Lu, you had no security as a kid. That's why you're craving it now.' He opened his mouth to continue but she cut him off.

'You've obviously taken temporary leave of your senses,' she snapped. She snatched her bag from the floor and then rounded on him. 'I asked for your help, Gabriel. Your *help*. All I wanted was some pointers on what might make a guy tick, some ideas on how I might propose in a fun way that Ed would like. I didn't ask for a critique of my life as I know it and I certainly didn't expect the suggestion that I undo all the changes I've made for the better. After everything they put me through. And everything I've done to put it right. You're meant to be my friend. Some friend!'

'Lucy…' His voice was shocked but she ignored it and turned to walk towards the door, leaving him standing at the table looking after her. 'Lucy, wait!'

She turned back towards him, oblivious to the interested stares from the other customers and the silence that had fallen as they turned to watch and listen. 'Just stay away from me!'

The door slammed behind her as she stormed from the café.

CHAPTER SIX

LUCY ignored the ringing telephone and took another batch of cupcakes out of the oven. The little kitchen in her flat was filled with the sweet smell of baking and cooking utensils were balanced on every available surface. Her hair was in an untidy bun on top of her head and the front of her T-shirt was dusted with flour because she couldn't be bothered to put on an apron. A couple of hours since her argument with Gabriel and at last she felt calm and focused. Cooking always did that for her. If she ever needed to think something over she gravitated to the kitchen. A lucky side-effect of her anger seemed to be heightened creativity. Some of her best cake creations had resulted from the most stressful moments in her life.

She glanced up as her mobile phone beeped and vibrated loudly on the counter with a text message, and she leaned across to turn it off with a jam-covered finger. She didn't even need to look at it to know it was Gabriel. He had never been able to stand it for long when they had an argument. She, on the other hand, preferred to keep her distance until she calmed down, and depending on the subject of the argument that could be anything from a few hours to a few days.

What he'd said about her parents had really touched a nerve. Her denial that they had anything to do with her desire to settle down was genuine. After all, she hadn't really interacted with either of them for years now. It hurt, too, that this had come from Gabriel, on whom she had always relied for justification of her actions.

She dripped red food colouring into a bowl of white icing and began to beat it with a wooden spoon. It streaked a lovely shade of pink. She wasn't an idiot. She'd always known she wanted a proper settled family one day. Her childhood had been so difficult it would be some kind of miracle if it hadn't shaped the person she was now. It wasn't so much this that bothered her as Gabriel's implication that what had happened years ago was the *only* reason for a decision she was making now. That getting married was the wrong thing for her to do but that she was incapable of seeing it. Why would he say that? Why was he being so horrible, seeming to try everything in his power to put her off the idea?

She began to deftly spread the icing over some heart-shaped shortbreads. Her childhood did affect her decision because it had contributed to who she was. But the reasons she wanted to get married now were present-day reasons, not past ones. Her age, for example. She knew she wanted children and she was nearly thirty. She wanted to get started on that sooner, not later, and she also knew she wanted to be married beforehand. Her work, her financial security—the business had really gained a foothold now; it was doing exceptionally well, far exceeding her expectations. And of course her relationship. She had been happy with Ed for a good length of time now. She knew his bad habits and she knew she could live with them. He wasn't Mr Perfect, but she honestly believed he was Mr Perfect For Her. He was fundamentally a good man, he was good to her and, very importantly, he supported her business ambitions wholeheartedly, even when she was having success and he was putting up with setbacks. She was just ready to take the next step; it was that simple.

But do you love him, Lucy? Really love him? Yes, she told herself, firmly. That wasn't up for debate. She squashed the nagging little voice that reminded her she didn't feel the same depth of passion for Ed as she once had for Gabriel. She was just a kid back then. She knew now there were different kinds of love, and the kind she needed for the life she wanted was the reliable, constant kind, wasn't it? She refused to let her mind explore what alternative to that there might be.

Yet however hard she tried to stop it her mind kept slipping back to what Gabriel had said. She was unable to brush it aside, put it out of her mind. She worried at it, picked at it. She liked to think she was fully in control of her life now. She was in the driving seat, no one else. *If that's true, then why not talk to your parents and test it?* The idea made her heart beat faster and her palms feel clammy, classic signs of nervousness. Slamming the empty icing bowl into the already-full sink, she finally made the decision that had been lurking at the back of her mind for hours now. The only way to prove to herself that she was really and truly her own person, to prove Gabriel wrong, was to talk to one of them. It would have to be her father, she supposed. She had no idea where her mother was except that it was somewhere in Las Vegas. She had her father's address stashed somewhere and Birmingham was only a few hours away. There was nothing else for it if she was to put the niggling doubts Gabriel had planted behind her.

Gabriel made himself put the telephone down. He'd left three messages now and had sent a couple of texts. She would speak to him when she was ready. She always did. But he couldn't shake the nagging feeling that he'd gone too far this time. He'd gone to meet her intent on encouraging her to follow her plans to settle down with Ed. To play the supportive best friend, just as he always did. Certainly not to betray his true feelings for her. But watching her talking about how she could do her best to persuade another guy to marry her had gradually, minute by minute, become unbearable. Ed took her for granted and patently didn't deserve her. If he did he would have married her ages ago.

Gabriel sighed miserably. He'd lost control. There was no other way to describe it. He'd wanted to try and talk her out of it, question her love for Ed, persuade her she was making a mistake, but he hadn't quite dared. He was too afraid of what she might say, that it would be something he didn't want to hear. And so instead he'd hit her below the belt. He had mentioned her parents for no other reason than to selfishly put a damp cloth over her excitement at the prospect of proposing. In doing so he hadn't considered for a second how she might feel about him throwing her family into the mix. He could kick himself. He'd been there throughout her childhood. He'd dried her tears when she'd run to the manor house to escape the rows. He'd dressed the cuts on her hand that time when she'd hurt herself cleaning up a broken bottle after one of the more physical arguments. She'd been just a kid at the time. What the hell had he been thinking dragging all that back up for her again?

He desperately wanted to go to her and apologise, make things right. But knowing her as well as he did, he knew there was no point trying to force her to talk until she was ready. He had to go to an important client meeting but he found it impossible to follow properly what was said. His mind was consumed by Lucy.

'Would you mind waiting? I won't be long.' Lucy leaned forward and spoke to the taxi driver before climbing out of the cab. She surveyed the house on the opposite side of the street. A tiny nondescript terrace in a nondescript street. She briefly checked the slip of paper in her hand. This was it; this was the place. His place. Her palms felt hot and clammy and she unconsciously rubbed them slowly against her coat as she walked towards the grimy front door. To knock or not to knock, that was the question.

Before she could back out, she raised her knuckles and knocked. Then knocked again, loudly.

He isn't home. Let's just get back to Bath, Lucy. Bad idea.

She banged this time with her fist and, bending to open the letterbox, called out, 'Dad!' for good measure. She could see through it into a dingy-looking hall with a brown carpet.

At last a shuffling sound could be heard and a shadow loomed behind the frosted glass of the front door. She caught her breath as the latch rattled and then as the door swung open her heart began hammering in her chest. And there he was. Old now and grey, with a few days' scruffy growth of white stubble and unkempt clothes. Her father. Not quite what she'd prepared herself for. In her mind she'd built him up to be some kind of monster, but this was the reality. A pitiful, scruffy old man. A stale smell drifted from the hallway behind him.

'Lucinda,' he said in obvious surprise. 'Well, well, well. What are you doing here?'

No endearments. No 'pleased to see you'. Just an indifferent tone. Had she really expected anything else?

'I was in the area,' she said lamely. 'Work…you know. I'm on my way back to the station. I thought I'd drop by and see how you are.'

The eyes looking at her from the heavily lined face were shrewd. 'Ten years long gone, and in all that time nothing more than a card or phone call.'

Lucy looked away with a jolt of embarrassment, and was immediately angry with herself for doing so. What did he expect after the way he'd treated her? By the time she'd finally left he was drunk every night. He'd rarely spoken to her except to hurl insults and she'd been cleaning, cooking, shopping, trying to hold things together. She'd tried to make him get help with his drinking but he'd been sinking in his own self-pity since her mother had left and he had no inclination to find a way out.

Then she'd got a place at catering college. A means of escape. And once she'd left she'd simply kept running, that was all. Instead of going back home when her course finished, she'd rented a tiny flat in Swindon because it was cheap. Working for a pittance in a local restaurant to build up her experience, she'd spent

CHAPTER ONE

THE hair on Rikki Johansen's neck prickled. She chalked it up to internal radar as she always *knew* when a certain doctor came to the orthopedic ward. The fact she had a teeny tiny crush on him was beside the point.

Dr. Dane Hendricks didn't look pleased, and the scowl on his face proved something was wrong. His agitated demeanor flashed a warning, and made her wish she could hide. With his broad shoulders squared, and an IV piggyback in his hand, his intense green eyes scanned the nurses' station for a victim. He hadn't spotted her yet. She ducked her head.

"Which nurse is taking care of room 416?"

Rikki had just started her shift that Thursday morning, and couldn't avoid him. She glanced at her clipboard. Yep, she was the lucky nurse about to get chewed out. Dr. Henricks's no-nonsense glare made her wish she could swap patient assignments with someone…anyone.

"Over here." She nonchalantly raised her hand and pretended to be distracted by more important business, thumbing through a chart. She leaned back in her chair. She was damned if she'd let him know how much he and his demanding, perfectionist ways scared her.

His long strides echoed off the linoleum. Each step closer brought a twinge of dread. Rikki clenched her jaw, preparing for the worst.

He shoved the empty secondary IV under her gaze. "Whose name is that?"

"James Porter?" she read from the small plastic bag. Had she passed the test? She glanced upward into his dead-serious eyes, trying her hardest not to blink.

"Correct. So why did I find this hanging on, Patrick Slausen's IV?"

Uh-oh. She jumped up from her seat, and almost bumped into his chest. He stepped back, training his no-nonsense stare on her.

At 7:15 a.m., not about to start making excuses about how she'd just come on duty and hadn't assessed her patients in room 416 yet, she opted to keep things short and to the point.

"I'll see to this immediately, sir, and write an incident report. Did you notice any adverse reaction from the patient?"

His glower sent a shiver down her spine. She tensed, waiting for the worst.

He adjusted his trendy glasses. "Lucky for you, he's fine." He turned. "I'm going to have a little conversation with your supervisor while you check things out," he said over his shoulder, digging his heels into the lime-tinted floor.

Great. Two months on the job at Los Angeles Mercy Hospital, not even off probation yet, and he was going to complain to her boss about her. What did it matter that it wasn't her fault? She was damned if she'd grovel to the self-assured orthopedic surgeon. She knew how to take a setback. Hell, her whole life had been one challenge after another. He wouldn't get her down.

Not today.

Not tomorrow. That is, if she still had her job tomorrow.

At least the patient was OK. It could be worse.

Though rare, medication errors did happen in hospitals, and as an RN it was her job to see that they didn't. But no one was perfect, and nurses needed to feel it was safe to come forward and admit when they'd made mistakes without losing their jobs. The right thing to do was to immediately report the error to the nursing supervisor, fill out an incident report, and notify the patient's MD. This time Dr. Hendricks had beaten the nursing staff to the task. The outgoing nurse could not have noticed what she'd done. No one did something like this on purpose.

The best line of defense was always to check and double-check medications with the med sheet. Never rush. Allergic reactions from wrong medications could be fatal. Rikki knew that as well as she did her own shoe size.

What had they drummed into her head in nursing school? Check for the right patient, the right drug, the right dose, the right time, the right route, and then do it all again, and again, before giving a patient anything. Obviously the night nurse had been distracted, but that was still no excuse.

Rikki rushed into 416A, to Mr. Slausen, a total hip replacement, and began her head-to-toe assessment while taking vital signs.

"Good morning, gentlemen," she said to both patients. "Get any sleep last night?"

They both grumbled from their day-old whiskered faces something about how the night nurses never left them alone. If she hadn't been so distracted, she'd have teased them to brighten up their day, like she usually did with her patients. *Oh, come on. Those poor night nurses get bored. They have to keep waking you up to give them something to do.* But making a joke was the last thing on her mind this morning.

She noted on the chart that patient Slausen's antibiotic was to be given every six hours. The last dose had been given one hour before her shift had begun. Thank heavens James Porter, his roommate in bed B, was on the same dose of antibiotic for his below-the-knee amputation. The error had been the right drug, the right route, the right time, and the right dose, but the *wrong* patient. A careless mistake. And there was no antibiotic hanging for Mr. Porter, which meant he'd missed a dose. Not acceptable.

She handed Mr. Slausen his bedside Inspirometer after listening to his breath sounds. "Here you go. Deep breathe. See how far you can raise the balls." He'd sounded a little too quiet in his left lung. "Try for the smiley face area. We've got to re-expand your lungs."

She glanced at Mr. Porter, watching and waiting for his turn for vital signs. "Do yours, too. It's very important after surgery." He reluctantly reached for the plastic contraption that bore a silly happy face that elevated to various levels with each deep inhalation. She knew it might be uncomfortable for a post-op patient to do, but it lessened the chance of pneumonia.

Rikki didn't let on anything was wrong but, in her opinion, Dr. Hendricks had every right to be upset.

Janetta Gleason sat quietly while Rikki explained the mix-up with the medicine and the patients. She'd quickly learned she had a friend in her supervisor. Fair and just, Ms. Gleason never jumped to conclusions. The silver-and-black-haired lady smiled with kind gray eyes from behind her cluttered desk. Rikki bet she'd worn that same close-cropped tight Afro hairdo since the 1970s.

"I told Dane…I mean Dr. Hendricks…it wasn't your fault. I told him I'd talk to Rita from nights."

Rikki relaxed and studied a wall filled with pictures of the woman's young grandchildren and thought how one day she wanted to have several children of her own.

"Thanks. I'm not sure he likes new nurses, and that mix-up didn't help matters."

"Yes, well, he does like things just so." She rolled her eyes. "In a perfect world…maybe…"

Rikki handed the incident report across the computer. As she'd listed Dr. Dane Hendricks as first to notice the error, he'd have to sign it. She hoped Janetta would take it to him so she wouldn't have to face him again.

She had her hands full with a fresh hip replacement. Not to mention teaching Mr. Porter and his family how to care for his amputation stump in order to get him fitted for a prosthesis. Then across the hall she had the lady in traction with a fractured pelvis—a very demanding patient who was constantly on the call light. Thank goodness her roommate was more reasonable to deal with. Though that patient's compound fracture of the femur with metal rod placement looked much worse. It resembled Frankenstein's head, with hardware and screws protruding from the flesh, but suspended with traction in a lamb's-wool-lined canvas sling. Not a pretty sight.

The only thing she had to look forward to today was the first-of-the month party in the nursing lounge where they celebrated for anyone who had a birthday. November was her month, and on Saturday she'd turn twenty-six. Being raised in the foster-care system, special days like birthdays sometimes got overlooked. Today at work it was a given, her name was on the cake. For some dumb reason it made her happy.

Janetta read the incident report thoroughly and nodded her head in approval. "I'll pass this information on to Dane and counsel Rita."

"Thank you. Dr. Hendricks is the last person I want to see again today."

"He's actually a very nice man. He's been through a lot the last few years."

"Oh." That had never occurred to her. Hadn't she cornered the market on challenges?

"How are things going with your foster-kid?"

"Brenden is doing great. Thanks for asking. How about you? Have you signed on to replace that empty nest you're sitting on?"

"Actually, I've attended all of the training classes. They assessed my home, made sure I had appropriate space and childcare arrangements, and issued me a license. So I'm good."

"Great. I'll see you in the childcare center soon, then."

"Right. Hey, wasn't it you who transferred here because of our family care center?" Janetta asked, while she nonchalantly signed the paperwork.

Rikki nodded. "Yes. That and the fact Mercy pays better, so I could afford my two-bedroom apartment and still have two dimes to rub together at the end of the month. And the childcare center has been a godsend with Brenden."

"We've always been progressive here, so we finally had to listen to our working mothers."

"Absolutely."

"I only wish they'd had it when I was raising my kids."

"Yeah, but someone had to be the trailblazers."

Janetta laughed. Her smile brightened her eyes. "And I'll finally get to take advantage of it when I start foster-parenting."

"See? There is justice in the world."

Janetta's face grew solemn. Her gaze drifted some-where deep within as if remembering something special. "Since Jackson died, I just feel like I need to give more back to the community." She forced another smile. "You seem to do a lot of that."

"Nah. But every little bit helps."

"And I commend you for volunteering."

"What goes around comes around. You know?"

"Karma?"

"More like the golden rule—do unto others…"

"Whatever your reasons, I'm impressed. Now, get back to work," Janetta said with a kind smile and a swish of her hand. "And don't forget to have some cake, girl!"

Dane knew what he had to do. He stripped off his specially made prescription OR goggles and placed them in the ster-ilization bin. He removed his blue paper cap, mask, and gown, and disposed of them.

An apology was in order.

He scrubbed his hands and threw some water on his face. After standing for three hours during surgery, he needed to shake out his legs. The nursing supervisor, Janetta Gleason, had explained the circumstances of his patient's medication error, and he'd realized he'd accused the wrong nurse.

Emma had had another upset tummy last night, and he'd spent two hours pacing with her in his arms. He knew the girls missed their mother, yet they never talked about her. Instead, they'd take turns with odd little ailments or aches that only a good long hug could cure. Unfortunately for him, too often it was in the middle of the night before his scheduled surgery days.

He loved holding their little sparrow-like bodies—so fragile and innocent. They were the best things to have ever happened to him, and since their birth four years ago, medicine had run a distant second on the priority scale.

He shook his head. Normally, he'd check out his data before leveling a full-on attack at a colleague, but he'd been tired and irritable, and then, damn, he'd found the wrong patient's medicine on his other patient's IV. Was it too much to ask for proper patient care? He'd jumped to conclusions and blasted the wrong nurse as a result. Well, he couldn't let his mistake lie. He slipped on a white coat over his scrubs.

Rikki. Yeah, that was her name.

He and the enchanting little nurse had made eye contact on several occasions on the hospital ward. She'd always offered a friendly though shy smile. He liked her huge brown eyes and glossy, butterscotch-colored hair. Not that he'd spent a lot of time noticing or anything, but she had an enticing piercing—a tiny diamond chip or crystal or something that looked like a sparkly, sexy mole just above her lip. At first he'd thought it was a fake stick-on thing, but over time he'd realized it was always in the same place.

It made him wonder what it would be like to kiss her.

Would he feel it if he pressed his lips to her soft, sexy mouth? What was that about? He'd been too busy to ask anyone out on a date for months, let alone make out. Why think about it now?

He threw more water on his face and headed out the door. *I've been working too damn much.*

As soon as he wrote the post-op orders and notified the surgical patient's family that the knee replacement had been a success, he'd go back to the fourth floor and seek Rikki out. He owed it her to make things right.

Dane glanced at his watch. Too late. She'd already be off duty and he needed to pick up his daughters from childcare and take them for dinner at Grandma's. His apology would have to wait until tomorrow.

Rikki rushed into the blood donor center at Mercy Hospital. She'd promised to donate platelets tonight, a two-hour process, and the lab closed at 7:30 p.m. The teenager from next door, who she occasionally used as a babysitter, had arrived late.

She'd been hydrating herself and taking extra calcium and iron for the last week. She'd avoided analgesics that thinned the blood as a side effect. She knew the hospital's oncology department was always in need of the blood component that played an important role in blood coagulation. Without platelets, many patients wouldn't be able to survive chemotherapy or emergency surgeries.

She'd donated platelets during the first week of her employment when she had been going through orientation and they'd mentioned there was always a shortage in pediatric oncology. Having waited the required fifty-six days, she was ready to donate again, deciding to make it a routine.

Do unto others…her favorite foster-mother had always said.

After filling out the paperwork and being grilled about her sexual history—practically non-existent, thank you very much—she scooted back into the large over-stuffed lounger. She prepared to watch a movie on her one birthday splurge, a portable DVD player, while the nurse started the process.

She knew the drill. Her blood would be collected from one arm, sent through the plateletphoresis machine where the platelets would be removed, and her own blood would be returned to her other arm. She recalled a weird feeling that made her flush all over and gave her a strange metallic taste in her mouth the last time she'd donated. The nurse had told her it was the anticoagulant they used in the machine.

To help pass the time during the long donation that night, she'd chosen her kindest foster-mother's favorite movie, *Monty Python's Holy Grail*. A classic. She knew it was silly, but the two of them had always gotten such a kick out of the film when she was a young teenager. And laughing was good for the soul, the sweet Mrs. Greenspaugh had always said. After a long string of not-so-great foster-homes, she'd finally gotten a break with a terrific older lady. It had come at a perfect time in her life, too. Adele Greenspaugh had taught her to appreciate her individuality, and to love herself.

Unfortunately, she'd died and Rikki had gotten sent to the worst home of her life when she'd been sixteen. All the confidence Mrs. Greenspaugh had built up the "do-good witch" she'd been sent to had torn down. Well, she hadn't broken her spirit, just knocked her off balance and made her a little insecure. The room blurred with a wave of nostalgia and misty eyes for "Addy," the name Mrs. Greenspaugh had insisted Rikki call her. She shook her head and searched for a tissue.

Rikki hadn't done nearly enough laughing in her lifetime, and with good memories and her favorite movie in tow, she'd decided to do some catching up tonight.

Just after the nurse had poked her and started the IV, the donation process began. She settled into her chair, and was about to start the movie.

A familiar voice made her freeze.

Dr Hendricks? She bent her head forward and looked around the donor equipment just enough to see his athletic frame. Pale blue dress shirt, navy slacks with leather belt on a trim waist…really terrific rump… Exactly what he'd been wearing that morning when he'd chewed her out.

What was he doing there? Surely he wasn't a donor. She sat back and tried to become invisible.

Unfortunately, even with several other loungers available, he chose the one right next to hers. Her heart did a quick tap dance, and she held her breath. Why did he make her so anxious?

He nodded at her.

She nodded back, resisting the urge to play with her hair.

Before she knew it, Dr. Hendricks had loosened his tie, unbuttoned his collar, and started rolling up his sleeves.

Rikki reminded herself to breathe.

He glanced at her, and his brow furrowed.

She squirmed, wondering what he was looking at.

"You don't usually wear your hair down at work."

"No. We're not allowed to." She ran jittery fingers

through near waist-length tendrils. Her thick, naturally wavy hair was the one physical feature she was most proud of, but under his scrutiny she doubted even that measured up to his high standards.

"I see," he said, giving no further sign of interest and snuggling back in his chair. "OK, Sheila, hit me with your best shot."

The blood donor nurse smiled. "With veins like yours, I could do it blindfolded."

"Don't get any ideas."

He'd obviously been through this routine before. The ease with which he spoke to people at Mercy Hospital impressed Rikki. She wished she had half of his confidence.

"Well, I gotta tell you, your hair looks a heck of a lot nicer like that than that floppy knot thing you wear at work."

She'd taken a shower and washed her hair after work, and realized that it was almost long enough to cut off and give to Care to Share Your Hair. The organization that made wigs for chemo children required ten inches. Soon she'd have to make an appointment to get it all cut off, but right now it took every bit of control not to preen over his backhanded compliment.

She shot him a mock offended look and caught a sparkle in his playful green eyes. Playful? Dr. Hendricks? Wasn't that an oxymoron? Time stopped for the briefest of moments, and it rattled her.

"Leave her alone," Sheila broke in, and offered a grin to Rikki. "He's just a big tease," she said as she tightened the tourniquet, flicked his vein with her finger and rubbed it with topical disinfectant.

"Well, you should see her, Sheila. Sometimes she sticks pencils in the bun, like chopsticks."

The nurse jabbed him with a large needle. He grimaced. "OK. I get your point. I'll shut up now."

"You should be ashamed of yourself. Rikki? Don't you dare let him do his imitation of Hank Caruthers."

Go, Sheila! Why couldn't she have such poise where Dr. Hendricks was concerned? But, hey, he'd noticed quite a bit about her at work. She fought off a smile.

Sheila finished her job and gathered her equipment to discard. She stopped briefly, growing serious. "How's your brother doing?"

"Things could be better. He's finishing up more chemo, so I wanted to make sure he had plenty of platelets available."

So handsome doctors who seemed to have it all together had brothers with cancer? Her heart tugged. She'd been focused on her own circumstances too much. No one made it through life without challenges, and Dr. Hendricks was no exception.

"I didn't realize your brother had cancer," Rikki said.

"Yeah, well, he's putting up a good fight."

"What kind?"

"Leukemia."

Her hand fisted on the soft rubber ball the nurse had given her to hold throughout the donation process. She forgot to let up, and her knuckles went white.

A few moments of strained silence followed. What else could she possibly say? *I'm sorry?* What did it matter how she felt about his brother having a life-threatening disease? She meant nothing to Dr. Hendricks.

"Has he considered a bone-marrow transplant?"

"He's adopted and no one in our immediate family is a match for him."

"I'm on the National Marrow Donor Registry. Have our lab check it out. I think there's a one in forty thousand chance he'll find a match."

Dane gave her a surprised but pleased glance. "That's a good suggestion. Well, we'll see how this next round of chemo goes."

Rikki gathered he didn't want to discuss the topic any further, and pushed the "play" button to start the DVD—anything to help distract her and chase away the awkward silence.

He stretched his shoulders and popped his neck before settling down.

"My daughters wear shoes just like that. Aren't they called Mary Janes?"

She glanced at her feet. "Yes." She flexed and pointed her toes. She'd spent one entire afternoon looking for her size of the unique shoes on the online auction network.

"I buy them for my girls because they're sturdy and have good support. Why do you wear them?"

"I like them?"

"Why don't those lacy black tights go all the way to your feet?"

How old was he? Didn't he know that leggings were back in? "They're leggings. They're not supposed to."

"I see."

If I don't look at him, maybe he'll leave me alone. She fidgeted with her hair.

"That's an interesting look with your denim skirt."

No luck. She tried not to sigh.

"I think my grandfather used to own an Argyle sweater like the one you're wearing."

Growing more uncomfortable each second with his examination of her style of dress, she tried to divert his attention. "It's the retro look. So, how old are your daughters?"

"Four."

"Both of them?"

"That would make them twins."

"Ah. Right. How nice."

"Nice? It's a nightmare. I mean, what am I supposed to do with two little girls? They want to play house and dress up and have tea parties. What about football? Playing catch?" He scrubbed his face. "Before they grew hair, I'd never tied a bow in my life. Now I'm forced to be a ribbon expert."

Rikki sputtered a laugh. "Can't your wife help?" She glanced at his empty ring finger, but that didn't necessarily mean anything these days. What if she'd said the wrong thing?

His casual expression changed along with the tone of his voice. No longer jovial, he spoke softly. "I'm a single father."

She'd gone and done it again, taken a friendly conversation and ruined it, just like her last foster-mother had told her. *"You always ruin things, Rachel Johansen. Learn to keep your mouth shut. You're lucky to have a place to live."*

She restarted the movie and wished she could disappear.

"What are we watching?" Dr. Hendricks sounded like himself again. Was he giving her a second chance to put her Mary Jane clad foot into her mouth? Well, if he thought her style of dress was strange, he was bound to make fun of her quirky choice in movies.

"*Monty Python*," she mumbled.

He grinned. "Good choice. I see we're members of the same cult."

She looked at him with surprise. He winked, and a quick flutter burst across her chest. Positive the simple gesture hadn't meant anything to him, she wished she could resist his charm half as easily.

Nurse Sheila came by and checked both of their arms. "Are these IVs OK for you two?"

Rikki nodded and smiled.

Dr. Hendricks glanced at one of his arms. "'Tis but a flesh wound," he said with a poor excuse for a British accent.

Rikki's quiet laugh drew his attention. She saw that spark in his gaze again, and it jolted her. Thick dark lashes that any woman would die for lined the green of his eyes. If it weren't for the fact that he wore small wire-framed glasses, he'd be flawless. But wasn't that part of what she liked so much about him, the fact that he wasn't quite perfect?

The next time he made her feel nervous at work, she'd just imagine him sitting on the floor, legs crossed, playing dolls with two little pixies. Her mouth twitched at the corners.

Rikki relaxed. And if he enjoyed the humor of *Monty Python*, he just might understand her quirky personality. Something about that possibility made her break into a smile.

He caught her. They grinned at each other, and her heart broke into another tap dance. The quick rush made her mildly giddy, and she liked it. And there was that look again.

"I believe," he said, removing his glasses and looking steadily into her eyes, "I owe you an apology."

CHAPTER TWO

AFTER a day off on Friday when Rikki rested, rehydrated herself, and spent quality time with Brenden, she arrived at work on Saturday morning invigorated and ready for duty. It was a hell of a way to spend her birthday, but she didn't have any other plans. The call light in 408 was already on at the nurses' station—the fractured pelvis lady.

Rikki flopped her clipboard on the counter and headed for the room. Her hunch was right and she discovered the usual suspect on the call light. But the woman wore a worried expression, and pointed towards her roommate, the fractured femur in bed B.

She rushed to the restless and coughing patient.

"What's up, Mrs. Turner?"

The woman squirmed and pulled at her hospital gown. Her left leg, suspended by traction and a splint, had been healing beautifully, considering the hardware sticking out of it. She hadn't complained of pain the day before yesterday when Rikki had last taken care of her.

No one had mentioned any complications with her condition in report, yet here she was, clearly in distress. Rikki needed to figure out what to do.

"Are you all right?"

The woman nodded her head and fussed with the sheets on her bed, trying to adjust her position but unable to move much with the traction holding her in place.

As it was the beginning of the shift, Rikki took vital signs. Mrs. Turner had an elevated temp and her pulse rate was close to one hundred. She breathed as though she was anxious, short and shallow. There was no obvious sign of infection at the surgical site.

Something caught Rikki's attention when the woman tugged on the neck of her hospital gown. A sprinkling of small purplish spots dotted the surface of her chest. Rikki peeked inside the loose short sleeve of the gown, where more spots could be seen under her arm and on the side of her breast. It wasn't a rash. A mental red flag went up.

"May I look in your eyes, Mrs. Turner?"

The agitated woman nodded.

Rikki gently pulled down the lower lid and discovered a few more of the same sort of spots inside the eye membrane. Another red flag.

"I need to call your doctor, but in the meantime I'm giving you some oxygen." She pulled the two-pronged plastic tubing out of the bedside bag and connected it to the wall oxygen, then fitted it inside the patient's nose. "I'll be right back."

She rushed past the roommate, thanking her on her way out while dredging up well-learned data from nursing school.

Fat embolism was a complication that sometimes occurred with severe multiple fractures, especially of long bones. Mrs. Turner had a fractured femur. Fat globules could be released from the fracture into the bloodstream and act the same as blood clots, which could migrate to the lungs, heart, or brain. If not dealt with immediately, they could prove lethal.

Rikki grabbed the patient's chart, remembering Dr. Hendricks was her doctor. Flipping quickly through the hospital phone book, she found his private line and dialed. She'd try calling him before the on-call doctor.

"Dr. Hendricks," he answered gruffly on the first ring.

"Doctor?" She was surprised he was in his office on a Saturday instead of in surgery. "Mrs. Turner in 408B has developed petechiae across her chest and inside her eyes. She's restless and her temperature and respirations are elevated. I'm worried it might be fat embolism. Can you take a look at her or shall I call your on-call resident?"

"I'll be right there." He hung up before Rikki could explain why she hadn't thought to call the doctor on duty—because she'd become flustered and her mind had gone blank when she'd seen whose patient Mrs. Turner was. Rikki rushed back to the patient's room to check the oxygen saturation, which to her relief was in the normal range.

Dr. Hendricks appeared out of nowhere, winded and ready for business, as though he'd taken the stairs from his first-floor office rather than wait for the notoriously slow elevator. His sandy dark blond hair looked disheveled, and his white doctor's coat wasn't buttoned.

"Mrs. Turner." He slowed his pace and had a calm smile on his face, though his breathlessness gave his sprint away. "How are you feeling today?"

"OK, I guess."

As he casually questioned his patient, he looked under her lids and peered down the neck of her gown, confirming what Rikki had told him. "Are you having any chest pain or trouble breathing?"

Mrs. Turner shook her head. "I'm just antsy. You know, anxious, because I've been stuck in this bed too long."

"I'd go a little stir-crazy, too, if I were you." He nodded at Rikki while he listened to Mrs. Turner's lungs through his stethoscope. "Take a deep breath," he told the patient. "Does it hurt when you breathe?"

"No, I just feel like I need to cough."

"Let's get a blood gas, stat," he said to Rikki. "How is her urine output?"

"Um…" Rikki hadn't thought to check her intake and output, and Mrs. Turner hadn't asked to use a fracture pan yet that morning.

He didn't wait for her response. "Get some IV fluids going—normal saline, 125 cc an hour. Get a urine sample to check for fat globules. I'll order a stat CT scan of the brain and lungs, and we'll start heparin therapy after the blood gas has been done. Page me as soon as the results are back."

Rikki flew out of the room and paged the respiratory therapist for the blood gas test, then rushed to the supply closet for what she'd need to start the intravenous line. She glanced over her shoulder and saw Dr. Hendricks scribbling on a green doctor's order sheet, and blanched when he glanced up and caught her. When he smiled and nodded, she flushed and scuttled back to the patient's room, trying not to feel flustered under his smoldering gaze.

In the midst of setting up the IV bag and tubing, Dr. Hendricks appeared in the doorway again.

"Here's my beeper number." He handed her a small piece of paper.

She snatched it with an unsteady hand. He didn't let go of his end of the paper, forcing her to tug and look up at his teasing eyes. He gave her a casual smile and said, "Good catch. This could have gotten ugly. Oh, and I've ordered IV steroids."

"You'll be fine." He called out to Mrs. Turner. "Rikki here will keep tabs on you until I get back."

He nodded again, and smiled in a naturally sexy way that made her toes curl, then left.

She stood quietly, shaken. Why did she let him have such power over her? Damn, denial was useless—she had a crazy crush on the man. There was no getting around it.

Thankfully, she had something to distract her, something much more pressing to attend to than Dr. Hendricks's make-your-knees-knock smile. She had a sick patient to care for.

Dane had finished his weekend rounds and discharged several patients. Mrs. Turner's computerized tomography revealed early evidence of fat embolism in her lungs, and she needed to be transferred to ICU and intubated until her condition came under control. If Rikki hadn't been on the ball, the patient's prognosis could have been much worse.

He put his hands in his pockets, deep in thought, and walked to his car in the doctors' parking lot. He glanced up to find a captivating vision before him. Rikki's hips swayed with a mesmerizing rhythm as she walked quickly to her car. She'd unwound her bun and, as if a pendulum, her ponytail kept counter-time to her strut in a most alluring way. He rushed and caught up with her.

"What's your hurry? Hot date?"

She spun around, looking surprised. "Oh."

He could get used to that wide-eyed liquid brown gaze of hers.

She'd changed into baggy camouflage pants and a tight T-shirt, revealing a modest chest. Her backpack matched the pants. Not exactly the sexiest outfit he'd ever seen, but on her it worked. The fashion statement was further evidence that he couldn't deny: he was a good ten years her senior. Could they possibly have anything in common? At least she wasn't wearing combat boots, just brown high-top canvas sport shoes!

"Um," she said, as though still trying to figure out what to say. "No. I have some errands to run."

"I see." He forced her to slow down, so they could walk together and talk. "Where are you parked? I'll walk with you."

Painful silence made Dane more uncomfortable than he'd been in ages. Had he forgotten how to make conversation with a woman? He definitely needed to get out more. Well, he could always keep the subject on business. "Again, I want to thank you for being on the ball with Mrs. Turner."

"Oh, you're welcome, but it's my job."

"And you do it well."

It was never a good idea to socialize with people at work, especially with the kind of thoughts Rikki Johansen put into his mind. But his daughters had a sleepover party that night, and he was free to have some adult time. Only problem was, he didn't have anyone to spend it with. And seeing the ortho nurse had given him an idea. Ah, hell, why not just dive right in?

He cleared his throat. "If you're not busy tonight, how about having dinner with me?"

The color drained from Rikki's face. She practically stumbled before coming to an abrupt halt, though she covered it well by searching the asphalt for the invisible stray rock that must have tripped her. "You want to have dinner with me?"

"I believe that's what I said."

More stunned silence.

"Are you involved with anyone?" he asked.

"Well, no. But…" She bit her lower lip.

"I know, it might be considered improper of me to ask you out, but it's not like I'm your boss or anything. We may work for the same hospital, but I don't sign your checks, and it's just dinner, you know?"

"I'm parked over here." She pointed to an older and well-worn car. "Um…"

"Listen, if I've put you on the spot, forget I said anything, OK? No hard feelings."

"No. It's not that." She glanced briskly his way, as though torn about what to say, and dug into her backpack for her car keys.

An odd feeling of discomfort prompted him to do more explaining. "I enjoyed watching the movie with you the other night, and I thought we'd started to get to know each other at the donor center. You seem like a nice woman and, bottom line, I don't feel like eating alone. That's all I'm saying."

He didn't want to pressure her into feeling obligated to go out with him. Though usually any woman he'd asked out jumped at the chance. Damn, had he gotten that rusty in the last few months?

Rikki still hadn't located her keys, and dug into several different pockets of the backpack in a frustrated manner. So how could he get out of this awkward mess he'd made and still save face?

"I'm not on call, but I gave you my beeper number earlier today. If you change your mind, beep me. I'll keep it turned on, just for you." Let her think whatever she wanted about the double meaning of "turned on." She *did* flip his switch—that, he couldn't deny.

But he had his pride. He'd dump the dinner invitation in her lap, and if she didn't follow through, he'd know she wasn't the least bit interested and forget about it. But, damn, he could have sworn there was something, some kind of chemistry between them. He'd definitely felt it. And he really did want to explore where it all might lead.

Maybe he'd been wrong?

He reached into his shirt pocket for his business card and handed it to her. "Don't lose that number." He attempted a dashing smile while feeling strangely insecure. "My cell phone number is on it, in case I don't answer my beeper."

She read the card and recited his number. "OK." She scratched her nose. "I'll see how things go."

Not the most encouraging answer in the world, but he'd settle for it.

No fancy automatic car opener for Rikki, she shoved the key into the lock, swung open a creaky and dented door, and slid inside behind the steering wheel. He noticed a child's booster seat in the back. Did she have a kid?

Right this minute he didn't care if she had three kids, he just wanted to take her out to dinner and have a good old-fashioned date with a woman. This woman. Male pride made him take the last word. "I know the perfect place for a great meal."

Before she could answer, he spun around, stuck his hands in his pockets and strolled slowly toward his new car in the doctors' parking section. He casually whistled, and hesitated long enough to make sure her clunker of a car started.

By six o'clock Rikki had grown restless. Nothing remotely interesting was scheduled on TV. She'd seen all of her DVDs a million times, and wasn't inclined to rent anything new. Her best friend had a rescheduled blind date she couldn't get out of, and had promised to celebrate her birthday with her on Sunday night.

Brenden sat quietly on the floor, playing with his favorite toy robot in his Superman Halloween cape.

She flounced down on her couch and put her fuzzy slippers up on the coffee table. Another Saturday night at home—but this time, it was her birthday.

She couldn't get Dane out of her mind. Wasn't he totally out of her reach? Had he really said he'd liked talking to her? Well, they'd had a good time watching the Monty Python movie, and they'd both laughed at all the same parts. She imagined his chiseled face. What would his close-cropped hair feel like to run her fingers through? Ha! As if she'd ever have the chance.

His beeper number repeated in her head. How often did mature gorgeous surgeons invite her out to dinner? Never!

Meghan, the teenager next door, had offered to watch Brenden as a birthday present—why not let her?

Oh, what the hell. She searched for his business card, and a sudden rush of jitters made her drop it twice. She stood tall and swallowed, picked up the phone as a stream of adrenaline trickled through her chest, and dialed.

When he answered, she realized she'd been holding her breath. "Dr. Hendricks?"

"Call me Dane. What took you so long?"

How had he known it would be her? She picked at her hair, flustered. She heard children's voices and lots of racket in the background, wherever he was.

"Daddy? Daddy?"

"Hold on a second, Rikki. OK, girls, behave tonight. Emma, don't be a tattle-tale about everything Meg does, OK? And Meg, don't give Emma anything to tattle-tale about."

She heard him kiss his daughters, and another woman's voice spoke up. "Don't worry, I'll take good care of them," she said. "We're going to play dress-up and bake cookies and watch movies."

What sounded like a herd of little girls clapped and squealed, "Yay!"

Rikki smiled. She'd never been to a sleepover party. Come to think of it, she'd never played dress-up either.

More kisses. More goodbyes. A door closed.

"You there?" Dane asked.

She snapped out of her memories. "Yeah."

"When shall I pick you up?"

Ever cautious as a single woman, she answered without thinking. "I'll meet you."

After he'd told her the location of the restaurant, a place she'd never be able to afford on her own, her nerves doubled.

Now it was her turn to play dress-up.

Dane sat at the bar at his favorite steak house in Beverly Hills, nursing a beer. He'd pulled some strings to get a last-minute reservation. It was an unusually warm evening for early November, thanks to the Santa Ana winds blustering through L.A. He almost left his sport coat in the car, but remembered that the restaurant required men to wear jackets.

He tapped his foot and checked his watch again. He'd always been a stickler about being on time, and it was a quarter after the hour. But with that old clunker of hers, Rikki may have broken down on the way. He should have insisted on picking her up, but something in her tone of voice had made him back off and let her call the shots. He dug into his pocket for his cell phone and scrolled through previous incoming calls to find her number. Just about to dial, he glanced up.

Rikki stood in the restaurant entry in a whirlwind of color. From her gauzy layered skirt to the two-toned baby blue and brown vest top, she lit up the room. Copper-colored sandals that laced around her calves reminded him of a film he'd once seen on the Roman Empire. He smiled.

She quickly brushed her hair to fight off the windblown look and glanced his way. He pushed off from his barstool and walked closer. He adjusted his glasses to take a closer look at the pleasing sight.

There were no less than six bead bracelets on both of her wrists, alternating blues with browns, and a necklace of several strands to match just about anything in the world. His daughters loved to make their own jewelry with plastic beads, just like hers. And right now he could almost see her in one of Meg's tiaras.

She blinked in recognition and her gaze skittered from his to around the lobby and back. In the upscale steak-house, where women flaunted their highly insured gems, she stood out as "different." Well, to hell with everybody. He liked how she looked.

Rikki's quirky outfit tickled him. She was the most genuinely unique person he'd met in ages. A smile of admiration stretched across his face as he approached. Something about the intentional hint of brown lace from her bra peeking above her scooped neckline pleased him even more.

"Hi," she said, with an insecure gaze upwards. "I had trouble finding parking."

The expensive valet-only parking must have had her walking half a mile from wherever she'd left her car. Why hadn't he thought about that? He should have put his foot down when she'd insisted she'd meet him here. No wonder she was late.

"No problem." He reached for her hand and tugged her toward the hostess. "We're ready for our reservation." A surprisingly pleasant surge of energy started where he held her small, warm hand in his. He could get used to that.

She'd gone to trouble for him, and he liked the results. He glanced appreciatively into her delicately made-up eyes, more lovely than ever. Soft butterscotch waves tumbled over her shoulders, and she nervously used her free hand to flip her hair behind her shoulder. She smelled of citrus-infused lotion, and her tantalizing mouth glistened with lipstick, as if daring him to kiss her. Maybe he would…later.

Struck with a sudden urge to skip dinner and get right down to dessert, he swallowed hard.

"Your table is ready."

"You ready?" He broke off his stare.

Rikki nodded. He gave her a gentle nudge at the small of her back to move her along.

Her dainty hips swayed as they snaked through the

crowded and noisy restaurant to their table. He liked the swishing sound the skirt made and the natural herbal scent of her hair.

Content with the thought of sharing dinner with his intriguing date, he couldn't help but think this could be the start of something. His mouth went dry and a quick response kept him from tripping on a chair.

When had been the last time he'd dared to think that?

Several patrons cast curious glances at Rikki. Maybe they thought she was some eccentric starlet, or a pop singer. Whatever their reasons for staring, she didn't let it faze her. Instead, she held her head high and squared her shoulders until the hostess seated them. He liked her attitude.

Rikki had never felt more self-conscious in her life. She'd only seen restaurants like this in movies. Perfectly coiffed women and tailored men filled the tables. She even thought she saw an actor from TV in one of the booths at the back.

No gawking.

Her multiple foster-parents had frequently brought in children for the extra income, not purely out of the goodness of their hearts, and a place like this would never be in their budget. She and a few friends had once splurged and treated themselves to a swanky restaurant when they'd graduated from nursing school, but she honestly didn't feel the food had been worth the price. She had her few favorite eateries, and they weren't anywhere near this side of town.

Dane looked relaxed and in his element while he perused the menu. "I recommend everything except the seafood. Stick with steak tonight."

"But I'm a vegetarian."

He bore the look of a surgeon who had just amputated the wrong leg. He shook his head. "No wonder you're so scra—er, tiny. Why didn't you tell me?"

Bristling over his comment, she stared him down. "You never gave me a chance." She closed her menu and put it on the table. "You didn't give me a choice, or a say in where I'd like to go. You didn't ask what I'd like to eat. You just said, 'This is where we're going,' and 'Be there.'"

Dane stiffened. He clutched the wine list and frowned, confused.

She saw the evening turning around the wrong bend, and that was something she couldn't take. After all, it was her birthday. Didn't she deserve a nice evening out?

She wanted things to be better than this, even though Dane had some explaining to do about the look he'd given her when he'd first seen her. Surprise? Horror? She wasn't sure which. *Well, get used to it, buddy, because this is me. I know who I am, how I dress, and what I eat.* If he wanted to get to know the real her, she wasn't about to pretend to be someone else.

Truth was, she wanted a chance to get to know Dane Hendricks too—a man who would most likely never have given her a second look if they'd passed on the street. For some odd reason she'd caught his attention at work, and now she'd like to see how long she could hold it.

"But that's OK." She smiled brightly, changing tack. "They've got lots of great side dishes and salads." She picked up her menu again. "I'll be fine."

He studied her with a confused gaze a few seconds longer. "By any chance, do you drink wine? I was going to order a pinot…"

"Chardonnay?" She offered an apologetic smile. "I only like white wine. Sorry. But I can have tea, and you—"

"No." He raised his palm. "Chardonnay it is. And for the record, I like petite women."

Petite sounded a heck of a lot better than scrawny. Yeah, she knew what he'd meant the first time. But she'd give him a second chance.

Dane quickly made up for things. He became her hero when he withstood the snooty look the wine steward gave him when he ordered the bottle of white wine against the expert's advice for a nice pinot noir. No two-buck house wine for him, which was Rikki's usual choice when she was paying. He ordered the finest Chardonnay on the wine list. And he also suggested to the waiter that they should add a few more vegetarian entrées to their menu when they ordered their meal.

While they waited for their meal, Rikki skimmed her repertoire of conversational topics. The files were frighteningly thin when it came to holding her own with a man like Dane. What could they possibly talk about besides life at Mercy Hospital? An idea popped into her head. She adored kids. He had kids. Why not?

"So, you must love being a dad."

He raised his brows. "It's the toughest job I've ever had. Fact is, I'd rather do back-to-back hip replacements than stare into my daughters' big green eyes and tell them no."

He had a point. Children could be ruthless with their miniature bodies and precious faces, and the thought of big Dane Hendricks being defeated by his daughters made her grin.

"Don't get me wrong. I love my girls. And it's my responsibility to be their dad. But do I love being a father? I'll be honest with you. No."

"Well, I love kids. Someday I hope to have a whole houseful of them."

"You may change your tune once you've had a couple." He shoved a piece of bread into his mouth and chomped vigorously.

"I'm a foster-parent. I've hosted half a dozen kids already, and right now I'm caring for a four-year-old orphan named Brenden Pascual. It's been tough, but very rewarding to know that I'm giving him stability when his whole world has been turned upside down."

"That's commendable. You seem to be a very caring person."

"Nah. It's just my way of giving back."

"May I ask you a practical question? What about child care? How do you manage that? I've had nothing but trouble with nanny after flaky nanny. And my mother can only handle the girls for so long."

"Why haven't you tried Mercy's child care? It's open for all employees. That's the reason I transferred over from St. Michael's."

He tilted his head. "You know, you've got a point. Maybe I will try it out. Thanks."

She sat a littler straighter. "Glad to be of service. And for your information, caring for foster-kids hasn't put me off kids at all. I still want several kids of my own one day."

"That's also very commendable. But as for me, I know my limits. I've met my quota. No more kids."

Despite their differences on views of family size, the rest of the meal was pleasant enough. They chuckled over their favorite scenes in movies, and realized they both liked to hike. Rikki discovered Sheila was right—Dane did a flawless imitation of Mercy Hospital's administrator.

The absurdity of him clowning around and his spot-on imitation set her off giggling until she realized people were staring. She used her napkin to cover her mouth and quieted down. Dane kept taunting her by whispering more Hank Caruthers-isms. He obviously enjoyed watching her squirm and snort.

After the meal they both agreed that pie was the only true dessert and decided to share. She didn't let on it was her birthday, and cake would be more appropriate. But she had to admit so far it had been a fairly decent date.

So why was she still feeling so uncomfortable with Dane?

After one large bite of mixed berry pie, a couple brushed past their table, and a familiar face from Mercy Hospital stopped.

Exquisite Dr. Hannah Young, sleek, statuesque, dressed to knock out whoever her date was in a tight little black designer dress, paused to rest her hand on Dane's shoulder. "Greetings. Fancy meeting you here," she said, as though it was some sort of inside comment about the restaurant being their favorite hangout.

Dane stood up quickly, dropping the napkin from his lap. "Hey, Hannah." They smiled warmly at each other and shook hands. She cast a cool dismissive gaze in Rikki's direction. "You know Rikki Johansen from Orthopedics," he said, and gestured toward her while he bent down to retrieve his napkin. Rikki had never seen him flustered before.

The doctor raised her eyebrows and tilted her head in Rikki's direction. Her message came through loud and clear. *What are you doing here with this gorgeous man? There must be only one reason. Hmm.* She made a quick calculated head-to-table glance, and her perfectly shaped brows twitched in disapproval. "Good to see you."

Rikki forced a smile, nodded and said a curt "You too."

"Well, I'd better get back to my date. See you Monday at the admin meeting, Dane. I hear Hank has another groundbreaking announcement."

"I'll be there." He passed Rikki a mischievous sideways glance as though on the verge of another imitation. "Hey, great seeing you, Hannah." Dane sat back down with new color in his cheeks. Was he embarrassed being caught in public with someone like her?

All the insecurities she'd tried to suppress for the night came charging through her shaky defenses. As always, she didn't measure up. Everything had been a mistake. How could she—an abandoned kid from foster-care—ever feel on an equal footing with Dane?

"Why can't you be like those other girls, Rachel Johansen?" her least favorite foster-mom had chided her when she'd begun expressing herself by dressing differently than her peers. "You ain't got no class and you never will."

She stopped in mid-bite of the last of the dessert as a wave of anxiety took hold, and pushed back her chair. "I need to find the ladies' room. Will you excuse me?"

He looked surprised, the way he'd looked when he'd first spotted her waiting in the restaurant entryway.

She didn't give him a chance to say anything. When she reached the full-length mirror in the restroom, she scanned herself head to toe. No perfect little black dress for her. No. How had she possibly thought she looked nice with her own rendition of urban fairy? All she needed was a laurel crown. What had she been thinking? She should have known better than to venture out of her safe little antisocial cave. But wasn't this how she'd always thumbed her nose at society? *Dress weird, be an individualist, show them you don't give a damn what they think. You don't want to fit in. Maybe they'll believe you. And while you're at it, maybe you'll convince yourself.*

But she did want to fit in with Dane.

Part of the dinner had been great fun, but at other times she'd sat stiff and self-conscious. Old habits never died. In each new foster-home she'd had to make a quick study of the family dynamics in order to survive. Her overall position anywhere she'd lived had boiled down to one thing—she had been a misfit. The families had either felt sorry for her, doted too much, making her withdraw, or had chided her for her mother's problems, expecting the worst. And when they had, she'd taken their challenge by messing up in school and dressing weird.

Rikki had quit intentionally failing in her studies once she'd been on her own, but the defiant style of dress had stuck even when she'd pulled it together and got the education she needed to become a nurse. It had become who she was—*different*.

If she was being honest, she'd admit that Dane had gone out of his way to try to make her comfortable. Hadn't he stuck up for her to the snooty wine steward and made her laugh with corny imitations?

Confused, she rubbed the line between her brows and paced. What should she do?

Her cell phone interrupted her thoughts. It was Meghan, her babysitter. "Brenden's throwing a fit," she said. "He keeps yelling, 'I want my mommy.' I can't calm him down."

Rikki took a deep breath. "He does that sometimes. I'm leaving right now. I'll be home within the hour." So much for trying to work anything out with Dane tonight. She'd go back to their table, explain the situation and hope for a reprieve.

When she got to the lobby, Dane had already paid their bill and was waiting for her. Obviously, he couldn't wait to get the date over with either. But his eyes were soft and he looked like a man seeking peace.

The truth about Rikki had been written on the bathroom wall. The mirror had said it all. She was a misfit and she and Dane didn't belong together. She needed to cut things off with him before they ever got started. And Brenden had given her the perfect excuse.

"Are you ready?" he asked.

She nodded.

"I thought we might go somewhere to listen to music or have a drink. What do you say?"

So he wasn't beating her out the door? It didn't matter—their date was history.

"I can't. My foster-kid is having a bad night." He wasn't the only one.

Dane straightened his shoulders and jiggled the car keys in his hand. "I see. Well, in that case, let me drive you to your car."

"Oh. No. That's OK. I can walk."

He reached for and held her elbow, not about to let her get away with her disappearing act. "Don't be ridiculous, Rikki."

Wasn't that what she was? Ridiculous? The whole

evening had been a ridiculous farce, except it hadn't been funny. This was her life, out of sync with Dane Hendricks and the rest of the universe. And the damn thing was, she'd wanted to belong.

Rikki relented. "OK. I'm about a mile away, anyway."

He chuckled, and took her hand. "You're something else, you know that?"

Oh, yeah, she knew that.

Dane stared at Rikki, who studied her brightly painted toes while they waited for the valet to bring the car. No spark responded from her hand in his this time around. Instead, she'd subtly removed herself from his grasp in order to keep her hair out of her face when the wind had blustered through the driveway.

What the hell had gone wrong? He'd done all the right things for a perfect date—chosen a good restaurant, expensive wine. Hell, he'd even dressed up. But then, so had she…in a most unusual fashion. Peacock-feather earrings would have been the perfect accessories for her outfit. But he liked how she looked. Hell, he liked her, but somehow he'd only succeeded in making her uncomfortable. What had happened to the old Hendricks charm?

Despite every effort he'd made to loosen her up, she'd seemed uptight throughout dinner. He'd thought he'd broken through when he'd done his imitation of their hospital administrator, but she'd accidentally snorted when she'd laughed and had grown self-conscious again. He'd thought the snort had been kind of cute, but how did you explain that to a self-conscious woman?

And then, with exceptionally bad timing, gorgeous Hannah from Oncology had shown up, which had seemed to intimidate Rikki even more. But Hannah could do that to just about anyone. And to top everything off, of all the rotten luck, without knowing Rikki was vegetarian, he'd chosen a steak house. Way to go, Hendricks.

And what kind of convenient excuse was it for Rikki to claim her foster-kid was acting up so she had to leave? But if it was true, wouldn't he do the same thing if one of his girls were in need? Nothing was more important to him than their well-being. Fact was, children complicated life, and he didn't need any more problems. And Rikki couldn't hide that gooey-eyed look whenever the conversation turned to kids. Rikki was a package deal he wasn't sure he wanted to get involved with.

At a loss for words he tipped the valet and assisted Rikki into his car. She'd gone stiff again, obviously ill at ease. Did he need this kind of aggravation? Hell, no. He'd already had enough for a lifetime.

"So where're you parked?"

She cleared her throat. "Go down this street and make a right at the stoplight."

He tried not to chuckle at how far away she'd had to park in order to avoid paying a valet. She really did tickle him. Or maybe it wasn't the cost. Maybe she was embarrassed about her old clunker of a car and had worried it would stall for the valet. *Knucklehead. Why didn't I insist on picking her up?*

Everything was his fault. He'd let his physical attraction to Rikki dictate his actions without thinking things through. He should have gotten to know her better before asking her out. Truth was, they weren't suited for each other. At this stage in life he was looking for someone to relax with, so why get involved with a woman who was a revolving door for foster-kids?

Rikki Johansen was a reckless-dressing, do-gooder, overly sensitive younger woman, and he'd had enough women giving him trouble. He'd been left to raise his two girls single-handedly when their mother, his ex-wife, had discovered how difficult it was to be a parent. One unstable female per lifetime was enough and Rikki was obviously a woman trying to make up for something—and just like with having children, he'd met his quota. No. He didn't need any more problems. Next time he wanted a casual date, he'd ask Hannah.

Angry with the mess the date had become, he double-parked when they arrived at her car. He glanced over at her pixie silhouette, and against every ounce of etiquette he'd ever learned, a sudden urgent instinct took over.

The instant the car came to a stop, without further thought, he leaned across the bucket seat, took her face in his hands and planted a kiss on her lips. She went still under his kiss, but didn't pull away. The moment drew out while he felt her soft, plump mouth beneath his. She leaned toward him, kissing him back, her hand placed lightly on his cheek. He'd made the right decision.

Every ounce of logic flew out of his brain as he pressed closer against her warm, moist lips. Did she feel the spark? The intensity of the moment jolted him. He backed off.

Her ruffled gaze met his in the dark of the car, searching for an explanation. He couldn't say why he'd done it. She didn't ask.

"Rikki, I…"

Rikki cleared her throat and reached for the doorhandle. "Thanks for dinner," she said, breathless. The wind practically blew the door open for her. She jumped out so fast that she caught her necklaces and broke a strand, sending beads flying all over the street. She didn't stop to pick up any of them. It took both hands and all of her hundred-pounds-soaking-wet bodily strength to close the door.

Dane got out of the driver's side, only to have Rikki raise her hand to wave goodnight. She slid inside her car faster than he could utter a sound of protest, and slammed the door.

After two false starts, while she refused to glance at him, her engine finally turned over, making a ragged metal and muffler song.

Speechless and confused, he slipped back inside his car, completely aware of the taste of her lips on his and her lingering herbal scent. He drove up the street, and watched through his rear-view mirror to make sure her car continued to run. She made an illegal U-turn in the middle of the road and drove off in the other direction.

He shook his head. *Women!*

The light changed to green. Something sparkly in the passenger bucket seat caught his attention. Damn, a reminder of the woman who'd managed to confuse him— a short strand of Rikki's fluorescent blue beads.

CHAPTER THREE

AT WORK mid-Sunday morning, Rikki's radar warned her that Dane was in the vicinity of the orthopedic ward. She'd lain awake half the night trying to figure out why she'd gotten so skittish with him. He'd been kind, attentive, even entertaining, but the restaurant had been completely outside her comfort zone.

Her lifetime of being carted from one foster-home to another had taught her to never get too comfortable anywhere. With the few families she'd cared about, she'd had to quickly learn how to let go. After a while it had gotten easy, especially if she never let herself get involved in the first place.

And Dane's kiss had struck like lightning, setting fire to her soul. Just the thought of it made her palms tingle. Out of self-defense she'd never allow herself to get comfortable with a man like him. She couldn't trust where it might lead.

Hearing his footsteps approaching, she dashed into one of her patients' rooms.

How could she ever face Dane again after last night? It wasn't anything he'd said. It was more what he hadn't said—the look he'd given when he'd first seen her in the restaurant lobby had told half of the story. The other half had come through when he hadn't bothered to tell her she looked great or even good, but she had sure read that approving gaze he'd given when Dr. Young had shown up. Just once in her life she'd like to be accepted for who she was inside, a person of value, not how she was wrapped.

"Nurse?"

She quickly realized she'd been hovering at the patient's door, watching and listening. "Oh! Hi, Mr. Tanaka."

Her patient had had a shoulder joint replacement and was being held captive in a torso cast with his left arm held at a shoulder-high salute and propped on a diagonal metal rod mounted from waist to elbow.

"How are you doing?"

She did a circulation check of his nailbeds, which checked out, and noted a pathetic look on his face.

"I need to take a walk. Will you help me?"

"Of course," she said. "Do you need to go to the bathroom?"

"No. I want to walk around the ward, to get out of this room. I'm going stir-crazy."

Oh, no. If she walked with Mr. Tanaka, she might risk running into Dane. But her patient had to come first, and if he wanted to walk, she'd assist him.

Rikki helped edge his legs to the side of the bed and swing them to the ground. She let his feet dangle for a few seconds while she covered his backside with another hospital gown. On the count of three she helped him to stand, and once he gained his balance and gave her the nod, they started on their trek around the ward.

Just as she'd feared, Dane still sat at the nurses' station, charting progress notes and writing orders. He glanced up before she could look away.

His brows lifted in a quizzical manner above his glasses, his stare steady with no hint of a smile. Was he thinking about the kiss, too? The sight of his handsome face and broad shoulders made her want to yell "Truce" and ask for "another chance" so she could explain why she'd lost all her courage last night. Surely, as a father, he must have understood she had a responsibility to Brenden first and foremost.

If she'd lost her chance at getting to know Dane because of that, so be it. She'd survived alone this long in her life, and she wasn't about to let a man like Dane throw her off course.

She blew Dane and his suspicious gaze off by focusing on Mr. Tanaka and his monster cast. Yeah, she'd take the easy way out.

"Why don't we make this walk a short one?" she said.

"No. If you don't mind, I want to circle the entire nurses' station," he said.

Feeling Dane's penetrating stare, she wished she'd worn her invisible uniform instead of the cornflower-blue scrubs.

She stayed by her patient's side to make sure he didn't bump into anything or knock anyone out with a quick move of his arm and cast.

"Have I told you about my granddaughter, the doctor?" he asked while they ambulated.

She nodded. "Yes, but not recently." She pretended to be enthralled while the old man repeated all the same information he'd given her yesterday, wishing she had eyes in the back of her head so she could see what Dane was up to.

When they'd finally made it back to the door of the patient's hospital room, she felt a tap on her shoulder. She turned to find Dane unnaturally close and dangling a length of her home-made bead necklace. His eyes stared deeply into hers. She felt suddenly parched and steadied herself on Mr. Tanaka's cast. Why couldn't she just shrivel up and die?

"I thought you might want these back."

"Oh." Brilliant reply. She mentally kicked herself for getting so easily flustered where Dane was concerned. What should she do now? Her face went hot with embarrassment. *Keep busy. Act like that kiss never happened.*

As her hands were engaged, guiding her patient, Dane tucked the beads into her smock pocket, never breaking his intense stare until he walked away.

With her heart sinking to her feet, she mumbled, "Thank you."

"Don't mention it," he said without looking back, dismissing her as thoroughly as she'd dodged him the night before.

Dane had presented her with intimacy she was far from ready to handle. Just the thought of getting involved with him made her toes curl.

She glanced at the beads in her pocket—so much for a fresh start. She'd never be able to mention her disastrous dinner with Dane to anyone. Unfortunately, the night of her twenty-sixth birthday would go down in history as a date to forget.

"So, as I was saying." Mr. Tanaka hadn't missed a beat. "My granddaughter, the doctor…"

On Monday evening, Rikki watched as long tendrils of hair got clipped from her head at the hairdresser's. Finally it had grown long enough to donate.

"Why are you cutting your hair, Rikki?" Brenden stood beside the pumped-up salon chair, watching intently as Randall did the honors.

"Because the Care to Share Your Hair program needs ten inches."

"And is it ten inches?" Brenden looked quizzically up at Randall, who nodded.

She'd read about the program last year online and had quit cutting her hair immediately. If she could make someone else's life a tiny bit better, she'd try. She glanced at Brenden's bright dark eyes, full of wonder. Wasn't that what it was all about? When you can't fix the state of your own life, help fix someone else's?

Brenden slapped his hands over his mouth and giggled. "You look funny."

"You think so?" Her hair could always grow back, but now that it had been cut, looking at a strikingly blunt and choppy style in the mirror, a whim popped into her head. Why not go all the way? "Can you cut my hair really short, Randall? I'd like to go spiky for a change."

"Sure thing," the hairdresser said. "Short is always in," he said in an exaggerated manner to Brenden, razor-cutting several layers to frame her face.

Cringing at the memory of her disastrous date with Dane, she hoped he wouldn't recognize her the next time their paths crossed. And as most men liked long hair, she'd go one step further off his dating radar by wearing ultra-short hair.

It wasn't her imagination that there had been a spark in his eyes when she'd sat across from him at dinner. His handsome square jaw and straight white smile had made the back of her neck prickle on several occasions that night. A face like that belonged on the cover of *The Journal of Medicine's Hunk of the Year,* not behind a surgeon's mask.

And the kiss. She shook away the thought.

She had to give Dane credit. When she'd admitted how far away she'd parked the car, he hadn't judged her but had merely seemed amused. In fact, he'd seemed apologetic as if he'd wished he'd picked her up, instead of letting her talk him into meeting him at the restaurant.

Why couldn't she ever let people do nice things for her? Because very few people had ever offered, and when they did, there were always strings attached. She wasn't a fool. He'd kissed her like he'd meant it. If she hadn't put a stop to it, he would probably have wanted to take advantage of her, sleep with her and never see her again.

But, wait, *he* had been the one to stop the kiss.

Oh, she could just die, remembering the sexy but confused look in Dane's eyes when she'd said goodnight and rushed out of his car as if she'd have turned into a pumpkin in another second. Things would never be the same between them, that was a given.

She glanced in the mirror and froze.

"Randall?" she said.

Deep in concentration, her hairdresser pursed his lips and primped and played with her rapidly shrinking hair. "Yes?"

"Are we almost done?"

"Yes." He lifted the long strands of what had been her hair. "This will make a beautiful wig." He laid them reverently on a special piece of paper on the counter and carefully wrapped them. "Let me get some hair paste so you can look sassy with your spikes. Do you like your itty-bitty bangs?"

"Let me see your itty-bitty bangs," Brenden chimed in.

It took all of her power not to gasp when Randall gave her a hand mirror to check out the back of her head. Definitely short. Outrageously spiky. Oh, heavens! But wasn't that what she'd asked for? She gulped and tried her best not to reveal her gut reaction. She made a second 360-degree sweep of her head with the mirror. OK, not so bad, just different. She'd get over the shock, she reasoned. "It's time for a change, Randall, and I *love* the cut."

"Now you look like me!" Brenden said, and giggled again.

By the time she'd gotten home that night, Brenden's bright disposition had changed. He'd become moody and restless.

"I want my mommy!"

Rikki peeled the boy off her leg and attempted to stand him on his own. He plopped into a heap, bumping his head on the carpet and crying more.

Rikki tried to get closer, but he rolled around and kicked at her feet. "I want my mommy!"

Knowing four was a stormy age for a child, and he'd most likely want to follow his will to the extreme, she let him be. What could she say—*you'll never see your mother again*?

After he'd made his desire to see his mommy and daddy unmistakably known, and had quieted down the tiniest bit, Rikki got a bright idea. Her only hope was what she remembered from her child development studies in nursing school—kids this age could suddenly change from sad to happy and back in a blink. A surge of optimism pushed her onward.

"Want to play a game?" She'd stocked her guest room,

now Brenden's room, with children's toys for both genders, as she never knew what sex she'd get as a foster-parent. It was bright and colorful and, in Rikki's mind, looked like a happy place for any kid. Maybe if she could distract him, he'd calm down.

"No!"

Undaunted by his resistance, she dragged him, crying and kicking, as if dead weight, to the room and flipped on the light. He wiped away his tears. His favorite toy, a talking robot, blinked red eyeballs at him. "Want to play?" the toy said over and over at Rikki's command.

He giggled half-heartedly at Rikki's craftiness.

She handed him the remote control and he dutifully pushed a yellow button. The robot rolled toward him. Brenden pushed the knob again. It rolled closer. "Let's sing!" it said. "The farmer's in the dell…"

Normally, that part always made him smile, but not tonight. Unenthusiastically, he pressed the green button. The robot turned round in a circle, all the while singing the song. Brenden's eyes looked glazed and watery. His cheeks were flushed and his hair was damp.

Rikki felt his forehead with the back of her hand. He was burning up. "Let me take your temperature, kiddo. You feeling all right?"

"My tummy hurts." He rubbed his runny nose.

Sure enough, he had a temperature and was most likely coming down with flu. She got the children's antipyretic and gave him the proper dose, dressed him in his jammies, and helped him brush his teeth.

Rikki found a book to read about wild things and angry little boys who needed to settle down and go to sleep. She growled and roared and pawed at the air while she read, much to his droopy interest. Before she knew it, he'd cuddled into the crook of her arm in the rocking chair.

She read several more books, and had fleeting thoughts about how Dane must have felt as a single dad of not one but two daughters. He'd said it was the hardest job he'd ever had. She agreed, but it was well worth the challenge to make the world a better place. He wasn't shirking his responsibility to his daughters either. Just knowing she wasn't alone in the realm of single parenting, and then realizing that Brenden had drifted off to sleep, buoyed her confidence.

Barely able to lift Brenden's sturdy little body, she managed to carry him to his bed. She picked up the phone and dialed her nursing supervisor's sick call message machine. "Janetta? It's Rikki Johansen. I've got a sick boy here. I don't feel right about leaving him in the employee sick bay. I'll have to miss work tomorrow."

Once he'd settled into his pillow, she cuddled behind him to offer comfort. He was alone in the world, and deserved to know the security of his mother's arms. Rikki couldn't come close to filling that gap. Heck, she prided herself on being able to bring kids into a stable environment, take good care of them, and pass them on to better homes when the time came. She'd gotten quite good at it.

Brenden was an orphan with no relatives in this country. She herself may as well be an orphan—she hadn't seen her mother since she'd been three.

Rikki worried about getting too close to Brenden. The boy snuggled deeper into her embrace, and soon they both fell asleep.

Three days later, when Brenden no longer had a fever, Rikki bundled him up and brought him to the child-care preschool center at Mercy Hospital so she could go back to work.

"I'll come and have lunch with you today," she promised him.

The reticent boy shoved his thumb into his mouth—something he hadn't done before—but didn't pull his other hand from hers while they walked toward the building. Perhaps he didn't feel completely back to normal?

"OK," he slurped.

As she approached, she recognized Dane's large, healthy figure, a tiny girl dangling from each hand. They looked up to him in adoration. One chatted non-stop. The other observed everything about her surroundings with wide pale eyes. Beneath similar dresses in different colors, they both had stringy legs with knobby knees. And, yes, both wore Mary Jane-style shoes.

Rikki tried not to laugh at the lopsided bows each wore on thin, straight blonde hair. Obviously Dane was still on a learning curve where hair grooming and accessories were concerned.

When he noticed her, he pulled in his chin and stopped. "Where have you been, and who have you got there?"

"This is Brenden. The little boy I'm fostering."

"Hi!" one of the girls piped up.

"Meg. We're not 'posed to talk to stwaingers," the other cut in.

"It's OK, Emma, I know Rikki," Dane said.

"I've been sick," Brenden piped up.

"So that's why you haven't been at work." Dane bent down to the boy's level. "Hi, Brenden. I'm Dane."

He'd noticed she hadn't been at work?

Brenden looked at Dane, not making a peep. His thumb

slipped out of his mouth and he let go of Rikki's hand. "Hi," he whispered.

"He had the flu. But he's all better now, aren't you, Brenden?"

The boy dutifully nodded.

"I see. Well, Meg and Emma are new this week, maybe you can all be pals. OK, girls?"

Emma stayed put, shyly fidgeting with her dress. The more outgoing of the two, Meg, rushed to Brenden's side. "Come on. I'll show you my *favwit* toys. Do you like to play dolls?"

Brenden didn't seem to mind that a girl his age was taking his hand. "I have my own bestest toys."

He followed her inside. Once Emma decided it was OK, she took his other hand.

"I've got to get on the job," Rikki said, ready to make her break from Dane.

"Why did you cut your hair?"

Her hand flew to her neck. "It was long enough."

"Long enough for what?"

"To donate to Care to Share Your Hair."

"Oh, I've heard of that organization. Hmm. So let me get this straight, you donate platelets, register with the national marrow donor foundation, give your hair for wigs for cancer kids, and take in foster-children. Are you trying to replace Mother Theresa?"

She looked at her toes and gave a coy smile.

"Oh, and one more thing—you make your own jewelry," he added in a softer voice.

She sputtered a laugh. He hadn't forgotten their date any more than she had. "That I do."

"I'm still finding beads in my car."

They stared at each other for a few moments. Had he forgotten the kiss? Some sort of understanding passed between them. Respect? He'd made the best with what life had dealt him, and so had she. They had a lot more in common than she cared to admit.

Rikki scratched her nose, and wished she could think of something else to say. "I'll be late."

"Listen, if you ever need any sage advice on parenting, don't ask me, because I don't have a clue." He shrugged his shoulders and gave an all-forgiving smile.

"I'll be sure to put you at the bottom of my list." Maybe they could be friends?

"Thanks for recommending the child-care center. The girls have loved it so far."

"You're welcome," she said, feeling vindicated with a new spring to her step. "And if you should ever need more advice on child-rearing, I'll be glad to assist."

He smiled. "Have a good day, Rikki."

"You, too, Dane."

Just when she'd thought he'd left her life for good, he paused.

"By the way," he said. "If the warm weather holds, the girls and I are planning a day at the park on Saturday. Thought we'd take a short hike. Maybe you and Brenden would like to come along?"

"I didn't think we did so well with dating."

"Who said anything about a date? Think about it. If you change your mind, you've got my number."

Damn. Why did he always leave it up to her?

CHAPTER FOUR

FERNWOOD PARK had never looked so good that Saturday morning. Perhaps it was the pristine fall air. Or maybe it was the verdant hills with Chinese elm, sycamore, and those beautiful ancient oak trees. Rikki smiled, content. Then again, maybe it was the company of Dane and his daughters.

Above the park in the Los Feliz Hills sat the newly refurbished Griffith Park Observatory, as if a regal reigning queen. In awe, Rikki wondered why she didn't come to the park more often.

It had taken every ounce of courage to pick up the phone and call Dane, even though he'd invited her and Brenden to tag along with him and his girls. As before, he'd lobbed the ball into her court and waited for her return.

He'd sounded surprised Friday afternoon when she'd phoned, but pleased when she'd taken him up on his offer. She'd told him it was because she knew of an easy hike and a special cave she sometimes visited on her own, and she'd wanted to show it to Brenden. Dane had been gentleman enough not to call her on her prevarication, and had accepted her excuse for coming. This time she gave him her address and he picked them up.

It had been two days since she'd seen him at the day care center, and the power he still had over her nervous system surprised her. A swarm of butterflies had taken flight in her stomach when he'd tapped on her door. Seeing his handsome face again had almost made her need to sit down. Having experienced her skittish behavior at the restaurant, he'd seemed to know not to push. Today's get-together was nothing like a date. No pressure. It was just a simple outing with the kids.

She wasn't the only one who'd lightened up when Dane had appeared. Brenden showed more signs of life and excitement than she'd seen all week. Maybe it was the fresh air?

Once at the park, Rikki directed Dane to the best place to park and helped all three kids out of the car, handing each of them their hooded sweatshirts.

"We're going to go up this way." She pointed to a hiking trail. "You three hold hands. I'll show you my secret hiding place."

The kids danced around, excited, and ran ahead. "We're going to a secret hiding place!" Meg shouted.

"It's where I go when I need to think," Rikki said to Dane, remembering the many times she'd run off to her cave when she'd been a teenager.

Fifteen minutes later, after an easy hike, they reached their destination—a small meadow where a natural cave sat secluded in the side of a hill.

"This is my peaceful place," she said, gesturing to the surroundings.

Dane nodded. He wore jeans and a black T-shirt with a flannel, brown plaid button-up overshirt.

The children rushed Dane, asking for their toys—a ball

and a Frisbee—and immediately ran to the meadow and started to play.

Rikki and Dane found a large rock at the entrance to the cave and sat a careful distance apart, distracted by watching the kids play. The rich, damp earth smell had her taking a deep breath. Chilled air seeped out of the cave. How many times had the solitude here comforted her?

"This is beautiful. I can see why you like it here." It was the first moment they'd been alone since their date. "What do you think about when you come here?"

She shrugged and smiled, wondering if she dared to open up. "Trust me. You don't want to know."

"Try me."

She couldn't quite bring herself to tell him her deepest thoughts. Why unload her past on an unsuspecting man she hardly knew? It would only chase him further away.

"Why do I suspect it has a lot to do with all those things you do?" He pointed to Brenden. "And the reason you want to be a foster-parent? Most women your age wouldn't consider it. They're too busy dancing, party-hopping, and looking for the next good time."

"I guess it's because I'm a foster-care graduate. I went to my first home when I was three. Just a little younger than Brenden."

"I see." He went on alert, a keen glimmer in his eyes.

He nodded and leaned closer. She could smell his spicy aftershave. Tempted to give in to his masculine appeal and tell him her whole story, she withdrew to the safe inner place she'd created early in life to help her cope. A place no one else could touch.

After a few moments of dead silence, he cleared his throat.

"About our date the other night…"

If Rikki hadn't known better, she'd think the usually self-assured Dane Hendricks had taken a nosedive into embarrassment. Had he thought about that kiss as much as she had?

She gulped and jumped in. "It was a little rocky. I'm sorry…"

"No. No. If anyone needs to apologize it's me." He took her hand in his. "I'm sorry I put you on the spot, that I picked a steak house without asking you, that I failed to put you at ease and, most importantly, that I kissed you when it was clear you weren't interested in me that way."

She wanted to protest—his kiss had made her fingers tingle—but found she couldn't quite form the words.

"I guess some people are just better off being friends," he continued.

Her heart sank with disappointment, but she knew he was right. They weren't suited to each other.

In the distance the girls' voices grew shrill, drawing their attention. They were fighting over a red Frisbee, neither letting go, one screaming, the other crying. Brenden looked on in silent curiosity.

Dane rushed them. "Knock it off, girls." His voice boomed through the fall air. The girls went quiet, staring at the ground mutinously.

Rikki skipped over and put a hand on each girl's shoulder. "Hey, you know what I do when I don't want to share?" The little ones looked up at her, still avoiding eye contact with their father. She could see the defeated look on his face. She needed to lighten the mood, and thought fast. "I play hopscotch! Come on, we'll all take turns."

She led them from the grass to a dirt and gravel patch

and used the toe of her hiking boot to draw the hopscotch lines, then searched for a small rock to be her marker. "Go on, you guys find your markers."

With the tense scene totally forgotten by all but Dane, the children scuttled around, searching for their very own marker. While they did so, Dane touched Rikki's shoulder.

"Thank you for that. I just feel I have to shout over them when they start arguing. Damn, I'm bad at this parenting business."

"No, you're not. You just haven't found your parenting style yet. It might work better to get their attention if you lower your voice when you get upset. They'd have to quiet down to hear what you say, and they'd see by your facial expression that you aren't happy with them."

"How old are you? How do you know all this stuff?"

She laughed. "I paid attention in child development in my pediatric nursing studies. That's all."

Dane shook his head and gave a smile. It buoyed her outlook on just about everything. The kids tugged on her hands, and she ran off to play with them.

A few minutes later the children were ready for tossing the ball and she left them alone. Dane sat on a small boulder, grinning at her. Her step felt light, though she wore heavy duty hiking boots.

"Something tells me you're a special lady."

"Oh, no, not me. Besides being a notable date-saboteur, I'm just a regular girl."

He gave a soft smile and scooted to one side of the rock so she could join him. "Not so. For one thing, you're stoic. Most of the women I've ever known lay it all out there. You hear their history whether you want to or not. You know what I mean?"

She tried not to grin at the implication that all women were yakkers. "I'll forgive you the stereotype."

He chuckled and tugged on the short hair at the nape of her neck. Soothing warmth tickled her shoulders. The caring gesture made her long for something.

"So, do you want to tell me about what it's like to be a foster-kid?"

Could she trust Dane with her truth? With every sad detail of her childhood? It would only make him feel sorry for her. No, she'd keep her past to herself. "You don't want to ruin our day, do you?"

Dane got her point. Rikki had no intention of opening up. "For the record, I have issues, too."

She lifted her head, surprised by his confession. "Hey, if I were a reluctant parent, I'd have issues, too."

He nodded. "I'm punching in the dark as far as the girls go. I have no idea how to be a good father. You saw how I screwed up just now. How am I supposed to prepare them for life?"

"It's the hardest job in the world. But hang in there. For the most part, you seem to be doing great."

Something about spending a non-date afternoon had opened Dane up. He kept talking.

"It's not just being a single parent either. I feel like I don't have any control over my life anymore. As a doctor, I'm used to fixing people. Break a bone? I can fix it. Need a new knee? I can give you one. But my own kid brother has leukemia and I can't help. I'm a doctor, damn it, and I can't help him. It drives me nuts."

"But there are doctors who can help him with his leukemia."

"Yeah. But his latest round of chemo hasn't helped

much. It suppresses the disease, but his bone marrow doesn't respond well enough. They say he needs a marrow transplant and, like I said, I can't even help him there."

"You should have the lab tap into the hospital donor center files for other possible donors. And don't forget the national registry. Check mine out. It's worth a shot. There's got to be someone somewhere who matches."

He sighed. "Yeah. Good point. I'll look into it." After a few more moments he said, "Have you ever thought about tracing your birth family?"

His warm breath tickled the side of her face. She felt chills down her neck.

"Maybe you have relatives somewhere."

"It's a scary thought at this point. I don't know anything about them, only my surname, and it's pretty common."

"Maybe I can help you with it."

"Thanks." She pulled back and looked up into his green eyes. "Maybe I can help you find a marrow donor for your brother. I'll ask all the nurses on Four North to get tested."

He smiled down at her. "You've got yourself a deal."

After a long delightful day, the warm weather cooled, and the kids had played themselves to exhaustion. They made a fast-food stop for dinner and said their goodbyes on her doorstep while Dane's daughters slept in the car. Brenden ran inside to use the toilet.

"I'm having a few neighborhood kids over tomorrow afternoon for a craft day. Maybe your girls would like to come? We'll be making simple decorations for Thanksgiving. They might enjoy it."

"You know? I'd really like to watch some football with Don tomorrow. I may take you up on that offer."

* * *

The next afternoon, Dane dropped off his daughters as planned. He looked rugged in old jeans and a worn shirt with his favorite football team's name on it. While he was distracted, saying goodbye to his girls, she took in every inch of him. Damn.

Later, when he tapped on her door, Rikki felt excited. Her heart fluttered and her cheeks warmed up. All the other children had gone home with their Pilgrim and turkey decorations made from toilet-paper rolls, glue, and colored construction paper. Meg and Emma were watching Brenden show off all the cool moves his robot could make in his bedroom.

"Hey," Dane said, on the other side of the screen door.

"Hiya." She opened it and let him in.

"So you survived?"

"I had six kids from the neighborhood, plus your girls, and I've got to tell you, Meg and Emma are really good kids. You should be proud of yourself."

"They didn't fight?"

"They were perfect angels."

"Are we talking about the same kids? Short, blonde hair, knobby knees?"

She laughed.

Dane's softened eyes crinkled when he smiled down at Rikki. She caught her breath, realizing he intended to kiss her. He dipped his head and gave her a gentle, warm kiss, covering her mouth for what seemed like eternity, but in reality lasted only a moment or two. Her head spun with the feel of his lips on hers.

Just as quickly, he backed off. His eyes were a darker shade of green and his smile was nowhere to be found. He looked deeply into her eyes. "Oops. There I go again." He held up his hands. "I know. We're just friends."

Reeling with the kiss, and the possibilities, Rikki searched for her voice and strung together the best thing she could think of. "Just friends."

After floating through Sunday, reality came crashing down for Rikki on Monday morning. Brenden woke up sulking and stalled every step of the way getting ready for and going to child care.

Rikki had barely made it out of the shift change nurse report when Janetta summoned her to her office. Rikki peeked around the door and found her supervisor on the phone. Janetta waved for Rikki to take a seat.

Rikki stretched her neck and shoulders, sat, crossed her legs and waited for Janetta to hang up.

"You look about as perky as a dead cat. What's up?"

"I had a rough morning with Brenden. He didn't sleep well last night. Ever since he woke up this morning, all he seems to want is his daddy." She bit at a rough fingernail.

"Aw, all boys are alike. Just rough-house with him. He's a boy—he wants to be thrown around, not talk. I've got two grandsons, I should know."

"Hmm. I'll think about that. So you wanted to see me?"

"Yeah. I just received a call from the donor center. They're requesting an interview with you some time today. I'll try to find someone to cover for you so you can go down to the lab, but I can't promise."

"Thanks. But I'm sure whatever it is can wait. It's probably about my next platelet donation appointment or something."

Before she'd finished her thought, the ward clerk's

voice came over the intercom. "We need muscle in room 411."

Raising her brows, Janetta stood. "We'd better check this out."

They arrived in the room to find a patient in a long leg cast and a neck brace on the floor. An apologetic and wild-eyed nurse explained, "I was helping him onto his bedside commode, and we both lost our balance. You're OK, aren't you, Fred?"

"I'm fine. I just can't get up."

A male LVN entered the room, and the four nurses lifted the patient up and assisted him back into the bed.

"Be sure to fill out the incident report," Janetta said to the nurse as she left. "And call his doctor. He may want to get an X-ray."

The rest of the day was busy with nonstop admissions, discharges, and patient care. Rikki never had a chance to go to the donor center, and promised to see to it the first thing next morning. She was exhausted by 4:00 p.m. and wanted to go straight home. Brenden was cranky and with-drawn when she picked him up from day care. There would be no chance to relax tonight.

Rikki loaded up the boy into her car, secured him in the car seat, and drove home.

Two hours later, things hadn't gotten any better. Brenden whined and moaned, and every time Rikki tried to get close, he pushed her away.

Her home training suggested giving the child time to adjust to his new surroundings, but Brenden's break-in period seemed to go on for ever, and felt like torture. After a few weeks of smooth sailing, he'd had a relapse. And tonight he continued with his favorite demand.

"I want my daddy!"

She'd failed at trying to distract him with puzzles, books, toss toys, children's DVDs, and ice cream. Nothing worked to bribe him out of his mournful mood.

"I want my daddy!"

She raked her fingers through her hair and thought fast. Since she'd been doting on him, he'd quit screaming for his mother. She'd noticed how quiet and awed he'd gotten whenever Dane had given him attention at the park on Saturday. He especially enjoyed himself when they'd played catch.

Maybe if a man were around to give him some attention, he'd quit begging for his father. It seemed like wacky logic, but Rikki was desperate, and her young charge seemed beyond miserable. She had to do something.

"I want my daddy!" Brenden dissolved into a heap on the floor.

Rikki grimaced and picked up the phone to call the only man she knew—Dane. The kiss that had made her knees go weak came to mind and she had to sit down. He'd been in surgery, sending new post-op patients to her ward all day, so she hadn't seen him.

There was no answer at his house and, suspiciously relieved, she didn't leave a message.

She hoped she could distract Brenden by baking, even though it was the opposite of what Janetta had suggested. Horseplay?

"Let's make your favorite cookies."

"I want my daddy!"

She opened a cupboard and handed him a measuring cup. "Here, I need your help."

An hour later, managing to minimally engage the boy,

the first batch of chocolate-chip cookies came out of the oven. She removed them to cool while Brenden watched with a blank stare. Someone tapped on her apartment door. She flung a dishtowel over her shoulder and rushed to answer.

Dane stood under the yellow porch light with both daughters in tow. The girls were dressed in pajamas, robes and slippers. One wore a Cinderella pattern, the other Sleeping Beauty. They looked tiny and vulnerable next to their huge father.

The sight of him made Rikki go off balance. Even Brenden lifted his head from his curled-up position, curious as to who was at the door. "Hi!" Rikki couldn't help her excitement.

"Hi," Dane said, with a serious face. "I need to talk to you."

"Something smells really good," Meg said.

"They're chocolate-chip cookies," Rikki said.

The girls rushed inside. "My favewit!" one of them said.

They ran over to Brenden, who quickly forgot about sulking.

"What's up?" Rikki asked.

Dane stepped cautiously inside her apartment. "I've just received a call from the hospital. They've found a donor for my brother."

"That's wonderful!"

He brushed his knuckles across her cheek. "You've got flour on your face." He stood quietly watching her, as though searching for the right words while she wiped at the smudge. "They found a donor with a matching cell type to Don's, and want to move ahead with the bone-marrow transplant as soon as possible. I got the call when I was giving the girls their bath a half-hour ago."

Her hand flew up to her mouth. "That's so fantastic."

"Once his current chemo treatment is finished, he'll be ready for the transplant. All we need is to get the consent of the matching donor."

"How soon will that be?"

Dane reached for her hand, his trembling slightly. "As soon as you sign the Intent to Donate."

Rikki stared at him, confused. Her fingers tightened in his clutch.

"I don't know why they called me instead of you first, but the head of the lab said you're the match. I think he tried to call you at work today, and he'll call again tomorrow. Or maybe he left a message here. I don't know, but I couldn't wait to tell you."

All the blood rushed out of her head. She'd been so distracted by Brenden's foul mood she hadn't checked her phone messages. Dizzy, she needed to sit down. He grabbed her arm and helped her to the nearest chair.

"I know this is a shock, but you're a godsend, Rikki. You're the one who told me it's a one in 40,000 chance and yet you match my brother. You're the perfect match. Isn't that incredible?" He grabbed her hands again and smiled at her.

Her mouth went dry. She tried to focus on Dane's face, but it was blurry. The process of donation had seemed so easy when she'd signed up with the national registry. While she was under anesthesia, a doctor would do a simple surgical procedure using hollow needles to withdraw marrow from her pelvic bones. Her marrow would be infused into Dane's brother and would travel to his chemo-suppressed marrow and would hopefully multiply and help him back to restored health. Wasn't that what she'd dreamed of doing when she'd signed up? Hell, she'd already committed to donating. What was one more signature?

Dane sat beside her and put his arm around her. "Think about it. Take as much time as you need before you sign anything tomorrow. OK? It's a huge commitment. If you agree, you'll need to get a medical exam. That's easily arranged. Listen, I'll watch the kids while you think this through."

On cue, the oven timer went off. Another batch of cookies was ready to come out. Without thinking, she jumped up and rushed to the kitchen to finish her baking. She'd attended a thorough information session when she'd originally signed up with the national registry, but it all seemed so distant. Now it was real.

Dane followed her to the kitchen.

Brenden took one look at him and blurted, "I want my daddy!"

Using potholders to remove the baking pan, she said, "I can't seem to make Brenden happy tonight."

"Is there something I can do?"

"Maybe just talk to him? I honestly don't know how to reach him." She glanced over her shoulder. "But your daughters sure know how to make him feel at home."

"My social butterflies." He smiled proudly. "I know they didn't get that from me. What the heck, let me give it a shot. I owe you after yesterday."

Dane seated himself on her mini-couch, making it look even tinier. With her mind spinning about her chance to help someone with cancer, she brought out the first batch of cookies and a pitcher of milk. Slowly Brenden edged closer to the group, and wound up standing next to Dane, staring and quiet. Dane offered him a cookie. He took it and nibbled.

"Hey, champ. What's up?" Dane reached out his hand for a high five, but instead the boy crawled onto his lap. Dane bounced him on his knee until Brenden giggled.

"Stop it." Brenden chortled.

Dane stopped instantly, for one second, then started right back up again with the energetic bouncing.

"I said stop it." Brenden laughed.

"Stop what?"

"You know."

"Oh. OK." Dane repeated the teasing pattern several more times, to Brenden's delight.

The light-hearted gesture made Rikki smile, though she worried and was preoccupied about her important opportunity. It was time to put all her good intentions to the test. She suspected what her decision about donating marrow would be, but the details had to be worked out.

Brenden hadn't ever looked this happy. When Rikki realized Emma and Meg would soon be invading the game, she moved right in. "Do you know what I've got?"

"What?" they both asked.

"Beads! Would you like to make your very own bracelets?"

"Yeah!"

Rikki guided the twins into Brenden's room and closed the door, giving the males a chance to bond. An hour later, they'd all made new jewelry and then wore them for a special tea party, and she'd read three books to the girls while they'd cuddled up on the bed.

Rikki snuggled with them, content. They smelled like bubble bath. A strange feeling wrapped around her until she thought she might cry. These precious little girls, so eager for female attention, had brought her a new kind of happiness. It reinforced her dream of having a big family. The more the merrier. No child left behind, all loved equally. And their uncle needed a bone-marrow transplant so he could be around to watch them grow up, get married, and have kids of their own one day. Basically, it was a no-brainer. She'd already made her decision.

"I have to pee!" Meg said.

When Rikki opened her door, she found Dane with Brenden on his back, riding him around the living room, intentionally shaking him off, making the boy laugh hysterically, and then faking an apology. "Oh, I'm sorry, champ. I don't know how that happened. Here, get on again."

The moment the boy did, Dane bucked him off again. Brenden howled with joy. "Now, you stop that."

Rikki smiled so hard at the sight of them rough-housing and having fun, her eyes watered. Dane's brother deserved a chance at life. She'd sign the consent first thing tomorrow morning.

When the girls finished in the bathroom, they rushed their dad and Brenden.

"My turn."

"My turn."

They dove onto their father's broad, strong back, and all three of them rode around her house on a bucking bronco tour until Dane collapsed from exhaustion.

"That's enough, kids," he said breathlessly. He plopped onto his back and lay sprawled on her floor. He'd taken off his glasses. His shirt had become untucked from his pants, revealing a flat stomach with a thin trail of light hair working its way up to his chest. She shouldn't have noticed it, but she couldn't help herself. Not only was he one appealing male, he was a natural at fathering, at least the playing-around part if not the tying of bows.

"Would you kids like to watch a short video?" Rikki suggested in order to give Dane a break and keep him around a while longer.

"Yeah," they sang out, knowing it was well past their usual bedtime.

No sooner had she set up the kids with the latest children's show, and started to sort things out in her kitchen, than Dane showed up, leaning on her kitchen door. It made her nervous.

She tossed the dishtowel over her shoulder and folded her arms. "How can I thank you?"

"I was about to ask you the same thing."

"What?"

"Something tells me you'll sign that consent." He gave her a long, appreciative smile. "And I haven't seen my girls shine like that in a long time. You've got a way with my kids."

Wait. Was he flattering her to get her signature? He seemed so sincere about everything, and she'd already made up her mind.

He waited expectantly for her response.

"So do you. Brenden really came out of his shell tonight. I'll have to call on you more often."

Dane stepped closer, his hair disheveled from playing with the kids. Rikki resisted a powerful urge to fix it. They made silly grins at each other. He still wasn't wearing his glasses.

A subtle change of expression overshadowed his charm.

"Taking on more parenting duties is the last thing I need on my plate right now. So don't get any ideas. OK?"

Stung by the reminder, Rikki pretended not to care. "Ah, no. Brenden is my responsibility."

"As long as we've got that straight." He seemed defensive.

"I will need to go into the hospital for the bone-marrow procedure, though. I'll need someone to watch Brenden that day at least."

"You've already made up your mind? Of course I'll watch him. It's the least I can do." He took another cookie from the batch cooling and chomped it down. "You make great cookies, by the way." He stepped closer and took the towel off her shoulder, tossing it onto the counter.

She wanted to be angry with him for steamrolling through with the marrow donation plans, and for being so blunt about never wanting more kids, but his close proximity made her heart race.

He put his hands on her shoulders. "For the record, I really liked how you were dressed the other night at the restaurant. I don't think I told you." His eyes bored into hers.

How could she stay mad at him?

"And I like your short hair." He took inventory of her spiky new look and smiled. "I like those hip-hugger jeans and this skimpy top, too." He tugged on the hem. "And right now, *friend,* I'd like to kiss you again."

Oh, what the hell. His green eyes sent shivers down her spine. Everywhere he touched, her skin prickled. She hadn't forgotten their kisses, either of them.

He pulled her closer and covered her mouth with a soft

touch of his lips, just like the kiss the other night on her doorstep. She wanted to protest—it wasn't the right time for this—but it felt so good. She crumbled against his chest. She went up on tiptoe, tilted her chin and kissed him back, sending a definite message.

He dipped his head, held her face with both hands and took possession of the kiss, investigating the tiny piercing above her lip with his thumb. He drew her closer. She wrapped her hands around his neck. He tasted like bitter-sweet chocolate as she ran her tongue along the soft lining of his lips. He slowly explored her mouth and melted away every last bit of hope that she'd be able to control herself.

A warm rush traveled over her entire body when, on a deep inhalation, their stomachs touched and she felt tingling down to her core. The pleasant awakening danced between her legs, up her spine and across her chest. Her kisses grew eager, and his hot hands roamed across her back and over her hips.

Her breasts tightened and peaked and she pressed into his firm chest to satisfy her need to be closer. He groaned, and caressed her tighter, while kissing the most sensitive spot on her neck. Shivers slid over every inch of her skin. Hot with desire and longing to feel more of his flesh, she reached under his shirt and ran her hands up his taut skin, lightly brushed in crinkly hair.

She had a strong urge to rip open his shirt and run her cheek across that hair, but controlled herself. Cheers from the living room made her realize the kids' video was already over. The last thing she wanted to do was end their embrace, but she kissed him once more then broke away.

"Want to have a sleepover?" *I only meant to think that!* She couldn't believe the bold words even as they came out of her mouth.

He tugged her back, hugged her close and kissed the top of her head. "Definitely. But not tonight. I've got surgery all day tomorrow, and its way past their bedtime. I'm going to have to take my girls home."

She totally understood and tried not to cringe. Determined to be more businesslike, she said, "You made such a difference tonight with Brenden. Thank you."

"And you'll make a huge difference for my brother."

She kissed his cheek, and regretfully pulled free from the warmth of his arms, ready to get back on duty as a foster-mother. An uncomfortable thought came to mind. "You're not just doing this because I'm donating bone marrow to your brother, are you?"

"Hell, no! And I'm insulted you think so. I came over here to tell you the good news. All the rest is just as much a surprise for me as it is for you. Trust me. OK?"

Had she ever been able to trust anyone in her life? Mrs. Greenspaugh came to mind. *"You're a good person, Rikki, my girl, and you've got to understand, there are other people in the world just like you—good at heart. But we all make mistakes."*

Dane scratched the back of his neck. "I have to admit, I enjoyed myself horsing around with Brenden, too." His smile grew mischievous. "But not nearly as much as just now." He lifted his brows. "Horsing around with you."

She grinned and felt her face grow hot. She mock fanned herself. "If you keep that up, I'm going to need to put on the air-conditioning."

"A quicker way to cool down is to take off your clothes." His eyes hooded over, and he scanned her from head to toe with what felt like X-ray bedroom vision. Oh, yeah, he liked what he saw.

"Rikki, I need you," Brenden called out.

In an instant, a completely different feeling blossomed in Rikki's chest—pure and simple joy. Something even more compelling than kissing a sexy man like Dane got all of her attention—her foster-son's voice.

CHAPTER FIVE

RIKKI straightened her clothes and burst through the door.

"Yes, Brenden?"

"Can you take the video out?"

"Sure."

"I like your friends." His smile, accented by deep dimples and chocolate-chip smudges, was the single most beautiful sight she'd ever seen. Dane's taut stomach ran a close second.

"Well, since you like us so much," Dane said, entering from the kitchen, "I've got Thursday afternoon off. Maybe we can all go and see a movie since Rikki will need to see a doctor."

After their kiss, her head went spinning with the possibilities. Things would get too complicated if they continued with their infatuation for each other.

"Are you sick, Rikki?" Brenden's face looked worried.

"No. I'm going to help someone else get better."

Dane said goodbye to Brenden, bundled up his girls, and sent a meaningful sexy look her way just before he put his glasses back on and opened the door. She fought off the magnetic force of his smile, and stopped herself from rushing over and planting another solid kiss on him.

Instead, she hugged the twins and promised another tea party soon.

When she stood up, their eyes met.

"I'll never be able to repay you for what you're doing for Don."

She gave a somber nod. "I'm not doing it to get repaid. I'm just glad I can help."

"I know, but nevertheless…"

Brenden leaned against her leg. As natural as breathing, she ran her fingers through his shock of hair.

She allowed herself to wallow in her little happily-ever-after fantasy for a few extra moments before Dane's words in the kitchen came back to ruin her mood.

Taking on more parenting duties is the last thing I need on my plate right now. Despite what he'd said, he was only staying involved in her life because she'd said she'd help his brother.

"So, I guess I'll see you soon," he said, turning to leave. He glanced over his shoulder with a mischievous glance. "For the record, you really look hot tonight."

She grinned as they walked away, and then sputtered a laugh when she heard Meg ask, "Does Rikki have a fever?"

She closed the door and switched off the porch lights.

The possibility of she and Dane getting involved sent a shiver down her spine. First, she needed to learn how to feel comfortable around him, and to trust he'd accept her for who she was. She knew she wasn't in the sophisticated league of Hannah Young, if that was what he was looking for, but she'd never want to be like her. She didn't want to just be a fling to Dane either and worried that he was using her to make sure his brother had a bone-marrow donor.

Addy? Why can't I trust anyone?

A lifelong lesson in self-defense urged her to form a plan. As she was donating her marrow to Dane's brother, she couldn't get involved any further with him.

Her decision was for the greater good, and this good deed required both physical and emotional sacrifice.

Brenden tugged on her leg. "Will you read me a book?"

She bent down to meet him eye to eye. "Of course I will." She ruffled his hair, pretending nothing had changed when her entire outlook toward Dane would never be the same. "But first you've got to brush your teeth."

Dane sat across from Janetta the next morning. "I realize Rikki had a few days off last week, and she probably doesn't have any paid vacation due, so I'd like to make sure she gets a check."

"I don't have a clue how we can do that. The only thing I can do is to arrange her schedule so she has a three-day weekend. Maybe you can arrange for the donor date to match?"

"That would work. Now that she has consented to the marrow donation, I've moved ahead and made all of the arrangements. It's an outpatient procedure." He rubbed his jaw. "She'll need a driver to take her home. I'll see what I can do."

Things had certainly gotten complicated. Rikki had gone from being the date from hell to his brother's savior, and he wasn't sure where his feelings fit in. She was so damn energetic and quirky, she kept him on his toes, and he liked being challenged by a woman. Not to mention her exemplary altruism. But she was already suspicious that the only reason he pursued her was for an ulterior motive—his brother's health.

Now that they'd kissed, his instincts about her being one damn appealing woman were right on target. He'd suspected as much on their disastrous date and again on that day in the park, but after last night he knew he wanted more of Rikki in his life. He'd have to work out all the other details later.

"Hey! Where did you go? You were saying?" Janetta said.

Dane snapped back into the conversation. "Oh, I'm just working things out in my head. I'll take a couple of days off work and reschedule a few elective surgeries to make sure I have time for both Rikki and Don. If she needs transportation home and someone to watch Brenden, I guess I'll have to do that, too. Hell, I owe her, and it's the least I can do."

"I'll say."

But it wasn't just his duty—he cared about Rikki, and wanted to make sure she was OK. Damn, that part had snuck up and knocked him sideways.

"By the way, this Thursday, she'll need part of the afternoon off. I've arranged for Dr. Prescott to give her a physical. If all goes well, we're good to go for the marrow donation on Friday."

"This Friday? Has she agreed to all of this?" Janetta sputtered her sip of forbidden coffee at her computer. "How am I supposed to do all the rescheduling now?"

"For the record, she is definitely on board with it. I'm sure you'll work something out, Janetta. You're the queen of scheduling." He stood to leave. He was due in surgery in fifteen minutes.

She rolled her eyes and shook her head. "Right."

"And maybe you and I can take turns calling her every

couple of hours on Friday night. You know, just to make sure she's all right."

"Why don't you just have her stay with you?"

"Now, Janetta, that wouldn't be appropriate. The rumor mill would go into overdrive if anyone found out."

"Honey, I've got news for you, it already has."

On Friday morning Dane picked up Rikki and Brenden at eight o'clock. Her scheduled appointment for hospital admission was nine. He'd have time to deliver the kids to the child-care center and get back up to the surgical oncology suite before anything officially started.

Rikki appeared at the door freshly showered, and she hadn't bothered to put any makeup on or do anything with her hair. She looked all of sixteen with big brown eyes and pale olive-toned skin. Skin smooth enough to stroke.

He cleared his throat. "You ready?"

She nodded. "As ready as I'll ever be."

"You haven't eaten or had anything to drink since midnight, right?"

"Oh, gee, Doc, I didn't know that." She crossed her eyes, stressing her point.

"All right, OK, I guess I'm as nervous as you must be."

She nodded, put on her warm-up jacket and zipped it up. "Everything will work out."

An hour later she was in a hospital gown and was handed a consent form for the operation.

"You know, I've always had to explain these things to my patients," she said to the nurse. "From this side of the gurney it does look scary. I know they've got to state every single thing that might go wrong but, gosh, possible nerve damage and-or death?" She looked at Dane for support.

"Everything will go as smooth as silk," he said, resorting to clichés to ease his nerves. The palms of his hands had gone clammy at the thought of Rikki going through the procedure and, worse, any potential complications. "By the way, I'm calling in my staff privileges. I've asked to sit in on the marrow donation. Is that all right with you?"

She nodded, swimming in the hospital gown, looking as though she was shrinking right before his eyes. "I'd like that."

"I thought you could use some moral support." He gowned up. "I promised my brother we'd all celebrate with a beer once the transplant is a success."

"How long will that take?"

"Two to four weeks. We'll keep our fingers crossed until then. Come to think of it, some prayers wouldn't hurt."

The anesthesiologist arrived in the room with her box of drugs—a short, exotically attractive woman with large dark eyes similar to Rikki's, accentuated by the OR cap. "I'm Dr. Armerian." They shook hands. After a wide, infectious smile, she got down to the business at hand. "Are you allergic to any medications?"

"Not that I know of."

"Good. I'll be using general anesthesia as you'll be in the prone position. It works best."

She continued with a whole series of questions, and Dane felt like an eavesdropper, learning so much about Rikki's medical history. Though many of the family medical questions couldn't be answered as she hadn't a clue whether heart disease or high blood pressure and several other ailments ran in her family or not. Being a foster-kid, she just didn't know.

The oncologist, Jere Rhineholdt, stepped into the suite and greeted both of them. He was a middle-aged man with broad features, graying hair and slouching shoulders. If seen on the street, no one would ever dream the unassuming man was a highly acclaimed specialist. "Are you ready?"

Rikki nodded. The nurse started the IV, stuck on the electrodes for monitoring Rikki's heart, and placed the automatic blood-pressure cuff set for every five minutes.

Dane knew Jere had performed hundreds of these bone-marrow aspiration procedures and was as skilled as any doctor could be. Still, his heart raced when he realized there was no going back.

"Rikki, I'm going to sedate you now." The anesthetist injected a small amount of medicine into her IV port.

Without thinking, Dane placed his hand over Rikki's shoulder to reassure her. She glanced up with trusting velvet eyes, and his chest squeezed. She felt so tiny, and he had a powerful urge to protect her.

The RN edged in front of Dane. "Are you sure you being here is OK with Hank Caruthers?" she asked teasingly.

Dane grinned at the reference to Mercy Hospital's administrator—the king of policies and procedures. Sensing the tension in Rikki's body, and wanting to lighten things up for her, he couldn't resist doing his infamous, though politically incorrect imitation. He'd gladly resort to clowning around if it would help her relax.

Rikki sputtered a laugh, along with everyone else—mission accomplished. With her eyes closed, she yawned. She hadn't gone completely out yet. Within a few more seconds she was deep asleep and had been skillfully intubated by the anesthetist. Dane helped the nurse roll her onto her stomach, though, with her lithe body, he could have done it by himself with one arm tied behind his back.

The surgical nurse washed and prepared her skin with antiseptic and placed a sterile field across her buttocks. Rikki had a delicate butterfly tattoo on her right hip, and Dane's mind went flying off topic for a moment when he first caught sight of it. He quickly reverted to professionalism, though his libido had definitely been piqued.

Dr. Rhineholdt donned double sterile gloves and reached for a scalpel. He made a tiny slit in Rikki's flesh above the right posterior iliac crest, her hipbone, and dabbed at a drop of blood with sterile gauze. He reached for a large-bore needle and used surprising force to ram it into her bone to collect spongy red marrow, reusing the small incision over and over as the point of entry.

Dane winced at each puncture. Thank God Rikki was unconscious. This step would be repeated two to three hundred times over the next couple of hours in order to collect a liter of bone marrow.

More blood beaded and trickled down Rikki's hip. The nurse repositioned a sterile towel to catch it. Rikki's tiny body got bumped and pushed with each collection, and Dane didn't think he could take watching it much longer. But he needed to be there for her. She didn't have anyone else, and he owed her. He took her hand in his, knowing she was unconscious and wouldn't even know. Somehow it gave him reassurance.

How different it was to be the surgeon and do what was necessary for the patient, as opposed to watching someone he cared about go through a tough procedure. He looked away as the needle was plunged into her hip again. What kind of person would go through this for a complete stranger?

Someone like Rikki.

After completing the procedure on the right side, Dr. Rhineholdt moved to her left hip and made a new incision. The marrow was collected into heparin-rinsed syringes and transferred to a container washed with anti-coagulant to prevent clotting. An hour and a half into the procedure, they'd almost filled the bottle to the 900-mil-liliter mark.

Dane noticed Rikki's blood pressure and pulse slowly dropping. The anesthetist had noticed it, too. "Are we almost done?" she asked. "I may have to wake her up soon."

"I need a full liter for the best results," Dr. Rhineholdt said.

"Blood pressure 80 over 50, pulse 45." Dr. Armerian increased the rate of the IV.

A knot the size of a fist formed in Dane's stomach. *Wake her up. Come on.* Her respirations were even and the oxygen saturation was 98 percent. With the other vital signs so low, the oxygen reading offered little solace. He rubbed her palm with his thumb then stroked her wrist in an attempt to stimulate an increase in her heart rate.

The oncologist made another puncture and collected 5 ml more marrow. The alarm went off on the heart monitor. Forty beats a minute. Blood pressure 75 over 45.

Dane clenched his fist and straightened his back. He shot an intense look at Jere. The anesthesiologist didn't wait a second longer. She drew up and injected into the IV an antidote for each ingredient in the sedative cocktail she'd given Rikki earlier.

Dr. Rhineholdt made one final lunge, and when he was done the nurse placed pressure on the two tiny incisions over each hip crest using sterile gauze. When the bleeding had stopped, she applied a bandage to both sides. The incisions were so small there was no need to stitch them.

Each ring of the monitor alarm robbed the air from Dane's lungs. He was responsible if anything went wrong with Rikki. He couldn't bear to have that on his conscience. So what if they didn't have enough bone marrow to complete the donation? Hell, it could be the difference between a successful bone-marrow transplant for his brother and a failure. Damn.

Slowly the monitor numbers edged upward, and Dane could breathe without a hitch in his chest. Rikki squeaked a moan around the endotracheal tube. The sweetest sound he'd ever heard from the toughest trooper he'd ever met— all five feet and one hundred and one pounds of her, according to her chart.

He stayed by her side throughout recovery, and was there when she asked for a sip of water.

"Hi," he said as he handed her the straw.

She sipped and swallowed. "Hi," she said with a hoarse voice and droopy eyes. "How did we do?"

"You did great. They're treating your marrow even as we speak, and Don should be getting the infusion tonight."

"That's great."

"You're great." He cupped her cheek with his palm. She gave a dry-lipped smile and sipped more water. Only because the recovery room nurse showed interest in the attention he gave Rikki did he stop. His attachment to the orthopedic nurse was none of her business.

The same recovery nurse monitored Rikki's vitals and when she noticed Rikki was fully awake said, "Doctor wants you to stay in the hospital overnight for observation."

"But I don't want to stay. I want to go home."

"They want to make sure your blood pressure doesn't go too low. You're only 90 over 60 right now."

"That's normal for me. I've got Brenden to look after. Please tell him to let me go home," she pleaded.

Reading the frustration on her face, Dane said, "I'll talk to him…" and left her bedside.

Fifteen minutes later, after pulling more doctor privilege strings, he reappeared, smiling victoriously. Rikki had fallen back to sleep, but her eyes popped open with an expectant, woozy stare when he touched her hand. "Well?"

"Dr. Rhineholdt said you can go home in a couple of hours on one condition."

"What's that?"

"That you come home with me."

"I can't do that!"

"Weren't you the one who wanted a sleepover?" he whispered with a sly smile.

Rikki wasn't about to let anyone know how dizzy she felt when she stood up. She used the recovery room bed to support her.

Once the nurse had gone over the discharge sheet and warned her about possible side effects from the procedure—the main one being fatigue, followed by back pain, with dizziness running a close third, oh, and don't forget to watch out for signs of infection—she signed the sheet and stood to dress.

The back of her hips ached as though she'd hiked twenty miles straight up and hadn't drunk enough water.

The orderly arrived with a wheelchair, and she gingerly slipped into it. Every bump and jiggle got her attention. She finally accepted the fact that there was no way she could watch Brenden by herself tonight.

Dane waited at the hospital curb with all three kids safely tucked into their booster seats in the back of his weekend car, an SUV. Her eyes widened at the sight of a typical family man, arms crossed and waiting, at the front of the discharge circle. He wore casual slacks and a yellow form-fitting polo shirt—an unassuming work of art.

A quick fantasy about her big family dreams eased the pain in her lower back. But she couldn't let herself go there. Maybe someday with someone else, but from now on she'd keep things with Dane on a strictly professional basis.

Dane rushed to her aid and helped her to stand, then guided her with a strong, secure hand to the car. He treated her as if she was fragile and precious, and the thought gave her chills.

"Hi, Rikki!" all three kids blurted in unison once she was seated in the front passenger seat.

"Hi, kids!" She gave a special smile to Brenden, who looked as if he was thriving with his new friends.

"We saw the penguin movie yesterday, and Dane said we could rent a movie tonight," Brenden said with an excited grin.

"Yay!" Meg screamed, quickly mimicked by Emma.

The twinkle in Brenden's eyes made Rikki's throat tighten.

Dane got into the car, filling up the entire driver's side.

"Are we ready?" He smiled as though they'd known each other all their lives.

"Yeah!" the kids' choir squealed.

Oh, yeah, her fantasy world responded. *I'm definitely ready for this.* If only this could have happened under different circumstances.

She dozed on and off during the drive until a short twenty minutes later they arrived at Dane's high-rise condo complex on Los Feliz Boulevard. She'd often driven by the two towers at the base of the Los Feliz Hills, but the only thing she'd ever thought about it was how the buildings stood out against all the other apartments and condos along the boulevard. She'd always assumed that Dane would live in a house.

They parked underground, and with Dane's assistance Rikki was able to get out of the high cab and wait while he released all three of the kids from their seats. "Hold hands," he said, obviously repeating a several-times-a-day mantra without a second thought.

"Come on, Brenden, we'll show you our toys!" Meg whisked the boy into the elevator and Emma announced she'd pushed the tenth floor button.

A comforting hand around her waist and another under her elbow made her feel as if she'd just come home from giving birth or something. Now, that was a fantasy she'd save and savor some time as a dream prayer just before she fell asleep.

"Watch your step," he said, when they reached a single step. "Hold the elevator open, please, Emma."

She liked how he spoke to his daughters with respect, not dictating their every move.

The girls were well versed in condo elevator skills, and

the door remained open until Rikki and Dane were safely inside. Then Emma pressed the "close" button, and they were on their way.

At a loss for words, she leaned comfortably into Dane's strength and warmth, a healing touch no pain medicine could ever provide, until they reached his floor. Just for now. Tomorrow she'd straighten him out on their new business-only status.

They entered a bright living room lined in subtle wallpaper with several oversized modern artworks decorating the walls like exclamation marks. Real oil paintings without frames—no prints for him.

The kids dashed down the hall.

Dane guided Rikki to a sage green wraparound leather couch that felt like kid gloves when she sat on it. One entire wall was filled with glass, and the light filtering through felt warm on her face. No drapes were in sight.

A small balcony with two lounger chairs faced the length of Vermont Avenue. Off in the furthest distance, thanks to the recent sweep-through of Santa Ana winds, a hint of sparkle made Rikki realize she was closer to the Pacific Ocean than she'd thought.

"Wait here while I get your bed ready."

"I don't need to lie down," she protested.

He stopped in mid-step and gave her an authoritative stare. "Yes, you do."

While she waited, she glanced into a small open kitchen area with kid-functional dining table. Next to it stood a sturdy, multicolored plastic children's toy kitchenette extravaganza. Rikki's heart squeezed at the thought that Dane's daughters came before any false pretense of adult sophistication.

Back in the living room she noticed he'd staked out a personal corner with an overstuffed recliner chair and reading light. A super-large TV filled up another part of the room. Functional, uncluttered living at its finest, and Rikki approved.

Dane reappeared with a pulse-jolting smile. "Your bed's ready."

"My bed?"

"Well, it's my bed, but you can use it today. I had my housekeeper put on fresh sheets just for you."

Her mouth went dry. He went out of his way with clean linen for her?

He assisted her to stand and led her down the hall. On the way they passed an office, the girls' room, where the kids were happily engaged in play, and a guest room. Wait, didn't she belong there?

He opened double doors into a cavernous master bedroom with a king-sized bed. No less than a dozen pillows lined the head, and the covers were turned down. Simple pale blue sheets waited.

She stopped short. "You didn't have to go to all this trouble on my account. I can sleep in your guest room."

He shook his head, looking exasperated with her self-effacement. "Just get in and shut up, will you?"

In her sweet dream about being a princess, Rikki crawled through what felt like molasses to get to an ornate door. She touched it and entered a foggy world of white, scented by tomato soup. Her stomach growled with pleasure. Someone tapped on her shoulder.

She squinted open her eyes and peeked. It was dusk, and Dane stood at the edge of his bed, a tray in one hand.

"I thought you should eat."

She sat up, vaguely remembering the dull pain in her hips, and ran her fingers through her hair. What must she look like? Did it matter?

"That smells dreamy. I'm famished."

"Good." He set up the tray over her lap, and sat beside her. "Brenden is having chicken strips, potatoes and peas with the girls. That boy can eat."

Rikki grinned. "Tell me about it." She forced a steady hand in order to take a spoonful of soup. She slurped and swallowed. "Tastes great."

"I didn't know if you wanted something more substantial or not, but I could throw a cheese sandwich together if you—"

"This is perfect. I can't thank you enough."

His eyes softened into a smile. He looked as though he was about to say something, but refrained.

"Dad?" Meg appeared at the door. "Brenden wants thirds."

"I'll be right there." She rushed back down the hall, repeating the news, while Dane tilted his head and lifted a brow. "Were you starving that kid?"

Rikki sputtered a laugh. "I think he has a hollow leg."

His eyes lingered on her. "I like when you do that."

"Do what?"

"You make a cute little snort when you laugh."

"I do not."

He stood. "You do…and it's cute."

Before she could protest further, he'd left and shut the door.

An hour later, she'd managed to clean up and walk down the hall. Dane sat in the midst of three rambunctious kids, playing a board game. The skilled orthopedic surgeon looked bewildered by the rules. His glasses where shoved to the top of his head. He rubbed his jaw.

"No, Dad. You're s'posed to take your turn *after* you spin the thingy, *then* you look at the card. Not first," Emma said, with arms crossed and an impatient stare.

Brenden covered his mouth and giggled.

"Hey," Dane chided. "Us guys have to stick together."

Brenden laughed harder and ducked his head.

Rikki's heart lurched at the sight. For someone who refused to have any more kids, he was a natural father. What a waste. But it didn't matter, because they were only business acquaintances from here on out.

Brenden noticed her first. "Hi, Rikki. Are you all better now?" The girls rushed her and threw their arms around her waist. She almost lost her balance.

"Careful, girls," Dane said.

Though stiff and achy, she smiled and hugged them. "Yep. I'm fine."

Dane jumped up. "Can I get you some water or tea?"

"I can get it myself. You go ahead and finish your game."

He tossed her a thanks-a-lot glare. She stuck out her tongue, smiled and walked to the kitchen to fill the teapot.

A short while later she felt him enter before she saw him. The fine hair at the base of her neck prickled. He leaned against the refrigerator in his socks. No wonder he'd snuck up on her. "I don't want you to push yourself too much tonight."

"Honestly, Dane, I'm just a little sore. No big deal." She scanned the cupboards to avoid looking into his eyes. She couldn't allow her infatuation with him to grow a centimeter deeper, and those bottomless green eyes might force her to. "Where are your teabags?" She reached for the logical cupboard closest to the stove at the exact instant he reached for the knob. His hand covered hers and held tight. Chills marched a two-step up her arm. She'd never been so physically drawn to a man in her life. Damn it! Why did it have to be under these circumstances? "This one?"

He stared at her and moved closer. "Right here." He opened it, still not releasing her hand from his, and reached over her with the other to retrieve the tea. "I have to tell you, you look great in my bathrobe." He rubbed his jaw. "I'd like to see you in one of my pajama tops, but I don't own any." His mouth slanted into a taunting smile.

Shaken to her core, she used the counter to regain her balance. Did he sleep in the buff? Why was he tormenting her? With her face on fire, she reached for a glass for water.

He knew what he was doing. He was taking advantage of her vulnerable state, and the thought of sharing his bed made her toes curl.

"I feel a little dizzy. I think I better sit—"

Before she could finish her sentence, he whisked her off her feet and carried her to the couch. His strong arms wrapped her in security and, with his heat and strength, thrilled her to her very center. His masculine scent sent her reeling. No! She couldn't let this happen.

"Don't move," he scolded. "I'll bring the tea to you."

She spent the rest of the evening trying desperately to keep her distance from Dane. Once she'd accidentally drifted off to snooze and had used his shoulder as her personal pillow. He hadn't pulled away.

Later, they all watched children's movies until her eyes

grew heavy and she gave in to sleep. The instant her eyes closed, Dane picked her up and carried her, like a crippled princess, back to bed. It felt fantastic and she didn't even think about protesting. Only for tonight, she promised herself.

Made snug and comfy by Dane's expertise with the blankets and pillows puffed just so, within minutes she drifted off into a deep sleep.

Some time in the early morning hours she woke up with her back pressed against the natural warmth of Dane's broad chest.

CHAPTER SIX

HAD he crawled into bed with her? His hand rested on her waist and one leg was protectively across her thigh. Fearful of what she might find, Rikki lifted her head and looked over her shoulder. Dane was on top of the covers and fully clothed but, still, how had he wound up there? She hadn't told him he could share the bed. Would she assume such an intimate notion? She savored the feel of him, just for a second, and almost dozed off again.

Under most circumstances she'd never agree to sleep with someone she hardly knew. But hadn't she thrown herself at him a few days back? Considering the extraordinary circumstances that had cast them together, they'd become close very fast, both professionally and personally. But she'd made up her mind about keeping their relationship strictly professional. She really should do something about Dane sleeping beside her.

Soon.

An hour later, after she'd dozed off another time or two, she cleared her throat. He gave a deep, contented inhalation. She cleared her throat again. He stirred and stretched long muscular arms. One eye popped open. He went up on his elbow, looking as surprised as she felt. His gaze darted over her, around the room, and back to her face, as though trying to get his bearings.

"Um. You're probably wondering how I got here," he said, reading her mind. She'd never seen Dane look sheepish before.

She rolled away from his grasp, leaving enough room for his twins plus Brenden to crawl between them. Pulling the covers tight to her chin, she faced him. "As a matter of fact, I was."

"You don't remember me bringing your pain medicine last night?"

"No." Was he fudging?

Recovering his composure, he yawned and rolled onto his back, folded his hands behind his head and stared at the ceiling. "You groaned like you were in a lot of pain, so I stuck around until you settled down. Only problem was I got comfortable on my favorite part of the bed." He pointed to the opposite side of the king-sized bed. "Way over there." He was now lying in the middle. "I guess I dozed off and must have migrated toward your warmth during the night."

Her warmth?

He glanced at her with an apologetic twinkle in his sleepy eyes.

"I'd say I was sorry, but I'd be lying." He gave a charming grin that would have knocked her socks off if she'd had any on. "This was so much better than sleeping on the couch."

She pulled the covers tighter to her chin. Why had all her bravado disappeared? Hadn't she been the one who'd requested a "sleepover" the other night at her apartment? But this was different—he'd actually slept in the same bed as her. And she'd just recently made up her mind about keeping whatever it was they had going on all business.

The implication slowly sunk in of the two of them lying together on his bed, and Rikki almost jumped off the mattress. She would have if she hadn't been tucked in so tightly and her hips hadn't still been tender.

He sat up. "Look, I'll give you some privacy. You can shower while I fix breakfast. You can even lock the door if that makes you feel better." Within a flash he'd left the room, leaving Rikki to wonder if it had all been a drug-induced dream. Nah, she couldn't have conjured up the penetrating warmth and sublime feeling of his broad chest spooned against her back, even if she'd tried.

The memory sent shivers all over her body. She couldn't dance so she made "snow angels" on his sheets, choosing to linger under the covers just long enough for the chills to settle down.

She'd get a hold of herself and, as hard as it would be, she'd make sure Dane understood from here on out they were nothing more than two people trying to get his brother well.

Dane had enough time to make a pot of coffee before the kids woke up. What the hell had he been thinking? He never should have sat on his bed and waited for Rikki's pain medicine to kick in. He'd woken up in a totally compromised position, and Rikki probably thought he was taking advantage of her. Never in a million years did he want to do that. He respected her too much.

Had he really thrown his leg over her thigh?

Like clockwork, the kids got up, and ringleader Emma switched on Saturday morning cartoons, taking his mind off thoughts of Rikki. Emma plopped onto her stomach, her head propped up on her elbows. Brenden, who'd slept in the guest room where Emma had thrown open the door on the way down the hall, followed. And Meg sandwiched herself in between them on the living-room floor.

The dynamic trio. What a sight. A thought flickered in the back of his brain. Was it a good thing or a bad one for his girls to become attached to a foster-child? They'd experienced enough loss in their short lives. How would he explain it to them if Brenden's relatives appeared and took him away?

He'd offer the kids cereal and save the last two eggs for Rikki's omelet. Orange juice and toast would be enough for him.

Damn, she'd felt great beside him. It had been ages since he'd cuddled up with a woman, and he hadn't realized how much he'd missed it until last night…with Rikki. He poured himself a cup of coffee and took a swig. Maybe it was time to think about having a woman in his life again. That was, if she was interested, he could get used to sharing a bed with her.

But what if things didn't work out? How devastating would it be for his daughters to lose another mother figure? Was it worth the risk of getting involved with Rikki?

When she sauntered down the hall, showered and completely dressed in her warm-up suit zipped up to her neck, the girls rushed her. "Hi, Rikki! Are you all better?" They hadn't wanted a hug from him that morning. Were they so starved for female attention?

She smiled and gathered both of their heads to her waist. "I feel great today." She played with their fine and frizzy hair and got down on her knees to look them both in the eyes. "Hey, may I comb your hair and braid it?"

"Yeah!" They jumped up and down. The poor girls had forgotten what it was like to have a woman fix their hair.

Brenden looked disgruntled.

"Hi, Brenden," Rikki said. "May I comb your hair, too?"

"Nah," he said, pretending to be annoyed yet looking pleased she'd asked. "Just do theirs. That's girl stuff." He put his chin back on his palms and watched TV.

Rikki found the girls' brush and started with Meg's hair, slowly brushing and smoothing her thin shoulder-length waves. Emma stared in reverence, patiently waiting her turn.

Dane pretended to be busy making toast, but he watched from the corner of his eye. Meg sat rapt under Rikki's spell, letting her part, divide, and gently tug her hair into compliance. The result: two spindly blonde braids and a bright smiling face.

His heart tugged at the sight.

"I want my hair like that, too," Emma said.

Rikki repeated the ritual with Emma. Dane wondered what was so hard about taking care of little girls that his ex-wife couldn't handle? What had proved overwhelming to her seemed second nature to Rikki. The simplest gesture of braiding hair, made both of his daughters ecstatic. And she'd managed to make sure Brenden didn't feel left out either. Three kids, all satisfied.

Though so young, Rikki was a natural mother and shouldn't be robbed of the chance. And he was a man who'd met his kid quota. Not exactly a perfect match. He needed to think things through before he made a huge mistake.

She glanced his way with velvet brown eyes and caught

him staring at her. All his doubts flew out of his head. The fact was, her mothering turned him on. How sick was that?

She blushed—another thing she did regularly around him—which also turned him on. She'd put the sexy piercing back in, and his mind drifted to that special little butterfly tattoo on her hip.

Holy hell, what was he thinking at eight in the morning?

He raked his fingers through his bed hair and turned away. Thank God the toast was done.

Later that day, Dane's mother offered to watch the kids so he could take Rikki to meet Don.

His brother was in isolation on the second floor oncology unit at Mercy Hospital, so they washed their hands, gowned up and put on masks and gloves, before entering his room. The chemo had suppressed his immune system, and the biggest threat to the success of the bone-marrow donation was infection.

Rikki tried to keep her shocked reaction to Don's frail appearance from reaching her eyes. Though closer to Rikki's age than Dane's, he looked several years older and was completely bald from chemotherapy. Her heart lurched at his fragile condition. She prayed her bone marrow would help him turn the illness around.

When they entered, Don brightened up. His wide grin, straight teeth, and a cleft chin could have tricked Rikki into thinking they were blood brothers. But Don had been adopted.

"Hey, bro," Dane said, natural as a daily routine. He lightly punched his brother's arm with a soft fist.

"Is this my match?" Don's eyes looked expectantly toward Rikki.

"Yes. This is Rikki Johansen," Dane said proudly.

She reached for Don's extended hand. "It's so wonderful to meet you."

"Hey, you're the lady of the century in my mind."

"Oh." She blushed, and Dane wrapped his arm around her shoulder. She glanced up to admiring eyes, but saw something deeper and it made the hair on her neck prickle. She couldn't let things between them go any further.

Since donating marrow, being left in Dane's care, and waking up in the same bed, he'd changed toward her. She couldn't quite put her finger on what the look meant, but hadn't Addy used to call it "smitten"?

Nah, it couldn't be. She must be suffering from anemia while she waited for her bone marrow to replenish itself, and wasn't thinking right. Most likely what she saw in Dane's eyes was nothing more than deep gratitude. And before the day was over she'd strike a deal with him. Their relationship would be nothing more than a working one.

After the forty-five-minute hospital visit, Dane took advantage of his mother's offer to continue to watch the kids. They made a quick stop at Rikki's house so she could change, then he took her to a well-known vegetarian restaurant on the Sunset Strip for a late afternoon meal.

"I'm not sure what you need to eat other than red meat to build up your red blood cells, but I trust you know what to do."

She'd changed into a bright pink short jacket that stopped mid-rib cage, and cropped, loose orange cargo pants. She'd put on makeup and had spiked her hair every which way and now it framed her face in a whirlwind. Somehow the total look worked for her. And the bare midriff drove him insane.

Each day he'd spent with Rikki he'd found himself growing more attracted to her unique look. And every moment since seeing her first thing that morning in his bed, he'd fought the powerful urge to kiss her again.

She was the most selfless person he'd ever met, and something from her past had groomed her to be that way. She hadn't opened up to him at the park, like he'd hoped. He suspected she hurt somewhere deep inside, and he wished she'd trust him enough to tell him about it.

She looked delighted that he'd taken her to a place where she fit in, and this time he was the one feeling out of his element.

"You're going to have to tell me what's safe to eat here," he said, leaning in close to her ear and catching a fresh flowery scent. One false move on her part and he'd nuzzle his nose in her neck, not giving a damn what anyone else thought. Come to think of it, on Sunset Strip, no one would give a couple necking a second glance anyway.

She laughed softly, her beautiful brown eyes sparkling in the late afternoon sun, and he couldn't resist kissing her another moment. He leaned in and brushed her lips with his. Zing! Right to the soles of his feet.

She quickly pulled back and he searched to the very depth of her *café au lait* eyes, seeing an answer he didn't expect. Compared to the woman in her kitchen the other night, the one who'd wanted to jump his bones, she'd changed. "No" was written in her stare, and she looked as regretful as he felt. They lingered in each other's gaze having a silent conversation. She requested understanding, and he made sure she knew he didn't like to be turned down.

A waiter coughed and cleared his throat.

"Will you be needing more time?"

Rikki sat up straight, forcing Dane to lose eye contact. "Oh," she said. "Actually, I know what I want." She ordered a bowl of hearty lentil soup and a spinach salad with fake bacon, and goat's cheese.

Dane picked up the menu and perused it quickly, thinking, *Now that I know exactly what I want, which has nothing to do with food, I can't have it.*

During the meal, Dane's demeanor changed. From the corner of her eye Rikki watched as he gulped down his grilled vegetable sandwich more out of frustration than hunger. She knew he'd wanted to kiss her earlier, and it wasn't fair to keep him guessing about what had changed between them.

"I've been doing some thinking about us," she said.

He stopped in mid-munch and lifted his head. Alfalfa sprouts bunched at the corners of his mouth.

"All my pre-training for the bone-marrow program cautioned about getting involved with the recipient and his family. I know it's too late with our kids, but I think we'd better stop things from going any further between you and me."

He set his sandwich down and wiped his mouth, regret settling in his eyes. "You probably have a point there, but is it that easy? One minute we're hot and heavy, heading for the nearest bedroom, and the next it's all formal?"

"I know it's crazy, but these are special circumstances."

"Can we just turn it off like that? Can you?"

"I'm not sure, but I think it's for the best."

He wiped his hands and mouth. "I want to go on record as being the one willing to get involved. I think we've got something good to share, but I'll respect your decision.

Can't say I like it much, but what am I going to do? You saved my brother's life."

She'd lost her appetite. Apparently he had, too. He motioned for the waiter to bring the check. She sipped some water, hoping to recover her voice. "Thank you for understanding."

He fished for his wallet and threw a wad of dollars on the table. "Fact is, I don't."

They drove in silence to pick up the kids, and as though feeding on the strain between them, Emma, Meg, and Brenden bickered and whined until Emma complained that Meg had hit her.

"No, I didn't," Emma whined.

"Yes, you did," Meg screamed.

Dane hit the steering wheel with his palm. "Knock it off." His voice boomed to the back of the car. The kids fell silent. "This is the stuff I can't handle," he said to Rikki through gritted teeth.

Feeling responsible for the thick tension in the car, Rikki used her favorite ploy with Brenden. Distraction. "I know it's been a long day for everyone. Would you kids like to make mini pizzas when we get home?" Had Dane even planned to take her back to his house? Did they need to stop at the market for supplies first?

With differences suddenly set safely aside, the kids all cheered as one. "Yeah!" Emma and Meg hugged each other.

Dane shook his head and sent her a sideways glance. "What's your secret?"

"Dumb luck."

Rikki opened the bedroom door at her apartment so Dane could carry Brenden to his bed. The twins were spending the night with their grandmother as Dane had to work. It was almost nine and the boy had fallen asleep on the drive home to Rikki's.

The thought of being totally alone with Dane in her house, after their morning encounter, made her knees go weak. Even though she'd made it perfectly clear that they had to keep things platonic, he wasn't taking any part of "no" easily.

Dane took great care to close the door without making a sound. "I'm on call, starting at midnight," he said, taking Rikki's hand and leading her to the living room. He drew her quivering fingers to his mouth and kissed them, sat on the couch and patted for her to join him. "I've got an idea how we can kill some time." There wasn't a hint of teasing in his emerald gaze, and her mouth went dry.

God give her the strength to resist him.

"Rikki?"

"Hmm?"

"I can't run my hands all over your body, the way I want to, because you won't let me." He had the nerve to lift his eyebrow in a most sexy way, testing her resolve. She blinked, but didn't cave in. "I want to know what makes you tick. Why you do all these great things for everyone else, but when it comes to you, you back away. Help me grasp how you can shut down so easily and move on." He stared earnestly into her eyes. "Help me understand you."

"I don't understand myself. How am I supposed to spell it out for you?"

"You can start by telling me what it's like to grow up a foster-kid."

Did he really want to know her? She at least owed the poor, confused man an explanation, but the words just didn't seem to form in her brain. She clasped her fingers and held her fists between her knees. Hunched forward, she ventured a glimpse in Dane's direction.

He sat quietly waiting, eyes steady and trained on her. "Sometimes it helps if someone else opens up first," Dane said. He tried to lighten things up with a huge understanding smile. "And as I love to talk about me, I'll go first." His smile stretched into a full grin. She couldn't help but smile back.

He grew serious. "You know, up until five years ago I had a great life. I graduated with top honors in high school and college, I led both my high school and college football teams to victory, and I only dated homecoming queens. I even married one. I got my MD, finished my residency and went through more training to specialize in orthopedics. Then everything changed." He raised an intriguing brow. "I'll tell you my story if you'll tell me yours."

She relaxed with a sigh. He was giving her a chance to find out about him so why not take it? As long as she could avoid telling him about her life, she'd go for it. Wasn't distraction the first line of defense? "What happened with the girls and their mother?"

With a do-you-really-want-to-know look, he paused for a beat. "She left. She was even less interested in being a parent than I was. We'd had a nice life together as a childless couple. Lots of friends, travel, parties. Then by accident she got pregnant. With twins! I thought we'd make the best of it. But she resented losing her shape, even though I thought she looked beautiful. She hated being on call twenty-four hours a day. Meg was colicky. Being a mother didn't come naturally to her. And then one day she said she couldn't take it any more, and left. I don't know if she regrets her decision, but I've never looked back. I thought I knew her. But I guess I really didn't."

"Maybe she knew it was for the best?" Wasn't that what *she* had always told herself? *Mom went away because she couldn't take care of me the way I deserved.*

"The girls were only two. Too young to remember her. I don't talk about her to them unless they ask. You don't know how close I've come to telling them she's dead. But someday, when they're grown up, after all the hard part is over, she may decide to come waltzing back into their lives, and I don't want to poison their attitudes about her. I'll let them make their own decisions about her."

He didn't want to bias his daughters against their mother. He didn't sound bitter, but she knew he must hold a grudge. It would be very hard for him to ever trust another woman. "You're an incredible man."

"Hardly. You see how I mess up with the girls."

"You're on a learning curve, that's all."

"Tell me about you, Rikki."

How could she not? He'd just told her things he probably hadn't shared with people outside his family. He deserved to know a little about her. "Let's just say I knew exactly how Brenden felt, being left with a stranger, when all he wanted was his mother and father. But I didn't even have a father that I knew of when I was taken from my mother."

He nodded and leaned closer. Even after the entire day together, she could still smell his spicy aftershave. Tempted to give in to his masculine allure, she withdrew to the safe inner place she'd created early in life to help cope. A place no one else could touch.

"I have such a vague memory of my mother. I remember long brown hair, cold bony hands, like she was skinny or sick or something. I remember the day she left." Her throat tightened, she could barely swallow. Her vision blurred.

I'll be good, Mommy. Please, don't go. "I remember saying something, protesting, when one of the men picked me up and I watched them take her away. That was the last time I ever saw my mother."

Rikki's eyes brimmed with moisture. She found herself enveloped in warmth and Dane's tight embrace. She curled into his chest and fought back her tears, feeling somehow safe from her past in his arms. "That was the first day I went into foster-care," she said, noticing the scratchy feel and special smell of his flannel shirt. "I was three years old. I lived in fifteen different homes, some for a few months, a couple for a few years. My favorite foster-mother died. After that I was a teenager and I just didn't give a damn any more."

"Oh, sweetheart." Dane kissed the top of her head and rocked her. "I can't begin to fathom all you've been through." He shook his head, like he'd finally realized the truth about her. "You're an incredible person."

She swiped at her tears and attempted to lighten the mood. "Maybe, but I dress weird."

His laugh rumbled in his chest.

"I've never felt like I fit in. Like there's something wrong with me and I don't know how to fix it. Everyone else had families. I was just the extra kid in the house."

"There's nothing wrong with you. You've had rotten luck, that's all."

They sat wrapped in each other's arms. Rikki never wanted to let go. She felt safe and protected. Had anyone ever made her feel like that?

But she'd made a decision to keep their relationship professional. She had to…to survive. Something in her heart knew that Dane was one home she wouldn't be able to casually walk away from, never looking back. And she couldn't bear the thought of being sent away one more time.

After a few moments Dane let up on their hug. "Have you ever wondered about your birth family? I mean, have you ever wanted to find them?"

"I've thought about it, but honestly? I'm afraid of what I might find."

"When Don was eighteen, he decided he wanted to meet his natural parents. It really hurt Mom and Dad, but they helped him search them out. When he finally found out who his mother was, he never went through with actually contacting her."

Rikki studied Dane's fine mouth and lips while he spoke. Was he saying some things were best left behind?

"I think he regrets it."

"What are you getting at?"

"I've been thinking," he said, playing with a lock of her hair. "Before leukemia messed up my brother's life, he was a damn fine police detective. Maybe he could help you locate your family."

"But he's so sick."

"Yeah, but he's got a lot of time on his hands, and having a project he could do over the phone or on the Internet might help his mental attitude while he recovers."

She laid her head back on his chest. "Everyone needs a purpose. You're right."

"So what do you say? Shall I give him the Rikki Johansen missing family case?"

She sighed, a total sucker for his charm. "OK."

Dane got called into the OR almost immediately after midnight. A multiple MVA had brought several severely injured patients to the ER via ambulance. He spent most of the night in surgery, doing an open reduction and internal fixation of both an arm and leg on one of the patients, while another surgeon searched for the source of internal bleeding.

Before he tried to get some rest at 8:00 a.m., he decided to check on his patients in the orthopedic ward. Any excuse to see Rikki again. He needed to make sense out of how he felt about her. Once Don was on the mend, they could pick up where they'd left off.

True, he was looking for a ready-made mother for his kids. True, she went all gooey-eyed around children, especially his daughters. It seemed like the minute she and the twins were together, Rikki slipped into mommy mode. She was perfect for them, and they adored her.

She also hadn't needed more than a few seconds to decide to donate her bone marrow to Don. Only an exceptional person did such a selfless thing—or someone who needed validation. After her history of one foster-home after another, he had a hunch what drove her to make the world a better place.

Special didn't come close to describe Rikki. And her appearance? Sure, it was different than his usual taste in women, but the fact was she turned him on. He couldn't get her petite body and soft skin out of his mind. But how did he *feel* about her? Did he care? *Really* care? Because she deserved that, too.

Rikki tightened her jaw and answered the call light. Javier had been buzzing every five minutes since she'd come on duty.

"Is it time yet?" he asked, the instant she walked into his room.

A known gang member and suspected drug abuser, he'd been in the hospital for two weeks with multiple fractures from a motorcycle accident. Though making progress with his injuries, his requests for pain shots hadn't waned a bit. Dane had recently increased the intervals and decreased the amount of painkillers to be given. Javier had caught on and was not happy about it.

"We're supposed to be weaning you off the shots and giving you pills. You can either take two pills now or wait another hour for a shot," Rikki said, standing close to his bedside, studying the orders on his medicine sheet.

In a flash he grabbed her arm and yanked her close, causing her to stumble and drop the chart. "I don't want no pills. Get me the damn shot. Now!"

Someone walked into the room and growled. The next thing Rikki knew, Javier let go of her and got jolted out of the bed by someone in a white coat. It was Dane. He'd practically lifted the patient off the mattress by his hospital gown with his bare hands, heavy casts and all.

"If I ever catch you laying a hand on her again, I'll cut your drugs cold turkey," he seethed through a clenched jaw. "And I'll have you arrested for assault." He shook him several times. "You got that?"

"Hey, Doc, I was just asking about my next shot."

"You're not fooling anyone. As of now, you're off shots. You'll get two pain tablets every four hours, no exceptions." Dane shoved the patient back onto the bed, lifted the chart off the floor, and reached for Rikki's elbow. "You OK?" Adrenaline made his eyes large and dark. They looked wild, like they had when they'd first kissed, only now it was with concern. "Did he hurt you?"

Flustered, but grateful that Dane had stepped into

what could have been an ugly situation, she nodded. "I'm fine, thanks."

Walking her out the door and toward the nurses' station, he cupped her elbow and said, "I would have broken both his legs again if he'd hurt you."

CHAPTER SEVEN

JANETTA GLEASON gazed over the top of her reading glasses. "OK, spill. What's up with you and Dr. Hendricks?"

From the doorway of Janetta's office, Rikki couldn't suppress a grin. "Nothing. We're friends, that's all."

"Every nurse on the ward is talking about how he practically swung in on a vine and saved you from that druggie, Javier."

"I could have handled it. Dr. Hendricks just happened to be in the right place at the right time. Anyone else would have done the same."

"Rubbish." Janetta motioned for Rikki to close the door and take a seat. "Any other doctor would have called Security and let them do the dirty work."

"Then I'm flattered."

"Are you feeling OK after the bone-marrow donation? You look a little pale. That was outstanding of you, by the way."

"I'm still a little tired." It wasn't exactly a lie. The fact that she'd stayed awake into the wee hours thinking about Dane, worrying she was letting the chance of a lifetime slip through her grasp, had left her sleepy that morning.

The marrow donation had her physically dragging, too.

It would take four to six weeks for her bone marrow to replenish itself but, all things considered, her hips didn't hurt nearly as much, and she was feeling good.

Who wouldn't be after spending so much time with Dane? And when he'd promised to break her patient's legs again if the guy hurt her, at first she'd been stunned, then had wanted to fly around the room, crowing. Someone gave a damn about her.

Something about the look in Janetta's eyes gave her the distinct impression her supervisor had just read every thought in her mind. Rikki's pleased grin had probably given her away.

"And how are things going with Brenden?"

How could she say enough about the little boy who'd stolen her heart? "He's wonderful. He really seems to be adjusting well to me now. Gosh, I hope to have lots of kids just like him someday."

"Any luck finding his relatives?"

"No. I think they're all in Central America. I don't know what the protocol is in that case."

"Well, things seem to be looking up for you. I'm glad."

"You know? I think coming to Mercy Hospital was the best thing to ever happen to me."

"Great. Then can you work an extra day this week? Cheryl Josephson needs Saturday off."

Between Dane's rescheduled surgeries and overbooked clinic hours, and Rikki's busy life with Brenden and work, they hardly had a chance to see each other over the next few days. The kids, however, saw each other daily at the hospital child-care center. Dane managed to call her a couple of nights just to say hello and see how she was, and she'd called him once to ask how Don was doing, but the shift in their relationship was painfully apparent. And it had been her doing. Old doubts started to creep back into her mind. She'd blown her chance with Dane.

She'd agreed to work an extra day that week, and on Saturday, for the first time, Brenden resisted going to child care. Six days in a row of pre-school activity were a lot to ask of a four-year old boy. She promised to make up for it on Sunday.

Welcome to the world of single motherhood and foster-parenting. She wondered if Brenden might be better off somewhere else. Still, she took pride in knowing she was making a difference in his life. She had been there for him when he'd lost both of his parents. And she'd be there for him until they found a permanent home for him, though the thought made her heart race and her throat tighten.

She hadn't been back to see Don since her initial visit, but had promised to stop by on her lunch-break today. She'd decided that as they already knew each other, she should be around to offer moral support while they waited for the new bone marrow to take effect. Don having one more person in his corner couldn't hurt.

After rushing through a shared egg salad sandwich with Brenden, she had to bargain with him to leave a few minutes early so she could see Don. Pizza and a video were on her agenda for that night. Considering he'd already begged for a day at the park on Sunday, the boy wasn't doing badly.

Having felt her strength return a bit more each day over the past week, she skipped off the elevator on the second floor to say a quick hello to Don. Down at the end of the hall stood Dane and Hannah Young, laughing and talking more like old friends than colleagues. Hannah kept putting her hand on Dane's arm while they talked, and he kept *not* removing it. Even from this distance she swore his eyes sparkled.

Rikki's stomach went sour. She'd made it clear they could only be friends, and he was already on the prowl. Before Dane had a chance to notice her, she donned the required isolation paraphernalia and slipped into Don's room.

He didn't look any better than before the bone-marrow donation. Maybe even a bit worse? She couldn't tell for sure, but today his skin had a grayish-olive cast to it.

His eyes lit up when he recognized her. "Hey. At first I thought you were one of my nurses."

She smiled and walked closer, trying to hide her ruffled state. "How are you doing?"

"OK, I guess. To be honest, I don't feel very different yet. But Dr. Young assures me it takes a couple of weeks or more for it to take hold."

So Dane trusted Hannah Young with his brother's life.

"Listen, since you're here, I've got some news for you." He reached inside the drawer of the bedside table and withdrew a messy batch of papers. "Dane gave me all your personal details, and I've been making some enquiries. I think I may have news about your birth family in the next couple of days. Have you ever heard of a Colleen Johansen-Baskin?"

Rikki shook her head. The thought of locating her family sent a chill down her spine.

"I'm trying to contact her. I'll let you know what happens."

"Wow, you didn't waste any time."

"I aim to please."

They stared gratefully at each other for a few seconds.

"Are you OK, Rikki?"

"Sure."

"Come on. I'm a cop, I can tell when something's not right."

"I'm upset with your brother, that's all."

"You want me to beat him up for you?"

She laughed.

"Hey, did you know that when I was a kid, I used to purposely tick off bullies just so Dane could save my butt? It used to make him feel needed."

She widened her eyes and giggled.

"He's that kind of guy."

"You mean Mr. Seems-to-have-it-all needs to be needed?"

"Yeah, he used to think I couldn't live without him. The point I'm getting at is sometimes he comes off as overbearing. Just tell him to back off."

No, that wasn't it.

"Other times he comes off as dense. So just tell him exactly what's on your mind."

Well, maybe… How could she explain to Don that even though she only wanted to be friends with Dane, she didn't want him to be "friends" with anyone else?

Before she could respond, Dane and Hannah entered the room, both wearing isolation gowns and masks.

Hannah hesitated when she saw Rikki. Dane smiled and tugged on Rikki's sleeve when he approached. "Hey."

"Hiya."

"Well, Don," Hannah said, after offering Rikki a cool

nod when she'd passed by, "I've got some news for you. Shall I wait until your guest leaves?"

"Nah. Rikki is my blood sister. Go ahead. Shoot."

"After an initial dip, your blood count numbers are picking up. I am cautiously encouraged that the procedure will be a success. We'll know more by this time next week."

"That's great news, Doc. Isn't that great, Rikki?"

"Fantastic."

"I wouldn't expect anything less from such a great source of bone marrow." Dane stood behind her and put both his hands on her shoulders, giving a gentle shake.

Something made her feel as though he wanted to kiss her, and maybe he would have if they'd been alone. Her crazy mixed-up worries about Dane losing interest since they were only going to be friends started to dissipate.

"So, Dane, where are we eating tonight? You owe me one, and I'm calling it in." Hannah's eyes drifted ever so quickly Rikki's way, but danced back to Dane, twinkling and flirtatious.

"Oh. Man, Hannah, I, uh…"

"You've owed me since last month when the Angels beat the Dodgers. Remember our bet? I'm calling it in. Tonight."

"Can we take a rain-check on that?"

"That's what you said last time. Not a chance, big guy. Do you want to sully your reputation around the hospital?"

Why was she doing this now, in front of Don and herself? Hannah obviously wanted to make her stand, and Rikki was damned if she'd give Hannah the satisfaction of knowing how it shook her up. But her lunch-break was up, and she had to leave.

"I've got to get back to work but, Don, it was great to

see you. And thank you so much for doing the legwork on that possible lead."

"Hey, Rikki, thanks for stopping by. Don't forget what I said about the other thing. And I'll let you know the minute I find anything out about your relatives." They shook hands, and Don gave her an extra squeeze before letting go. "I'll never be able to thank you enough."

"Just get well. That's all I ask."

Rikki brushed by Dane, who looked perplexed behind his mask but had mumbled "yes" to Hannah's blatant advance. No sooner had they set the boundaries on their "friendship" than right in front of her he'd accepted a date with another woman. Had he no regard for her?

Then she passed Hannah and imagined a smirk beneath the doctor's mask. Some women were horrible.

Self-doubt snuck out of its hiding place and ushered Rikki out the door.

"I'll call you tonight, Rikki," Dane said, surprising her.

"I won't be home," she said, trying to temper the anger in her voice.

At midnight, her phone rang. After the fourth ring, and only because she was afraid Brenden would wake up, Rikki answered.

"Hi," a very-tired sounding Dane said.

"What's up?"

"I've been at the hospital all evening. Don has spiked a temp. He's septic. We've got him on massive amounts of antibiotics, but we've got to watch out for kidney damage. I don't get it—he was doing so well earlier. God, I wish there was something more I could do for him. I feel so helpless."

Immediately forgiving Dane, worry had her sitting up

in bed and switching on the bedside light. "Is there anything I can do?"

"No. He seems stable right now. I just wanted to talk to someone—to you. You seemed upset this afternoon, and I wanted to explain about that bet thing. But you ran off so fast I didn't have a chance."

"My lunch-break was over. I had to get back to work. And you could have called me."

"You told me not to." After a pause, he said, "I need you to know Hannah doesn't mean anything to me. She put me on the spot and I couldn't say no. So I bought her a sandwich in the hospital cafeteria. That's all."

Relief, like a cup of cool water, gave Rikki new hope. But, in all honesty, if Dane wanted to date someone it was his prerogative. She'd made it very clear they would only be friends.

"Listen, the girls are with my mom, and I could use some company."

She'd laid the groundwork for friendship. Wasn't that what friends were for, to be there when they were needed?

"I'd really like to see you," he said.

Truth was, she wanted to see him with all her heart, couldn't get him out of her mind for one second, but she didn't want him to think he could just walk all over her whenever he wanted to. That he could change the rules because he didn't like them. Hadn't Don warned her about Dane being overbearing? Didn't he understand that when she said no, she meant it?

"Well?"

Plus, she had her pride and self-respect to consider... "Yes. I'd like to see you, too." *So much for pride and self-respect, and everything else that made sense in her life.*

Dane tapped on her door within the hour. The moment she opened up, he took her in his arms and smothered her with a kiss. His warm lips and hot breath, combined with the cold night on his coat, gave her chills. She didn't have time to wonder why he had such power over her good sense. All she knew was she was glad to see him. And from the way he felt, he was glad to see her, too.

He pushed the door closed with his back and continued covering her face with kisses. As though she'd been starving for his touch all her life, she welcomed him, kissed him back, matching his desire with her own.

"Damn, I've missed you."

"Me, too." Why did his presence always reduce her to a two-syllable drone?

His hands wandered across her back and over her hips. Hungry dark green eyes searched her face, neck, and breasts.

He slid out of his jacket. "I need you."

Did he really think she was that easy?

He wrapped her in his arms and pulled her close to his chest, his heat radiating all over her. She looked up and their mouths joined in a fiery caress.

Apparently, she was.

He angled his head to kiss her again, deeper, more forcefully. His hot breath melted her resolve to keep him at a distance. Their tongues met and she tasted Dane's passion, felt it budding in her center.

Every reasonable thought flew out of her head, along with her last whimper of protest. He walked her backwards to the bedroom, lifting her at the halfway mark.

Maybe in the past she'd have been scared of such a big man overpowering her, but not Dane. He may have been large, but he knew how to be gentle. He carried her as if she were delicate china, even as his zealous kiss tested her strength.

He grazed her lips and nibbled as he spoke in a rasping voice. "I know you said we should just be friends, but that's not all I want with you."

She met his gaze and understanding passed between them.

"If you're not sure about this, you better tell me now, because in a few more minutes I can't predict what I'll do."

"I'm definitely not sure about this." She gasped for air and reached for his collar to bring him back to her mouth. "But don't stop," she said, fisting her hands in his shirt before he crushed against her lips.

"What about your hips?" he said over her mouth.

"They're fine," she whispered breathlessly. "Just keep kissing me."

The next few moments were a whirlwind of desire and heat. He placed her gently on the bed, careful not to hurt her back.

He removed his glasses and yanked off his shirt. The vision of his large, muscular chest lightly dusted in tawny hair took what was left of her breath away. He knelt on the bed, passion flaming in his eyes. Her insides turned to warm honey.

She unbuttoned and yanked at her clothes, while he unzipped and pulled off what was left of his. The sight of him in all his naked masculine glory set her heart pounding. Flaring with passion, all she wanted to do was touch him, run her hands across his chest and arms and down to his thighs. His large, thick thighs were made for sprinting and football. She wanted all of him, next to her, on top of her…inside her.

He studied her nakedness with near reverence. The tiniest twitch of his brow and tightening of his jaw assured her he liked what he saw. His huge hand covered her entire breast, yet she felt more than enough for him. She budded and his thumb lingered over her, circling, teasing her, sending chills across her chest and down to her tummy.

He kissed her shoulder, doubling the wave of tingles from her breasts up to her scalp and down her spine. She shivered with excitement under his touch, hopelessly unable to contain her response.

His chest and arms were hard, like marble, his stomach lean and firm. She pulled him down to her, but he stopped her.

"What?"

Before she could protest, he flopped onto his back and pulled her on top of him. "Just in case your hips are still sore."

"Oh." She'd totally forgotten the week-old procedure and the leftover tenderness. "Guess I'll be on top." Somehow, even though stark naked with the man of her dreams, she was able to produce a coy smile.

He grinned up at her.

She straddled his waist and leaned forward to kiss him again, and again, while his hands explored her hips, thighs, and back.

She arched. He took a breast into his mouth, sending chills down to her toes. Then he tasted the other. Her eyes closed to better isolate the sensation. She could barely tolerate the pleasurable waves rolling across her body. She smiled and cooed.

Wanting more, she wrapped her thighs around his tall erection and nearly drove herself mad by gently gliding up and down over the soft, firm skin. A throbbing heat started in her core and grew in intensity until she couldn't stand not having him inside her another instant.

"Did you bring protection?"

He scrambled for his wallet and dutifully produced a condom.

She did the honors of sheathing him and gingerly slid on top until he filled her, sending her nerve endings helter-skelter. She had to move, couldn't help it.

His chest, stomach, and thigh muscles tensed with their lovers' rhythm. She pressed his shoulders to the bed while their hips rose and fell. Warm pleasure burrowed deeper and deeper until she'd taken him all in. She heard a groan, but was so lost in the sensations she couldn't tell if it was hers or his. Their tempo quickened and the liquid heat rapidly turned to flame. She held onto his shoulders, threw her head back, gripped and tightened around him, begging for release.

Their eyes met in primal frenzy—his were wild and dark with passion. She could hardly focus. He guided her hips exactly where he needed them. A perfect place for her, too. He stayed there, working and moving, as long as she needed him, until fireworks launched from her center out to her fingertips and down to her toes.

He let out a guttural growl when he climaxed. The force sent her into more pleasurable spasms, and they moved together until they could breathe again…until they were sated and back in a semblance of control.

"Come here," he said, gathering her snugly to his chest beside him.

She cuddled into his hold and dreamed of feeling this way with him often and regularly. She sighed.

He kissed her ear. "That was fantastic."

She sighed again, this time with pride. She wanted to say, *It's never been this way for me before*, but instead simply said, "Me, too."

His heartbeat lulled her. His breathing subtly lifted and dropped her head. Who cared if nothing made sense? If she'd just made the biggest mistake of her life, letting Dane closer than anyone else in the world? Within minutes she dozed off in the comfort of her friend turned lover's arms.

The next morning, the phone woke them. Rikki untangled herself from Dane's grasp, and was surprised to hear Don's voice. At 8:00 a.m. he sounded chipper.

"Rikki? I've made contact with that Colleen woman in Pennsylvania."

"Wait, wait. How are you feeling, Don?"

"Oh. Much better. My fever broke last night. Those drugs did wonders."

Dane sat up with an inquisitive stare.

"That's fantastic. May I come to visit you today?"

"I was hoping you would."

"Let me speak to him," Dane said, interrupting and taking the phone.

Rikki's eyes flew open. Did Don know about them?

He didn't give her a chance to protest. "Your fever broke? Fantastic. What did Hannah say?"

Rikki jumped out of bed to get dressed before Brenden had a chance to wake up and find her naked with Dane. She grabbed her clothes and rushed into the bathroom. Dane watched her every move while listening to his brother and answering all his questions. "We've been dating for a few weeks, since before we found out she was your match."

Never in her life had a man looked at her like that. It was a combination of pure sex, fascination, adoration, possession, and entitlement. Well, maybe she was reading a lot into his interested gaze but, whatever it meant, it made Rikki want to ignore good sense and jump right back into bed with him to repeat last night's acrobatics.

He couldn't seem to get enough of her. He'd devoured her inch by inch, sending her out of the sexual stratosphere. And where had that guttural wail come from? Good thing Brenden was a sound sleeper. She'd never dreamed of being ravished by a man before, but Dane, in his hunger and eagerness to please, had shown her how spectacular it could be.

Oh, God. She couldn't let her physical attraction to him interfere with seeing things for what they were. He'd said he needed her. Nothing more. At some point during the night he'd said how great she was with his daughters. He'd even said she'd saved his brother's life. But not once had he uttered a word about wanting or loving her. And since their first date he'd made it perfectly clear how he felt about having more kids. They weren't compatible, and she must never forget it.

Was she nothing more than a practical solution in Dane's chaotic life? Well, that wouldn't do.

Glancing over her shoulder at the handsome, appreciative and grinning Dane, watching her every move while he lay naked in her bed, Rikki had to admit it could get tricky to remember what she'd just vowed never to forget.

Later that Sunday they'd picked up Emma and Meg from Dane's mother's house, and had brought Brenden along, promising them all a picnic in the park after a stop at the hospital. Brenden had reminded her she'd given her word they'd go to the park on Sunday afternoon.

As they all held hands and walked into the lobby, Rikki couldn't help but think what a portrait they made.

It was Rikki's turn to call in a favor, and she had a plan. She let Emma press the elevator button for the fourth floor, promising that Brenden could push it on the way down and Meg could push the "close doors" button going up or down if she wanted to.

When they arrived on the orthopedic ward they marched straight to Janetta's office. She sat engrossed in paperwork, this being her on duty once-a-month weekend.

"Hey," Rikki said.

Janetta glanced up. A surprised look quickly replaced her glare of concentration. "Hi, Rikki. Dane. Kids. What are you doing here on your day off?"

"I'm about to ask you a favor. Can we leave the kids here while we visit Dane's brother in Oncology?"

The grandmother of five looked unfazed. "Sure. Just tie them up and put them over there." She nodded toward the corner of her office with a grin.

The kids giggled.

"You can't tie us up." Brenden made himself the spokesman.

"Oh, OK. Well, then, here." She handed each of them a pad of paper and some pencils. "You can help me figure out the scheduling."

Rikki smiled, and caught Dane staring at her. Her face flamed, as though she'd just met him for the first time.

"Thanks," Rikki said.

"Be good for Mrs. Gleason, kids," Dane added.

"If you're not back in half an hour, I'm sending out for pizza and you're paying for it," Janetta said with wink and a cheer from the kids. "Oh, and I'll add in a tip for my services, too."

Dane reached for Rikki's hand when they walked toward the elevator. He didn't seem the least bit hesitant to let anyone at the hospital see them together as a couple. She resisted getting too optimistic about what it could mean. After all, she'd already gone back on her promise to herself to keep things platonic. Knowing better than to let her guard down, she'd let Dane into her life. It was probably a huge mistake.

After they gowned up on the oncology ward, Don seemed eager to see them. His coloring was better than the day before, and he seemed to have more energy.

"I feel like a prisoner in here," he said.

"Until we're sure the procedure has been successful, and your labs stabilize, you may as well get used to it. By the way, Mom said she's coming over later for a visit, too."

"Good. I hope she brings some home-made food."

"Well, that's a good sign, if you want to eat."

"Yeah, I'm hungry. A couple of my cop buddies may come by, but they don't like all this isolation business. The least I can do is offer them food."

Don waved for Rikki to come look at his laptop.

"See this? I sent an e-mail last night, and got a response this morning. This woman, Colleen Johansen-Baskin, had a sister who had a kid around the time you were born. She lives in Philadelphia, but said her older sister moved out west and dropped out of touch with the family."

Rikki read the e-mail and her chest quivered. There was a phone number offered by a complete stranger with an invitation to call. She closed her eyes to still her nerves. Did she want to open that door? How much more could she stand to open up?

Dane's warm hands grasped her arms. He pulled her against his chest, and she laid her head back. He kissed her forehead through his mask. "Think it over."

"She could be your aunt. It's amazing how easy it was to track her down," Don said, a proud grin on his face.

He searched for a piece of paper, and scribbled out the number, then handed it to Rikki.

Tears welled in her eyes when she took it. Dane turned her round and cradled her. She'd never had a real family. She'd always been the outsider. Why hadn't they come for her after her mother had been taken away?

She wrapped her arms around Dane's waist and nuzzled her face into the side of his neck, wanting to stay there for ever.

"If Don can find my potential family in only a few short days, why can't they find Brenden's?"

"Good question. I wish I had an answer. Maybe it has something to do with them not being in this country? Don't forget, sometimes people don't want to be found."

She knew that desire well. How many years had she lived hiding in the shadows? But since she'd met Dane, he'd almost convinced her it was better to be found. Just the thought made her tremble.

A nurse entered the room with the next dose of IV antibiotics for Don.

Dane reminded his brother that his favorite football team had a game on TV that afternoon. Rikki told Don he could call Ms. Baskin for her if he wanted, as she probably wouldn't get around to it any time soon. *Because I don't have the guts to make contact.* After visiting a bit longer, they said their goodbyes and left.

Unsettled with the possibility of finding blood relatives, Rikki withdrew to her safe place—the cave in her heart—and kept Dane at a distance the rest of the day.

On Monday morning, Rikki had just finished changing a dressing on a second-day post-op foot amputation when she was called out of the patient's room.

"You've got a phone call," the ward clerk said.

Rikki took the receiver. "Hello?"

"This is Claire Brodsky from Children's Services. I wanted to notify you that though we haven't been able to locate Brenden Pasqual's blood relatives, we have found another foster-family for him."

The air left Rikki's lungs. She couldn't even form the words to respond.

"They are a Hispanic family with two children around Brenden's age, and the wife is a stay-at-home mom. The situation is ideal and they are eager to take him in for as long as necessary."

Her thoughts swirled around in the sudden dizziness overtaking her. *But I'd keep him for as long as necessary, too.* All she could manage to say was, "How soon?"

"We'd like to pick him up tonight."

She fell into the nearest chair. Her palms went clammy. The room blurred. "Can we wait until the weekend?"

"We feel it would be in the boy's best interests to move in with the Gomez family as soon as possible. Of course, we appreciate all you have done for him, but you knew you were only keeping him on an emergency temporary basis, and you've had him for almost three months."

Three months wasn't nearly long enough in Rikki's estimation. Knowing better, she'd let him get under her skin and had hoped to keep him permanently.

"If we are unable to locate his relatives and if they don't want him when we do find them, the Gomez family is interested in adopting him."

Her mouth went dry. She swiped at tears dripping down her cheeks and chin. "Is there any way I can apply to adopt him?"

"Well, Ms. Johansen, certainly you can apply, but I'll be honest—little Brenden has a chance to be with a ready-made family and they share his culture and background. It's the best possible circumstances for him, given the situation. I couldn't guarantee your application would be seriously considered as you are single and so young."

"But he's such a great kid. I want him to be in a good home."

"You can trust that we've found an excellent home for him. We here at Children's Services want to thank you for your help, and we will definitely be contacting you again for future short-term foster care. What time would be good to come by tonight?"

Never? Oh, God, she wanted to bolt. She wanted to pack her clothes and run away with Brenden. He'd just gotten used to being with her and now they wanted to upset him again with more strangers. Dear God, what could she do?

"I'll need some time to get his belongings together, and I'd like to have one last dinner with him to say goodbye." Her voice cracked on goodbye.

"Would eight be all right?"

* * *

Rikki could barely make it through the rest of her workday. She didn't know who to turn to. Who could possibly understand how she felt?

Janetta? She'd only just gotten her first foster-care ward. She wouldn't understand yet how hard it was to give a child up.

Dane.

He'd seen her eyes light up every time Brenden giggled. He'd been with her the first night Brenden had really opened up. His daughters were the boy's newest best friends. And in her heart she knew Dane, the man who never wanted another child, had a soft spot for him.

On her afternoon break, Rikki snuck off to Dane's office. Fortunately, he was there.

His nurse had just left the room. She and Rikki knew each other from around the hospital. "Something is up," the nurse said. "A month ago he'd have read me the Riot Act for not telling him a patient had cancelled. Today he said, 'No problem.' Can you believe it? Dane Hendricks saying 'no problem'? I'd sure like to know what's going on in his life."

Rikki had seen a change in Dane, too, but she wouldn't let herself think about what it could be from. Certainly she didn't have anything to do with it. Or did she? But today the only thing on her mind was Brenden.

She stood in his doorway. One look at her, and Dane jumped up from his chair and rushed around the desk. "What's wrong?"

The words stuck in her throat. "They're moving Brenden to another foster-home."

Dane wrapped her in his arms and held her close. "Oh, no. Rikki. Honey."

"What am I going to do?"

He didn't offer any solutions. He just stood there and hugged her as close as he could. "Sweetheart. Whatever you need, I'll be there."

In her wildest dreams she wanted to ask Dane to marry her so they could adopt Brenden and be one big happy family, like they'd seemed to be on so many occasions over the last couple of weeks. If only dreams could come true. But her prayers had never been answered when she'd been a child, begging for a real mommy and daddy and family all of her own, so why would things be any different now? And Dane would never consent to more children, let alone a new wife!

"I could use some moral support."

"You've got it."

"Will you have dinner with us and help me say goodbye?"

"Of course. Anything you need."

"Brenden?" Rikki ruffled his hair, trying her hardest not to cry again. She'd picked him up from day care and treated him to his favorite ice-cream cone, even though it was cold outside and it might spoil his dinner. They'd gone directly home after that, Rikki knowing and dreading what she had to do.

"Yeah, Rikki?" He looked up with his soulful dark eyes from his bedroom door.

She bent down. "Remember when the nice people brought you to me?"

"Yes," he whispered.

"They said I could watch over you until they found a good home for you."

His face twisted in thought. "Are my mommy and daddy alive now?"

"No, honey. But they found a whole new family for you, and they want you to go and live with them."

"Don't you want me any more?"

Her heart shattered. "Of course I want you. I cried when they told me you were moving away." She'd gone through this how many times before with other foster-children? She'd learned her job was to care for them, and then let them go when the time came. She'd prided herself on knowing her job and being good at it. What was different this time?

"I'll be good. I promise."

That was it. Brenden's circumstances reminded her so much of her own. She started crying again and dropped to her knees beside him. Oh, God, she knew exactly how he felt. Her heart ripped in two.

Tears brimmed on Brenden's lashes. One fat teardrop rolled down his cheek. "I don't want to go."

"I don't want you to."

They hugged each other as if they'd disappear if they let go. And sadly in a few more minutes Brenden would disappear from her life. How would she bear it?

"They said I could come and visit you sometimes." Rikki's voice broke so often she had to start the sentence a second time.

"I want my mommy!" The boy dissolved in tears. He dropped to the floor in a puddle, just like the night he'd first arrived. She tried to pick him up, but he was dead weight.

I'll be good, Mommy. Rikki remembered lying in a heap on a cold linoleum floor writhing and crying. *I'll be good, Mommy. Please, don't go.*

But she'd never seen her mother again. And now Brenden was being taken away, too.

Dane held Rikki while she shook and wept in his arms after the Children's Services' representative had bundled Brenden up and left. She cried so hard, he thought she'd melt.

"You don't do this with every kid, do you?"

She shook her head. "Brenden was different."

He couldn't think of one thing to say so he just stood there and held her, offering tissues from time to time. A tight band of anxiety circled his chest; he could hardly breathe. He pinched his eyes closed and rocked her.

When she'd settled down the slightest bit he lifted and carried her to the bed. She curled into a ball. He rinsed a washcloth with cool water, wrung it out, and placed it on her eyes and forehead. He sat next to her and patted her hip. He'd do anything to take away her pain. The most selfless, giving person he'd ever met didn't deserve to suffer like this. She'd never had anyone to support her, to love her no matter what, to ease her suffering. God, it made him ache inside to think how alone she'd always been.

And now she'd completely withdrawn from him. If he could only chip through to her heart, he could be sure about the new feelings he had for her.

He sat on the bed and gathered her into his arms. Her eyes were tightly closed beneath the washcloth. Her hands were balled into fists. He rubbed her shoulder.

"I get the feeling there is some horrible thing that keeps holding you back in life. Tell me, Rikki. Tell me about your mother. Please?"

She stirred in his embrace. "I can't."

"You've got to tell someone. Share it with me. Come on."

She cleared her throat and lifted the cloth. Her eyes looked distant, focused on somewhere he couldn't begin to see. "I remember being alone a lot. I remember the day my mom left. She told me to go hide in the closet and not make a peep, like a good girl. She would tell me to do that sometimes. I thought it was a game. Sometimes I'd fall asleep, and when I woke up she'd be asleep on the couch. The last time I was in the closet I heard pounding on the front door, men's voices, and my mother sounded scared, so I came out. The big men were leaving with her."

He felt the cords in her neck tighten. He cupped her jaw and gently tilted her face. No amount of tears could wash away the tortured grief he saw.

She bit her lower lip. "I remember saying, 'I'll be good Mommy, please, don't go,' then one of the men picked me up and I watched them take her away." She'd finally let go of her tightly held secret—he could feel her body relax as a flood of tears ran down her cheeks.

He clenched his jaw to fight off the ache in his chest, but couldn't hold back a wave of emotion rooted in love and respect for her. His eyes grew moist, but he blinked away any trace of tears. He needed to stay strong for Rikki. He needed to be there for her, no matter how much it hurt.

"That was the last time I ever saw my mother. And as irrational as it seems, I can't help thinking if I'd only been good and stayed in the closet, maybe things would have been different."

"Oh, God. Honey, what a burden to carry around all your life." His voice was high with pain.

They held each other and she cried several minutes more. For the first time in years he revisited his own grief. When his wife had left, it had been a different kind of hurt, the kind that came with broken trust. He hadn't felt this much raw pain since he'd found out his brother had leukemia. He desperately needed to help Rikki feel better, as much for his own sake as for hers.

Would finding her family help? He cleared the lump in his throat. It was worth a shot.

"Don talked to your aunt this morning. We're positive it's her because she laughs just like you."

She gave a half-hearted laugh, and he was pleased his ploy had worked. She hadn't protested so he'd continue. "She said when your mother died, your grandfather had cancer and your grandmother was too overwhelmed and couldn't take you in. It wasn't that they didn't want you."

Rikki went completely still. He knew she was listening.

"Colleen, your aunt, was three thousand miles away in college and was too young to help out." He laced his fingers through Rikki's limp hand. "She said it has haunted her all these years, and she'd love to meet you. Your grandmother died shortly after your grandfather, so your Aunt Colleen and her children are all you have left."

What else could he say? She looked so tiny and fragile, whimpering from time to time. What thoughts were going on inside her head? He longed to erase every bad thing that had ever happened in her life. Had she heard a word he'd said about her aunt?

"Does she know how my mom died?"

"Apparently, no one could stop your mother from using drugs until she overdosed. Sweetheart, I'm so sorry."

He needed to make her feel better. He wanted to

promise her the world, but knew he might regret it if he promised too much. For the first time since his ex-wife had left, he wanted to trust a woman, to have someone in his life again, someone to share his beautiful daughters with. He wanted to make someone else happy. Whatever it took.

"I thought maybe we could fly out to Pennsylvania and meet her. I'd pay for everything."

"I don't know, Dane, I'll have to think about it. You don't owe me anything, if that's what this is all about."

"I owe you more than you can ever imagine."

Rikki was more than a wonderful person, more than a fantastic lover. He lifted her slack hand, kissed her fingers, felt her waning life force and ached to make her feel better.

She was his friend.

His lover.

He'd fallen in love with her, and he wanted her to know.

Rikki wiped her eyes with the washcloth. She looked at Dane with sorrowful dull brown eyes, eyes he wanted to make sparkle again. How could he not trust her?

As though she'd read what was on his mind, she whispered, "Just be my friend."

CHAPTER EIGHT

DANE finished his Monday morning hospital rounds and headed for his office. It had been a week since he'd promised to be Rikki's friend. His body ached for hers, but he knew he had to back off, give her time to catch up with him. He'd always been impulsive. Want something? Go after it. Something was wrong? Fix it. His life had been one long list of accomplishments. Check. Check. Check. Until his marriage had fallen apart and his brother had gotten leukemia.

And then he'd met Rikki. He'd found what he'd wanted in a caring person who was good with his daughters. He was lucky enough to be sexually attracted to her, too. It was supposed to be a win-win situation. He'd gone after her without regard to her needs. He hadn't come close to thinking things through, with all the possible consequences.

Maybe it was time for him to broaden his vision to see the whole picture. Since he'd become a father he'd learned life wasn't all about him any more. And now that he'd met Rikki, he understood her needs had to come first.

The last seven days had been the edgiest in his life since waiting to hear if he'd made the cut for medical school. Yet if Rikki only needed a friend, he'd be that for her. She deserved it…and much, much more. If he could just hold out a little longer, maybe she'd start to see the bigger picture, too.

She was going through hell getting over Brenden, not to mention deciding whether or not to meet her only remaining relatives.

He and Rikki saw each other every day, and it was obvious that his daughters loved her. Yet, for her sake, he kept a safe distance.

Dane had a busy clinic waiting for him, and the sooner he got started, the better. He rushed into his office and grabbed the first chart his nurse had left on his desk. A stack of messages begged for his attention, too, but they'd have to wait until later.

He washed his hands and was about to walk out when Hannah appeared. The somber look on her face made him tense up.

"Do you have a minute?" she asked.

"Of course. Is this about Don?"

"I'm afraid so."

"Let's go back into my office." A sinking feeling made him need to sit down.

"His labs have been plummeting. His white cell count is practically non-existent. Normally, we'd see a rally by now with a successful engraftment." Her voice was strained and she blinked nervously. "If things don't change soon…"

Everything stopped for a moment. The room went quiet, his pulse paused, he didn't breathe—he couldn't. Then, just as quickly, life switched back on. His brother might be dying and he had to deal with it. He pinched the bridge of his nose, squinting hard to help think of some way to fix everything.

"Damn it all to hell."

Don. The kid he'd been insanely jealous of when his parents had first brought him home. His adopted kid brother, the scrawny tag-along who'd driven him nuts in high school, was dying. How many times had he saved him from bullies? His kid brother had been his biggest supporter in his football days, too. Yet Don could never even make the C string.

Was it only the luck of the draw in life for one to be so strong and healthy and the other so susceptible to disease? Don had been a sickly kid, yet had overcome most of his physical challenges. The day he'd become a police officer, after six weeks of grueling academy training, had been the proudest time in his life. He'd taken on a tough job and performed it well and received respect from his peers.

Though Don had always been frail, he'd always made up for his shortcomings with wisdom. Dane had learned to respect the kid who'd bugged the hell out of him. And more than anything, he wanted to know Don until they were both cantankerous old men.

"We could try another bone-marrow transplant," she said.

"No. Don was adamant. Damn. I've got to see him."

"You won't like what you see."

Somehow Dane had made it through his morning clinic and rushed to his brother's room during lunch. Hannah had been right—what he found shocked him. How could someone change so much for the worse in forty-eight hours? Don looked ancient.

Despite everything modern medicine had done for him, Don looked very sick. Burning up with fever, dehydrated, in pain, ghostly white, he lay listlessly in his bed as if he were a shriveled-up old man. He was only thirty. He'd never have the chance to get married and have kids, or take the trip to Europe he'd always dreamed about, or retire from the police force.

"Hey, brother," Dane said.

Too weak to respond, Don merely nodded at Dane.

"We've been here before. We'll get you through this. You'll pull through."

Dane wasn't sure if he believed what he'd just said, and from the distant look in his brother's eyes, he could tell Don wasn't sure either. Still, he needed to say it for both of them.

"All my papers are in order," Don whispered in a rasping voice. "They're in the file cabinet in my office."

"Don't talk like that. This is just a temporary setback. You'll pull through."

Don stared at Dane with wise, feverish eyes. Dane couldn't fool him. This was his last chance for a miracle.

Dane offered him a sip of water and prayed the bone-marrow donation would kick in.

"OK, bro," Don said in a weak voice. "It's confession time. You go first."

"What are you talking about?"

"I'll start. I paid Billy Maarschalk off to pretend he was going to kick my butt that time your football team lost to Los Vergennes High School. I thought if you could stop another bully from hurting me it would make you feel better."

"You're lying."

"Nope. Now it's your turn to spill. Tell me about Rikki."

"Honest?"

"If I'm lyin', I'm dyin'." Don gave an ironic laugh.

"She's great with kids."

"You are so full of it, bro."

"Hey, shove it. OK, the truth. I've never met anyone like her, and I can see a future for us. But she insists we should just be friends. What can I do?"

"Leave it up to me."

They exchanged knowing smiles and drifted into silence. Dane sat by Don's bedside for another hour, just to let him know he wasn't alone, until Don fell asleep.

Dane called his nurse and asked her to cancel his afternoon clinic, knowing he'd have hell to pay tomorrow. But he couldn't go on today. Maybe his physician's assistant could see some of the patients who'd already shown up.

Completely drained, all he wanted to do was get away from the hospital. He needed to think everything through. He needed solitude and, thanks to Rikki, he knew exactly where to go.

Janetta called Rikki into her office and gave her the update she'd just heard from the ICU supervisor. If things didn't turn around in the next couple of days, they were starting a last-ditch course of chemo for Don.

Rikki's stomach cramped and she got light-headed when she heard he'd relapsed. She clasped the corner of the desk until her knuckles went white. The bone-marrow donation had failed. She had failed. Don was in grave danger of dying.

Rikki wanted to rush to Don's bedside, but the family had requested no visitors, according to Janetta.

She called Dane's office. She had to speak to him. His nurse told her he'd cancelled his afternoon clinic and left for the day.

The ICU nurses' station said he hadn't been there for a few hours. She called his cell phone, but he didn't answer. Frantic to see him, the minute she got off work she drove to his house. He wasn't home. No one was at his mother's house either.

On a whim, she drove to Fernwood Park. He'd liked it there when she'd shown him her secret thinking cave. She'd thought about going there the day after they'd taken Brenden away, but Dane had kept her busy with his girls. They'd gone back to the spot on several occasions with the kids since she'd first taken him. Maybe he'd go there?

It was worth checking out.

She parked her car, threw on her jacket and scarf, as the early days of December had taken a turn toward colder weather. She strode along the hiking trail, though at four-thirty in the afternoon daylight was already turning to dusk.

She marched up a small hill to the crest, winded from the climb. When she stopped to catch her breath, she saw him. Dane sat on a rock in her cave bundled in a coat, stripping the bark off a twig. His face was devoid of expression.

Her heart jumped at the sight. Hurt couldn't begin to describe the distant look on his face. He'd crawled somewhere deep inside and left a "vacant" sign in its place.

"Dane!" she called, and rushed toward him.

He glanced at her but went right back to skinning the twig. Sullen. Withdrawn. Beyond her reach.

What could she say? How could she help him deal with

the possibility of losing his brother? She'd never had a brother or sister and couldn't imagine how difficult it must be for Dane. Though she still had vivid memories of losing her mother, and even after twenty-three years, the pain had never stopped.

"Dane, are you all right?" She approached him and held out her hand. He reached for it in a half-hearted manner. His eyes barely made contact with hers. His cold fingers went flaccid in her hand and he let his hand drop from her grasp.

After a few seconds of silence, he broke the twig in half and tossed it on the ground. His face had turned to stone. His eyes were lifeless. He didn't utter a sound.

"Do you need me to watch the girls for you?"

"They're with a friend."

Rikki fumbled to find words, avoiding the helpless feeling that threatened to take over. "There must be one last thing we can try to help Don get better."

"I don't know. All we can do is wait and see how the chemo turns out."

She wanted to cry at the sound of his defeated words. Don was young. Surely he had another trick up his sleeve.

Resting her head on Dane's thigh, she wept. She'd never felt more involved in anyone else's life than with Dane. His pain was her pain. It frightened her.

Dane didn't move, but sat as though he were carved out of granite. She forced herself to stop crying, swiped at her tears and looked Dane in the face. "I'm so sorry."

Several minutes passed without another word. Rikki remembered how as a teenager when she'd come to this cave, needing time to think, she'd wanted nothing more than to be left alone. To never be found again.

She bit her lower lip and searched Dane's eyes. He stared coldly off into the distance. Did he even realize she was there? Maybe her presence reminded him how the bone-marrow transplant had failed. With all hope taken away, maybe he blamed her.

If she could only read his mind.

Rigid and withdrawn as he was, she suspected her presence might bother him. He needed time to himself.

That's how she'd always wanted it to be when she'd come here. *Leave me alone. I'll tell you when I'm ready to talk.* The way he hardly acknowledged her right now, he probably would just as soon be left alone, too.

She remembered Addy's sage advice. "Timing is everything." Maybe Dane didn't want to be found today, but hopefully tomorrow would be different.

She stood and without another word and all the respect she could offer, she kissed his cheek. He didn't even flinch. She backed out of the cave to give Dane the space he needed.

When he wanted comfort, she'd be there for him. Now was not the time.

Dane watched Rikki leave without saying goodbye. He couldn't bring himself to call out to her. His voice had disappeared after he'd cried and yelled so loudly he'd thought the granite might cave in. Nothing he could do could make his brother recover. All they could do was wait. He'd never felt more helpless or alone in his life.

And Rikki had just walked away. It seemed strangely reminiscent of how his wife had bailed out of their marriage when the going had gotten too tough. Rikki was so busy trying to fill up the gaping hole in her soul by doing things for others that she'd missed the point about healing herself first. She wouldn't be able to love anyone until she did. Well, that was something she'd have to figure out for herself. Right now he had his own healing to deal with.

They were friends. More than friends. He shouldn't have to explain to her how much pain he was in. If she really cared about him, he shouldn't have to stop his grieving to fill her in on all his anger, denial, and self-doubt.

He'd about reached the death and dying bargaining stage when she'd arrived, but his pact with the big guy in the sky hadn't been anything he'd wanted to talk about just then. And how far would he go to save his brother's life? Would he offer his own?

Truth was, the answer was no. There were people and things he wanted to live for.

Damn. Not only was he a coward, he was a failure. And now Rikki had walked away, too, which made him a loser on top of everything else. His thoughts were jumbled and confused. If he could only figure things out. Why couldn't he think straight?

He stood up to run after Rikki, but it was too late. She was long gone.

The last thing he could handle today was history repeating itself. And the one thing he hadn't done when his ex-wife had walked out years ago had been to have a good stiff drink. Considering how this day had gone, he couldn't think of a more appropriate way to end it.

Rikki lay spread-eagle on her bed, staring at the ceiling. She'd cried out all of her tears hours ago and now, emotionally drained and numb to the world, she lay motionless.

Dane didn't want her around. Would he ever want her around again? It had made sense to leave him alone to think things through. How long should she expect to wait for him to call her or come to see her? As difficult as it would be, she'd have to bide her time. For once she'd lobbed the ball into his court, and it was up to him to make the call.

She'd come to her senses and quit blaming herself for the bone-marrow donation not working. She'd done her part, and the rest was in the hands of fate. For some reason the engraftment hadn't been successful, and she'd have to deal with it.

But poor Don. She couldn't give up hope that the chemo would work this time.

Her eyes welled up again when she thought about Don, and what it meant to him. Life and death was the part of nursing she'd never been able to figure out. That was probably why she preferred to be an orthopedic nurse. Broken bones could be fixed, shattered joints could be replaced, but cancer was another story altogether.

She'd thought over her situation with Dane, too. He'd filled up her life with so many wonderful things. She'd grown more confident than she'd ever been since meeting the nitpicking, demanding, and overbearing orthopedic surgeon. He had great kids. She absolutely loved them.

And she loved him.

Dear God, she'd let herself fall in love. The thought made her want to curl up into a ball and hide.

A sudden rapping on her door pulled her out of her thoughts. More knocking. She sat up. Her heart pounding, she rushed toward the door.

"Dane? Is that you?"

"Yeah. Open up."

Maybe he was ready to talk. Maybe she could console him now. She opened the door with a burst of optimism. His belligerent glare put a quick end to any renewed hope.

Disheveled, he pushed his way into her living room. He smelled of alcohol and seemed a little unsteady.

"I hope you didn't drive yourself over here."

"I took a cab."

He wore the same coat he'd had on at Fernwood Park. His ash-blond hair fell onto his forehead and stuck out at the sides. She wanted to smooth it down, but was afraid to try to touch him. His glasses were smudged and sat crookedly on his nose.

"You know what your problem is?" he said, turning and pointing his finger accusingly at her.

Stunned—suspecting he was drunk—she didn't say a word.

"When it comes to really giving, Ms. Philanthropist." It took him a couple of tries to say it right. "When it comes to giving, you don't have the foggiest idea how," he said with a slight slur.

"What are you talking about?"

"You're so busy trying to help everyone else that you've never fixed yourself."

What? How was she supposed to respond to that? Dazed, she took a step back. How dared he? He'd been sitting in a bar all evening, ruminating over the big questions in life with a bartender, and suddenly he had everything figured out? She didn't deserve to be lectured to by a drunk.

"I won't let you put down my charitable efforts. I think I add something to the world, instead of sucking life out of it like most people."

"Oh, get over yourself. You don't get it, do you?" He straightened his glasses and looked her straight in the eyes. A fruity alcoholic aroma permeated the air. "I needed you today, and you left me. Was it too much just to be there for me? Just because you couldn't cut off your hair, or give me your platelets, it didn't mean there was nothing you could do for me. I needed you to *be there*, but you left."

"I'm not a mind-reader, Dane. You hardly acknowledged me. I assumed you wanted to be alone. I would have wanted to be left alone if I were in your shoes."

"You're just like my ex-wife." He barreled full speed ahead. *"If life gets tough, I'm outta here."*

"That's rubbish, Dane, and you know it. I'm nothing like her."

"Then why did you leave me?"

"I already told you, I thought you wanted to be left alone."

"Wrong answer."

What the hell was he getting at?

He jabbed the air with his finger, widening his belligerent stance. "All the great things you do in the world won't make any difference until you fill that gaping hole in your own heart."

He'd totally withdrawn from her at the park, and now he was drunk, waxing poetic, and forcing his opinions on her. He acted like she'd better listen to his pearls of wisdom or she'd live her life in vain. What kind of pushover did she think she was?

Anger snaked up her spine. She straightened her shoulders.

"You know? A month ago, I might have agreed with you, but that was the old me. And yes, you would have been right back then, but I'm going to surprise you with this next part. I admit it. Knowing you has made me a better person."

Now she'd gotten his attention. He lifted his head, tried to focus his gaze. "Then why don't you trust me?"

She stumbled backwards. Be honest. Put it all out there. He deserves the truth. "I'm afraid."

He stood, his arms akimbo. "Get over it."

"It's not that easy."

"Make up your mind to trust me."

Damn, Don had been right about Dane being overbearing. "How am I supposed to decide to just start trusting?"

He combed his fingers through his hair. "I'm the one whose wife walked out. I should be the one who can't trust. But I know a good thing when I see it. We're good together."

She lowered her voice. "Dane."

"I'm willing to take a risk on us, but you've got to meet me halfway. One day we're close, the next day we're distant. I can't take it. You're so closed off. How can I know for sure I love you, if you won't let me in?"

Her mouth dropped open.

"Make up your mind to trust me, because I'm quite sure I have feelings for you."

Oh, God. She wanted to run for cover. Anxiety thrummed through her body. It was now or never, and she couldn't take the plunge. Tears filled her eyes and she pleaded for understanding. "I'm afraid."

A new expression appeared on his face. Resolve? "Then I can't help you." He tapped his fingertips on his chest. "Don't ever forget you were the one who walked away today."

She couldn't take this. Her hands flew to her ears.

He grabbed her arms, lowered them and stared into her eyes. "I can give you what you need, and you know it."

She couldn't let him be in control one more second. He deserved to know her reasons for being afraid to love him. She swallowed. "Not true."

"What are you talking about?"

"I'm looking for a man who loves me for impractical reasons. Not because we'd make a great team. I want you to love me because I'm everything you never thought you could love. I want a man who wants kids as much as I do. Not a man who is a decent parent because he feels stuck with two gorgeous daughters who deserve his devotion. Not because those girls need a mother. I don't want a man who doesn't have a clue about what blessings he's got," she said.

He let her go. Perhaps she'd hit below the belt, but he'd been fighting dirty, too, and it was true. She may as well let him know it.

He stepped back. "I know what I've got, and what I want. Ah, hell." He swiped the air with his hand. "This is all too much to handle. My brother may be dying, Rikki. I don't need this added aggravation." He headed for the door.

"My heart breaks for Don, and your family, too. I've tried my best to help out. I'd like to see him, but you aren't allowing visitors outside the family now."

Dane stopped in mid-wobbly step, registering what she'd said. "I'll arrange for you to see him if you'd like," he said quietly.

"Yes. Thank you. And, please, give my love to the girls. You've done a superb job with them."

He pointed a finger at her. "When you come to your senses, you know where to find me."

"Ditto."

So this was how it would be—an emotional stand-off. He walked out the door. She closed it and leaned against it.

Her heart raced in her chest and she didn't think she could breathe. Had she done the right thing, or had she just blown the greatest gift she'd ever been offered?

Right now, too confused to think one more thought about Dane, Don had to come first.

There was another tap on her door. She opened it. Dane looked chagrined. He scratched his jaw.

"I need to call a cab."

She snorted. "No, you don't. I'll drive you home."

CHAPTER NINE

R$_{\text{IKKI}}$ and Dane didn't say a single word on the whole fifteen-minute drive to his house. She steered her car with a death clutch from tension, but she was damned if she'd break the ice.

So they'd come to a crossroads and neither could compromise. It was crystal clear they couldn't be together. Finally, they'd *gotten* it.

When she pulled into the high-rise condo driveway, Dane looked like he wanted to say something. He quickly brushed his fingers through his hair, got out without looking at her, but bent back down. "I'll tell the nurses in ICU you have my permission to visit my brother any time you want."

"Thank you," she said, staring straight ahead, determined not to even glance at him.

He closed the door and walked unsteadily toward the lobby entrance.

An urgent need drove her to honk the horn. He turned around, looking confused. She jumped out of the car.

"Could you call the hospital now?" She spoke to him over the hood of the car. "I'd like to see Don tonight."

He nodded, as though, at just before midnight, her request seemed completely rational and normal.

"Thank you." She slipped back into the car, hoping her car hadn't left any oil drippings on the perfectly manicured driveway.

Just past midnight Tuesday morning, Rikki arrived on the Mercy Hospital ICU oncology unit. The lights had been dimmed and, like a barricade, every patient room had a nurse seated behind a desk. Despite the hour, the noise level was no different from the busy day routine. Nurses called across the unit to each other. The ward clerk answered the non-stop phones and called questions to nurses. Orderlies bustled around, delivering equipment or patients on gurneys.

No wonder intensive care patients got so little sleep in the unit.

Rikki found Don's room and started to gown up for the visit. His nurse recognized her as being a fellow nurse at Mercy Hospital. "Dr. Hendricks just called. Go ahead and go inside, though Don hasn't been very responsive tonight."

Her mood sank even further.

They'd changed tack, started more aggressive medical intervention, and hoped his bone marrow would respond. Rikki wanted to cry, but held her emotions inside for Don's sake.

She quietly took the seat beside his bed. Several IVs were attached to ports in his arms and chest. He wore an oxygen mask and seemed to be struggling to breathe. She glanced at the monitor on the wall. His heart rhythm looked normal, though his pulse was too fast. The last blood-pressure reading was as low as hers. He normally ran much higher.

Disillusioned, she touched his hand. He looked flushed and dry, as though he had a fever. When he opened his sunken eyes, they were glassy and deep green—almost the same color as Dane's.

Her heart ached when he recognized her and gave a forced fearless grin beneath his oxygen mask.

If only things could be different. "I guess I let you down," she said for openers.

He gave a dry swallow. "No. You didn't." The hissing oxygen mask muffled his already weak voice. "You gave me your best shot, and I'll always be grateful to you. Now I'm giving my own marrow a pep talk to go forth and multiply, just like the good book says."

The room went blurry. She squeezed his hand.

"And the only way you'll ever let me down is if you don't call that aunt of yours," he continued.

She gave an ironic chuckle and gave him an I'm-glad-you-don't-ever-give-up look.

"Promise?" he asked, with hopeful eyes.

"OK. I promise." Desperate to find something to do for him, she searched for a lemon-glycerin swab in his bedside supplies, lifted his oxygen mask and quickly wiped his mouth to help moisten his lips. Afterwards, just before she replaced the mask, he smacked his lips like a man who'd taken a huge drink of icy water.

"Thanks."

"No problem."

"No. I mean…thanks for everything." He made a weak attempt to squeeze her hand. "You're my blood sister."

Nothing could stop her now. The tears flowed and she could barely focus on his face, but she smiled and clung to his arm.

They sat quietly for several moments.

"You gonna marry that brother of mine?"

Oh, God, what could she tell him—that they'd just yelled and screamed at each other and would probably never talk again, let alone consider marriage? Never lie to a dying person—her nurse's training took over. "Actually, I think we just broke up."

"Damn. Sometimes he's difficult, Rikki, and I know I told you he was overbearing, but he's a good guy." Don took a great deal of effort to shift onto his side in order to make eye contact with her. "The thing is, I've never seen him look at a woman the way he looks at you. And you look pretty damn speechless around him half the time, too—at least, as far as I can tell. Not that I'm an expert on relationships or anything, but I'd say you two were a perfect match. You know, in the old polar-opposites-attract kind of way."

More tears. If she could only get past her fear.

"What's the matter with you tonight? You're going all female on me."

Rikki smiled and shook her head. "Your brother. He's such a jerk."

"What has he done now?"

"It's not what he did, but what I couldn't do."

"I'm in the dark here. You've got to give me more."

"He doesn't understand why I'm afraid to take our relationship to the next level."

"Oh. The old 'what if' game."

"What do you mean?"

"*What if* I let my guard down, and it doesn't work out? *What if* we fall in love and get married? *What if? What if* the chemo doesn't work?"

Well, that certainly put things into perspective. She was afraid to let herself fall in love, and Don was dealing with life and death.

"*What ifs* never pay off. If your heart is telling you to love him then listen to it. You can't sit on the sidelines and call it a life. Jump in."

She wished she wasn't wearing a mask so she could kiss him, then figured what the hell, untied it and kissed his forehead anyway.

"*What if* my chemo *does* work?"

"Then I'll be the first one dancing at your welcome-home party."

From where had all the energy come, or, for that matter, the wisdom? He was supposed to be sick and distracted—possibly dying! But he'd detected something Rikki had yet to realize. The look Dane often gave her, the one that brought her to her knees, was something much deeper than a prelude to sex. He did love her in a special way, and everyone else could tell. What an idiot she'd been.

Don had worn himself out with his speech. He repositioned himself on his back and grew very quiet, as if he were in pain. She wished there was something she could do to comfort him. The nurse came in with a gazillion bottles and meds, and she hoped one of them was for pain.

Not giving a damn what the nurse would say, Rikki raised her mask and kissed Don again, hoping it wouldn't be the last time she ever saw him. One of her tears splattered onto his forehead. She wiped it off with her thumb.

"Now, if you'll excuse me," he said, "I've got to visualize my bone marrow multiplying and my white blood cells fighting off any trace of the bad guys. It's chemo time!"

"That sounds like a grand plan."

"Yep. Think positive."

"Mind if I do the same?"

"Mind? I'm depending on it. Now, remember what I said," he whispered, glancing fondly up at her.

She squeezed his hand once more. "I'll never forget."

On Friday afternoon, Rikki had just finished starting an IV on a pre-op patient when Janetta called her into the office. "I just got word from my ICU source that Don Hendricks has undergone a strong rally. He may be in remission."

Rikki fell into a chair and wept with joy. She'd gone by to see him for at least a few minutes each day that week. She'd been careful to time her visits for when Dane wasn't around. Mostly they'd spent the time in silence, but Rikki knew Don appreciated her being there—the way she should have been there for Dane.

"This is so wonderful, I can't believe it. I mean, I thought he was getting his color back and looking stronger, and I hoped, but I was afraid…"

Janetta stood and gave her a businesslike hug. "Never give up praying for miracles."

Rikki wanted to click her heels and run to the ICU, but she had patients to care for. She'd stop by after work and give Don a big hug, but only if Dane wasn't around.

On Sunday afternoon, with Don's constant urging echoing in her ear, Rikki found the piece of paper he'd given her, picked up the phone and dialed.

"Hello? Is this Colleen Baskin?"

"Yes," the voice all the way across the country replied. "Who's this?"

"My name is Rikki, uh, I mean, Rachel. Rachel Johansen. My mother's name was Mara. I think you might be my aunt?"

"Oh, my God. Is it really you?"

Rikki paced her living room as she gave Colleen dates and told her what she knew of her mother. "I went into foster-care when my mother had to do some jail time. I never saw her again, but I do have one snapshot of her." She conjured up in her mind the one photograph of her mother she'd memorized as a child. "Let me see, she had dark brown hair and eyes. She wore her hair long. I used to love it when she smiled at me."

She heard sobs on the other end of the phone. "Mara was a beautiful girl, Rikki. Did you know she was a home-coming queen?"

"No!"

"She had everything going for her, and then she met a slick and dangerous man named Richard Figgen. I suspect he was your father. He took her away from us, made her afraid of everything, got her into drugs, and I hold him responsible for her death."

Rikki's mind spun out of control. Her father had a name? There wasn't one on her birth certificate. How odd that when Rikki had wanted to change her birth name from Rachel, and Addy Greenspaugh had gone with her to do it legally, she'd chosen the name she'd always wanted—Rikki. She'd thought she was being daring to take on such an unusual name. At fourteen, it had meant everything to her to be different and cool. It had also helped to separate her from her dismal past. She had become her own person that day.

Maybe somewhere in the back of her mind she'd

recalled hearing her mother talking to her father, Richard…Ricky? Maybe she'd wanted nothing more than to connect with her father on a deeper level by changing her name.

Her stomach twisted up and she needed to sit down.

"So my mother was an addict?" She bit back her tears.

"Only at the end of her life, Rikki. There's so much more I'd love to tell you about her. She was a great older sister to me. It all changed when she moved out to California, though. He made her afraid of everything."

"If you don't mind, I'd like to keep in touch with you."

"Rikki, honey, I'd love to meet you. I told that wonderful man Don to tell you to come and visit me."

"Maybe this summer on my vacation?"

"Yes! And in the meantime, give me your e-mail address. I'll scan some pictures and send them to you. I have so many stories to tell you, not just about Mara but about your grandparents, too. You would have loved them."

An hour later, Rikki hung up, feeling connected to a distant yet loving family for the first time in her life. She had an aunt and cousins. She belonged somewhere, with people who looked like her and wanted to know everything about her life.

And she had to admit, after all the years of denying she needed a blood family—because she'd figured out who she was without one—it still felt incredibly good.

Two weeks later, the invitation came. Don telephoned Rikki with new vigor in his voice.

"What's up, blood sister?"

"Don! I heard you'd been discharged from the hospital. How are you?"

"I'm feeling great! Listen, you made me a promise that when I beat the odds you'd be the first to dance at my homecoming party."

"I remember."

"So bring your dancing shoes this Sunday, two o'clock."

When Rikki arrived on the brisk mid-December afternoon the number of police cars parked around the neighborhood stunned her. As she made her way into Mrs. Hendricks's back yard, the uniformed presence gave a military feel to the party.

Don had touched a lot of lives, and the huge crowd of well-wishers proved it. She knew firsthand how he'd touched hers. He'd pointed her in the direction of her estranged family. But hadn't it been Dane's original idea? He'd put Don on the task to keep him occupied while he'd been recovering. She had Don to thank for getting her in touch with her aunt, and she needed to thank Dane, too. *If* she saw him today, and *if* she had the guts.

Rikki and her aunt had both ended up crying when it had been time to end their phone conversation. Don had helped her make sense out of her mother's addiction and eventual death. Yes, people had free will and sometimes their choices were bad. Sometimes the choices killed them.

Armed with new information, after all the years she'd spent wondering who her father was, she no longer had a burning desire to find out about him. And if her hunch was right about why she had chosen her name, she might consider going back to calling herself Rachel. Maybe.

How many more things could change in her life?

Don had clued Rikki in on how Dane looked at her like no other woman. How could she not have recognized the look of love? One of his glances could send shivers through her body and, more, his look touched her soul. Dane was the special meant-to-be man in her life, and she prayed it wasn't too late to salvage what they'd shared together.

Rikki glanced up in time to see the twins. They broke away from their grandmother's hands and ran toward her, throwing their arms around her waist. Rikki bent down to kiss each of them. "I've missed you, sweeties."

"Why don't you come see us any more?" Meg scolded, with clear eyes and an innocent face.

What could she tell them?

"I'm sorry." She fumbled through a million things to say, but only managed an apology. "I promise to make it up to you."

"I miss you," Emma, the quiet and sensitive twin, said.

Rikki kissed the little girls again. "I've missed you, too." And Dane.

She noticed they wore the bead bracelets she'd made for them out of her special clay the last time they'd spent the afternoon together.

A relative Rikki had never met came to gather up the girls and led them back inside for a group game.

They went willingly and waved goodbye, and Rikki hoped with all her heart she would be able to keep her word about seeing them soon. A twinge of fear threatened to take hold. Her eyes stung and the world went blurry again.

Tears came easily most days now. Rikki couldn't believe she had so much to cry about, but after each crying jag she felt better and more focused. She'd rebelled against her nature for years by stockpiling her sadness. Crying cleansed her and helped her see life more clearly, especially the bit about being a part of Dane's life.

Quickly wiping away her tears before anyone could see them, she found Dane in the crowd. Tall, broad shoulders, strong arms, the handsomest man she'd ever known, he stood a half-head above most of the other men at the party. He held a cup of punch in his hand and was laughing, as if someone had told a really good joke.

They hadn't seen each other since she'd switched to the night shift, and she'd missed him, thought about him day and night, and wondered if she'd passed through his mind from time to time over the last couple of weeks. Had he totally given up on her? She hoped not.

Don was surrounded by well-wishers and wore a surgical mask for protection against germs. She worked her way to the front and gave him a huge hug and kiss. He grabbed her like a long-lost friend.

"Your nose is cold," he said.

"Yeah? Well, put on some music so I can warm up. I believe I owe you a dance?"

They laughed and hugged again, and another batch of guests pushed their way toward the man of the hour. She worried Don might get worn out soon. She backed away, then drifted out of the group.

Her gaze came to rest on Dane, sitting across the yard. Today was the day she'd promised herself to tell him how she felt—no matter how afraid she was.

Dane received a long and drawn-out hug from Hannah Young, and a wave of insecurity almost knocked Rikki off her very high-heeled ankle boots. She caught her balance and stood up straight. Hannah could offer all the sexy hellos she wanted, but Dane belonged with her.

* * *

Dane peeled Hannah off and turned to the gaudy, irreverent banner the police officers had brought. *Born to Protect and Serve. Don Hendricks. RIP. NOT!*

Yeah, it was sick cop humor all right, but it made Don laugh, and so it made Dane laugh, too. The thought of how close Don had come to dying still made Dane shake his head. He blinked back the nagging moisture that all too often fogged his vision these days. He lifted his gaze across the lawn. One lone person stood on the other side.

Rikki.

The sight of her made his heart jumpstart. He couldn't help the response. The cloudless bright blue sky with the dependable California sun sparkled through her spiky butterscotch hair. No Mary Jane shoes for her today. She'd outdone herself in party attire, with black high-heeled ankle boots and some sort of baggy high-waisted dress rippling in the breeze around her knees. Her only warmth was from a black velvet bolero-length jacket. She looked great. A faint smile crossed his lips. God, he loved her individuality.

He loved *her*.

He backed away from that thought, remembering how she'd disappointed him. He'd trusted her, and she'd let him down with her pitiful excuse about being afraid. He wouldn't allow history to repeat itself where women were concerned.

Rikki didn't approach him. She hesitated, as though waiting for an invitation. Dane wanted to rush to her and hold her for comfort, but didn't move, just stayed seated. When he'd stared at her for a while she lifted a tentative hand and waved. And when it became apparent to Rikki that he wasn't budging, she walked toward him.

Her high heels kept digging into the grass, making her

approach long and awkward. He worried she might twist her ankle or fall. To distract himself, he went back to staring at Don's banner until he heard the sweetest voice he could ever remember.

"Please, don't ask me to leave, because I won't."

Her delicate hand rested on his shoulder, and without thinking he bent his head and rubbed his ear over her cool knuckles. She circled in front of him and sat on an adjacent stool. She smelled like flowers. She reached for and held onto his hand as if she never wanted to let it go. He never wanted her to.

"I could use some fresh air," he said. "What do you say we blow this party?"

She scrunched up her face. "We're outside. It's, like, sixty-five degrees."

"Do you want to or not?"

Some sort of battle went on inside her head for the next few seconds before she gave a mischievous glance. "I'll drive."

He stood and smiled. "Sounds like a plan." He took her hand and walked her to her clunker. They got inside, not saying a word. She started it up, needing three tries to get the engine to turn over, and drove up the street. He sent her a silent message.

She slanted him a sideways glance, as though she'd read his mind, made a screwball turn to get on the right freeway, and with a little extra adrenaline in his system, they headed in the direction of his condo.

He wasn't sure what would happen once they got there. He really didn't want to argue any more. Though he knew one thing for certain: he didn't want to spend any more time without Rikki. Evidently Rikki was on the same wavelength. She parked the car in one of the visitor spots and got out.

"I'm going to fix you a cup of that tea you like so much," she said matter-of-factly.

He gave a noncommittal nod. "Fair enough."

Again, they didn't say two words in the elevator, but he had to admit that having her near made him feel alive again. He unlocked his door, and she breezed by and straight into the kitchen, as though she lived there. He leaned against the wall in silence and watched her refamiliarize herself with his cabinets. He kept his hands where they'd be safe, in his pockets, while she filled the teapot. He couldn't trust that he might want to touch the wisp of hair on her neck, or circle her perfectly shaped ear with the silver piercing with his fingertips, or turn her face so he could stare into her huge brown eyes until he needed to kiss her while she waited for the water to boil.

No. He'd stay right where he was, stoic and withdrawn.

Rikki had never been more flustered in her life. Completely unsure if Dane wanted her there or not, she went about her business. Even if he didn't want her around, she longed to be near him and, yes, she did love him.

The realization made her fingers clumsy and she ripped a teabag and had to throw it away. She loved him with all her heart and, no matter how hard she tried to deny it, she couldn't help but love him. He'd have to throw her out of his condo in order to get her to leave today.

Something made her glance over her shoulder. She tried not to come undone at Dane's penetrating gaze. She'd seen that look before, and it usually had nothing to do with asking her to leave. The fine hairs on her neck and arms prickled. How did he manage to have such power over her?

She couldn't hide the small tremor in her hand when she gave him a clanking cup and saucer. He smiled appreciatively when he took it. No. There was far more than appreciation in his gaze. She had to turn away before she got her hopes up. She picked up her own cup and gave a quiet sigh. She needed to gather her composure, or before long she'd burst.

He took off his jacket, kicked off his shoes and sat on the couch. She sat at the opposite end, and they drank their tea in strained silence. She followed his lead and unzipped her boots, removed them and wiggled her toes. Who'd decided that ultra-pointy shoes should be in style anyway?

She drank more tea then placed her cup on the end table and ventured a look at Dane. He sat, staring at his cup. With sudden conviction she needed him to know how she felt about him.

"I've really missed you and the girls. It felt like a whole part of my life had disappeared after our argument."

He looked up, expressionless.

"The fact is, I didn't realize what I was feeling because I'd never felt it before I met you." She attempted to swallow something the size of a dry sock, realizing it was time to *show*, not tell.

She scooted over to him, removed the teacup from his grasp and placed it on the table. She took him into her arms and drew his face to hers, his warm breath caressing her skin. He didn't resist. With every ounce of compassion and love she felt for Dane, she kissed him gently. He came to life after the kiss, pulled back and gazed longingly into her eyes.

"I've missed you more than you'll ever know," she whispered, and pressed her lips to his again.

Apparently at a loss for words, he drew her closer and kissed with purpose—a hungry kiss that made Rikki's heart race. Over and over they made love with their mouths. Fiery kisses that burned a path to her very center drove her to lie back on the couch and pull Dane with her. He dove into her neck with more hot kisses, and she wove her fingers into his hair in a futile attempt to control her response. She inhaled his clean scent and savored each and every touch of his lips.

"Before this goes any further," she said, breathlessly, "you need to know one thing."

He lifted his head and looked at her with unfocused, hooded eyes.

"What if I told you that I love you?"

"I might tell you the same thing back."

"Well, I just hope you realize that I'm the most worthy person you'll ever meet to love."

For the first time that day, Dane smiled. "You want to know what I've been thinking?"

"I'm almost afraid to ask, but what?"

"You *are* the damn most worthy person I'll ever love."

She caught her breath from sheer joy. They'd finally told each other. She pulled his face to hers and captured his smiling mouth with her own. His tongue welcomed her and they danced through several more minutes of steamy kisses until she wanted more than anything in the world to be naked with him.

CHAPTER TEN

"Why do you always insist on carrying me in here?" Rikki asked, nuzzling her head into Dane's neck, thrilled down to her toes to be swept away by his strong arms and warm chest.

"Because you're so cute and liftable."

"Liftable? Is that even a word?" She giggled and snorted, embarrassing herself.

"Yeah, it's a word. I created it just for you. Liftable makes me feel…uh… Damn horny is what it makes me feel." He carried her down the hall and into his bedroom.

After yanking back the bedspread, he gently placed Rikki in the center of his bed and proceeded to unbutton and remove her dress. She kept perfectly still and, mesmerized by his attention, stared at the passion in his eyes— quickly getting lost. She co-operated when he lifted the dress over her head, and felt a tickling in her belly when he unhooked her bra.

Her breathing quickened at his reverent gaze. The look abruptly changed to hunger and need, sending a shiver to her core.

Dane peeled down her stockings then swept his hands up her thighs until he reached her lace underwear. She tightened her muscles in anticipation. The breath caught in her throat when Dane drew out the moment by running his palm across her stomach, and down, grazing her mound. Heat flicked between her legs when she shimmied to assist him with removing the garment. Yeah, she'd made the right choice in panties today.

The desire in his eyes alone made her want him, but his touch turned her longing to need.

She didn't speak, not wanting to spoil the moment.

Dane rose up on his knees and unbuttoned his shirt, then pulled his undershirt over his head as quickly as humanly possible. The sight of his broad shoulders and muscular chest dusted with tawny hair made blood rush to the surface of her skin. Warm and willing, she watched as he undid his belt and removed his slacks and briefs, releasing himself.

The man was gorgeous, but what excited Rikki even more was that he wanted her. And she'd missed being with him. Nothing had ever been like it.

The need in his dark green gaze kept her spellbound when he hovered over her on his hands and knees. Would she ever grow tired of staring into those eyes? The intensity frightened her as she outlined his chest, shoulders, and arms with her palms.

After a hungry smile crossed his lips, he swallowed. "You're so beautiful."

She couldn't bear being apart another instant and reached for him. He welcomed her into his tight embrace. Now skin to skin, she reeled with sensations at every point of contact. She inhaled his masculine scent and felt his erection on her thigh, then pressed into it.

They clung together, kissing and rolling around on the

bed for several minutes. His hands explored every part of her, tickling, brushing, grazing, kneading—hungry to touch her more deeply. And she let him.

Swept up by his touch, she wrapped her legs around his waist, pulled him closer, and he entered her, rocked and withdrew. She savored his exquisite, slick feel and opened to bring him deeper, then tightened to hold him in place. She let him withdraw and moved to bring him back.

Ready. Wet. Nerve endings on fire. Deeply in love. Deep inside. They didn't bother with protection. They belonged together, like this. For ever.

Their tongues and lips tangled, nonstop. His warm palms traced a trail over her tightened breasts. She moaned with pleasure when he lifted and cupped all of her. He tested her pebbled nipples first with his thumb, then his tongue. She arched and he drew her into his mouth as his hips drove deeper inside her. On and on they grappled and lunged, heightening their sensations…their need.

Later, amidst wild breathing and restless desire, when she didn't think she could bear another second of pleasure, he brought her to the brink. She coiled tighter than she could ever remember. Dane made several quick thrusts, and she strained against him, higher and higher, before shuddering her release. The world broke loose, and she descended into a freefall of sensations.

He slowed down…and stopped.

"I love to feel that. To know I brought you all the way."

So wrung out, Rikki couldn't respond. She groaned her continued pleasure. He laughed and growled back at her. And when her spasms calmed down, he moved deeper inside, as though determined to keep her with him. He worked her quickly back to frenzy and, fisting the sheets in her hands, she came again. He felt like steel and she took him as deeply as she possibly could, until he pumped liquid heat into her.

They collapsed in sated bliss, staying as close as possible. And Rikki knew without a doubt that this was where she belonged for the rest of her life.

A few minutes later Dane stirred from his contented trance. He searched for and kissed Rikki's fingers. He stared into her huge, dreamy eyes. He knew what he had to do, and there was no time like the present.

He nervously nibbled and sucked on her fingertips. "I only thought I'd been in love before, until I met you. You came out of nowhere one day at the hospital, and I thought, Wow, who is that woman? I felt our chemistry immediately."

Her eyes were huge with amazement.

"You surprise me. You make me laugh. I adore your crazy get-ups and spiky hair." He tugged on a tuft of it.

She shook his hand off as if he were a pestering brother. "Stop it. Go on."

"You've taught me how to care about people besides my immediate family. Damn, I can't tell you how much you've added to my life."

Big tears filled her eyes; her lips trembled with expectation. "You're doing great. Go on."

"You want more?" He wanted to please her, to make her understand how much he loved her. He remembered the phrase she'd said she needed to hear the night they'd broken up, and repeated it. "I love you because you're everything I never thought I could love. With all my heart, I *want* you to be my wife more than anything else in life. I *want* you to be mother to my daughters." He dove into her eyes, searching for her soul…her honest answer. "I *need* you to love me, and I *want* you to be the mother of all my future children. So, what do you say? Will you marry me?"

Without hesitation, Rikki squealed, "Yes! Yes!"

He laughed before he grabbed her and smothered her mouth with his.

They settled down, Dane realizing the momentous significance of what he'd just asked. His life would never be the same. He was ready for it. Hell, it had changed the day he'd followed a scrawny, frustrating nurse out to her car in the Mercy Hospital parking lot and asked her out for dinner.

They lay silently in each other's arms for several seconds, deep in thought.

Rikki was shocked that Dane's proposal had included children. "What changed your mind about having more kids?"

"You."

She smiled reassuringly. "You're a good father."

He laced his fingers through hers and kissed her knuckles.

"You know?" he said.

"Hmm?"

"Don will be very happy about us getting married."

"I know," she said. It occurred to her that she hadn't told Dane about her aunt. That even though Don had tracked her down, she'd never thanked the person who'd instigated finding her in the first place. "And by the way, I believe I owe you thanks."

"Well, I know I'm great in bed, but there's no need…"

"Oh, get over yourself." She playfully slapped his arm. "Besides, it takes two to make great love." She rose up onto one elbow, facing him. "No, what I'm saying is I need to thank you for putting Don on the task of finding my family. It was your idea."

He lifted his brows in understanding.

"I've talked to my Aunt Colleen on the phone, and even though I haven't met her yet, I feel like I have a real family now."

Looking more than pleased with himself, he kissed her arm.

"You're welcome. And soon I hope you'll feel like you have a real family with me and the girls, too."

Her heart clutched at his statement. "I already do." God, she loved him. Their eyes connected. Gratitude. Understanding. Love passed between them.

And before long, they were ready to make love again.

After a brief nap, they woke up hungry. Rikki wrapped herself in one of Dane's sweatshirts, put on some of his socks, and drifted toward the kitchen. She'd plopped her purse on the table and her cell phone had fallen out. The red missed-call light blinked. She'd left it on vibrate for the party. She decided to check her messages.

It was from Children's Services, and they asked her to return the call.

She quickly dialed their number, excitement whirling through her. Would Brenden be coming back?

"Yes, Ms. Johansen, I'm glad you called. We have a fourteen-month-old baby in need of emergency shelter. Are you available?"

Dane wandered into the living room, searching for his shoes.

"Can you hold on a moment, please?" Rikki covered

the phone speaker. "Dane! They want me to take in another child."

Dane knew this was a defining moment. He'd just told her he loved her and wanted to marry her. It had been a full disclosure proposal. She'd always be taking in foster-children, like other people took in stray cats. He knew Rikki's dreams of having a big family, too. Hell, they hadn't used birth control all afternoon. He understood what he was getting into.

No need for conversation. He gave an encouraging nod. She almost jumped up and down when she told the person on the other end of the phone she'd be available within the hour.

While Rikki quickly showered and dressed, Dane called his mother and explained why he wouldn't be coming back to the party. With loud conversation and chatter in the background, obviously still surrounded by family and friends, she agreed to keep the twins for the night and assured him she understood.

Don broke into the conversation. "You'd better have a good reason for bailing on my party, bro."

"The best, brother. I just asked Rikki to marry me."

Dane had to hold the phone away from his ear for the loud catcall Don made. If he hadn't been sure about Don being on the mend before, he knew now.

When Don settled down he spoke in a raspy voice. "Pencil me in as best man."

Dane smiled into the phone.

They drove to Rikki's house, where she rushed to make the guest room suitable for the toddler. He offered to help her attach a bedside rail on the child's bed while she placed colorful stuffed toys along the wall. She rushed around putting in electrical socket protectors while he put clamps on the handles of every single lower cupboard and cabinet. It brought back memories of when his daughters had been younger. Now he had a new love and a future wife, and he'd do whatever it took to make Rikki happy.

"So tell me about her," he said.

"All I know is she's fourteen months old, and her name is Lily Chow."

No sooner had she said that than the doorbell rang. He followed her to the other room. The same woman he remembered from when they'd taken Brenden away stood on the other side of the screen with a small bundle in her arms.

"Won't you come in?" Rikki swept open the door and the woman entered with a beautiful little girl in a white hooded windbreaker, matching coveralls and shoes with bunnies on them.

Dane's heart pinched at the sight. A beautiful, helpless child needed shelter, and Rikki wanted nothing more than to help her. Truth be told, so did he.

"This will only be a temporary stay, two to three weeks. Her father was arrested for spousal battery. The mother is in the hospital and he's going to jail. No immediate relatives in Los Angeles beyond an uncle who's a known drug dealer. Until Mrs. Chow can get back on her feet, Lily here needs shelter."

Damn, did the child understand what was going on?

Rikki grinned a heart-melting smile, and reached for the little girl. "May I?" she asked the woman.

Lily's black eyes widened, but she didn't protest…at first. Once the transfer had been made into Rikki's arms, the little girl looked back at the Children's Services representative. Then she wailed.

Rikki bounced and patted, walked and sang to the child to calm her down. It didn't help. But she seemed less flustered than when she had first been faced with Brenden.

The representative handed Dane a suitcase. "Are you living here?"

"Me? No. I'm just here for moral support."

"Well, if you intend to spend the night in this household, we need to do a background check for our records. Maybe you should consider taking the training classes and apply for a license."

"He's a doctor," Rikki broke in over the crying child's racket.

"I'm an orthopedic surgeon at Mercy Hospital."

"That doesn't make you any more qualified to be a foster-care provider than anyone else," the woman said with a flinty glance.

He scratched his jaw. "If you have the paperwork I need with you, why don't you give it to me now?"

Had he ever in his entire adult life expected to hear those words coming from his mouth? And, more importantly, had he ever seen Rikki look more surprised and happy? His proposal hadn't even drawn that kind of response.

Dane held the squirming Lily while Rikki signed all the necessary documents for the transfer of the child to foster care. The representative handed Dane a packet of forms for him to fill out at his leisure and, bidding them both good night, she prepared to leave.

"I'll be in touch in the next few days with an update on Mrs. Chow's condition. In the meantime, take care, and thank you," the woman said, one foot already out the door.

When they were alone again, Dane and Rikki looked at each other expectantly. Lily stopped fidgeting long enough to realize the woman had left, and went back to fussing. A few inconsolable minutes later Dane thought an alien force had inhabited him when he heard himself say, "Here. Let me take her."

Having not made any progress in consoling the child, frustration in Rikki's eyes, she gladly handed Lily to Dane. He was right. She did need a break.

He took the wailing child into his arms and placed her on his shoulder. "This used to work with Meg and Emma when they were teething." He rubbed Lily's back, patted her bottom, paced the living room, and started to sing Hush Little Baby.

Rikki's jaw dropped. She stared at him as though in awe. "Both my girls were colicky," he explained.

He'd learned a few things over his years as a parent. And who knew how many more children he'd wind up with? Loving Rikki meant having a big family, sharing his home with foster-children, and maybe a few more of his own?

For the first time in his life he felt ready for it. And when he glanced at Rikki's beaming face, the rewarding look of love only proved his point.

He rubbed Lily's back and patted her bottom, bouncing her up and down with each step. He drew a hushed breath when she settled down, and he continued to sing. Happier than he could remember, he smiled at the woman he loved, and she smiled back. He sent a special message through the lullaby, followed by a wink. "Daddy's gonna buy you a diamond ring."

EPILOGUE

FOUR months later…

Rikki followed Dane into the donor center. It had been a few months since he'd last donated platelets. She had decided to keep him company as he'd been in surgery all day, and she'd hardly had a chance to see him the previous day. Her shift had ended at four, and she'd had a doctor's appointment after that. They'd met up in his office and walked downstairs together.

"Hey, Dr. Hendricks," Sheila, the donor center nurse, greeted him. "Have a seat right here." She glanced at Rikki. "You won't be donating, right, Mrs. Hendricks?"

Rikki shook her head, wondering if she'd ever get used to hearing those incredible words. *Mrs. Hendricks.* "Not for a while."

"What's new, Sheila?" Dane asked, sitting down.

"Same old, same old. How about you?"

"Today was arthroscopy day," he said, loosening his tie. "Four knees and two shoulders."

"Sounds exciting."

The nurse walked off to gather her equipment while Dane rolled up his sleeves. He leaned over the chair to give

Rikki a kiss. She closed her eyes and welcomed him. Would she ever grow tired of kissing her husband?

"How did the ultrasound go?" he asked. "I'm really sorry I couldn't get out of surgery to be there."

"That's OK," she said, patting his arm. "The ultrasound tech thinks he might be a boy."

"Our kid was giving the male salute?"

She giggled. "Well, not exactly, but enough to make the tech think *it* is a *he*."

Dane grinned and leaned back when Sheila reappeared to start his IV. "Did you hear that, Sheila? We may be having a boy."

She smiled at both of them. "You two work fast."

Rikki felt a blush come over her—they'd only been married three months. Dane made a big deal out of patting her thigh. "Yep," he said, with a wink. "Now, hit me with your best shot."

Rikki snuggled back into the adjacent chair and held his free hand while Sheila prepared to insert the intravenous line. Nervous for him, she twiddled with her hair. She'd been growing it out again so she could donate to Care to Share Your Hair again. Growing like crazy with the extra hormones of pregnancy, it had already reached mid-neck.

"I've been thinking. If we have a boy, I want to name him Don."

"That's great, but these tests aren't one hundred percent sure, you know," Dane said with a grimace when the needle pierced his skin. "'Tis but a flesh wound," he blurted out, his knee-jerk response.

She snorted. Would she ever grow tired of his corny sense of humor? She settled back on her chair while Sheila taped him up. "I just know it's going to be a boy. I'm positive."

"Well, it's always best to have a back-up plan, you know, in case things don't turn out as you expect."

"OK." She crossed her arms and legs and pumped her foot, while thinking.

After a few moments of silence Dane asked. "So, what do you suggest we name the baby if she's a girl?"

She tapped her finger on her lip and stared up at the ceiling. She lifted a brow and gave Dane a coy glance. "I have a great idea."

"Well?"

Rikki reached over and kissed him between the eyes. "How about we call her Don?" She grinned, totally pleased with herself, and kissed him again.

He looked confused, as though he thought she might have lost her mind.

"D-A-W-N. Dawn."

MILLIONAIRE IN COMMAND

CATHERINE MANN

USA TODAY bestselling author **Catherine Mann** lives on a sunny Florida beach with her flyboy husband and their four children. With more than forty books in print in over twenty countries, she has also celebrated wins for both a RITA® Award and a Booksellers' Best Award. Catherine enjoys chatting with readers online—thanks to the wonders of the internet, which allows her to network with her laptop by the water! Contact Catherine through her website, catherinemann.com, find her on Facebook and Twitter (@CatherineMann1), or reach her by snail mail at PO Box 6065, Navarre, FL 32566, USA.

All my love to my flyboy husband Rob. Even after many years and four children, you still make my heart flutter!

One

Phoebe Slater brought a baby to the millionaire military hero's seaside welcome-home gala.

Undoubtedly most of the guests plucking canapés and champagne from silver trays at this high-profile affair could afford nannies. Of course the Hilton Head Island wealthy could also afford tailored tuxedos and sequined high-end dresses as they mingled the evening away in the country club gardens by the shore. Her basic little black dress had been bought at a consignment store to wear to the few mandatory cocktail parties related to her position as a history professor at the University of South Carolina.

Of course she usually didn't accessorize with baby drool dotting her shoulder.

Phoebe jostled the fractious five-month-old infant on her hip, smoothing down the pink smocked dress. "Hang on, sweetie. Just a few more minutes and I can feed you before bedtime."

As waves crashed in the distance, a live band played oldies rock, enticing guests to the dance floor with a Billy Joel classic. Even South Carolina's governor was dancing under the silver silk canopy with his wife. Darn near gawking, Phoebe stumbled on the edge of the flagstone walkway.

Definitely this was a party for the movers and shakers in the political world—as well as on the polished wood dance floor planked over the sandy lawn. She untangled her low heel from between two decorative rocks. She wasn't here to socialize tonight. She'd come to find little Nina's father.

If only she had a better idea of what he looked like.

Her longtime friend and old sorority sister— Nina's biological mother—had told Phoebe that Kyle Landis was the baby's daddy a couple of months ago when she'd asked for "just a little help" with Nina while she went on an audition for a dinner-theater production in Florida. Bianca had been so excited to get her prebaby body back, insisting this was her chance to provide a better life for her daughter.

Who could have known Bianca wouldn't return?

Phoebe hugged Nina closer, all the more determined to make sure this precious baby had a stable life. Which meant finding Kyle Landis, a man she'd never met in the flesh. She'd hoped to ID him by his Air Force uniform, but the place was packed with tall, dark-haired guys decked out in formal military gear. Medals gleamed in the moonlight.

Cupping the back of Nina's bonnet-covered head as the little one finally dozed off, Phoebe scanned the sea of faces, their profiles shadowy with only the illumination of moon, stars and pewter tiki torches. She only had an older photo to go by, a picture tucked deep in the bottom of the flowered diaper bag slung over her clean shoulder. No way was she going to disturb Nina by looking, not now that the baby was nearly out for the count.

He used to appear in the newspapers frequently when his late father had been a senator. Then his mother and brother had stepped into the political spotlight, too. But the family kept Kyle out of the media's scrutiny as much as possible for safety's sake because of his tours of duty in war zones.

The crush of people grew thicker, faces tougher to see. As much as she hated to draw attention to herself, she was going to have to ask for help finding—

"Can I get you something?"

The deep voice rumbled from behind her as if in answer to her very thoughts, jolting her with a clear shot of sexy bass on the salty ocean breeze. Lordy, the waiter must rack up tips with that bedroom voice of his. She glanced over her shoulder to ask for a napkin—she'd forgotten the burp rag again, damn it.

Her smile froze.

Captain Kyle Landis—in the flesh, all right.

His dark brown hair was trimmed military short, mellow blue eyes creased at the corners from a deep tan she knew he'd earned in a Middle Eastern desert. A broad forehead and strong jawline gave him a masculine appeal just shy of harsh.

She should have realized the guy would be even better looking in person. He was a lucky son of a gun from an established old Southern family—handsome and rich, with a smoky voice to boot. He'd even reportedly survived a crash unscathed. His muscled chest in a blue uniform jacket sported at least double the medals of most here, perhaps only outdone by his stepfather, a general.

What were the odds of Kyle finding her tonight, instead of the other way around? But then, as the guest of honor, maybe he felt obligated to make sure everyone else was having a good time.

"Can I get you something?" he repeated, a cut-crystal whiskey glass cradled in his hand.

An older woman angled past, whipping a full, ruffled train against Phoebe's leg. The scent of strong perfume made Nina sneeze. She readjusted the baby, wishing they were at home in her bentwood rocker rather than here with this man. "I actually don't need help anymore, since I was looking for *you*."

A dimple dug into his cheek with his one-sided smile. "I'm sorry, if we've met before, I'm not remembering."

That dimple would have been charming if she hadn't already heard from Bianca to be wary of his prep-school-polished sense of humor. She might be out of her financial league here, but she was a smart, determined woman.

Phoebe forged ahead, needing to say something before he turned her over to a bouncer. "I'm not here for myself."

He glanced behind her quickly, then focused his full, deep-blue-eyed attention on her face again. "Which one of my pals are you with? We don't get many chances to meet the wives."

"I'm not married." But she had been. She shoved away even the thought of Roger before the inevitable stab of pain could steal her focus.

Kyle's gaze flicked briefly to Nina, then away. So much for him recognizing his child on sight.

To be fair, he didn't even know about Nina's existence. Bianca had insisted early in the pregnancy that, while she wasn't sure if she wanted to keep the baby, she would inform the baby's father. Then later said she'd chickened out, then couldn't find him and certainly didn't want to send this kind of news to him overseas through his family.

As if Bianca would've even gotten past personal assistants to talk to anyone in his famous family. It had been a major challenge to gate-crash this shindig, but no security could outdo her determination.

That drive—along with channeling some acting tips she'd picked up from Bianca—and Phoebe had convinced them all she was the caterer's assistant's wife. Easy enough to do, since she was more the friend-next-door than the flashy-leading-lady.

Nothing could stop her, not now that Kyle had come home. Somebody had to tell him about his new "little" responsibility and since Bianca was MIA, that left it up to her.

Might as well get this over with. "Is there somewhere we can step aside to talk?"

"I'm sorry, but my mother would haul me back in by my ear if I tried to duck out of my own welcome-home party." He angled closer, the fresh scent of his aftershave teasing her nose. "Maybe later, though?"

Undeniable interest flared in his cobalt-blue eyes, his full attention fixed on her.

Holy crap. Could he actually be hitting on her? She'd prepared herself for any possible reaction from him—except that.

She jolted back a step, holding up one hand. "Wait, that's not what I meant."

And even if he were interested enough to actually contact her, what if it took him a week to call? She didn't have another week to waste waiting for him to phone her back.

Nina didn't have a week.

Phoebe patted between the baby's shoulders, praying she would stay asleep. The last thing she needed was a colicky nuclear meltdown. "I have to speak with you for five minutes out of earshot of everyone else. I promise I won't keep you long and you can get back to your welcome-home party. Perhaps you could just escort me to the door? Then you'll know I'm truly on my way out of your hair."

"Fair enough." He set his drink on the bar behind him. "Do you need some help with the kid?"

Instinctively, she backed farther away until her butt bumped a column plant-holder, jostling the fern on top.

Laughing, he held out both hands. "Hey, no need to freak out. I won't drop her. I've never been much of a kid person, but I'm getting practice lately with my nephew."

Nina had a cousin. How wild to think about, and imagine them playing together happily. Nina needed a life full of people who loved her. And the sooner Phoebe cleared this up, the sooner Nina would be settled. "We're fine, but thanks for asking. Just lead the way and we'll follow."

"Let me know if you change your mind."

He turned his broad shoulders sideways to slide past a pair of tuxedo-clad teens sneaking refills from the champagne fountain. Kyle plucked the glasses from their hands on his way by and passed them to a man from the catering staff.

He led Phoebe around a corner and stopped in a small, empty alcove with a spindly iron bench and two more large potted ferns on Grecian-pillar stands. The party noise muffled down a notch, although the laughter of a nearby couple made her itchy for a room with a door to close. The nook just past an ivy-covered trellis wasn't totally private, but it would have to do.

Stepping away from his towering presence for a bit of breathing room, she eased the diaper bag down onto the iron bench and rolled the kink out of her shoulder. "Do you remember someone named Bianca Thompson?"

His eyes went from friendly to reserved. "Yes, why do you ask?"

Nearby laughter swelled as two trophy-wife types ducked into the alcove, one with a silver cigarette case in her hands and the other weaving tipsily behind her. "Oh," the woman said, tucking her cigarette case surreptitiously behind her back, "excuse me."

Kyle's easy smile came back. "No problem, ladies. I think there's another bench just past the palmetto tree wrapped in lights."

"Thank you, Captain." The woman flashed a smile back, "advertising" with a length of too-tanned leg through the gown's excessive slit.

Phoebe watched them disappear faster than the after-waft of their cologne. She turned back to Kyle. "You don't deny knowing Bianca?"

"This is getting strange here." He scratched the back of his neck. "You need to cut to the chase… What was your name again?"

"Phoebe—" She paused as a uniformed waiter tucked into the alcove, stopped short and then spun back around to leave, apparently looking for a place to ditch work undetected for a few seconds.

Good luck with that, buddy, because apparently there wasn't a quiet place to be found at this crammed-to-the-gills gala.

She hefted Nina's limp—and growing heavier by the second—body higher onto her shoulder. Her sweet weight and baby-shampoo-fresh scent tugged at her heart with a reminder of just how important this meeting was to both of their futures. "Phoebe. My name is Phoebe Slater. Bianca and I were sorority sisters, but we've stayed in touch over the years."

Although not as much as she would have liked during the past two months. She still could hardly believe Bianca would just drop off her baby daughter and not look back.

"Nice to meet you, Phoebe," he said, one eyebrow

arching up with the implication his patience had about run dry.

Time was up. There wasn't ever going to be the perfect setting for this kind of revelation. She resisted the urge to clutch the baby tighter and bolt. This wasn't her child, but she loved her as dearly as if they shared the same blood. In fact, this would be her only chance at motherhood—however brief. When her husband she'd loved more than life had died, all hopes of being a mother had died with him.

No blue eyes would distract her from protecting Nina, no social brush-offs would dislodge her from her mission. She would do anything, *anything* to secure Nina's future.

Phoebe braced her shoulders and her resolve to push forward with her plan, even if it meant making a deal with a blue-eyed devil. "Meet Nina, your daughter."

Damn.

Another gold digger.

Party noise droning behind him like the buzz of aircraft engines, Kyle rocked back on his heels, his polished uniform shoes squeaking. He'd worked in intel during his Air Force career, but it didn't take an investigative mind to determine something was *way* off with this woman.

The second he'd seen Phoebe Slater sidle past security, he had been gut-slammed by her appeal. He still couldn't pull his eyes off her beacon-pale blond hair, clasped back simply, and her wide mouth that didn't need lipstick or collagen to make it kiss-me sexy.

The kid had given him a moment's pause, but his attention had shifted fast enough back to the totally hot female. He'd initially sized her up as a down-to-earth sort with unadorned appeal, a simple but intriguing woman. Not so simple after all, apparently.

Perhaps she wasn't a gold digger. Maybe she was just a deluded psycho.

He tucked his fisted hands firmly behind him, glad now he'd chosen a locale that was only semi-private, rather than totally secluded. "Ma'am, I'm certain we've never met before tonight, and I'm even more certain we've never slept together." He would have definitely remembered her. "As cute as your kid is, she's not mine."

Phoebe Slater visibly bristled, her chocolate-brown eyes darkening. "She's not my daughter. I'm just caring for her while her mother—Bianca Thompson—is away at an audition in Southern Florida. Bianca and I went to school together before she started pursuing her acting career, and I became a history professor. But that's all beside the point." Her throat moved in a long swallow. "I'm here because Nina needs her father. She's five months old now."

The hairs on the back of his neck prickled.

He *had* slept with Bianca Thompson, but he'd used protection—he always did. They hadn't known each other well. It had been more of an impulsive hookup on both their parts, over a year ago, before he'd left for a year-long deployment to Afghanistan.

Just about the right timing.

His gaze snapped to the kid blinking groggily at him with light blue eyes just like his mother, brothers… Damn. Plenty of people had blue eyes, and plenty of people knew what his family looked like. And those same people would know about the Landis family's hefty investment portfolio. His youngest brother had even had a false paternity suit filed against him by someone he'd actually cared about.

Kyle bit back a curse. He needed to stop this conversation now, until he could regroup with some more information on this woman. Preferably in a place where he didn't have to worry about everyone from the press to the governor of South Carolina overhearing.

"Ma'am—"

"Slater. I am Phoebe Slater." She rubbed soothing little circles between the baby's shoulders, swaying back and forth like a pro.

Impressive. He knew from his brother and sister-in-law how tough it was to keep a little rug rat quiet at this age.

"Okay, Ms. Slater, let's schedule a time for this

conversation when we're not trying to speak over a band and we're certain not to be interrupted—"

"And this is Nina." She angled sideways so the baby's chubby-cheeked face was fully in view.

Cute kid. But that was irrelevant. "I don't think this is the—"

"Her mother is Bianca Thompson.

She'd said that already, but hearing it again made him really look at the baby. She didn't have Bianca's red hair. The baby had dark brown hair. Like him. "Where is Bianca? Why am I talking to you instead of her?"

His suspicions mounted as he tried to put the pieces together before this blew up in a very public setting. His mother had gone to a lot of trouble putting together this shindig commemorating his homecoming. It meant a lot to her, since this also marked the end of his military commitment. In two weeks, he would start his new career as the head of the Landis Foundation's international interests.

He didn't want his family upset needlessly by a scene. Family was everything.

His eyes flicked uneasily back to the baby, looking too darn cute in her pink dress.

"I was only supposed to watch Nina until Bianca settled in at her new place in Southern Florida. Then weeks turned into months. When she stopped calling, I got worried and notified the police to file a missing person's report. Which then brought child services into the picture, and if I don't figure out something soon—" Phoebe's chin quivered briefly before steadying again "—they're going to put Nina into the foster care system."

He wasn't sure what she was up to anymore, but truth be told, even a conversation with a crazy woman was more engaging than the small talk he'd made tonight with people who were mostly here for the free food and a chance to rub elbows with politicians. Phoebe Slater was anything but boring.

"So you want me to take in this child, with no proof of who you are or who this kid is."

"Just hear me out." Her eyes turned a deeper shade of brown, panic glinting.

His instincts went on alert. If this woman was a crook—or a psycho—the kid could be in danger. That changed things entirely. "You know, maybe I should hold the baby after all, while we check into things."

"You're doubting me now, aren't you? Smart man."

She secured the sleeping baby and leaned to dig through the voluminous diaper bag on the bench. Good Lord, he could have stuffed all his military gear in that sack.

His eyes dropped to her hips, to the sweet curve of her bottom as she rifled past diapers and a bottle. Was she really a college professor? He'd certainly never had any profs that looked like her.

What a waste to have all that appeal packaged in a woman he couldn't go anywhere near. She straightened and turned back to face him, drawing his eyes upward.

"Okay, Captain Landis, I thought you would want proof. And well you should." She pulled out a file of papers. "I've got her birth certificate, photos and a notarized letter from Bianca stating I'm a babysitter for Nina, authorizing me to get medical attention for her. I even included a copy of my driver's license."

He took the file from her and flipped it open, angling so his shoulders blocked any passersby from possibly seeing the contents. He scanned the first page, with pictures of Bianca Thompson holding a baby with wide blue eyes.

The hair on the back of his neck prickled again. He turned to the next page and read through the birth certificate…

With his name in the "father" box.

He exhaled hard. True or not, he still needed a second to process seeing his name in that context. Not that he had anything against kids—he liked his nephew well enough. He'd just planned to leave perpetuating the Landis name to his brothers.

Thumbing to the last page, he found a copy of Phoebe Slater's driver's license. The picture was unflattering, to say the least, with eyes deer-in-the-headlight wide and no smile, but without question it was her.

All of which proved nothing, in and of itself. Why

the hell hadn't Bianca notified him? She had plenty of contact numbers. He may have been out of the country, but his family had all been firmly here on U.S. soil.

The more he thought about this, the less it made sense. *If* the little girl was his, he would move forward and take responsibility. Landises didn't shirk their responsibilities. But, for the child's safety as well, he needed to investigate this claim *and* this woman further.

He closed the file and tucked it under his arm. "I'm going to need some time to look over this. I can't just take home a child because you say—"

She laughed, her breath gusting a straggled strand of blond hair. She scraped it away and behind her ear. "No, you completely misunderstand. I don't want you to take her. I got the message loud and clear from Bianca that you're not interested in settling down. And truly, I love this little girl." She rested her cheek on top of the baby's head with unmistakable maternal affection. "I want to be her mother. I want to adopt her, if at all possible."

He should be relieved…but something was still off. His instincts from battling overseas bellowed loud and clear that there were more land mines ahead. "Then why are you here?"

"I'm here to keep Nina out of the foster care system," she said, her words tumbling together as she blurted, "I'm here to ask you to marry me."

Two

Phoebe bit her lip, cringing inside over having blurted the "proposal" rather than easing him into the idea the way she'd mentally rehearsed.

Too late to call back the words now. The band segued into a Motown ballad, the crooner's tune filling the silence while she waited for Kyle's reaction. Not for the first time, she cursed Bianca for disappearing, while praying that her old friend hadn't landed in some kind of trouble. Or worse.

Meanwhile, she had to make use of whatever allies she could find, and please, please she hoped Kyle would fall into that category. She searched his face for some clue of his feelings, but he guarded his emotions well.

Finally, he raised a hand shoulder-high.

She tensed, wondering, waiting and definitely keeping her trap shut for now. She was a thinker, a plotter, damn it. Bianca was the impulsive one.

Kyle spanned a broad palm along Nina's back protectively, his gold college ring glinting in the flickering candlelight. "Let me hold the kid for a minute."

Relief gusted from her so fully that she hadn't even realized she'd been holding her breath. She'd hardly dared hope it would be this easy for him to connect with his daughter—

Then the glow from the pewter tiki torches revealed the glimmer of alarm in his eyes, quickly covered as he flashed a pacifying smile.

Damn.

He thought she was off her rocker to the point he feared for Nina. As if she would do anything to harm this child. Although she'd surely screwed up in pushing so hard and fast for his help.

"I'm not crazy, and I'm the last person who would ever hurt Nina." She cradled the sleeping girl closer until he relaxed his hands, if not his stance. "I didn't mean to spring that last part on you so bluntly, but you were ready to leave and I don't have time to be subtle."

"Is there a *subtle* way to ask a total stranger to marry you?"

Phoebe ignored his sarcasm. "Child services is going to take her since I can't find her mother. I just need to buy a little time until I can settle things for Nina."

She didn't know what else to do. Nina had no one except her... And this man. Her father.

"I still think you're half-cracked, but I'm listening." He folded his arms over his chest.

Was he settling in or blocking her exit? Either way, she needed to talk fast.

"Okay, so maybe the marriage idea seems extreme, but I'm desperate here." Backing off the proposal seemed prudent since she had a serious aversion to ending up in a straitjacket. "My primary concern is keeping Nina secure. She's already had too much upheaval, with Bianca dropping out of her life so abruptly."

"This is a lot to digest," he said, his voice neutral, his eyes still watching her guardedly.

His military aura swelled unmistakably. He might not be thinking of himself as Nina's father, but he clearly would stand between the baby girl and any perceived threat all the same.

Her frayed nerves snapped. "If you can think of another alternative to keeping her out of the foster care system, I'm more than happy to climb on board."

He cocked a thick, dark brow. "Excuse me for

being slow on the uptake, but I didn't know until ninety seconds ago that I even had a child."

"If you'd stayed in touch with Bianca after you deployed, you may have—" She bit her tongue to keep from saying anything else, when she longed to shout out her frustration as she saw her last hope for help slipping away.

His eyebrows slammed down and together. "You can't actually be blaming me because Bianca kept this a secret. If what you say is even true. I had my hands full fighting a war."

Her anger defused and sympathy slid into the void. "I'm sorry. You're right. This is a lot to take in and I don't mean to be combative."

His jaw flexed as he paused to gather his composure. "Arguing won't get us anywhere."

"I completely agree."

Still, he kept his post in front of the arbor trellis, sprawling ivy cascading down the sides like spiky tentacles ready to snag her in place. "Regardless of what came before, we need to decide on a plan of action from this point forward, which I absolutely refuse to talk about in a place where anyone could overhear. There are no less than seven people from the press attending this shindig my mother put together to welcome me back."

He had a point there. While press coverage could be helpful in finding Bianca, it could also bring the wrath of child services down on her head. She had to strike a delicate balance here.

At least Kyle was still talking to her. Maybe he would have an idea, and if not, then she could bring up the marriage idea again with more finesse. It was outrageous, sure, but not that totally out there. She reassured herself for probably the thousandth time that this wasn't a totally crazy idea. Although she could imagine her long-dead parents wincing over her whole plan.

She'd thought this through. People got hitched in Vegas every day for far more flimsy reasons. Wedding vows meant next to nothing to most people these days.

And they would certainly mean nothing to her ever again.

She started toward him. Their cubby of space went darker as another person strode under the ivy-covered arch, snapping Phoebe back into the present. She needed to be on guard for those press people he'd mentioned. Backlit, the shadowy figure was still obviously a woman.

"Kyle, dear, there you are." An older blond woman stepped into the glow of the flickering light. She rested a hand on his arm, manicured nails tipped white.

His mother.

Even if Ginger Landis Renshaw weren't famous for her political prowess as a former senator and then secretary of state, Phoebe would have noticed the family resemblance. Their hair color was different but their faces, their smiles, were the same.

Somewhere in her early fifties and carrying it well, Ginger smoothed a hand over her simple red Chanel evening gown, almost managing to disguise her curiosity. "Our guests are beginning to ask where you've run off to."

"Mom, we need to find an empty room and talk. Immediately." He stepped aside, clearing the view for the woman's gaze to fall squarely on Phoebe.

Ginger's blue eyes darkened from curiosity to concern. "Kyle? What's going on?"

"Not now, Mom," he said quietly, his voice urgent. "We need to move this to a room, preferably one with a closed door."

She straightened with a take-charge efficiency that had won respect around the world during her secretary-of-state days. That political sway continued now in her tenure as ambassador to a small but politically powerful South-American country. "Of course. This way."

She tucked out of their garden nook and sliced a path straight into the country club. A quick flick of her hand had the manager rushing ahead to unlock his office. Phoebe followed, unable to squelch her awe at this woman who made things happen so effortlessly.

Damn it. Forget awe. She would stand down anyone for Nina if need be. But she hoped she would find an ally in a political powerhouse.

The door clicked closed behind them, sealing them inside an office with looming dark furniture and heavy tapestry upholstery. The scent of furniture polish and fresh-cut flowers coated the air thickly.

Ginger turned toward her son but looked at Phoebe and gestured toward a wingback chair. "Have a seat, dear. Even little babies can grow quite heavy when you've been holding them for too long."

Phoebe blinked back her surprise and sat. Disobeying this woman wouldn't dawn on her, and her feet were throbbing. All the same, she wouldn't relax her guard for even a second. Winning his mother's support was just as important as gaining Kyle's trust.

Ginger pinned her son with a questioning stare.

He scratched the back of his neck. "Mom, it appears I may have left a child behind when I went to Afghanistan."

Kyle knew one thing in this crazy, mixed-up night. Give a Landis a crisis and they start things cranking at Mach speed.

He had no more than announced the possibility of this child being his and his mom had spun into action. She'd called for her trusted assistant and gathered the rest of the family. So much for keeping things secret.

With four Landis brothers, two of whom were

married, that made for quite a group packed into the country club office. His brother Sebastian sat at the sprawling wood desk, putting his legal eagle-eye and degree to work reviewing the documents. The rest of the family seemed transfixed around the wingback chair where Phoebe fed the little scrap of a kid a bottle. Kyle paced. He damn near wore a hole in the Persian rug as he moved restlessly behind his brother. Sebastian was a year younger than Kyle, but his quiet soberness had always made him seem older. They needed his calm efficiency right now.

Sebastian closed the file and glanced up somberly. "Is she your daughter?"

Kyle stopped in his tracks and dropped to sit on the edge of the desk, his foot twitching. "It's a distinct possibility." A possibility that still sucker-punched him harder than the missile that had taken down his aircraft in Afghanistan. He pinched the bridge of his nose briefly before his hand fell away. "If she's really Bianca Thompson's daughter, the timing of our, uh, week together lines up."

"A week, huh?" A rare hint of humor lit his normally serious brother's eyes.

Kyle wasn't in the mood to laugh. "We hooked up when I was in between rotations overseas. Neither of us was interested in anything long-term."

"You never are." Sebastian looked away and back at the papers.

Yeah, he wasn't known for serious relationships, but at least he understood himself, rather than sending out mixed signals. "Which makes it all the more ironic that Phoebe would toss out a marriage proposal to me."

"I think it makes her seem like a more logical type." Sebastian kept his voice low enough that the cluster of people a few feet away wouldn't hear. "If she knows your reputation, then she has no reason to worry about you growing attached to her or the baby."

"She said she only tossed it out there in desperation. That she didn't really mean it, and could I come up with something else." Still it rattled around in his head. "You got any suggestions?"

Sebastian scrubbed a hand over his face, a near mirror image of Kyle's. "I think the first order of business is finding out if she's really yours. I've never been one who could see Great-aunt Whoever's chin on some infant, but I have to confess, she looks just like a Landis."

The uncertainty was already chewing him up inside. "Any idea how long it takes for the results of a paternity test?"

"Gotta admit, I've never needed one." His eyes slid over to his wife with obvious affection. Their son had been born a few months ago, a surprise pregnancy after the crushing loss of the baby daughter they'd adopted, only to have the birth mother change her mind. "Jonah should know, though."

Their youngest brother had always been a hell-raiser, so much so that after a while it became tough to distinguish between truth and reputation. Kyle had always understood his younger brother better than the rest of the family, although the military had helped him rein in his wilder impulses.

And yet still, somehow, he may have screwed up. "The sooner we can clear this up, the better."

"What do you know about her?" Sebastian nodded toward Phoebe, who was lifting the baby up to burp, a hand towel from the bathroom draped over her shoulder.

"Nothing at all." Kyle flipped open the manila file folder again and thumbed through the papers. "I'd never met her, but those photos of her with Bianca look real."

"The private investigator I keep on retainer will be able to verify her story by morning. The fact that she lives and works in state makes things easier all the way around." Sebastian tapped the documents spilling out across the desk. "Everything seems authentic and in order though. We'll see soon."

Not soon enough. "So, we're stuck for now." Kyle lowered his voice, even though no one across the room seemed to be paying any attention to them. "Either she's on the up-and-up helping out a friend, in which case she needs help, so the baby stays. Or she's a nutcase, in which case for the baby's safety, she has to stay."

"Be careful, my brother." Sebastian leaned closer. "There's a lot of money at stake here."

Sebastian's wife glanced over her shoulder. "Men are so cynical."

Damn, he could have sworn they were keeping their voices down. Could Phoebe have overheard them too? Not that they'd really said anything that mattered. She should expect they would have her investigated.

The wife of their oldest brother, Matthew, stepped aside, opening the circle as she caressed the slight curve of her stomach. "They're right to be concerned," Ashley said. "I've seen some sad cases of how heartless people can be when it comes to the needs of a child."

Their youngest brother, Jonah, snorted, lounging on the other wingback chair, one leg draped over the armrest. "Who are you condemning here? The baby's mother or Phoebe?"

Ginger rested a hand on the back of Phoebe's chair and shot her sons a censuring stare that hadn't lost its impact over the years. "I'm sorry you had to hear that. My boys should be more diplomatic."

Kyle watched his mother win over Phoebe with a few well-chosen words. There was no doubting who wore the diplomatic mantle in their family.

"I'm not offended," Phoebe said. "In fact, I'm relieved that you're all being practical about this. That bodes well for Nina, and I have nothing to hide."

Jonah twitched back an overlong lock of hair from his brow. "Lady, I have to confess, this all sounds a little hinky to me. You wouldn't be the first person to want a piece of the Landis lucrative pie."

"I'm not here for money." She patted Nina's back steadily until the baby burped, then lowered her to the crook of her arm. "I only need time. I want to keep her out of foster care until we can find her mother, and if we can't, then it's my hope I can adopt her."

Jonah tugged his dangling tux tie free…not that it had even been tied before they stepped back here for the family confab with Phoebe. "Then let the legal system sort it out. If you're best for her, that's where she'll land."

Ginger waved her rebellious youngest son up from the chair and motioned for pregnant Ashley to sit.

Ashley smiled her appreciation as she sat with a heavy sigh. "It's not that cut-and-dried. I was lucky."

Phoebe smoothed her hand over the baby's head with obvious affection, but her face creased with concern. "Yours is a success story, then?"

"My foster sisters and I found a wonderful home with 'Aunt' Libby and were better off. Claire's biological mother wanted to keep her, but was too young and didn't have the money. Starr's parents were criminals who refused to relinquish custody. My parents gave me up." Quiet Ashley grew more fervent as she spoke. "Not all of the girls who were placed with Aunt Libby came straight there from their biological parents, though. Most foster parents are well-meaning, big-hearted people, but there are some…" She shook her head in obvious disgust.

The defender in Kyle, the military part of him that had spent the past six years of his life protecting, made him want to pluck the kid up and keep her safe from the world.

How much stronger would those feelings become if it turned out the baby was his?

Phoebe rested her cheek on Nina's head. "I don't want to run any risk of Nina landing in an unloving home for even a day."

"Exactly," Ashley agreed. "Some people don't have choices. There are options here for little Nina."

His mother nodded. "I've already spoken with my assistant and she's scheduled a paternity test."

"On a weekend?"

Apparently Phoebe didn't grasp his mother's ability to move mountains.

Ginger toyed with one of her diamond stud earrings. "We'll have an answer before child services opens on Monday morning."

Time to test how far she was willing to go with this. He put his hands behind his back, military bearing tough to shake even with his separation papers in the works. "Since you all seem so certain Nina is mine, we might as well start moving her things into my wing of the house."

"Excuse me?" Phoebe's eyes went wide with alarm. "Um, Nina and I are already settled in our hotel, but thank you."

Kyle braced a hand across the door. "If there's even a chance that's my daughter, I'm not letting you just walk out of here with her."

Phoebe looked around nervously, then bolstered, her arms locked around Nina. "I'm not leaving her behind."

"I don't expect you to." *Nobody* was going anywhere until he had answers. "You'll both be staying with me at the family compound."

Three

She didn't have a choice but to go with him, and she knew it. Sitting in the back of Kyle's Mercedes sedan beside Nina in her car seat, Phoebe just wished she'd foreseen this twist in the plans.

His broad shoulders, encased in the uniform jacket, spread in front of her in the driver's seat. He guided the luxury car through the security gate into the Landis family beach compound. As the gates swung closed behind them, she shifted closer to Nina, the infant asleep and drooling in her rear-facing car seat. Morning was going to come early after this late night and she needed any edge she could scavenge to soothe her already frazzled nerves.

By appealing to Kyle for help, she'd also made herself vulnerable. One call from him to child services could steal her few days' window to secure Nina's future. She hadn't felt so powerless since she'd watched helplessly while her husband had drowned.

Her gaze skimmed nervously ahead to the beachside Hilton Head mansion owned by the Landis family. Kyle had told her that his lawyer-brother and wife had a home a few miles away, and the oldest brother, a senator, and his wife had an antebellum mansion in downtown Charleston. Kyle had kept his gear in the third-floor quarters of the mansion since he'd deployed so often.

She'd rubbed elbows with plenty of affluent families at the college fund-raisers, but she'd never visited anywhere nearly this opulent. In spite of insisting she didn't need money, a hotel over the weekend would have taken a chunk out of her account. She had to keep her savings intact for any legal fees she might need in adopting Nina. Staying here was the fiscally smart thing to do.

She'd seen photos from a *Good Housekeeping* spread when she'd looked up the Landis family on Google for more details, and she'd read about their diversified fortune that increased under the savvy care of each generation. But no picture could have prepared her for the breathtaking view. On prime oceanfront property, they'd built a sprawling white three-story house with Victorian peaks overlooking the Atlantic. A lengthy set of stairs stretched upward to the second-story wraparound porch that housed the main entrance.

Latticework shielded most of the first floor, which appeared to be a large entertainment area. Just as in Charleston, many homes so close to the water were built up as a safeguard against tidal floods from hurricanes.

The attached garage had so many doors she stopped counting. His sedan rolled to a stop beside the house, providing a view of the dense green bushes behind them and the Atlantic shore in front of them. An organic-shaped pool was situated between the house and beach, the chlorinated waters of the hot tub at the base churning a glistening swirl in the moonlight.

He put the car in Park and reached for the door. "I'll get your things from the trunk while you unload the munchkin."

Kyle stepped out before she could even answer. Apparently he'd inherited his mother's take-charge attitude. Phoebe walked around to the other side of the Mercedes, security lights activating like sunrise coming early, and unhooked the carrier from the car-seat base so as not to wake Nina.

He lifted her small suitcase and duffel with a

porta-crib out of the trunk. "You sure do travel light compared to most women I've met."

"I had only planned to stay overnight." She'd pretty much counted on getting his support and then heading home in the morning, a naïve fantasy now that she saw how complicated things were becoming as reality played out. "I have a job to get back to in Columbia."

He gestured toward the sprawling staircase. "Then you can leave Nina here."

She hesitated at the bottom step, suddenly claustrophobic about entering his house. Sheesh, it wasn't like he could lock them away in the attic. "I won't abandon her."

"And neither will I," he said with unmistakable determination, which made her glad for Nina.

If she could trust him.

She looked away from his persuasive blue eyes and back up the length of stairs. This would be temporary, until he left on his next assignment, then she could resume her life. "It seems we're at an impasse."

"What about your job?" His intoxicating bass drifted after her shoulder as he followed her up the outside wooden steps.

"I'm teaching all my classes online this semester anyway." She'd adjusted her schedule to be with Nina, seeing this as her once-in-a-lifetime chance to take care of a baby. Little had she known when

Bianca dropped off her daughter… "I can work from here until we have things settled."

Until he left.

She would have her life back on track shortly. His job, along with his track record for short relationships, would have him out of her life soon. And she really didn't have any other options if she wanted to keep Nina.

She pointed to the cluster of live oaks and palmettos framing a two-story carriage house. "Who lives there?"

"My youngest brother, Jonah. He's finishing up his graduate studies in architecture. He stays here between internship trips to Europe."

White with slate-blue shutters, the carriage house was larger than most family homes, certainly bigger than her little apartment in downtown Columbia. "It's lovely."

She understood he came from money, but seeing Kyle's lifestyle laid out so grandly only emphasized their different roots. Phoebe gripped the increasingly heavy car seat with both hands as she reached the top of the stairs. The tall double doors opened before Kyle could even reach forward.

His lawyer brother, Sebastian, filled the entrance, their appearances close enough to be mistaken for twins. Except the lawyer didn't have Kyle's laugh lines. "You finally made it."

Kyle deposited her bags on the polished wood floor. "I drove slower because of the kid. Where's Mom?"

"Still at the club with the general closing out the party so it's not as obvious we're gone." Sebastian eyed Phoebe and Nina briefly then looked back at his brother. "We need to talk."

Kyle ushered her into the cavernous foyer. "As soon as I get them settled."

A woman, the wife of the lawyer brother, stood waiting in the archway leading to a mammoth living room with a wall of windows overlooking the ocean. "I can show her around." The woman—Marianna, she'd been called back at the country club—swept a loose dark curl from her face. "You'll want to put the baby to bed. I'll take you to your rooms."

Phoebe glanced into the hall where Kyle had deposited her bag. "Did the porta-crib make it inside?"

"Don't worry," Marianna reassured her. "Everything's taken care of."

Still, Phoebe hesitated. What did the brothers need to speak about that she couldn't hear? Suspicion nipped her ragged nerves, but there wasn't anything she could do about it, especially in her exhausted state. Maybe she could ferret some information of her own from this woman while Kyle was out of the room.

She smiled back at Marianna. "Thank you, I appreciate your help."

Marianna extended her hand for the diaper bag.

"Let me. Those things weigh a ton. Come on and I'll show you to the nursery."

"There's a nursery here?"

"My husband and I live a few miles away, but Grandma Ginger keeps everything we need here if our little guy needs to nap. Ginger's second husband, Hank Renshaw, also has grandchildren from his daughters. Between us all, we make good use of that room. You'll find everything you could possibly need in there."

Still, Phoebe hesitated. Giving Nina a room here, even a temporary one, seemed such a huge step. One she should have been happy about.

Marianna hitched the pink-flowered diaper bag over her shoulder. "There's a nursery monitor so you can hear the least little peep if she needs you."

Even swaying with exhaustion, Phoebe hesitated. "I don't think I could leave her to wake up alone in a strange place."

Marianna's face softened with understanding. "There's also a daybed in the nursery if you would rather sleep in there with her."

"Show me the way."

Marianna started the winding walk through pale-yellow halls until Phoebe wondered if she would be able to find her way back out of the Landis world again. Beach landscapes mingled with framed family candids that added a surprise touch of hominess to the designer decor. A grandfather clock ticked, their footsteps muffled by the light patterned Oriental rugs.

Phoebe couldn't take the silence any longer. Besides, she would never learn anything from the woman this way. "Aren't you going to ask me if I'm lying? Everyone else doubts me."

Marianna glanced back with a reassuring smile, her thick dark hair swishing like the clock's pendulum. "I believe you're telling us the truth about Nina being Kyle's daughter."

"How can you be so certain?"

Marianna gestured to a portrait on the hall wall, a painting of an infant boy. Undisguised love shone in her eyes. "That's my son, Sebastian Edward Landis Junior. And very obviously Nina's cousin." She tapped four other framed images of babies along the way, all with striking blue eyes. "These are of Matthew, Kyle, Sebastian and Jonah when they were little. There's no mistaking the Landis look."

She totally agreed. The deep blue eyes, the signature one-sided smile…they all had it, as did Nina. "If you see the likeness, why can't they?"

"Because I'm evaluating with maternal eyes, and so are you." Marianna stopped in front of a closed door, her hand resting on the brass handle. "We see them in a way nobody else ever will."

Marianna's words stabbed her with an inescapable reality. "I'm not her mother."

"You're willing to do anything for Nina. In my eyes, that makes you her mother." Marianna looked at her with an understanding. "The family will want a paternity test for legal reasons, of course. They're that way about details, but truly it will protect Nina's interests as much as their own."

"Those results take a while, don't they?" Would they know soon enough to satisfy a family court judge?

"Nothing takes long when you're a Landis. They're an impatient bunch and have the money on hand to see that their wishes are met speedily. Don't worry. You'll get your answer quickly."

Marianna swept open the door to reveal an airy nursery, decorated in neutral sea-foam-green, a white crib on one wall with a coordinated white daybed tucked under a window. A fat, delicious-looking rocker and ottoman took up a corner underneath a mural of fairy-tale characters. "Here we are."

"Thank you for showing me the way." Phoebe stepped inside with mixed feelings, wishing she could have given Nina all this and more.

Marianna kept her hand on the open door. "I'm sure Kyle will check in when he's done talking with Sebastian, but I really need to head home now so the sitter can leave. I don't like being away from little Edward too long. Good luck."

"Hopefully I won't need it."

With a smile and a quick squeeze of her arm,

Marianna seemed to sense her worry. "It will be fine. You'll both be fine. You'll see."

She closed the door behind her. The click reminded Phoebe of her plans to learn more from the woman. She hadn't found out much more than confirmation of what she'd already known in her heart. Nina was a Landis.

Long after Marianna left and Nina was tucked in her crib, Phoebe sat on the daybed, hugging her knees and staring out at the ocean, unable to sleep. Too many questions, uncertainties, fears churned in her mind like the curling waves, rolling and retreating only to crash right back over her again. One thing shone through as clearly as the moonlight slashing away at the murky depths.

The Landises had power.

The kind of money and impatience that could buy an overnight paternity test could surely oust anyone who didn't belong in their elite world. With no blood claim to Nina, and Bianca gone, Phoebe could easily find herself at odds with Kyle all too soon.

After having been helpless while she'd watched her husband leave her, she couldn't tamp down the reflexive fear of having someone she loved taken from her again.

Parked behind the desk in the family study, Kyle scrubbed a hand along his bristly face that had long ago gone past a five-o'clock shadow. Early morning rays from the sun were just beginning to poke through the horizon and past floor-to-ceiling windows. Answers were piercing through just as surely.

Sebastian slept on the butter-yellow leather sofa in front of built-in library shelves of warm oak, but Kyle kept watch for the updates that had been coming in from the private investigator over his BlackBerry throughout the night, while doing some checking on his own. Money and the Internet provided a wealth of fast information.

So far, everything about Phoebe Slater's story checked out. She did, in fact, work at the University of South Carolina. She'd been a history professor on campus for three years, but for the fall semester had abruptly shifted to teaching only online classes—right about the time Nina would have entered her life full-time.

Bianca Thompson had indeed gone to school with Phoebe, and Bianca had given birth to a daughter named Nina.

He cradled his BlackBerry in his hand, staring at the latest report. The one that had surprised him.

Phoebe was a widow.

The circumstances of how her husband had died were simply listed as accidental drowning. That explained the haunted look that never left her eyes, even when she smiled, which was only when she looked at the kid.

This was getting complicated.

He shoved restlessly to his feet, pacing, farther and farther away from the desk until he found himself making his way through the halls, toward the nursery where Marianna had said both Nina and Phoebe were staying. The door was cracked slightly open. The baby slept on in the crib his mother had set up for her grandchildren. They'd expected Matthew and Ashley's baby, due this winter, to be the next addition.

Who could have foreseen this?

He stepped deeper into the room—and stopped short.

Phoebe sat curled up in a corner of the daybed, asleep with her cheek resting against the windowsill. The sheet and coverlet twisted around her, attesting to a restless night. She still wore her little black number from the party, but she'd kicked off her strappy heels. The delicate arches of her bare feet called to him to stroke up her legs, explore the softness of her skin.

Her white-blond hair streaked over her face, the silver clasp discarded on the bedside table. Given they both wore the same clothes from the night before, they could have been a couple ending a long, satisfying night together.

Except she wasn't here for him. He started to back out and his uniform shoe squeaked.

Phoebe jolted awake. She shoved her silky blond

hair away from her eyes, blinking fast, adding to her sultry morning-after appeal. "What? Nina?"

Kyle held a finger to his mouth. "The kid's still sleeping," he said softly, striding closer. "No need to get up yet, unless you want to go to shower and change." He really didn't need an image of her showering seared in his brain. "I can, uh, keep an eye on her."

He had his BlackBerry. He could still work from here.

She tugged a strap back up her arm. "I only meant to close my eyes for a second after I put on her pj's, and then I was going to unpack and put on something else. I must have fallen asleep."

"You have reason to be tired after yesterday, traveling with a baby on your own, then sleeping sitting up."

She shifted free of the tangled covers. "I didn't want her to wake up in a strange place and be scared."

An image of the little tyke's face scrunched up and crying sucker-punched him. Damn. And he didn't even know if she was his yet. "I really, uh, don't mind staying here with the kid while you sleep or shower."

"Her name is Nina."

"I know."

"You keep calling her 'the kid' or 'rug rat' or other generic things." Phoebe swung her slim legs from the bed, her simple black dress rucking up to her knees. "She's a person—Nina Elizabeth Thompson."

"I know what her name is." He dragged his eyes

away from the enticing curve of Phoebe's legs and back to her equally intriguing face. "I saw her birth certificate. She's Nina."

Nina. A person. His eyes went to the crib where the little girl—*Nina*—slept on her back in fuzzy pink, footed pj's, sucking on one tiny fist in her sleep. A plastic panda teething toy lay beside her head.

For the first time in a crazy-ass night, he stood still long enough to think beyond the weekend. What if Nina turned out to be his? What if—as Sebastian had warned him—the courts still opted to put her in a foster home for even a short period of time? No. Freaking. Way. He had to stack the odds in his favor, in Nina's favor, just in case this little girl belonged to him.

Damn. He was actually considering Phoebe's proposal.

His hand fell to rest on the crib railing. He glanced over his shoulder at Phoebe. "You've given this paper marriage thing some thought."

"I haven't thought of much but that." She stood, her eyes wary. "Does this mean you're thinking about it, too?"

"I won't turn my back on my responsibility." He gripped the railing tighter. "We still have to wait for the paternity test. If she's not mine, marrying me won't help you. Bianca could have lied to you."

"She didn't." Phoebe crossed to stand beside him

and rested a hand on top of his. She squeezed his fingers lightly. "Nina is yours. I know it."

Her touch sent a jolt through him, just a simple touch, for Pete's sake. But her soft skin and light vanilla scent along with the pooling gratitude in her eyes had him downright itchy. He needed distance. Fast.

He stared at her hand pointedly and scrounged up some sarcasm. "I don't want you to do something stupid like fall in love."

She jerked her hand away and shook it as if it burned. "With you?"

"Who else have you asked to marry you?"

She laughed, then laughed again until her giggles tripped on a snort. The baby stirred and Phoebe went silent in a flash. He gripped her elbow and guided her back out into the hall, the doorway to the nursery still open.

She sagged against a wall alongside framed portraits of generations of baby Landises. "Don't worry." She gasped through a final laugh. "There's not a chance in hell I'll fall in love with you, but thanks for helping to lighten the mood for me."

What he'd meant as sarcastically funny suddenly didn't seem quite so humorous. "You're quite a buster there."

"I feel certain your, uh, man parts and ego will survive any potential busting."

"You seem mighty confident," he pressed, not

even sure why, since she appeared so damned confident in her ability to keep her distance. "We've barely
met. What have I done to make you dislike me so
much? Not to sound egotistical, but I happen to have
a lot of money. I've been told I have a pretty decent
sense of humor, and I haven't noticed my face scar-
ing off small children or animals."

"Other than the money part, the same could be said
of me," she pointed out logically. "So since you already
have plenty of money and don't need more from a wife,
should I worry about you falling in love with me?"

Damn. She was good.

He couldn't stop a begrudging smile of respect at
how she'd taken him down a notch. "Touché."

"I'll take that as a no."

"It's nothing personal. You're a beautiful, smart
woman." A hot, sharp woman, a distinction that was
even more pulse throbbing.

"Of course. Just as it wasn't personal when I
laughed at you."

"Point well taken. I'm years away from being
ready to settle down." He had his hands full launch-
ing his new life and career outside the military.
"What about you?"

"I was married before."

He knew that already, of course, but letting on
would make it clear he was already having her investigated. "Nasty divorce, huh?"

Her face went devoid of emotion, completely. He'd seen the look before on shell-shocked soldiers, numbing themselves for fear even the smallest emotion would shatter them to bits.

"He died," she said simply. "There's no room in my heart to love anyone else, not when he still fills every corner."

He exhaled hard. He knew that kind of love existed. He'd seen it with his parents, and again when his widowed mom remarried. He'd also seen how torn up his dad was over having to divide himself between career ambition and family. "Wow, that's hefty stuff there. I'm really sorry. How did he die?"

And why did he need to know more about it?

She looked down, staying silent.

Damn it, he needed to know everything about her. He had a short time to make an important choice, a majorly life-altering choice. He was used to making snap decisions in war, but he did so with as much intel as possible at his disposal. This shouldn't be any different. It wasn't personal.

"Phoebe, if we're going to get married, I should know. It will seem strange if someone thinks to ask and I don't have the right answer. For Nina's sake, we would need to make it look real."

"He drowned." A flash of undiluted grief bolted through her brown eyes like a lethal lightning strike.

Then her face went blank again. She pushed away from the wall, away from him. "I should get back to Nina."

She spun on her heel, giving Kyle her back. She couldn't have been any clearer. Discussion over. Stand down. But he had his answer. That flash of grief in her eyes, followed by her abrupt shutdown left him with no doubts about where she stood on the subject of her ex-husband.

She was completely committed to another man.

That should have made the possibility of a paper marriage easier to contemplate, but damn, what a tangled mess. The door clicked closed behind her, and he reminded himself to take things one step at a time. First, he had to give a blood sample later today and wait for the paternity test results.

Although his instincts now shouted loud and clear that Phoebe Slater was telling the truth.

Four

"Marry me."

Kyle's demand—not request—bounced around inside Phoebe's head hot on the heels of the preliminary paternity results. Overwhelmed, she sagged in the front seat of his Mercedes, Nina asleep in the back after the exhausting day at the doctor's.

Butter-soft leather cradled her in luxury but offered little comfort for the stress knotting her neck. "Are you sure this is what you want to do?"

"Now's not the time to lose courage." He turned on the engine and adjusted the climate control for the muggy fall afternoon, all efficiency with a calm she envied. "I've talked it over with Sebastian and you were right about this being the fastest, most efficient way to secure Nina's future."

She stared through the windshield at the busy hospital complex parking lot. Her eyes were magnetically drawn to mothers with their children.

Mothers *and* fathers, too. "How long?"

"We'll get married on Monday—tomorrow." His jaw flexed with the first signs of stress.

A closer look revealed the pale hint under his tan.

She fisted her hands to keep from touching him, comforting him. She understood well how overwhelming this could all be, becoming a parent out of the blue. "No, I mean, how long would we keep up this charade? Who will we tell?"

"My family already knows what's going on. But beyond them, we would need to keep up appearances for Nina's sake."

"Appearances?" Holy crap, she'd meant fake marriage. Not pretend-to-be-real fake marriage.

"We'll need to live together, at least for a while." A slight grin eased the deep lines around his mouth. "But since I live at the Landis compound, we'll be surrounded by family to protect you from your lecherous husband."

She tucked her tongue in the side of her mouth to keep from laughing, but she couldn't keep from smiling...until she thought about the next hurdle she should have considered before moving forward with this half-baked plan of hers. "What will your family think?"

More importantly, how would they react to her and Nina in their lives full-time? Her smile faded.

"You'll be welcomed as a Landis. And my mother will adore you simply because you love her…uh… granddaughter."

"That's a relief, at least." Nina would never be alone and abandoned again. "I wouldn't want things to be awkward when I bring Nina to visit."

"Visit?" He cocked a dark eyebrow and put the car in Reverse. "You'll need to stay at the house for at least a couple of months. At that point we could maintain two residences and claim work conflicts."

"Months?" She pressed a hand to her forehead.

He nodded curtly. "Long enough to get official custody worked out. Or until Bianca returns." His fist tightened on the gearshift. "If we don't hear from her, we can start divorce proceedings after a year."

"And about Nina?"

"I'll want visitation for me and for my family."

"Of course." She went weak with relief as he backed the car out of the parking spot. It must have been hard for him to concede full custody. Even though he hadn't known his daughter long, Phoebe had been around the Landises enough to recognize they took the notion of family loyalty to a whole new level.

Thank heavens, he wasn't going to fight her over custody. Tears burned behind her eyes and she blinked fast to hold them back, along with the urge to throw her arms around him in gratitude.

He was far too foreboding at the moment for a hug, his normal grin and lightheartedness nowhere in sight. Maybe he needed some reassurance, too. "I want to sign a prenup that makes it clear I have no claim to any Landis assets. Can your brother draw one up right away?"

"Except I will provide for Nina."

"Whatever you think is fair. I'm just so relieved you're not going to take her away."

"It's obvious from everything I've seen and learned about you that you've got her best interests at heart." He put the car in first gear, focusing his attention in front, his jaw flexing again, faster. "I'm in no position to be a full-time father with the travel load that comes with my job."

"Of course, that's totally understandable." Although she would have given up any job for Nina, had in fact made major concessions in her own work world. But she wasn't going to argue with him.

She did, however, want to ask him how he felt about all of this. Wasn't he frustrated over marrying a woman he barely knew? How did he feel about having a daughter, for crying out loud?

His resolute face shut her out as he steered onto

the road. He was doing what needed to be done, fulfilling obligations. She should have been relieved over his emotional detachment.

Instead, she just felt hollow inside. "I need it to be indisputably clear I'm only interested in Nina's well-being."

"Okay, then. I'll let Sebastian know so he can draw up the papers."

So cold and businesslike. Nothing in the arrangement resembled her emotional engagement to Roger. He'd proposed at the beach, no ring, no money, no complicated legal dealings to wade through. Just simple declarations of how much they loved each other and wanted to spend the rest of their lives together.

Yet, tomorrow she would be married to the man next to her. She'd gotten her way. Nina would be as safe as she could possibly arrange.

So why did a year suddenly sound like forever?

"By the power vested in me by the State of South Carolina, I now pronounce you husband and wife."

The jowly justice of the peace's proclamation resonated hollowly in Phoebe's ears, as if she was watching some kind of drama, far removed from her place beside Kyle. He wore a uniform again, a less formal version this time, but still with a jacket and tie for their courthouse wedding.

Everything had felt surreal since they'd rushed

through the paternity test over the weekend, verifying what she'd known in her heart for certain since laying eyes on Kyle Landis. *He was Nina's biological father.*

Once Kyle had heard the paternity test results confirming she was his, he hadn't hesitated. Things had taken off at warp speed from there as he arranged for a Monday-afternoon wedding and an appointment with a family court judge shortly thereafter. The building complex made for one-stop shopping. This military man sure knew how to take command and move mountains.

Her fingers clutched around the bouquet of mango calla lilies with yellow roses. One of his sentimental sisters-in-law had thrust it into her hands—Ashley, the pregnant one married to the oldest politician brother. The other wife, Marianna, jostled her son on her hip, while Ginger stood beside her general husband and proudly held her new granddaughter, Nina.

Phoebe was a part of this family now, even if in name only.

The justice of the peace closed his folder containing the vows, a South Carolina flag and American flag behind him. "You may kiss the bride."

Phoebe looked up sharply at Kyle, any feeling of being a distant observer gone in a snap. Surely nobody expected them to go through with that part of the ceremony. Except the magistrate.

Kyle's face creased in a one-sided smile and he dipped his head toward her. She barely had time to register his oldest brother smothering a laugh before Kyle's mouth touched hers. Firm and gentle all at once, he kissed her. Her eyes closed, her ears roared and she lost track of everyone around her.

It had been so long since she'd felt a man's lips against hers. *Too* long. All her buried sensuality smoked back to life, steaming through her at just a simple, closed-lips caress. She wanted to open for more, more of this, more of him. Dots sparked in front of her eyes and she realized she'd forgotten to breathe.

He eased away slowly, thank goodness, so she had time to regain her balance. She clutched her bouquet, the floral scent teasing her with romanticism, and she opened her eyes. Kyle stared back at her for just an instant and then offered his elbow along with his typical lighthearted grin. She couldn't help smiling in return. Maybe, just maybe they could wade through this tangled mess.

As they turned toward the gathered family, Ginger held Nina out for them to hold. Kyle hesitated. Only for a second but long enough to bring her back to reality.

Phoebe thrust her bouquet of roses and lilies toward him and took the baby from Ginger. "Come here, sweetie. You were so good, so quiet."

She smoothed Nina's floral pinafore, adjusting the bonnet and booties until it seemed the momentary awkwardness had passed. But she hadn't forgotten. In spite of his speed in stepping up to the plate—honorable though that was—she could see he hadn't connected with Nina in any real way.

Not exactly the dream wedding day she'd fantasized about as a child, although she did feel like she was playing dress-up. She wore a knee-length gown borrowed from her new sister-in-law. The woman had graciously offered for Phoebe to keep the simple drape of pale yellow—with a Versace label. Marianna had insisted it didn't fit her anymore since she'd given birth to her son.

Nina grasped the strand of pearls resting on Phoebe's collarbone, Roger's gift to her the day they'd exchanged vows. Their wedding had been a simple affair, as well, but she hadn't minded. There'd been so little money in those days. He'd sold one of his first-edition books to pay for the necklace.

A fresh ache stabbed through her over the thought of never having Roger's baby. Nina was her one chance at motherhood, for however long that lasted.

A camera flash went off from a corner of the room, taken by a photographer hired by the Landises and soon to be released to the press. She blinked against the continuous barrage of flashes. At least the pictures had been staged by them, along with a story stating simply that Kyle had married his daughter's guardian.

She'd never seen such choreographed control before.

Kyle angled down conspiratorially. "Welcome to living with a family full of politicians. Watch what you say, and don't ever, ever chew with your mouth open. Well, unless you want it plastered on some Internet blog before you've swallowed your food."

Nina reached to pat his face, more of a thumping actually with her drool-covered palm, then she giggled and stuffed her plastic panda teething toy into her mouth. He was so charming with adults, why did he freeze with Nina? Or was it all children?

Regardless, he would be jetting off again soon to his base for some mission and she would be alone again with Nina. She just had to make it through a few days, not much time to ache for another kiss.

Ginger gave her a one-armed hug that seemed genuine and not just for the photo op. "Welcome to the family, dear."

"Thank you." Phoebe paused, lowering her voice. "But you know this is only temporary."

Her new mother-in-law gave her shoulder a final squeeze. "You're a Landis and you're an important part of my granddaughter's life. We'll worry about tomorrow when it gets here."

Panic constricted her breathing and the diamond-studded band on her finger seemed suddenly too tight. She should be happy. Everything was going just as Kyle had said it would, with his family accepting her even knowing the full circumstances.

Once the photographer had been ushered out, Marianna stepped alongside her with a supportive smile. "You look exhausted. Let's finish up the paperwork so you can get out of those heels."

If she could just go back to her apartment for even a little while and regroup. "You're so thoughtful to have loaned me your clothes, but I can't keep borrowing from you forever. I'll need to go back to Columbia. Nina and I are out of—"

Ginger waved a manicured hand. "No worries, dear. I've already taken care of everything. There are clothes waiting for you at the house. You can choose whatever you like. Marianna arranged for a complete nursery to be set up closer to your room and ordered clothes for the baby." She ticked through the list with a thoroughness that likely made governmental issues run more smoothly but felt a little steamrollerlike at the moment. She clapped her hands together. "Now if you'll pardon me, I need to pop in upstairs to speak with a judge friend of mine about something that came across my desk last week."

Ginger strode out of the office and into the hall with a fast, efficient click of her high heels.

Phoebe sagged with an exhale and turned to Marianna. "She set up all of that to happen while we were here?"

Marianna leaned closer, jostling her baby son more securely on her hip. "Money, influence and a personal assistant make things move much faster." Like with that overnight paternity test. "She means well and is usually right. You might as well go with the flow for now. If you have a stand you want to make, you'll be better equipped to do so well-rested and with a full stomach."

"You're encouraging me to leave?" She hadn't expected to find such total support within the Landis camp for whatever decision she made.

"I'm simply telling you that if you intend to fight, you would be wise to choose your timing well. The Landises are all charming—and stubborn. Of course, you're a Landis now."

"Temporarily."

Marianna didn't answer.

Realization seeped in with the full weight of what she'd done. The sense of claustrophobia she'd felt on her first night at the family compound squeezed tighter. The Landises had accepted Nina because of her blood tie. However, it was also a double-edged sword.

They didn't know Nina. So they didn't love her, not really, not yet. But they wouldn't let her go.

Kyle tossed the bouquet on the clerk's desk and picked up the pen.

The final paperwork sealing this marriage waited

in front of him by the blob of yellow-and-orange flowers. Today should have taken care of all problems by securing Nina's future. His kid. His child. He still hadn't sorted through all that in his head, beyond moving ahead and taking care of his responsibilities. However, instead of smoothing out his life, this ceremony had introduced a new problem—not totally unexpected—but certainly surprising in the magnitude.

He *wanted* his wife. One kiss had made that more than clear.

His grip tightened around the pen, darkening the stroke of his scrawl. It was all he could do not to send everyone away so he could seal a deeper, fuller imprint on Phoebe's mouth and in her memory. The scent of her lingered on his shirt from the brief brush of her breasts against him and left him aching to explore. He'd found her attractive from the first time he'd seen her at the welcome-home bash. He'd even wanted to ask her out on a date.

Then they'd started talking, he'd met Nina and here they were.

At least Phoebe looked as stunned as he felt by the kiss. Thank God, he'd scrounged up enough control to keep his hands to himself so he wouldn't give the photographer an unexpected headliner. He glanced up from the paper over to Phoebe standing with Marianna. The yellow silky dress hugged the subtle curve of Phoebe's breasts, gliding over her slim hips in a way that made him wonder what she wore underneath.

Kyle checked over his shoulder fast to make sure the photographer hadn't slipped back in.

He'd been lucky to stay out of the spotlight this long, but now that he was out of the military, he was fair game for the media hounds. Although he had to admit Phoebe certainly made for a beautiful subject for the photographer with her cool, blond good looks.

Phoebe shuffled Nina over to Marianna and glided toward him, drawing his eyes to her legs. He flipped the pen between his fingers. Maybe this marriage could have some unexpected benefits. Who could fault him for sleeping with his own wife?

Her heart might well be buried along with her dead husband, but if that kiss was anything to judge by, her sensuality was alive and well.

Phoebe held out her hand. "May I have the pen, please?"

"Yeah, right." He passed it over and she leaned by him, a whiff of her floral shampoo drifting from her loose blond hair. An image flashed through his mind of the silky straight strands splayed across a pillow while he peeled her clothes away.

He tugged at his suddenly too tight tie.

Phoebe nudged aside the bouquet to rest her wrist on the table as she signed her name. She tucked her tongue in her cheek. He could still taste the hint of coffee from her lips.

Coffee, for crying out loud. Who would have thought the simple brew would taste so sexy? His heart rate spiked.

She finished her signature with a curly flourish at odds with her no-nonsense air.

Regardless, it was official. They were married. His eyes narrowed. And he fully intended to consummate this union as soon as he could romance his new wife into his bed.

Kyle slid the papers across the table toward his mother's assistant and focused his full attention on his wife. "Have you eaten anything today?"

The family would understand if he and Phoebe opted out of any scheduled big gatherings for some time to get to know each other. He seemed to recall a quiet little café near the courthouse. He'd eaten there before with his mother's judge friend, later took the judge's daughter there for a date.

Hmm…perhaps not a good idea to take the new wife to an old date site. Moving on to plan B.

Phoebe pushed her hair behind her ears with a sigh. "It's been a busy day."

Was she thinking about her first wedding? Understandable, but he needed to divert her thoughts of the man who still had such a prominent place in her mind.

"I would offer to take you out, but I imagine

you're exhausted. The rug rat looks like she needs to stretch her legs. What do you say I pick up some takeout along the way and we spend the afternoon on the beach at home? There's plenty of space away from the rest of the family so that it will be just the three of us, relaxing by the shore, getting to know each other."

"That's really thoughtful of you." Wariness lit her dark eyes. "I would like that, very much."

"Then let's get moving. Once we're past the press no doubt waiting outside, we'll be home free."

Smiling reassuringly at her, he palmed her back. This time he prepared to steel himself for the jolt of awareness sparked by the feel of her under his palm. He ushered her out of the office, into the long corridor toward the elevator. He vaguely registered the footsteps of his family following and talking with each other. Cameras started clicking again from a small pack of reporters clustered behind a security guard blocking them from pressing closer.

His oldest brother, Matthew, broke away and started speaking with one of the reporters, diverting their attention by offering up a couple of sound bites. Apparently an interview with a U.S. senator trumped snagging more photos of a surprise wedding.

Kyle smiled. Thanks, bro.

He focused his attention forward, intent on getting Phoebe and Nina home. Anticipation ramped inside him. For the first time since Phoebe Slater had blasted into his world, he had control of his life.

Nina's future would be secure.

And for however long this marriage lasted, he and Phoebe could have one hell of a totally legal affair. No worries about emotional entanglements for either of them.

He stopped in front of the private side elevator designated for employees and special guests. He jabbed the button just as the door slid open to reveal one person already inside.

Damn.

A leggy redhead in her twenties blinked in wide-eyed surprise. Then smiled with recognition.

The timing couldn't have been worse to run into one of his exes. The judge's daughter. The one he'd dated briefly in the past.

Leslie? No. *Lucy* took the bouquet from him. "Okay, Kyle Landis, you're officially forgiven." She lifted the flowers to her nose and inhaled deeply, thrusting her breasts out none too subtly. "These are just gorgeous, you charmer. Calla lilies and roses, no less. I didn't know you were so romantic."

Phoebe bristled visibly beside him, stepping away from his palm at her waist. He needed to implement damage control before some reporter with a telephoto lens and great hearing put together a new headline.

He rushed Phoebe and Nina into the elevator with

Lucy and pushed the Close button. "Uh, Lucy, I'd like for you to meet—"

Lucy laughed, talking right over him. "I was just going to leave you an 'eat dirt and die, you scumbag' message, but since you've apologized so nicely with flowers," she lifted the bouquet to her nose briefly, "I'll forgive you for breaking my heart."

Five

Stuck in the elevator with Kyle, most of his family and a towering redhead holding *Phoebe's* bouquet, she mentally thumped herself for being so gullible. Bianca had warned her of Kyle's ladies'-man past, damn it.

Phoebe resisted the urge to back into a corner. Pride starched her spine. Pride, and a need to carry this off for Nina's sake.

He braced his shoulders, his uniform stretching over his chest. "Phoebe, this is a friend of the family, Lucy Cooper. Lucy, this is my wife, Phoebe." He gestured to his daughter and said simply, "And this is Nina."

The bubbly redhead turned…well, as red as her

hair. Her mouth opened and closed a couple of times, and Phoebe actually felt sorry for the woman.

Lucy's eyes dropped down to the flowers in her hand. Her mouth went tight. "I guess these must be yours. My mistake." She thrust the bouquet toward Phoebe. "Congratulations. And good luck."

There was no missing the sarcasm coating her words more thickly than her cloying cologne soaked the enclosed space in the elevator. Phoebe couldn't bring herself to be angry at the woman for spoiling the day. She'd found out firsthand today how quickly a single kiss from Kyle Landis could persuade a woman to ignore warning signs.

The elevator doors swooshed open again blessedly soon and Lucy didn't even offer a good-bye before making tracks out into the back hall, toward a glowing exit sign.

Jonah inched forward, scratched his head. "At least she didn't ask about the kid."

Sebastian coughed into his hand. Or laughed. But Phoebe wasn't feeling the love. She couldn't avoid Kyle—they were married, after all.

However she could damn well resist his charming smile. "Kyle, I've changed my mind about dinner. I don't think I'm in much of a beach mood anymore."

Seven hours later, Phoebe dropped back onto her bed in the guest suite with an exhausted—exasperated—huff. At least she'd made it through the large family dinner, even if she hadn't been able to bring herself to eat much. Tempting thoughts of how they could have spent the evening tormented her. Images of lazing the hours away together on the beach, getting to know each other. After the Lucy debacle, he hadn't bothered bringing up cozy meals together.

She rolled onto her stomach and picked at the white piping around the dusky-rose-colored pillow sham.

Just a family friend.

How clichéd.

It was obvious *Lucy* had expected more out of Kyle, from the way she'd gushed all over the flowers. Phoebe's flowers, now discarded on the other pillow. She plucked a rosebud from the bouquet, releasing a fresh whiff of the fragrant perfume.

Stroking the bloom along her mouth, she glanced through the open side door to the connected sitting area Ginger had converted into a permanent nursery just for Nina. All that trouble and money, as if she and Nina would be staying here, made her nervous.

At least the local judge had been able to connect with a Columbia judge and they'd worked out an agreement granting temporary custody to Kyle and Phoebe Landis. Even thinking of her new last name made her shiver. She'd been Phoebe Slater since she'd married Roger. She'd kept his name even after he'd died. Before that, she'd been Phoebe Campbell. Phoebe Campbell wouldn't have been able to make things move so quickly, either, and right now she couldn't bring herself to resent the Landises for their privileged ways when it kept Nina secure.

The rest of the day had been a blur after leaving the courthouse. Ginger had had a meal ready back at the house, and neither Kyle nor Phoebe had asked to be alone.

It shouldn't matter that Kyle was a flirt with a vast dating history. She didn't intend to *stay* married to him. She only cared because of Nina, damn it, and didn't want a constant parade of countless women marching in and out of Kyle's life. Phoebe swung her feet off the edge of the bed and padded across the hardwood floor to Nina's new nursery, so much nicer than the little dressing-room nook back at Phoebe's apartment and more personal than the luxurious green nursery down the hall for visiting Landis and Renshaw grandkids.

Nina wasn't a visitor anymore.

Did she miss her tiny space back in the apartment? Phoebe had poured her heart into creating the little garden haven, complete with painted puckish fairies that reminded her of Shakespeare's *A Midsummer Night's Dream*.

This space was tastefully decorated in pinks and browns to coordinate with the already rose-colored walls. Little ballet-shoe accents rounded out the decor. Without a doubt, the Landises had more to offer Nina financially. But what about love?

Her fingers tensed along the cherrywood crib railing. Losing her husband had taught Phoebe too well how priceless and precious—and fragile—love could be. All this money wouldn't mean anything to Nina if she wasn't wrapped in affection, as well.

Ginger Landis Renshaw might be a loving grandmother, but she'd given no indication she intended to be anything other than a grandparent. And Kyle? Phoebe had definite questions and concerns about his ability to take care of Nina, if he even wanted to beyond some sense of appearances. She took her responsibility to Nina seriously.

The room darkened and she glanced up to find Kyle standing in the opening as if conjured from her thoughts. He'd changed from his suit into well-fitting jeans and a white button-down shirt with a South Carolina palmetto tree stitched on the pocket. His rolled-up sleeves exposed tanned forearms sprinkled with dark hair. Masculine arms. Even out of uniform, he made her mouth dry right up with want.

She tore her gaze away from him and gestured around the transformed sitting area. "This is lovely. The little ballet shoes are precious. Your mother and Marianna went to a lot of trouble to create this space just for Nina, when there's already a nursery here in the house."

"Marianna's an interior decorator. In fact, she decorated the whole house."

"She obviously knows her way around little-girl fashions." She trailed a finger along the tiny pink-satin slippers hanging from the wall over a mirror. "Did you need something?"

"I noticed you didn't eat much at supper. I've brought you food."

She thought of earlier, when they'd planned a picnic on the beach and considered a polite *no thanks*, but she was hungry. She simply needed to keep her guard in place. "Thank you. That's very thoughtful."

"I promised you a meal and I keep my promises." He nodded his head for her to follow him. "Let's step out onto the porch off of your room. The food is set up there so you can hear Nina if she needs you, but we won't wake her by talking."

He turned without waiting for her to answer, a man used to people following his orders, damn his broad shoulders and perfect butt. Need crackled to life inside her again with a reminder of just how much he'd moved her with one quick kiss. And she had gone so long without more than just kisses.

Stay strong. She needed to keep things simple between the two of them. Complications could spell big trouble down the line when it came time to say their farewells.

He swung the double French doors wide, out onto the veranda. "Prepare to feast."

Phoebe blinked in surprise, stopping short of the wrought iron table set with linen, silver, roses and the warm glow of a candle protected from the ocean wind by a hurricane globe. A wooden rail surrounded the balcony, the waves rolling hypnotically only a staircase away. Her dress from the wedding swirled around her legs in sensual swipes.

"This is so much more than I expected." She peeked under a polished cover and found a steak and lobster dinner, the scent of warm melted butter steaming lightly upward. "Much more."

The table was set so beautifully she'd expected some dainty, tiny offerings, and while the food was still decoratively presented, she was surprised at the hearty portions.

Kyle held out her chair. "I thought you might be hungry."

She edged past him to take her seat, her shoulder brushing him briefly before she settled into the chair. His forearms skimmed her side as he tucked her under the table, the crisp tanginess of his cologne drifting on the breeze and more enticing than any finely cooked fare.

She had to fight off the sudden urge to tip her

head back against his shoulder, to revisit the taste of his mouth on hers…

"I am hungry." Ravenously so, suddenly.

Well, if she couldn't feed her senses the way her body craved, at least she could enjoy this meal. She draped a linen napkin across her lap, eyeing the cup of creamy crab soup.

Kyle motioned toward two wine bottles in silver ice buckets. "Would you prefer chardonnay or merlot?" He smiled. "Don't worry, I'm not planning to get you soused and press for my marital 'rights.' The cook just wasn't sure which kind of wine we would prefer with a surf-and-turf meal."

Marital rights.

The words brought to mind an image of the two of them tangled in Kyle's sheets, taking the attraction to a heated conclusion. Blinking back the thought, she spooned up a taste of the creamy soup instead— and held back her moan of appreciation. Then again, maybe she'd just needed an excuse to release the tension inside her at the thought of a physical relationship with the man seated across from her.

Her senses sang to life begging for more of this, of everything. "I really should keep my head clear to listen for Nina."

And to be sure *she* didn't get soused and claim *her* marital rights.

"One glass then?"

She couldn't resist *everything*. "Chardonnay, then, please."

He filled her wineglass halfway, then poured the merlot into his. He held her eyes with his while she tasted. *Damn*. There was a difference in the good stuff. How much of this would it take to ruin her for cheap wine for the rest of her life?

He set his glass back on the table. "I'm sorry about the mix-up with Lucy at the courthouse."

Phoebe tucked her tongue against her cheek while she considered what to say. She was upset, but probably not for the reason he thought. And she couldn't change anything. Better to take the high road. "You have nothing to apologize for. It's not like you were seeing some other woman while we were engaged for all of twenty-four hours."

She tried a smile, hoping the conversation would veer away from the woman.

"You're being very reasonable." He watched her through narrowed eyes.

"Did you expect me to throw a jealous fit? I seem to recall you already warned me against falling in love with you." She leaned forward on her elbows. "I'm a very good listener."

He threw his head back and laughed, that sexy sound of pure *Kyle* winding around her with the wind. "Just so you know, the wedding ring on your finger put an end to my friendship with Lucy."

"I noticed how fast she ran out of the elevator."

"I meant that as long as you're wearing my ring, I won't be seeing anyone else."

Now, that surprised her… If she could even believe him. "Bianca warned me you were a charmer."

His face hardened for the first time since she'd met him. "You think I'm BS-ing you? I may have a lot of flaws, but I do not lie."

"You really expect me to believe you're going to be celibate for the entire marriage? For a whole year?" She wondered how long he really expected that to last? Did he have plans to walk away that she didn't know about?

"Aren't *you?* What makes you think I have less self-control than you do?"

She opened her mouth—and closed it again. She didn't have an answer to that. And truth be told, as much as she cautioned herself against being gullible, she believed him on this one. Phoebe nudged aside her soup and stabbed the steak.

He swirled his merlot in his glass, watching her. "Celibacy doesn't make for much of a wedding night."

"I don't know about that." Although just the mention filled her mind with what the night could have held. Had he chosen his words with that intent? "Nina is safe for now. That means the world to me."

He finished off his merlot. "What about when Bianca shows up again?"

The bite of steak palled in her mouth. She swallowed thickly. "I only want the best thing for Nina. That would be to have her parents' love and want to take care of her."

"Even if that means giving her up?"

Her fork clattered against her plate. "Are you threatening to take her away?"

His one-sided smile returned with a dry twist. "Hardly. You're a terrific mother. But me? Ask anyone and they'll tell you I'm a crappy candidate for fatherhood."

Curiosity nipped.

"You say you're always honest, so tell me. What do you have against children?"

"Why would you say that?" he asked evasively. "Marianna and Sebastian have never voiced any complaints about me with kids."

"You pick Nina up, you carry her, even play with her, but you're always holding something of yourself back. I know it's early yet, but it seems like you distance yourself from her."

Kyle attacked the rest of his steak. "That's just your imagination."

She reached across the table and touched his wrist, stilling his hand. "I've heard too much about acting from Bianca over the years not to have picked up something. You're good, but you can't fool me."

He stared at her fingers for two crashes of the

waves before setting aside his fork. "Little Edward isn't my brother's first child. They had a baby girl before Edward, but lost her before her first birthday."

She gasped. "How awful." Her heart ached for the lovely woman who'd been so kind to her. "I can't imagine how devastated I would be if something happened to Nina."

"Sophie didn't die." But his face still creased with pain. "They'd tried for years to get pregnant, then decided to adopt. Four months after Sophie was placed with them, the birth mother changed her mind. They went through hell."

She'd assumed the extra portraits of children that didn't look like Landises were the grandchildren of Ginger's second husband. Now she realized one of the little-girl images must have been that adopted daughter. So that's why Marianna had noticed she loved Nina as much as any biological mother could. "I'm so sorry for what they went through."

"The birth mother sends them periodic updates and Sophie looks happy."

As she studied his pained expression, she realized it wasn't totally about hurting for his brother. He'd loved the little girl, too, and grieved when she was taken away. She stayed silent so he could just talk.

"My brother and his wife may be happy now, but after all they went through..." He shook his head slowly. "They even divorced at one point. My brother is a steady sort, good marriage material. Me? Not so much, even on a good day."

His line of logic wasn't going where she'd expected. She struggled to follow. "You're afraid of letting your family down?"

"I would do what I have to, but I saw from my sister-in-law, from my mother, too, how much more is needed to make a marriage and family work. I'm not cut out for that."

She almost blurted out her disbelief at his assumption, told him that he was copping out, but held the words back at the last second. He said he didn't lie to people, and maybe strictly that was true. But she suspected he was lying to himself. Men weren't always great at admitting their fears, especially if one fear involved turning his heart over to a child. "You're really content to live your life alone?"

"I have a big family around me, and a satisfying career. I have a good life."

"You seem to be forgetting one thing."

"I'm sure you'll tell me." At least his smile returned. He held her gaze over the candlelight, the flame flickering inside the hurricane globe and casting flecks in his beautiful blue eyes.

She touched his wrist again, lingering, feeling his pulse throb against her thumb. "You can't escape the fact that you're already a father."

His eyes locked on hers. Intense. Inscrutable. Her

fingers stroked along his wrist when she'd meant to let him go.

"And you're a wife."

He stood slightly, leaned across the small table and she knew what was coming but couldn't find words to stop him from—

Kissing her.

His mouth fit over hers, more familiar this time, but the tingle showering along her nerves was still surprising in its intensity. She'd hoped her reaction at the courthouse had been an anomaly, some kind of mixed-up reaction to memories from her first marriage, but damn, she fit her mouth against his and wanted. *More*.

She parted her lips and he growled his approval until she could taste the rich bouquet of his merlot. His hands stayed on the table, her fingers around his wrist. He only touched her with his mouth, his tongue. The spicy soap scent of him stirred around her in the breeze, reminding her of the moment when she'd first met him and his voice stroked her senses as, temptingly, his mouth moved on hers.

She should pull away, prove she was strong and resolute the way she'd planned this afternoon. Phoebe lifted her hands to push against his shoulders.

But he pulled away first.

Her head swam and she couldn't even blame it on the drink, because he had honored her request to stick with one glass. Her only consolation came from watching his chest rise and fall as rapidly as her own. She needed to get her head together. She refused to let him win her over easily as he must have done with women in the past, like Bianca and Lucy.

Phoebe drained half her water goblet while he reclaimed his seat. She had to think. Focus on what was important.

She had to keep her head clear and her wits about her at all times. She hoped this dinner would be over soon so she could start figuring out how to deal with her desire. "Um, when do you report back to your base?"

"I've already finished up all the paperwork." He watched her, his chest still pumping. "It'll be official next week."

"So you're on vacation." And when would that vacation end? She wasn't even sure where his base was. She was married to a stranger, a totally hot stranger who turned her inside out with his kisses. The mere thought rattled her, leaving her feeling disloyal to her ex. "Rest is a good idea after such a long deployment."

"I'm not on vacation." He straightened in his chair, his eyes narrowing. "I've turned in my papers now that I've fulfilled my commitment to the air force. We were going to announce it after the party. But then you showed up with Nina, and we've been distracted since then."

A roar started in her ears, her pulse louder than the waves rushing in with inevitability. "What exactly does this mean?"

"As of today, I'm no longer in the military. I'm taking over a branch of the Landis Foundation." He spread his hands wide. "As of now, I'm totally at your disposal."

An hour later, Phoebe stood in Nina's new nursery, toying with the decorative silk slippers tacked to the wall. Control slipped away as fast as the tears down her cheeks.

What had she gotten herself into?

Swiping the back of her wrist under her eyes, she looked into Nina's crib at the sweet baby she loved so much. Phoebe adjusted the light blanket, smoothed back a dark curl...saw Kyle's one-sided smile as the infant grinned in her sleep.

Life was marching relentlessly on without her first husband. Her emotions had spiraled so far out of control she didn't know how she would ever retrieve them. Now Kyle and all the myriad temptations he presented would be with her twenty-four/seven as she settled into a family life she'd never had and that Kyle clearly didn't want.

She touched along her kissed-tender lips and searched back over their few conversations prior. What had she misunderstood to make her believe he was still in the air force, due to zip off into the wild blue yonder sometime soon? Maybe she'd just heard and believed what she'd wanted to where Kyle was concerned, desperate for a way to secure Nina's future. She hadn't looked beyond that to understand all the ways she could be hurting both their hearts to put them through this sham of a marriage.

Now it was too late to go back. She could only steel herself, forge ahead.

And try not to think about how much she wanted him to kiss her again.

Six

A week later, Kyle stood outside the nursery door, double-checking the monitor to make sure the thing was actually working. He pulled it away from his ear, looked at the buttons, clicked a couple back and forth. Yeah, he could hear the white-noise music playing low in the background.

Good God, the baby gear was more complicated than some of the intelligence equipment he'd worked with in the air force. In another week he would start with Landis International. For now, he was already unofficially working from home, but soon the traveling would start.

He hadn't lied about being at Phoebe's disposal. He just hadn't mentioned there was a deadline to that since his new job would take him on the road even more than his old one. That didn't leave him much time to win Phoebe over, into his bed.

Kyle started down the hall, eager to move forward with his next plan for persuading her they should enjoy all the benefits a wedding license brought. For the past week, he'd wined and dined Phoebe at the most romantic places he could think of, a challenge to do when considering the kid-friendly aspect. The opera had been a no go, but then he didn't really like opera. He'd even persuaded Phoebe to fly upstate on the family jet for an outdoor history fair at Halloween. He'd thought Phoebe would enjoy the historical aspect, and Nina sure looked damn cute in her little princess costume. He had to admit the kid was easier to take along than he'd expected.

Of course, he didn't really know what to expect from a child her age. He should probably get one of those parenting books or surf the Internet for kid-care articles because, his choice or not, he was a father now, which meant doing his best. He was also a husband, something he intended to focus his full attention on for the rest of the evening on their first adults-only date.

This time he would be careful not to lose control of the conversation the way he had during their wedding-day dinner on the porch. He believed they could enjoy a fun and sexy relationship. Anything more would only complicate things for both of them, not to mention Nina.

He jogged down the stairs and around the corner to the home office where Phoebe was camped out in front of the computer. A couple days ago they'd made a day trip up to Columbia for her things, including her computer for work teaching her online classes. She'd unpacked her academic gear into the honey-brown wood shelves flanking a scenic window with brocade drapes. Phoebe had added her computer to the overlarge partner's desk and parked a baby swing in the corner.

He took a minute to study her, enjoying the way her straight blond hair shimmered with every move of her head, however slight. She looked every bit as enticing in jeans and a formfitting green cotton shirt as she had in the little black number she'd worn the night they met.

While she stared at the screen, Phoebe plucked at the hair band she'd slid around her wrist—as he'd learned was her habit. He'd also learned how much he enjoyed discovering new things to entice her out of her somber reserve.

Her earthy practicality appealed to him, chasing away any initial doubt anyone might have had about her being after Landis money. She liked to walk on the beach without her shoes and bring Nina to the public park. While nannies pushed designer-clad tots in fancy strollers, Phoebe let Nina roll around on a blanket in the grass to, as she said, see the world up close.

He even liked the way her history professor side would come out at odd moments with a sudden tutorial on a historic building they drove past or a surprise lesson on the French Huguenot influence in Charleston. Jonah had snickered the first time she'd launched into one of her diatribes, but by the end, even he'd been wound up in her stories.

He couldn't remember wanting anyone this much before. "Hey, professor. How's paper-grading going?"

She glanced up, her smile quicker lately. "I've just about finished the backlog of work."

He set the nursery monitor on the corner of the desk, anticipation ramping. "Ready to take a break?"

"I'm at a stopping point. What do you need?"

He *needed* to persuade her they belonged in bed together. "Let's go for a drive along the shore."

Her face lit with enthusiasm, then she looked at the monitor. "Nina might need me."

"It's only a drive, nothing elaborate or far away. Just some grown-up time away from work. I've already spoken to Jonah and he's on his way over from the carriage house." Ginger and her husband were in

D.C. for business. "He can call us or the housekeeper if he has any questions. Nina's asleep and seems out for the count." He held up the monitor, bobbling it back and forth in front of her. "I looked and listened."

"I didn't hear you." She eyed her receiver—the set had come with an extra—for the nursery monitor as if it had betrayed her.

"I was very quiet. I didn't want to wake her up." He rotated her chair toward him. "You deserve a break. Come on."

She tucked her tongue in the corner of her cheek as she always did when mulling something over, an increasingly sexy habit that left him aching to get her alone out of the house.

Phoebe gripped the arm rests with a resolute smack. "Okay, you've convinced me. Let me just save my work." She clicked along the keyboard then rolled the chair away from the desk, rising to her feet.

Stopping mere inches away from him.

Her vanilla-sweet scent tempted him to skim his knuckles down her cheek. Just one stroke. Except he didn't want to pull his hand away. She stared up at him, her pupils widening, pushing at the brown until the colors blended.

A clearing throat sounded from across the room. Damn.

Phoebe blushed.

Kyle dropped his hand to squeeze her shoulder

and turned to find Jonah lounging in the open doorway. Long hair brushed his shoulders, their rebel brother marching to his own tune, as always. "I'm ready to report for diaper duty, bro."

Kyle passed over the nursery monitor. "Thanks. I owe you."

Phoebe snagged a pencil. "I'll have all her instructions written down in just a min—"

Jonah whipped a piece of paper from his back pocket. "Already taken care of. Kyle left me a very detailed list." He glanced at his older brother. "You know I'm not ten anymore, right? Now go, both of you."

"On our way out." Kyle wrapped an arm around Phoebe's shoulders and shuttled her out of the office into the hall.

"You actually know Nina's routine." She glanced up at him, surprisingly not pulling away.

Progress.

"Isn't that why you brought her here?" He steered her down the long corridor, enjoying the familiar feel of her against his side. "To give Nina a father?"

Her smile faded and she tensed under his arm. "Has your private detective uncovered anything new about Bianca?"

"A few facts, none of them particularly helpful or I would have told you right away." He wished he had all the military intelligence equipment at his disposal now, but he could only keep tossing more money at private detectives.

What a mess for the kid. If Bianca had just gone off to party, then she didn't care about her child. And if she were dead… Either way, Nina needed them.

He was realizing more and more every day that he wouldn't let Bianca keep his child from him ever again. Even if she returned, he would still play a major role in Nina's life. "Bianca got fired a week into the rehearsals. Then it seems she just disappeared. No credit card use, nothing. But there's no indication she's met with foul play, either."

"That's a relief at least." Phoebe grasped the banister on the way down the winding inside stairway that led to the garage.

"At least the judge is on our side with the temporary custody order."

She glanced over her shoulder at him. "How long do you think we'll need to keep up this charade?"

"Let's just take it a day at a time." He swept open the garage door. "Or rather, one evening at a time." He palmed her waist on his way past the SUV for towing the boat and on down the line of family vehicles.

Phoebe tapped his hand on her shoulder. "Kyle? Kyle, that's your Mercedes."

"We're not taking it." He passed his car and stopped in front of their ride for the night. "I leased this for a few days."

A 1965 Aston Martin convertible.

"Oh my God," she gasped. "James Bond style."

He opened the passenger door and passed her a scarf. "Let's make it a ride to remember."

After settling in behind the wheel and maneuvering out of the estate, he opened up the engine on the shoreline road. She threw her head back with an abandon that stirred thoughts of uninhibited sex. He downshifted around a curve, houses spacing farther and farther apart until there was nothing but shoreline stretching ahead.

She hooked her arm along the open window, her hair and the scarf streaking behind her. "This is amazing."

"Wait until I drive you along the shores of Greece."

She laughed, along for the fun of the daydream. "Then we could go to the Parthenon. I've always wanted to see it for real."

"I can make that happen tomorrow."

Phoebe pulled her arm back inside. "Nina has a well-baby checkup."

"Then we'll go the next day." He slowed the vintage car, angling off to the side of the road, easing to a stop. He needed to recapture the joy on her face from earlier. "What else is on your tourism wish list?"

Her face creased with incredulity. "Well now, if we're dreaming, let's dream big." Her eyes tracked fast as if she was overwhelmed by the possibilities.

"I'd want to see all the regular stuff, Big Ben, the Eiffel Tower, but mostly I want to see the street-side cafés, the people, the feels and tastes of the…" She shook her head, scooting down in her seat. "I'm being silly."

"Not silly at all. Seeing the world has always helped me put life into perspective." His job as head of the international offices for the Landis Foundation offered a lot of travel, the main reason he had been all right with ending his military career.

Phoebe wrapped her arms around her waist as she took in the open marshlands on one side of the car and boats bobbing on open water on the other. The humid air hung heavy through the evening and brought cooler weather. "Thank you again for the outing. I can't believe you planned this for me. It's perfect." She turned her head along the back of the seat to look at him. "You've really been wonderful all week. I appreciate your trying so hard."

"Don't go getting soft on me now. Remember that love talk we had."

She thumped his shoulder, laughing. "Egomaniac."

He laughed along with her, wondering how in the span of just a week it could have become so important to him to see her smile. Her eyes held his. She stilled, waves crashing in the silence between them. He angled to kiss her and found she was already on her way over to meet him halfway.

A kiss. Just a kiss but the feel of her soft lips against him stirred him more than… Hell, he didn't want to think about anyone else. Only her and how damn good she felt against him. Her breasts brushed his chest, and he had to feel her skin. Now. He skimmed his hands under the hem of her cotton shirt and stroked up her back, urging her closer to him. Not near enough.

The sexy sound she made—a high sigh, half moan—sent his hand higher to span her back and feel every available inch of her. His heart rate kicked into overdrive faster than the Aston Martin, all systems go. He'd waited for her ever since that kiss on their wedding day, but it felt as if he'd been waiting forever.

If he could guide her across to straddle his lap—

She nipped along his mouth and rested her cheek against his, her breath gusting over his ear. "We can't do this."

His pulse was more jacked than if he'd run all the way here, but he slowed his breathing to try and rein himself in. He'd hardly done more than kiss her, yet she had a way of shredding his restraint. He caressed up and down her back, massaging. "I have birth control in my wallet."

Phoebe buried her face against his shoulder. "That's not what I meant. It's too soon. We've only known each other a week."

Hadn't he thought the same thing a few seconds ago? But he couldn't bring himself to fuel her argument. "We're married adults."

Arching back, she cupped his face, her hands firm. "Do you have a hearing problem? I've only known you a week."

The real answer knocked around inside his head. "You're not over your dead husband."

She flopped back in her seat and shouted to the open sky, "Damn it, Kyle, I've only known you a week!"

"How long had you known him?" Frustration—and, hell yeah, jealousy—made him push when he damn well knew better.

Phoebe hesitated so long he wondered for a minute if she was simply going to blow off his question. He was just about to start the car again when she sighed.

"I'd known him all my life," Phoebe said softly. "He told me he loved me the first time when we were seven years old and I fell off my bike. We had a great marriage right up to when he died five years ago." She looked down. "That probably sounds corny to a cynic like you."

It sounded exactly like the sort of unconditional commitment a woman like her deserved. "My parents had that kind of marriage before he died. She loved him so much I didn't think she stood a chance at finding it again. But man, was I wrong." Her stillness stopped him. "What?"

The moonlight illuminated the confusion in her eyes. "You're making an argument for falling in love twice, but I'm not supposed to fall in love with you."

Ah, crap. "Wait, uh…"

"Gotcha." She winked.

And that surprised the socks off him. "You're wicked, Phoebe Landis."

"Not really."

Something had shifted between them when she'd opened up enough to talk about her past and, all jealousy aside, he wasn't letting that progress slip away. He draped an arm over the steering wheel. "Oh, I think you've got a seriously untapped bad girl in there."

She tightened her wispy scarf around her head again. "Well, I can tell you for sure you won't be tapping any of that tonight."

He let his gaze wander over her, begrudgingly enjoying this bold, confident side of her. At least her eyes didn't have that haunted look anymore. In fact, with her swollen lips and tousled hair, she appeared vibrant. Vital. And very, very touchable.

Good thing he already had his hands on the wheel.

Kyle cranked the engine. He would let her go for now, but he had hopes for a lot more next time. "Lady, you're killing me here."

"Somehow, I believe you'll survive until morning."

"I'll be thinking of you all night." And he'd already arranged it so when she climbed in bed, she would find a surprise gift that ensured she would think of him, too.

Seven

"Thanks, Jonah," Phoebe said softly, walking up the side steps to the porch just off her suite. The sandy wind stung her legs, her skin still overly sensitive from one sensory-igniting kiss. When he didn't answer, she moved closer, reassured by the steady drone of the nursery monitor on the table.

Her brother-in-law sprawled in a chair at the table, his head back and eyes closed. His laptop computer also rested on the table, open to a full-screen shot of a girl with a backpack, a panoramic mountain range in the background.

Curiosity drew Phoebe closer… Jonah's eyes

snapped open. She stepped back, embarrassed to be caught staring at him when he was apparently resting his eyes. "Pretty girl."

"Nice ride?" he asked, dodging her comment and clicking the photo closed.

What was his life like when he wasn't surrounded by his ambitious and well-connected family? "Lovely ride. The shoreline view is gorgeous. Thank you again for keeping an ear out for Nina. Did she give you any trouble while we were away?"

He glanced past her as if to check for Kyle. She was alone, though. Kyle was putting away the Aston, since she'd bolted from the vehicle as quickly as she could rather than risk being tempted further.

Jonah passed her the nursery monitor. "The munchkin didn't make a sound the whole time. But don't worry, I still looked in on her twice."

She tapped the top of his computer. "Checking your MySpace?"

He tucked the laptop under his arm. "Grad school paper. Thank goodness for laptops." Jonah winked on his way past and down the steps, looking so much like Kyle—except for the longer hair. "G'night, Phoebe."

He loped across the manicured lawn toward the carriage house, keeping his secrets. She wondered if Kyle knew more about the girl on Jonah's screen saver. They seemed such a close family. How easy it would be to grow too comfortable here and forget it was all temporary.

Phoebe wrapped her arms around her waist, wishing it were that easy to hold together the pieces of her tattered control. She'd played things light with Kyle after his kiss. She'd sensed that would be the best way to gain some much needed distance.

His surprise ride along the shore in the vintage auto had touched her far more than any five-star dinners. Without question, the quirky car pick appealed to the history buff in her. He'd chosen his venue well for softening her up.

Time to return to reality. She eyed the nursery monitor, then raised it to her ear. Lullaby music played in the background, but she needed to see her girl to be sure. She creaked open the nursery door, leaned inside and, sure enough, Nina slept soundly as Jonah had said. The little one sucked her bottom lip, snoozing away.

Phoebe closed the door softly, suddenly awake and restless. Maybe she should try to get more work accomplished, except she couldn't scrounge up enthusiasm for chaining herself to a desk, especially after the open-air outing.

Might as well just curl up in bed and try to sleep, since Nina would be awake early. Phoebe pivoted toward her bed…and stopped short.

A large gift, wrapped in rose-patterned paper, rested on top of the pink-and-white accent pillows.

Cocking her head to the side, she approached the package warily. Who?

She plucked the card from under the bow and found it simply read: *Enjoy! Kyle.*

Her skin began tingling again in excitement as she picked up the briefcase-size box, testing the weight. Heavier than she would have expected. She didn't dare shake it without knowing if it was fragile. She peeled back a piece of tape slowly, careful not to tear the paper. It had been a long while since someone had surprised her with a present.

Phoebe parted the floral wrapping, taking her time in the unveiling…of…

A laptop computer.

Her nerves tingled hotter, tighter, his thoughtfulness touching her as firmly as any stroke of his hands. How had he pulled this off? She glanced at the porch. He must have left the gift with Jonah to place on her bed.

Kyle had put even more planning into the evening than she'd first realized. He must have noticed her struggling to balance work with caring for Nina. The new computer would make her life so much easier. Possibilities bloomed in her mind. She could even write on the patio, with Nina in her swing.

Phoebe smoothed her hands along the box, the night stretching long and lonely ahead of her. She knew full well what she was missing in turning him away.

Her cell phone rang from inside her purse. She

looked at the clock—11:42 p.m.—and smiled. It could only be Kyle this late at night.

She fished the phone from her bag and, yes, his number scrolled across the faceplate. Dropping onto the edge of her bed, she answered. "Thank you so much for the computer. I should say it's too extravagant, but it'll help me spend more time with Nina so I can't bring myself to say no."

"I was counting on that. And you're welcome." His bourbon-smooth voice intoxicated even through the airwaves.

She sagged back on the pile of pillows. "Why are you doing all of this? I would have taken care of Nina without all the kindness." Silence vibrated through the phone and over her nerves. "Kyle?"

"I'm here. And I think you know exactly why."

Her mouth dried up with the possibilities, dangerous possibilities that could threaten her objectivity. "Sex would complicate things between us. We wouldn't be able to go back. That could make things very awkward living together."

"Would it help you to know that my new job is with Landis International? I'll be traveling a lot, starting next week."

He would be leaving soon? She inched up higher on the pillow stack, not sure how she felt about this latest revelation. "All this romance has been about a short-term affair?"

"You've made it clear you aren't interested in any emotional commitment." He paused while his words sunk into her brain, tickling her mind with the possibilities. "Five years is a long time to go without sex."

There was only one way to deal with Kyle. Surprise him, keep him as off balance as he kept her. If that was even possible. "Who says I've lived like a nun since my husband died?"

"Are you sure about that?"

"Of course I'm sure." She'd dated and even tried to take things to that level, only to bail before making it to the bedroom. "I've learned to take care of those needs on my own."

Had she really just said that out loud? At least she'd managed to shock him silent. She gripped the phone until her fingers turned blue.

"Damn, Phoebe," he growled low. "You're trying to kill me, aren't you? Because an image of you 'taking care of yourself' could definitely give me heart failure."

She burrowed deeper into her pillows, her face heating with embarrassment—and stirring excitement. "I can't believe we're even having this discussion."

"Then I'll let you go…for tonight. See you in the morning."

She thumbed the off button and clutched the phone between her breasts, right beside her pounding heart. Her way of dealing with Kyle proved to be a double-edged sword. In spite of her best intentions and how little time they'd known each other, she wasn't sure how much longer she could hold out against the allure of Kyle and a short-term affair.

Four days later, Kyle buckled the seat belt in the Landis family jet, preparing for takeoff.

Finally, he had Phoebe to himself after an evening of family attendance at a diplomatic dinner in D.C. at the infamous Watergate Hotel. Phoebe had agreed to come along when she'd realized they could fly there and back in the same evening. Nina would only be with a sitter for a few hours, mostly asleep. Time management had been better for Phoebe overall with the computer, so she'd agreed.

His pulse kicked up a notch just remembering their phone conversation the night he'd given her the new laptop. Finding ways to romance his wife had been an exciting challenge, but he was beginning to get a sense of the things that appealed to the history major in her. He'd initially planned on skipping the D.C. function because of the distance from home, and the temporary custody order mandated that Nina stay in state for now.

Then he'd thought of the family's private jet.

The event had been important for Landis contacts and he'd been surprised how much he enjoyed having her by his side. His brothers and their wives had stayed in D.C. to visit longer with their mother and her husband. Sebastian and Marianna had a sitter who traveled with them. Maybe next time Nina could go with them and they could spend the day in the Smithsonian—

Next time?

He should be focusing on the present and the stunning woman in the seat next to him. Her hair sleekly upswept, Phoebe stared out the window at the night sky as they left the nation's capital behind after an evening of dancing.

The vibrantly red satin gown hugged her elegant curves, the strapless cut revealing a hint of the gentle swell of her breasts. Landis diamonds around her neck and dangling from her ears refracted the muted overhead light as if the stars from outside had come inside. The European ambassadors hadn't been able to keep their eyes off her.

The intercom system crackled to life. "Mr. and Mrs. Landis," the pilot's voice filled the cabin, "we're at cruising altitude. You are free to walk around."

Kyle unbuckled his seat belt and strode toward the galley kitchen. "There's a midnight snack here if you're hungry."

He'd planned ahead for this private time with Phoebe. The pilot was in front behind a closed partition, and a sleeping compartment was built into the back behind another partition. He really didn't need to think about the bed a few feet away. Not yet, anyway.

Phoebe unbuckled her seat belt and stood, stretching with a sensual moan of pleasure that shot straight to his groin.

"Thanks, for the food, for the whole evening. This is so surreal," she twirled in the middle of the floor, her hand sweeping toward the sofas lining one wall and the rows of leather seats on the other, "having a babysitter while we jet up to D.C. for dinner and dancing, home before Nina even wakes up."

"I'm glad you enjoyed yourself. You look…" He took in the curve of her exposed neck, her creamy skin glowing against the deep red strapless dress. "Absolutely amazing."

"And thank you again. You look very handsome yourself, Mr. Landis." She stepped closer to him, toe to toe, and tugged his tuxedo tie straight again. "Do you miss your uniform?"

He stilled under her touch, careful not to startle her away. "Do you?"

Some women were downright groupies when it came to military men. The person inside didn't matter to them, only the trappings that came with the job.

She patted his chest once before backing away. "You're just as good-looking in the tux as you are with the medals, and you know it."

His chest still bore the phantom feel of her touch,

his skin warm under the stiff fabric. But he was making progress, so he let Phoebe have her space. He pulled the protective wrapping off a silver tray of brie, bread and fruit, and opened a chilled bottle of sparkling water. "You must really think I'm egotistical."

"I think you're confident and sexy and exasperating." She plucked a purple grape from the platter and popped it into her mouth. "So you're okay with hanging up your uniform?"

He barely registered her words, so caught up in watching the way her pink lips moved, enticing him to kiss the sheen of juice from her lips. Then he saw she was waiting for his answer.

"Sure, I feel nostalgic about turning a page on that chapter of my life, but honestly, I never planned on the air force being a career."

"Then why did you join up if you always intended to get out before retirement?" She leaned a slim hip against the marble counter dividing the kitchen from the seating area.

His gaze lingered on that hip as he imagined his hand molding to fit the curve of her waist and trail lower to explore.

He filled two cut-crystal glasses with ice, then water. He wanted something stronger, but he needed a clear head around this woman. "It was about serving my country, about giving something back."

"That's really admirable." She studied him with

curious eyes before looking away self-consciously. She reached for her water glass. "I read up on you before I came here, and I saw that you were in a plane that was shot down. There wasn't a lot of information in the article. The writer noted something about withholding details to protect you while you finished your tour of duty. I wondered if the crash had anything to do with your decision to get out of the service."

That day smoked to life in his memory like a dark but distant cloud. "Definitely not the highlight of my life, but I know I was lucky. Not a scratch on me. Apparently someone lurking around on a mountain shot down the plane. Everyone survived the crash landing, but we had to abandon the site to hide out from rebels. So the rescue mission took a while longer."

Her hand flew to her neck, her face creasing with concern. "Those hours must have been horrifyingly long for you. How did you get through it?"

He spread brie over a cracker slowly, his mind awash in memories. "We all opened up an MRE—meal ready to eat—and thought about our families back at home. As I sat there, crunching on the rat-nasty crackers, I kept remembering how Sebastian and I used to eat peanut butter and marshmallow sandwiches when we were kids."

"That must have been frightening wondering if you would see them again."

It had been total hell. He offered her the cracker and cheese, surprised to see his hand was steady.

He lost himself in that past memory to distract himself now, as he had in the desert. "This one time when I was about ten and he was nine, we spent most of the summer playing in a forest behind our house. Well, it seemed like a forest, anyway. It was probably just a few trees with a bike path."

"Haven't you always lived at the Landis compound?"

"My grandparents used to live at the compound. We moved in when Dad got out of the air force and ran for senator. Dad said we needed the extra security the place afforded, but I sure missed the freedom of our old digs."

"That sounds like a haven for children." She brushed a cracker crumb away from the corner of her mouth absently, her eyes locked on him.

Kyle picked up his water glass, swirling the lime around and around. "We would hang out in 'our woods' all day long. We'd pack marshmallow and peanut butter sandwiches, take a gallon jug of Kool-Aid. And we dug tunnels."

"Tunnels?" she nudged gently.

"We dug deep trenches, put plywood over the top, then piled dirt to finish it off." He could almost smell the musty little cavern. "We were lucky we didn't die crawling around in there. We could have suffocated, or the roofing could have given way if someone had accidentally stepped on one of those boards."

Shivering, she wrapped her arms around herself, plumping her breasts in an understated but alluring display. "What did your mother say when she found out?"

His eyes flicked over her neckline and he closed his hands against the impulse to learn the shape of her firsthand. He knocked back half a glass of water. "My mother never knew about the tunnels. She would have grounded us until we left for college if she had." And they would have deserved it. His mother had been tough but fair. "We made Jonah stand guard and let us know if she was coming."

"How much did you have to pay him not to snitch?"

"Who said we paid him?" He winked. "He's the youngest. He did what we said."

She leaned closer for another grape, her vanilla perfume drifting over him. "And your oldest brother, Matthew?"

"He's too much of a rule-follower. We never let him in on the secret. I was especially into it—I would sneak out there on my own sometimes. Sebastian says it's no surprise I went into the military."

"So you're all four even closer now that you're adults." Her gaze danced down to her glass of water. "I envy that kind of love and support."

"We're lucky. I was lucky that day in the desert. I

thought about those sandwiches a lot while I waited in that trench in Afghanistan." What would he think about if the same thing happened today?

Without question, he knew his mind would be packed with images of Phoebe and Nina. They'd both filled his world so damn quickly, an unsettling notion given how short a time they'd both been in his life.

Phoebe rested her hand on his by the silver platter. "It's really honorable that you served your country. You had any number of options and you still chose to give back."

He flipped his hand to link fingers, her soft skin, her warmth, and just that fast he found himself imagining how much softer her skin would be under the dress. "Or maybe I just didn't know what to do with myself after graduation."

She shook her head. "If that had been the case you could have simply lived off your trust fund."

"Boring." He shrugged off her compliment, uncomfortable. He stroked his thumb over her wrist, enjoying the way her pulse leapt under his touch.

Her pupils widened with awareness, but she didn't pull away. "What about your new job? Will it keep you from being bored?"

This whole conversation was getting deeper than he'd intended. He didn't want anyone picking around inside his brain, getting closer, especially when he knew his lifestyle and hers ultimately wouldn't be compatible for anything more than a casual affair. They needed to keep emotions well clear, for Nina's long-term benefit. He also needed to get this conversation, this whole outing, back on track.

Still holding her hand, he tugged her nearer until her breasts brushed against his chest. His body tightened instantly in response. "You know what would keep me from being bored right now?"

Her head tipped back, exposing her neck as she stared up at him with intense dark eyes. "Stop it. I want to talk. If you really want to stand a chance at getting me in bed, then be serious for just five minutes."

Phoebe's words stoked his barely banked desire. "You're entertaining the possibility of us in bed?"

Eight

Standing in the jet cabin with her emotions as firmly in the clouds as her body, Phoebe couldn't deny it any longer. She wanted to make love to Kyle. And yes, there was a part of her that was comforted by the fact that he would be leaving soon. The aftermath would be simpler with time to regroup. Maybe, just maybe she could keep her heart safe this go-around.

The whole outing had been surreal from the start. She'd never imagined flying in a private jet, wearing such extravagant jewels or hobnobbing with international dignitaries in a historic hotel ballroom. But the man more than the accessories had made the evening. Kyle had been at his charming best, his smile and strength reminding her at every turn of the pleasure waiting a simple stroke away.

If she dared.

She knew without question if she didn't take this chance now, she would regret it for the rest of her life. Kyle was right. She was on fire with unfulfilled needs, needs growing increasingly painful the more time she spent with him.

Committed, nervous—excited—she flattened her hands to his chest again. "As soon as we land, I want us to be together, to consummate this marriage."

His eyes went sexy lidded as he slid his hands around her back, angling her hip-to-hip against him. "Who says we have to wait until we land?"

The possibility of having him now, here, sent a surge of thick longing through her veins. But her ever-present practicality tapped her with reservations. "What about the pilot?"

"He's behind the partition and has his hands full flying the plane. Even if he needs to switch to auto-pilot and open the door for some reason, he would announce himself over the intercom first," Kyle explained. His hands roved up the zipper along her spine and down her bare shoulders, callused fingertips rasping over her skin with tantalizing masculinity. "The bedroom in back isn't large, but we'll have privacy, atmosphere and protection."

Need gathering speed inside her, she eyed the small door behind the seats. She hadn't paid much attention to it on the flight down since his brothers and sisters-in-law had been along. She also hadn't realized then that she and Kyle would be flying back alone.

Very alone. No more waiting and second-guessing.

Delicious anticipation sent her arching up on her toes until his mouth waited a whisper away from hers. "Then, yes, I'm more than *entertaining* the idea of us going to bed together."

His hands spanned her waist and he lifted her up onto the counter island. He stepped between her legs, his breath warm and seductive against her brow. "Stay right there, just where you are, so I can touch you," he sketched his lips over her brow, "feel you," he kissed over her cheekbone, "take my time with you."

He sealed his mouth to hers, his tongue searching, soothing and exciting all at once. The thready reins on her restraint snapped. She'd been thinking of him, of this, ever since that night he'd given her the laptop, the night he'd told her she would be in his dreams. She looped her arms around his neck, desperate to get even closer still. The silk tuxedo lapels under her soothed along the overheated flesh of her exposed shoulders, the fabric a sexy, extravagant luxury for such steely strength.

His fingers traced just below the diamond necklace, dipping between her breasts far too briefly.

Dragging in breaths between frenzied kisses, she inhaled the scent of his aftershave, gloried in the scratch of his rougher cheek against her skin.

Hot sensation spiderwebbed over her skin, a network of exquisite pleasure from the barest of touches. He cupped her face, brushing kisses over her eyes and cheeks while he stroked her exposed shoulders until her breasts ached for his attention. She linked her ankles behind his knees and urged him nearer, as close as he could come with her gown bunching between them.

Growling his appreciation, he inched the hem of her dress up to her knees, freeing her to wrap her legs around his waist. He cupped her bottom and lifted her off the counter.

She squealed into his mouth, then held on tight as he walked across the cabin toward the door. He opened the door to the sleeping compartment, angled inside and kicked it closed again with a final click. The double bed invited with its thick burgundy comforter that brought out the warm glow of mahogany accents and brass-globe lighting. Dim light, but just enough for her to make out the hard lines of desire etched in Kyle's features as she sprinkled kisses over his face.

He lowered her to her feet, sliding her body down his with sensual precision. "Patience, Phoebe."

"Later." She swept aside his tuxedo jacket, burning to see him, *have* him.

He tugged the zipper on her dress down her spine until the air gusting from above chilled her back. She trembled in delicious anticipation. *Finally.* His warm, bold hands tunneled inside, lower, lower still until he cupped her bottom and brought her against him for another moist, searching kiss.

Rational thoughts scattered as quickly as their clothes hit the floor—both his clothes and hers—and before she knew it, cool air blasted over her bare breasts. She tightened in response, her senses humming as surely as the engines powering them through the night sky.

His eyes roved her body as she stood clad in nothing more than her champagne silk panties and a fortune in diamonds. "What was that I said about patience? I can't seem to remember right now."

Reveling in the mutual attraction, she kicked aside her dress pooled at her feet and savored staring at a gloriously naked *man.* If she'd had more space, she would have stepped back and simply admired him. Instead, she traced the angular line of his jaw, down to the hard plane of his collarbone, over his pectorals. His muscles jumped under her fingertips.

He stepped closer, his skin sealing against hers, the hot, hard length of his desire pressed to her stomach. Kyle walked, backing her until the edge of the mattress hit behind her knees. She toppled onto the bed and he followed her down, ducking his head in the tightly confined space.

The small cavern with curved walls, engine droning, gave her the sense of being closed off from everyone and everything. They were truly in their own private haven.

He stretched over her, leaning on his elbows to hold the bulk of his weight off her. She hooked a leg around him, pulling him full out on her. She wanted all of him, the full-bodied experience of him blanketing her.

He palmed just below her breasts, stroking his thumbs along the sides, then around to her already tight nipples. The pressure of his gentle torment made her ache for more and she arched against the warm pressure of his leg between hers. His blue eyes darkened to near violet, broadcasting just how much he wanted her, too.

Her eyelids went heavy, and she couldn't stop them from closing even as she mourned losing the vision of him over her. Other senses heightening, she inhaled the tangy scent of him mixed with the musk of desire. Part of her felt the frantic edge of passion clawing to get free, but she gritted back the impulse to rush. Reality would take over soon enough.

She felt the hot gust of his breath an instant before he took her mouth. He kissed her, long and well with the talent of a man who knew how to please.

Tasting the pungent, buttery flavor of brie, she

explored just as deeply. He stroked her breasts with persistence until she wriggled against him, hungry for deeper pressure. And she could tell without question he wasn't unaffected. The hard swell of him throbbed and she ached to learn the intimate feel of him.

Phoebe slid her hand between them and encircled his hard length, slowly caressing until he rolled onto his side, taking her with him. She considered tumbling farther so she could be on top. A quick glance told her the angled ceiling was low enough that if she lost control and arched back she could bump her head. A definite mood buster.

She draped her leg over his, understanding now why he'd shifted, and she found she liked the equality of power in the position so very much, especially when he hooked his thumb along the low waistband of her underwear. Her hand stilled, every nerve ending focused on where his search would lead him next....

Yes.

Two thick fingers dipped inside her panties, his touch cool and welcome against her overheated flesh. He stroked, parted, found the tight bundle of nerves. Her hands fell away and she gripped the comforter, tighter and tighter until her muscles burned.

Faster, but softer he circled until frustration knotted within her. She nipped his lip. He growled lowly, trailing his mouth away, along her neck. She gasped, again, and couldn't stop the moan that followed. If she didn't find relief soon, she might well scream.

"No more teasing. Finish this. Patience is for later, remember?"

"Whatever you say, whatever you *want*." He traced the curve of her ear, his promise stroking her senses as surely as his hands, his tongue, even the enticing brush of his body against her.

Still, he wouldn't allow her the release she craved. She let go of his hip and tried to slide her hand between them again to torment him as fully as he was tormenting her. He clasped her wrist, halting her progress.

A whimper slid past her lips. "No more."

"Do you want to stop?"

"No! I mean, no more playing." She stroked the full length of him.

He groaned. "We're in agreement on that."

If nothing else.

But she didn't want doubts or darker thoughts now. She needed—deserved—this stolen moment of pleasure with him. He thumbed either side of her panties and skimmed them down. His hands came back up and somehow he'd palmed a condom. Before she could chase that thought further to a time when she'd considered getting pregnant, Kyle sheathed himself and pulled her to him again.

Side by side, he nudged against the core of her, entering, stretching, her body oh-so-sensitive from such a long stint of abstinence. Gasping, she went bone-less from the sheer pleasure of the thick pressure. She slid an arm over him, her fingers threading through his close-shorn hair.

He whispered in her ear, words of encouragement, of how much he wanted her, how she turned him inside out. Each sexy sound stroked her emotions as smoothly as he stroked her body while they rocked against each other.

She'd wanted him since hearing that sexy voice of his for the first time. It had been so damn long since she'd even felt desire, much less pursued it. The rippling, sweet surge of sensations stormed through her as she writhed against him. She pressed her face against his neck, grasping him with frenetic hands, her nails scoring down his back.

Too soon, the storm gathered in that tightening swell and as much as she wanted to delay, she lost control. She clasped him closer, harder. Her teeth clamped into his shoulder with the force of her completion exploding through her. He thrust harder, faster, drawing out her orgasm until every nerve tingled, damn near burned until he followed her over the edge.

Slowly, she realized her arms were locked around him, the vent chilling the light sheen of sweat slicking her body and his. He rolled to his back, hugging her to his side. His chest still pumped heavily and she couldn't have found the air to talk even if she knew what to say. She wasn't even sure what to think.

She was too busy being scared. Because without question, she'd found so much more than she'd expected to experience here with him. Ever with anyone. At an earlier, freer time in her life, she might have taken a chance on this man with potent kisses, restless feet and a carefree smile. A risky proposition, to say the least.

With Nina's stability at stake, Phoebe feared she couldn't risk another night in his bed.

After their jet landed and they gathered their luggage, Kyle opened the car door for Phoebe, enjoying the way the moonlight played with her loose hair. Hair loose and fluffed from lovemaking.

Before they'd even had time to steady their breathing, the pilot had called over the loudspeaker, announcing they were preparing to land. Phoebe had launched from bed and shimmied into her dress again.

He'd known she had a passionate nature beneath her cool exterior, but he hadn't had a freaking clue how much steam waited to be tapped. His body surged with the memory of how she'd fit against him, of how she'd responded. Of how damn hot she'd looked wearing nothing but diamonds and a light sheen of perspiration. His back bore the marks of her pleasure.

And he looked forward to adding more as soon as they both recharged with a few hours' sleep.

He slid into the driver's side of the Mercedes. "We'll be home soon. I've already arranged for someone to come by in the morning to watch Nina so you can sleep in."

She looked at him sharply. "Thank you, but I'd rather not. I've already spent enough time away from her."

He drove out of the small airport's parking area and onto the main highway. "I can see how that would be upsetting for Nina."

"It's more than just not wanting her upset. She's had enough shuffling in her life as it is." Phoebe shoved her hair back from her face, frustration sparking in her eyes as clearly as the diamonds refracting the dash lights. "Don't look at me like I'm being overprotective."

Had he done that? "Sorry." He reached across to tunnel a hand under her hair and massage the back of her neck. "I only wanted to make sure you had enough rest."

She tucked her tongue in the side of her mouth. "I'm the one who should apologize for snapping. You were just being thoughtful." She sank back into the seat, easing away from his hand. "I'm so afraid of doing something wrong with her. Before Nina came into my life, I knew so little about babies. As Bianca started depending on me more and more for babysitting, I did research to make sure I had all the most current information."

Good God, if she inched any farther away from him she would fall through the open car window. What the hell was up? Suddenly her speed in getting dressed and out of the jet seemed like evasion rather than efficiency.

He needed to keep her talking and hopefully clear the furrows from her brow before they got home. Before they went to bed. "How did you and Bianca end up friends—and staying friends? You're both so different."

"We met in a theater history class in college. Roger was a theater major, too, and I took the class to be with him." Streetlights whipped past on the nearly deserted road. "We met Bianca and we all hit it off. She's more the flamboyant type and I crewed backstage for a couple of productions, building sets, making costumes."

"What about Roger?" He stomped back any residual jealousy and watched her out of the corner of his eye.

"He was a playwright, a really gifted one." She thumbed her wedding ring around and around. "I've always thought he would have made it big if he'd lived."

He couldn't miss how she talked about both Bianca and Roger being the spotlight sort yet didn't seem to see her own special individuality.

"We all three had such big plans and dreams in those days." She looked down and he wondered if she felt some of the same jealousy he'd wrestled with. "I'm not really sure why I've kept in touch with her, but I'm glad I made the effort for the occasional lunch out to catch up. Otherwise, I never would have known Nina." She looked over at him, full on for the first time since they'd made love. "What are you thinking?"

"That maybe you kept up the friendship with Bianca in spite of your differences because you weren't ready to let go of your husband." Downshifting around a corner onto a two-lane road, he hated the image coming together in his mind. "Being around her made you feel connected to him. This way, you don't have to let go and move on."

Pain flashed through her eyes. "Wow, that's pretty insightful for a card-carrying member of the testosterone club."

"That's me—Mr. Sensitive." What would have happened if he'd met Phoebe instead of Bianca? "So you've researched Mommying 101."

"There's a lot of information out there, scary information."

He pulled up outside the security gates leading into the Landis compound. "You still look worried."

"Of course I'm concerned about her future," she said as the iron barriers swung open. "We may have kept her safe today, but until we know where Bianca stands, there's still so much uncertainty. I guess what worries me most is the uncertainty. If Nina is meant to be with Bianca, of course it will break my heart to let her go, but it's more important that she be settled somewhere, securely, permanently."

"Even if it's with Bianca?" He guided the car along the winding drive, oak trees and palmettos lining the way.

"Even if. There are so many frightening studies out there right now about attachment disorder. Have you heard of it?"

"Only in very general terms. It has something to do with kids not bonding, right?" He pulled up outside the garage.

"A lot of the studies focus on babies that are neglected or abused. When they don't learn to bond as babies, it affects how they can bond as children and adults." She turned to face him, her face shadowy in the dark garage as the door closed behind them. "Nina hasn't been neglected or abused, but some of the studies also suggest there could be attachment issues when babies are shuffled from caregiver to caregiver, never having a chance to bond with anyone."

"And that's what you worry about with Nina."

She stared down at her hands, twisting the diamond-studded wedding band around her finger again. "All babies deserve security. I would do anything to keep her safe. *Anything*."

Just that fast, it hit him. Even if he'd met Phoebe before, she might not have even consented to a date. She'd only married him because of Nina. Her loyalty to Nina—to her dead husband even—might not extend as far as him.

Anger crackled inside him over the idea of just how far she may have been willing to go to secure Nina's future. "And was tonight about doing anything to make sure you don't lose Nina?"

Her eyes went wide and her mouth fell open. "Are you insinuating I would sleep with you just to keep Nina?"

Kyle scrubbed a hand over his unshaven face, reason poking through his anger. "Of course not. I know you better than that." His hand fell away and he cupped the back of her neck again. "I'm trying to figure out why you're pulling away after some of the most amazing sex ever."

She looked away, but at least she didn't dodge his hand this time. "This is difficult for me, being with someone again." A long swallow moved her throat. "You've always had a large family to depend on, so maybe you don't get what it's like losing the only person in your world. We only had each other. He was a foster child and both my parents died before I finished college. Dad died from complications during a routine surgery and Mother basically grieved herself to death."

"I'm sorry." He started massaging her neck again, finding deep and unrelenting kinks.

"It was a long time ago, but I still miss them. Especially at times like this. They would have enjoyed Nina so much." She smiled bittersweetly. "But you understand that, don't you, having lost your father?"

He nodded, his dad's death still as tough today as it had been when he was a confused and grieving teen. How much worse it must be to lose a spouse. "How did your husband die? You said he drowned, but there must be more to the story than that."

She blinked fast even though her eyes were dry. "We'd both been working too hard. I was finishing up grad school, and he took on a second job to help pay my tuition. We decided to spend an afternoon at the beach. The day was beautiful, sun shining, but the wind was heavy, making for red-flag swimming conditions. So we just picnicked."

"What went wrong?"

Fresh tension kinked in her neck under his fingers all over again. He resisted the notion there might be nothing he could do to help her through this.

"Two tourists tried to surf the waves in spite of the warning. One of the guys got caught in the riptide and called for help."

"Your husband answered the call." God, he couldn't even resent the guy anymore.

"He would have made it out, too, but the surfboard hit him on the head. It was a freak accident."

Still, she blinked fast against dry eyes and he realized she'd already cried herself dry over the man.

"You really loved him."

She nodded simply, reaching up to link her fingers with his. "Love that strong doesn't just go away." She cleared her throat and plastered a brittle smile on her face. "So don't worry about me misunderstanding what happened back in the airplane. I understand our marriage is short-term. You've made that clear enough from the beginning."

"What if we stayed married?" The words fell out before he'd even formed the thought. But once said, it made total sense. "We've got a great thing going here. Amazing sex, a friendship, security. We're both so independent we won't need to live in each other's back pocket. You want clear? Okay, let's stay married."

She watched him with sad eyes. "What about love? You might find it one day and be sorry."

"No," he insisted, backing away from even the thought. "I have my future mapped out and it's too transitory for any woman to put up with. We'll have different expectations in a partnership."

He didn't know why this mattered so much, had never thought about extending the marriage before now. But the possessiveness fisting in his chest wouldn't retreat.

Kyle angled closer, the perfect argument coming to mind to win this battle. Defeat was suddenly, deeply unpalatable. "You could have more children one day. You're a natural mother."

She gasped. In shock or horror? "Are you presenting yourself as a sperm donor?"

"What if I'm offering that, and more?" His question filled the space between them with possibilities.

And she didn't say no outright. Confusion scrolled across her face and he prepped his next line of persuasion. Victory hovered so damn close—

The phone rang from the depths of her bag.

She startled in her seat. "That can only be about Nina this late." She avoided his eyes and dug in the bag at her feet until she found her phone. "Hello?"

"Phoebe?" a female voice shrieked so loudly from the other end of the line Kyle could hear clearly. "Phoebe, is that you?"

The voice slammed him back in his seat. It couldn't be. Not now. But Phoebe's terrified eyes confirmed what he already suspected.

Bianca was alive and well on the other end of that phone line.

Nine

Frozen in the front seat of the Mercedes, Phoebe gripped the phone, terror and relief warring within her. Kyle tensed beside her and she feared he might reach for the receiver.

Her fingers trembling, Phoebe changed to speak-0erphone. "Bianca? Is that you?"

"Of course it's me," her college friend, Nina's mother, answered. Her perfectly modulated voice filled the car. Any accent had long ago been smoothed away in her theater training. "I'm standing outside your apartment. I've been ringing your doorbell for the past five minutes and the neighbors are starting to get pissed. Wake up and let me in."

Bianca was in Columbia? Where had she been all this time? Wherever she'd been hiding out, she must not have read a newspaper if she didn't know about Phoebe and Kyle getting married. The news had been splashed all over South Carolina and beyond. Diplomats from around the country had congratulated them last night at the D.C. dinner party.

A marriage they'd consummated, the scent and feel of him still lingering under her satin gown. Had it only been a few short hours ago they'd left for Washington, D.C.? Good God, her world was blowing apart faster than she could gather up the pieces.

At least Bianca seemed oblivious to all the changes that had gone on in their lives, which would give them a few precious hours to get their thoughts together before Nina's mother burst through the door. "I'm not at home. I'm in Hilton Head—with Nina."

She couldn't even think about the upheaval this would cause for Nina. She'd just been settling into the Landis home and their new—more secure—life. Phoebe's belly clenched.

"Hilton Head?" Bianca asked. "What are you doing there?"

Phoebe glanced at Kyle beside her in the parked car inside the lighted garage. How would Bianca react to the news they'd married? Even more important, didn't Bianca care what had happened to her child? Of course not, or she wouldn't have simply disappeared. "I'm taking care of *Nina*."

"Oh, how's the kiddo doing?"

The throwaway tone grated along Phoebe's already raw nerves. It was obvious Bianca was unharmed and had chosen to fall off the face of the earth.

Phoebe resisted the urge to throw the phone as maternal anger mushroomed inside her. "Nina's fine. Since you left her with me last summer, she learned to roll over. She's almost sitting up on her own."

"Good, good. Thanks for babysitting. Do you have an extra key hidden around here somewhere? It's not under the flowerpot like it used to be, and I really need a place to crash."

Babysitting? Babysitting! Two months—nearly three months now—went way beyond some kind of nanny gig, especially with an infant.

"I took the key with me when I left my apartment." She'd closed up the place but had kept paying rent. She'd planned on going back, but deep down she'd always thought Nina would be with her. Now Nina had both her biological parents in the picture, which left little room for a *babysitter.* "Uh, Bianca, I'm in Hilton Head with Kyle Landis. When you didn't come back, I brought her here to her father."

She watched Kyle's jaw flex, his face stark and hard, anger darn near rolling off him in waves. Nina would have a fierce defender in her Landis father. Silently Phoebe sent up a prayer of thanks that she could count on him now.

"He's back from Afghanistan?" Bianca's voice breezed from the phone. "Wow, cool, I was planning to get in touch with him."

How could she be so blasé about letting Kyle know about his daughter? Would Nina have ever had the chance to know this big and wonderful family if Bianca hadn't told Phoebe?

He gestured for her to keep talking.

Phoebe swallowed down the wad of fear clogging her throat. "Well, you can come to Hilton Head and talk to him in person."

"He's probably mad, isn't he?" Bianca asked, hesitancy tingeing her voice for the first time. "Could you just bring Nina back here?"

Phoebe's patience snapped. If Bianca thought she could steamroll over her old, quiet friend, she was in for a rude awakening. "I can't do that, Bianca. You abandoned your daughter. Kyle has temporary custody."

"Phoebe," Bianca gasped, "what in the hell have you done?"

"You didn't leave me any choice when you walked out on your child."

"Fine, I'm getting a hotel for tonight. I'll meet you in Hilton Head tomorrow."

It was less than three hours' drive. Nothing would have stopped Phoebe if it were her child, and oh, God, she could lose Nina now. "Call when you get close to town and I'll give you directions to the house."

Bianca hung up without another word.

Phoebe stared at the phone in her hand, a chill settling all the way to her bones. Her teeth started chattering. Vaguely, she heard Kyle speaking to her, offering up soothing words about how everything would be okay. But she couldn't think of anything but checking on Nina.

Phoebe tossed aside her phone and bolted from the car. Bunching her dress up, she raced into the house, up the stairs, not stopping until she reached Nina's nursery.

The crib was empty.

Kyle heard Phoebe's scream.

He sprinted into the nursery and found her clutching a baby quilt to her chest as she stood by the crib. "Where's Nina?" Panic lit her eyes as she looked frantically around the nursery. "You said she would be taken care of. I shouldn't have left her for even a second. Oh, God, do you think Bianca lied and she's already taken her?"

Kyle cupped her shoulders. "Calm down, it's okay. Nina is in the main nursery. The sitter put her there and went to sleep on the daybed. Nina hasn't been alone for even a second since we left."

Phoebe sagged with relief. He pulled her to his chest, understanding her fear and vowing for her—for Nina—he wouldn't let anyone harm one hair on their heads. She shuddered against him, and it ripped him up inside to see his normally cool wife fall apart.

With a final trembling sigh, she straightened. He only had a second to register her damp eyes before she charged out and into the hall. Her high heels clicked along the hardwood floors as Kyle followed her to the green nursery his mother kept for all her grandchildren.

Phoebe cracked the door open slowly—warily?—and peered inside. She slumped against the door frame, her eyes closing, releasing two fat tears. "Thank God."

Kyle stopped behind her and peered through the door at the baby fast asleep in the spindled crib.

His daughter.

He allowed himself a selfish moment to just stare at Nina and reassure himself she was okay, she would be okay. He memorized her features, a face he should have studied more fully before now.

She had the Landis chin and hair. If she were awake, he would be staring at his own eyes. But beyond that, he knew she liked her feet uncovered and she giggled when he waved her favorite panda-bear teething toy in front of her face.

It was so damn little to know. He should know more. He *would* know more. He wouldn't be that part-time parent jetting off for months only to find out his child had met a milestone while he was gone. He had options, damn it.

She was his daughter.

He loved her. And in the morning, he could lose her to a woman who didn't think anything of disappearing for nearly three months. He'd never known this kind of fear before, not even when he'd been shot down in Afghanistan. The full impact of that crushed his chest until he damn near couldn't breathe. He couldn't even imagine what kind of hell Phoebe must be feeling. His wife had loved this little girl for months.

He started to reach for Phoebe, but she stepped deeper into the room. She quietly called out to the sitter, gently waking her, smiling her thanks and telling her she was free to go to the guest room across the hall.

Once the sitter bustled past him and into the other room, Phoebe curled up in the corner of the daybed as she'd done her first night here.

Watching her distance herself from him, Kyle realized he wasn't just in danger of losing his daughter, he could also lose his wife.

"I'm here to pick up my daughter."

Bianca strode into the foyer of the Landis mansion, flicking her wavy red hair over her shoulder with a gesture Phoebe recognized as calculated to catch male eyes. It usually worked.

At least today, Kyle seemed oblivious to Bianca's dubious charms, currently encased in skinny jeans and a lime-green tank top. His barely banked anger steamed behind his eyes. Nina didn't seem to notice the tension, however, as she patted him on the face with her panda-bear teether clutched in her chubby fist.

Even as tense as things were between her and Kyle, Phoebe was relieved to have his support in this stand-off with Bianca. He'd called the rest of his family this morning and they would all return within hours.

Kyle palmed Phoebe's back. "Let's all step into the living room and talk. There's a lot to go over from the past few months."

Bianca eyed the wide-open entryway, her deeply tanned fingers gliding over a blue-and-white Fabergé egg by a crystal vase of lilacs. She strolled deeper into the living room. A wall of windows let sunshine stream through and bathe the room in light all the way up to the cathedral ceilings. Hardwood floors were scattered with light Persian rugs around two Queen Anne sofas upholstered in a pale blue fabric with white piping. Wingback chairs in a creamy yellow angled off the side. The whole decor was undoubtedly formal, but in an airy, comfortable way.

Phoebe feared Bianca was seeing dollar signs.

But if she'd only wanted money, wouldn't she have come to Kyle right away?

Bianca spun on her spiky green high heel and extended her arms. "My baby." She gripped Nina so firmly Phoebe had no choice but to let go. "Aren't you beautiful, and so big?"

"Yeah," Kyle muttered, "they grow. As a matter of fact, they grow a lot if you don't see them for nearly three months."

Phoebe rested a hand on his arm, wary of angering Bianca, especially when they didn't have a clue what she had in mind. "Where have you been? Do you realize how worried we've been?"

"Were you worried about me, or did you just care because of Nina?" Lifting an eyebrow, she hitched the baby on her hip awkwardly. Nina squirmed and threw her panda-bear plastic teether on the floor. "It doesn't matter now. I'm back and ready to see my girl."

Kyle stood, feet braced, in the archway between the living room and foyer as if blocking any chance of escape. "You fell off the face of the earth so completely we thought you might be dead. You still haven't told us where you were."

"Sorry about that. I went to the islands with this important director. He said he had a part for me." Bianca pried Nina's fingers off her giant gold-hoop earrings. "He lied, the scum, but I got a vacation out of it. Mothers need vacations. I'm all rested now and ready to snuggle with my little girl."

Phoebe resisted the urge to grab Nina and run. "You can't just abandon Nina for months and think I'll trust you to take care of her."

Bianca looked back and forth between Kyle and Phoebe standing close together. "Ah, I see how it is." She jostled Nina uncomfortably as the baby tried to climb down. "You've got Kyle now and if you lose the kid, you lose him. He's quite a catch. I can see how you wouldn't want to give all that up."

Phoebe bit back the impulse to snap at Bianca. Kyle was more than some "catch." He was about so much more than his bank balance. He was an honorable man who cared about his family, took his responsibilities seriously and even appreciated the simple beauty of beachside rides in an open-air car.

Kyle scooped up Nina's plastic teething toy from the floor and lifted Nina from Bianca's awkward hold. "Phoebe and I are married."

Bianca blinked fast, speechless for once.

His daughter secured against his chest, Kyle waved the tiny panda bear in front of Nina's face, soothing her into precious baby giggles. "She came to tell me about Nina, and we found we had a connection."

"You expect me to believe you two fell in love? You're kidding, right? Phoebe's totally locked in the past with Roger." Her painted lips curved with a hint of condescension as she turned to Phoebe. "And let's be honest, girlfriend, you're not exactly Kyle's type."

Phoebe rocked back a step at the blatant cruelty of her so-called friend's words. She'd maintained the friendship with Bianca because she was outgoing and vivacious, a force that had pulled Phoebe out into the world when she'd felt isolated by grief. And yes, maybe she'd had blinders on where Bianca was concerned because she'd been part of happier times in Phoebe's life. But the blinders were off now.

Bianca winked. "Maybe you can get something in the divorce settlement. You married him to help his daughter, after all. What?" She blinked with overplayed innocence. "That's why you married him, isn't it? It's not like the two of you knew each other."

A brief flash of anger iced Kyle's eyes before he smoothed his features into a neutral mask. Phoebe admired his calm, his skill in putting feelings in the background to remain focused on solving the problem. She could see well what had made him such an effective warrior.

Kyle's gaze pinpointed on Bianca. "What do you really want?"

"My baby."

Cold fear sprinkled goose bumps over Phoebe's arms. "The courts have given Kyle temporary custody. You left her. We'll need to go back to court to settle that."

"That's really upsetting." Her look went calculating. "You actually care about her already? She is a pretty kid."

Her worst nightmare was unfolding. Again, she was losing someone she loved, and while she tried to console herself that at least Nina was alive, Phoebe still couldn't erase an image of the baby crying out for her at night and wondering… The pain went deeper than tears.

Bianca, however, blinked big, fat tears down her face. "I'm so sorry. I've been so stupid, but I really thought I could make a better life for Nina. I'm not good enough for her, not like you and your family."

Was Bianca acting or had Phoebe grown more cynical?

If only she didn't know what a damn fine actress Bianca could be. Had she been using those acting skills on Phoebe all this time, too? Had the entire friendship been a lie? Perhaps Kyle was right that she'd clung to Bianca out of a need to hang on to the past with Roger. She'd allowed herself to be blinded.

Phoebe gathered her shaky poise. "Where are your bags? I'll show you to your room."

Bianca shook her finger. "No, no, no. I'm not staying here under your judgmental eyes, with you recording every misstep I make. I'm staying in a hotel and Kyle's paying." She passed Kyle a card. "Here's the number so you can call with the specifics."

She hitched her bag higher on her shoulder and twitched toward the door. The closing door echoed in the silence.

Swaying, Phoebe could have sworn all her bravado melted from her. She grabbed the wingback chair behind her and sat heavily.

Kyle paced around the living room with Nina, still waving her panda toy in front of her face. "Phoebe, I don't want you to worry. We'll play this out in the legal system. The judge isn't going to reverse the custody arrangement on a whim, and I doubt Bianca has the staying power to hold out long-term."

Phoebe wasn't so sure. The cynic inside shouted Bianca was ready to dig her spiked heels in deep. But she let Kyle continue to spell out his plans, realizing that taking charge seemed to keep him calm.

She watched him stride back and forth across the room, Nina cradled confidently against his chest. When had he grown so comfortable with her? There was no mistaking the connection as Nina stared up at him with adoring blue Landis eyes. He waved her favorite panda-toy teether in front of her face, joggling the beads in the panda's clear belly around in a gumball-like display. Nina loved that toy.

And Phoebe couldn't deny the truth any longer. She'd fallen in love with Kyle.

Ten

He'd never felt so out of control.

An hour after completing their meeting with the judge, Kyle clenched the steering wheel, driving the Mercedes along the dark shoreline with Phoebe beside him. The car seat in the back was empty.

The judge had awarded Bianca one-night-a-week temporary visitation with Nina, starting today. The judge had given them the next month to gather information or work out an agreement before he revisited the case.

Thank God for Sebastian's artful negotiations or things might have played out so much worse. He'd managed to wedge in a provision. Kyle would pay Bianca's expenses and hire a nanny to stay with Bianca and Nina during the twenty-four-hour visitations. At least they had the reassurance the baby would be cared for, and Bianca couldn't skip town with Nina. They'd all stayed at the courthouse until arrangements had been made with the sitter they'd used during their D.C. trip.

He'd done everything possible for now. And still, it didn't quiet the roaring inside him. The sun sank as hard and fast as his gut. What if they still lost Nina? The love he felt for his daughter slammed through him all the more once he had to watch Bianca walk away with his little girl. Seeing the devastated expression on Phoebe's pale face at the loss had only hammered home his failure.

His headlights swept around the next curve, sharper than he'd expected, and he forced himself to slow down. He wouldn't be any good to Nina or Phoebe if he totaled the car. His hands shook so hard he decided to pull off the deserted road until he regained control of the fears broadsiding him.

Kyle guided the sedan onto a secluded parking area sandwiched between dunes with towering sea oats. The wind tore in off the ocean, bits of spray pinging on the windshield.

His hands fisted against his knees, tighter, tighter again as if he could somehow hold back the swelling frustration inside him. Muscles tensed and bunched up his arm until he slammed his fist against the dashboard with a curse.

He welcomed the bolt of pain that shot up his arm. He considered giving the leather a second go...until he saw the tears streaking down Phoebe's face.

Ah, hell. Those tears hurt him far more than if he'd broken his hand. "I'm sorry, Phoebe, so damn sorry."

Sorry for more things than he could even put into words right now. He gathered her against his chest, and she didn't even protest, just sagged against him. A choking sob caught in her throat. She gripped his suit coat until her fingers dug into his shoulders, the same fears and frenzy radiating from her that he felt inside himself. He thumbed away two tears streaking down her cheek, rested his head against her brow, murmuring whatever consoling words he could scavenge out of his own stark arsenal.

Phoebe burrowed closer, turning her face toward his caress, toward him. "Touch me," she whispered, her voice hoarse and agonized, "hold me, make the emptiness go away."

Kyle stilled. She couldn't possibly be suggesting they...

But then she pressed a kiss into his palm, her lips moving against him as she spoke, "I can't stand one more moment thinking about what happened. I need you to give me something else, something wonderful, to think about."

All his frustration gathered force with a purpose—giving Phoebe the distraction, the outlet, even a momentary relief from the pain. He guided her face up to his. Their mouths brushed. *Held.*

Phoebe's fists unfurled from his suit coat and her fingers crawled across his back to clamp him closer. Passion exploded inside him, feeding off all the frustrated emotions that had stockpiled within him since Bianca's out-of-the-blue call. Hell, since Phoebe had shut him down after sex in the airplane.

Kyle slid his hands up to cup her face, to fit their lips more surely against each other, to deepen the kiss and contact and connection. All the frenzy of the day channeled into the moment, seeking an outlet.

He grazed his fingers down her back to cradle her hips, guiding her onto his lap the way he'd fantasized about doing when they'd made out by the shore in the Aston. But, where that night had been about seduction, this moment was about release.

She slid over his legs, her pink-cotton wraparound dress bunching up around her hips. The fabric parted along the side at the wrap, exposing her rose-colored panties. He slipped his fingers along both hips, twisting the silky fabric until the underwear… snapped. He brushed aside the scraps until she pressed against him, moist and hot.

She sprinkled desperate kisses along his mouth, his jaw, nipping and tempting with her tongue and teeth. The last rays of sun faded. The dusk of night sealing them in darkness, heightening his other senses as he inhaled her vanilla scent mixed with the musk of sexy want.

Her panting breath synced up with his. Phoebe tore at his belt, making fast work of his fly and freeing him from his boxers. She stroked him, already throbbing and hard in her hand. The touch of her cool fingers spiked his need. He clenched his teeth, scavenging for bits of his shredded control long enough to fish his wallet from his back pocket. His eyes adjusting to the dark, he plucked out a condom.

She rocked her hips against him, her body bare and welcoming. His jaw flexed, his throat moving in a slow swallow as his lashes went heavy for an instant and he fought the urge to close his eyes.

He tore open the packet. "Wait."

"No patience tonight." She snatched the birth control from his hand.

"I agree."

"Now shh…" She rolled the condom along the length of him, urgently, efficiently.

Phoebe straddled his lap, kneeling over him as she positioned herself. He cupped her buttocks and guided her down on him until they sat together, connected. Cradling her in his palms, he thrust and she writhed and they moved in tandem, knowing each other's bodies and needs better this time.

She squeezed her arms tighter around him, echoing the clasp inside as well that urged him closer and closer to completion as surely as her breathy moans and sighs and demands for *more, harder, faster. Now.*

Wind rolled in off the ocean, carrying salt and sea spray through the vents. Their mating was raw and sweaty and intensely consuming. It went beyond sex. It was different being with Phoebe, and that scared the crap out of him, because if she left, nothing would be the same, nothing would be as good.

Her moans grew louder, louder till the sound of pleasure filled the car. She clawed at his shoulders, anchoring herself deeper as he watched the shadows play across her face, watched her come apart. Her breasts thrust forward with the powerful arch of her spine again and again, her neck exposed in a graceful arch. He felt the damp strength of her release. She contracted around him, massaging him…over…the edge.

His head dropped against the seat rest. He rode the surging release rolling in wave after wave of expanding explosions. He wasn't even sure anymore if the roaring in his ears came from the ocean or his own body.

He combed his fingers through her hair, her face tucked against his neck. They hadn't solved anything out here by the ocean, but at least she wasn't crying anymore.

He dropped his chin to rest against her head.

Damn it all to hell, what a time to understand her powerful connection to her dead husband. Because right now, Kyle knew he would find a way to make her love *him,* no matter how long it took.

Phoebe had to do something, anything.

The pure helplessness of waiting to see Nina home again safe and sound was eating her alive. Sitting cross-legged on her bed, she clicked through the keys on her laptop computer, surfing the Internet for anything she could find on child-custody battles. She needed to arm herself with as much knowledge as possible. Kyle, too, had his laptop out, but he'd set up on the patio outside her suite. Only a few more hours and they would pick up Nina.

Neither of them had strayed far from Nina's room. Did he feel closer to their daughter here, too? She couldn't even hazard a guess. Since they'd made such frantic love in his car, Kyle had completely shut down. He'd spent most of the night working at his computer, even after his family had returned. He'd surprised her when he'd climbed in bed with her at about two in the morning, making slower, more thorough love to her with his body, his mouth, his words, but said nothing about his own needs or pain. But being with him hadn't distracted her from worrying about Nina as much as it had rocked her to the core.

She'd felt Kyle's hurt for his daughter, the raw edge to his lovemaking. That shared connection had dissolved her defenses against him, leaving her open and so much more vulnerable than she'd ever imagined.

Then she'd woken alone. Gazing across the room to the open balcony door, she found him on the porch back at his computer. He'd pulled away again, and she didn't know why. She could understand his frustration over losing full custody of his daughter, fears of the next judge's hearing upsetting Nina's world even more. But his retreat seemed motivated by more than that, since it had only grown deeper after they had made love.

She swung her feet to the floor and padded across to watch him through the open French doors. A light breeze fluttered the whispery curtain and lifted her hair, the air muggy after the night of rain.

What would Kyle do if she walked up behind him and massaged the tension out of those braced shoulders of his? Maybe it was worth the risk to find out. She stepped outside only to pull up short when she saw the deep furrows in his brow. "What's wrong?"

"Take a look at this." He turned his laptop screen toward her, displaying an image of Bianca at a beach party, dancing between two men, an umbrella drink held over her head. "Does that seem like Bianca was working to make a better life for her child? Check out the time stamp."

Less than a week ago.

"There are more. Lots more. And not just drinking, but drugs and even a sex tape that, uh…" He pinched the bridge of his nose, shaking his head. He clicked the drop-down menu to save the latest Internet site, his jaw flexing but his eyes still flat and emotionless. "It appears she didn't spend much time wasting away missing her child."

The crowded party and cabana sure looked like it provided phone service, yet she'd never bothered to call. Phoebe pulled out a chair and sank down beside him. "Why didn't the private investigator find these?"

"Most of them are from the past week. And I have some, uh, skills from my military intel days." His fists clenched on the table, his wedding band glinting in the high-noon sun. "Damn it all, I should have been doing this myself from the start."

"You've been doing everything you could to take care of Nina from the first moment you met her." She slid her hand over his fist. "This is scary stuff. Thank goodness you found it now."

He slipped his hand from under hers and clicked through more computer commands. "I need to do more. Time's running out."

"When do you leave to start your new job?" It seemed he'd already left emotionally now. The fragile common ground they'd just begun to share seemed to be slipping away as surely as the cresting waves pulled sand from the shore.

"I've pushed back all my meetings until we get things settled with Bianca. I meant that time is running out for Nina."

"What if it takes a while to settle the custody issue?" A frightening possibility they both needed to face.

"It won't," he said curtly. "I won't let it."

She touched his wrist, trying again to break through the icy exterior that only cracked during sex. "Some things are beyond even the control of a mighty Landis."

"The great thing about being a Landis is that we're all equally as determined. I have a wealth of support when it comes to being there for Nina."

"When it comes to your daughter, there's no replacement for you."

He turned suddenly-haunted eyes on her. "You think I don't know that? I've already told the family I'm not taking the job heading up Landis International. I have options, and I intend to make the most of them."

She was stunned at this abrupt shift in his life plan. "But surely you can just postpone it. You won't be happy nailed down to one place, you've said so yourself. There has to be a better compromise. Let's talk this out."

"There's nothing to discuss."

She leaned closer, refusing to let him push her

away. She'd fought for Nina and she would fight just as hard for him. "Kyle, damn it, you're the one who keeps preaching to me about not shutting down, about coming back to life."

Something smoked through his eyes and for a moment she thought she might have truly gotten through to him. Then his beautiful blue eyes iced over again.

He shoved his seat away, iron grating across stone tiles. "This isn't about me. We're in the middle of a custody battle. Unless we work together, presenting a unified front in our marriage long-term, we could well lose Nina for good." He closed his laptop and stood. "We should get moving so we're not late picking up Nina."

He left her sitting on the porch alone and confused. As she sat, stunned at the loss of lighthearted Kyle with his bolstering one-sided smiles, his words trickled through, about staying a married couple long-term.

Finally he'd committed to staying together, yet she'd never felt farther apart from him.

Eleven

Sitting in an antique rocker in the living room, Phoebe cradled Nina in her arms even though the baby had gone to sleep at least fifteen minutes ago. She hadn't been able to let her out of her sight since they'd picked her up yesterday. The room was silent but for the rustling of her mother-in-law at the coffee table, pulling Thanksgiving decorations from a plastic storage bin.

Phoebe couldn't help but be warmed by the lack of pretension in such a powerful world figure. Wearing a lightweight orange sweater set—and blue jeans—Ginger Landis Renshaw could have been any other grandmother preparing for the holidays with her family. What would it have been like to have such a woman to turn to after Roger had died? Or when she'd been wrestling with what to do after Bianca had disappeared?

Kyle was sequestered with his brother. Maybe he would find some comfort and reason there since Sebastian would understand the pain after having lost his adopted daughter. Heaven knew Kyle still wasn't listening to her. His emotional retreat from her stung more than she could have ever imagined a few weeks ago. How had she opened herself to so much pain again?

Phoebe rested her cheek against Nina's head and inhaled the sweet scent of baby shampoo, watching her mother-in-law lift out a brass cornucopia. "That's a beautiful piece."

Ginger glanced over her shoulder with a smile before placing the horn of plenty on the mantel. "It belonged to my first husband's grandmother. She loved the holidays. She also gave me the most exquisite family Nativity, a magnificent collector's piece. It's in a museum now, but I had a replica made for my grandchildren to enjoy."

"How lovely to have such long-living traditions in your family." She glanced down at the wedding ring Kyle had placed on her finger, over the spot that had once worn Roger's simpler gold band. "Forgive me if this is too personal, but did your husband—the general—ever have a problem being reminded of your first marriage?"

Ginger turned slowly and leaned back against the cool hearth. "Hank and I have been friends for years, back when we were both married to other people. I helped him with his children after his wife died. He helped me after I lost Benjamin. This love we've found came later and certainly surprised us both, pleasantly so."

"No jealousy then?"

"None. That doesn't mean we got over losing a spouse quickly. When I say it took us a long time to find each other, I mean a very long time. Years. Yet here we are, blending our Nativity scenes and families." She patted Nina's diapered bottom. "I look forward to setting up the crèche with my granddaughter someday."

"Make sure you take pictures, lots and lots of them." In case Phoebe wasn't a part of her day-to-day life anymore. Regardless of Kyle's talk of working together, she didn't have faith in the long-term hope for their relationship.

"I have photos in the album of my boys setting up the Nativity with their grandmother. In fact…" She leaned into the container, sifting through padded ornament holders. "I believe the replica ended up in here with the Thanksgiving decorations."

Ginger straightened, holding a velvet bag in her

hands. "Here we go." She sat on the edge of the sofa and began withdrawing the wrapped pieces. "Matthew and Kyle used to argue every year over where to put the Wise Men. Matthew is such a traditionalist like his father. He wanted them right there in the manger. Kyle, however, pointed out that the Wise Men really didn't show up until two years later, so they should be positioned somewhere outside the manger."

Phoebe rocked Nina, eyeing the trio of porcelain figures and envisioning a young Kyle dreaming of the Wise Men's world travels. The reproduction of the antique crèche still looked vintage, with an Old World style to the rich-hued paints.

Ginger cupped a camel in her hand. "Every year, my little smart-aleck son would cradle those three porcelain antiques and shake his head, saying, 'Two years, for Pete's sake. That makes 'em the three wise slackers, if you ask me.'"

"That certainly sounds like Kyle." At least the Kyle she'd known a week ago. Would Nina have his sense of humor, as well as his smile? Would they see that humor again?

Ginger placed the camel behind the three kings. "He always has joked to cover when he's uncomfortable with emotions. His father being gone so much bothered him deeply, but Kyle always shrugged it off as if it didn't matter."

Could he be shutting down as a different defense

mechanism against uncomfortable—hell, painful—emotions? He was all action, without a doubt, and she'd learned long ago men sometimes overcompensate with actions at the expense of words and feelings. "Kyle turned down the job with Landis International."

Ginger didn't look up, just continued to arrange the figures on the coffee table even though it was weeks too early for Christmas decorations. "I was disappointed to hear that. I take it he seems to think he can't be a good father and travel the way he wants."

"He even hinted that leaving would be the same as what Bianca did." She thought back to the time she'd expressed her fears about attachment disorder and how that must have fueled Kyle's concerns. "Have you ever talked with Kyle about this? Maybe he'll listen to you."

Laughing lightly, her mother-in-law shook her head. "If I've learned anything in all my years parenting and in politics, it's that you can't tell people anything and have them accept it as truth. They have to come to the conclusion on their own."

"But you told *me*."

"You were almost there on your own and you already had all the pieces in place."

Phoebe tried to understand where Ginger was going with her trip down memory lane, but the way she saw it, things looked so damn bleak. "Are you telling me this so I can give up on Kyle?"

Ginger leaned back on the sofa, her blue eyes wise but kind. "I'm helping you so you can show him the pieces he needs to put it together." She gave the camel a final nudge so it lined up alongside the magi. "It may take a while, even a long while, but don't give up. Some people see the pieces differently, but as long as you're both talking about how to work it out, you'll find the answers that are just right for you."

Phoebe looked at the porcelain set resting on the coffee table. She could almost see the four Landis siblings taking turns arranging the figurines, the brothers so alike in looks, but different in many ways now that she knew them better.

And what about her? How would she have displayed the scene? No matter how many times she jostled it around in her head, she couldn't recreate what she'd put together before. Her mind kept envisioning things differently, from the perspective of a mother, with Kyle's quirky, slacker Wise Men off to the side.

Slowly her vision cleared and the image of how her life should be came together again, differently than before, with Roger, but no less wonderful. She wanted a future with Kyle, a unique life together that they built, not some attempt to recreate the past. Something was going on with Kyle, but not for a moment did she believe he didn't care.

The time had come to truly take command of her life and be the wife and partner Kyle deserved.

* * *

Kyle sensed a new determination in Phoebe as they sat around the table in the courthouse mediation room to discuss the first round of custody specifics with Bianca. Kyle had buried himself in paperwork in the hopes that he could make this right.

He'd vowed he would do anything to make Phoebe happy and look toward the future rather than the past. Keeping Nina absolutely topped the list of securing everyone's happiness. After they'd crossed that hurdle, he would do everything in his power to be the best husband and father possible—even if that meant nailing his ass to a desk in Hilton Head.

He just hoped the evidence they'd found about how Bianca had spent the past months would turn the tide in their favor. So much depended on the judge's final verdict, and Sebastian had told him that could swing either way. Still Phoebe sat next to him exuding quiet confidence, her chin high and shoulders square.

Bianca huffed a ragged strand of hair off her brow, thumbing through the stack of documents in front of her. "This is all so complicated and official."

Phoebe leaned closer to Bianca. "You have to understand we only want to keep Nina safe."

"That's what I want, too," Bianca rushed to answer. "I just want to play with her."

Kyle started to reach for the file of damning

photos. Phoebe placed a hand on his arm. "Wait a moment." She leaned on her elbow. "Bianca, do you truly want custody of Nina?"

The confidential tone in her voice was soft. Non-accusatory. And completely caught him off guard. What the hell was she doing? Even ever-stoic Sebastian tensed in the leather seat.

Bianca scratched mascara from the corner of her eye, her gaze darting around nervously. "What kind of mother doesn't want custody? Even you want her and you're not her mom."

"No one here is judging you, Bianca," Phoebe continued with admirable calm. "We all want what's best for Nina and best for all of us, including you. Why not let go of who you think you should be. Be who you are and let's work from there."

Kyle's neck started to itch. Phoebe had said much the same thing to him when he'd told her about turning down the job with Landis International.

Phoebe reached across the table to Nina's biological mother with an openness Kyle didn't think he could have scavenged.

"Bianca," she pressed gently. "What's really going on?"

Bottom lip quivering, Bianca squeezed Phoebe's hand. "You're going to think I'm an awful person. All of you." She looked around the table. "Nina's sweet and I do want to see her. But I want to be an actress. That's all I've ever wanted." She blurted, "I need money."

Sebastian's eyes narrowed.

Anger gelled inside Kyle as what he'd feared and expected played out. "You want a payoff."

Phoebe touched his leg lightly under the mahogany table, patting his knee reassuringly to quiet the storm brewing inside him.

"No, no." Bianca raised both her hands defensively, her long, manicured nails reflecting the halogen bulbs overhead. "I'm not bribing you. I wouldn't do that. I may have flaws, but I would never sell my baby. I just want a decent shot at being an actress. I've got an audition in Bollywood and I can't afford the plane ticket. All I want is a plane ticket."

Bollywood? In India?

Kyle stared at her in shock. She was already making plans to jet? To leave their daughter all over again? But on the plus side, all she wanted was a damn plane ticket. Less than a thousand dollars. If Bianca was interested in bribing them, she would have asked for a hell of a lot more than that.

Bianca twisted her hands in front of her, a blur of fuchsia nails and silver rings. "I realize you're pissed because I didn't tell you about Nina, but I knew if I came to you, you would get all wrapped up in making a family. I mean, God, all you talk about is family,

family, family." She glanced up quickly. "No offense meant to any of you."

Sebastian smiled, one-sided. "None taken."

"Anyway, I didn't know what to do and Phoebe's so smart and logical, I knew she could take care of everything. I'm not like her. I'm not cut out to be a full-time mom, no matter how much I love the little cutie."

Kyle vaguely registered his wife murmuring something about how glad she was to take care of Nina, furthering his sense that Phoebe undoubtedly had Bianca's number.

Had Bianca even somehow set this whole thing up, arranging circumstances so Phoebe would come to him? Kyle couldn't go quite that far, but he could see he had sure sized this up way wrong from the minute Bianca had walked into the Landis home.

Sebastian began speaking with Bianca in his best soft and reasonable lawyer tones, explaining the ins and outs of what it meant to sign away her parental rights. But Kyle was focused on Phoebe, who had somehow seen a way through this tangle and found a way to unknot the threads and restore order. From her quietly outrageous idea to get married, to seeing through Bianca's bad-girl exterior to the more complex—albeit still selfish—person inside.

He hadn't needed to blast forward with his background search on Bianca and level the field in a manner that would set bad blood between them for the rest of Nina's life. What more had he missed from Phoebe with his charge-ahead attitude that apparently kept him from slowing down long enough to pick up on important nuances?

He didn't know yet. But he looked forward to finding out one day at a time. Days and weeks and years of building a life and getting better as he learned more about her.

Starting today by telling his wife the most important detail, a detail his charge-ahead brain had wrongly plowed right over as insignificant. Once he got Phoebe alone, he intended to make sure that she heard, believed and never forgot.

He loved her.

Phoebe closed the door to Nina's nursery, Kyle behind her. She still couldn't believe they'd stumbled on Bianca's real agenda and it had been so easy to address.

Although now that she thought back, it made total sense. If Bianca had been after money, nothing could have stopped her from getting through to the Landis family. They should have realized that from the start. The talk with Ginger had helped her trust her instincts.

Bianca had seen the pieces differently than Phoebe would have ever guessed.

Phoebe leaned on the wraparound balcony, tipping her face into the sea breeze. Kyle pulled up alongside her, his leg pressed against hers intimately.

Where would they go from here? More passionate sex that turned her inside out…only to find herself alone afterward? No, damn it, she'd learned. No more hiding in her dusty academic world. She would fight for herself, for this marriage, as firmly as she'd fought for Nina. Even if it took time.

She turned to face him, leaning an elbow on the railing. "Bianca surprised me today. She grew up. I'm relieved for Nina."

The cool breeze seemed to soothe the hot frustration of the last few weeks, easing the ache inside her. She just wished she could share some of that peace with Kyle.

"We accomplished what we set out to do." His voice wrapped around her with the same warmth it had that first night at his homecoming party.

Was it her imagination, or was there a hint of the old Kyle in his tone? She peered over at his strong profile as he looked out at the water.

"We accomplished it with a solution that's outside the box." Just like she hoped he would find for himself.

Like she hoped he might see for their future.

"You fought for us, for both of us, and I love you for that."

"If we keep thinking outside—" The word stuck

on her tongue as her thoughts rewound and her heart picked up speed. "What did you say?"

That strong, handsome profile of his turned until he looked full-on into her eyes. "I said I love you."

Her jaw went slack. She'd been expecting to dig in for a long haul, work to build a relationship that would lead to love, the way Ginger had found her second chance with her longtime friend. There were still so many pieces left to move.

"Kyle, are you sure? Wait, of course you're sure. You pride yourself on always being honest." Her head began spinning as fast as her heartbeat. "You were right that I was hanging on to the past. I was looking to recreate that, which is impossible. That was a unique love, just as my love for you is unique. By expecting this to be like the past, I almost missed how absolutely awesome the present could be."

Kyle frowned. His hands landed on her shoulders, steadying her. "Wait. Back up a second. Did you just say you love me, too?"

Oh, she had. And why hadn't she thought to say that straight away to him? "Yes." She looped her arms around his neck, the truth of that simple fact shining through. "I am totally and completely in love with you. I know it's only been a few weeks. I'm the one who said things take time."

"I seem to recall you shouted it in the Aston."

That gorgeous, lopsided grin of his returned, making her knees ridiculously weak.

"I did, didn't I?" Ah, but she would need that stubbornness to go toe-to-toe with her hardheaded Landis man. "My point is, I do love you. It came on me differently this time, but I know just as surely that this is real."

"Phoebe? Quiet, my love."

His love? She would never grow tired of hearing that. "Yes?"

"I should have realized sooner what was happening between us. God knows, you've rocked me more in a million ways than anyone has before from the first time I saw you, to the first time I kissed you, made love to you. Something about the way you handled things with Bianca finally got through my thick skull until I could see just how perfect you are, how perfect we can be together. I would be a damn fool if I let you go." His smile dug a dimple in his cheek. "I may have been slow on the uptake, but I'm not an idiot. I love you, Phoebe Landis, and I want to spend the rest of my life with you and our daughter and any other children we decide to add to our family."

"And I want to spend the rest of my life with you."

He tucked her closer against him, their bodies a perfect fit. "We'll start house-hunting here, for a place of our own."

A final problem tugged her with worries about

long-term happiness. "But you love your job, the thrill of international dealings."

He tunneled his fingers into her hair. "I love you and Nina and the life we're going to have together more."

"I don't think I'll ever get tired of hearing that."

She arched up on her toes as he leaned down, his kiss wonderfully familiar and even better every time, as they built on the desire she'd felt the first time his sexy voice had stroked over her. How much more would she have to look forward to in the future?

His hands slid down her sides to loop low around her waist as he kissed along her jaw, his late-day beard a sweet abrasion against her skin. The scent of his aftershave mingled with the salty air, swirling inside her like dreams of their future unfolding. And just that fast an idea took shape inside those possibilities and plans.

Phoebe nestled against his chest, looking out over the ocean. "What if Nina and I traveled with you?"

His muscled arms tensed against her and he didn't answer at first, the waves rolling and receding while his heart thudded steadily under her ear. She stroked the hair at the nape of his neck. "Kyle?"

"I thought you would want the home and hearth here, stability for Nina."

So had she. At first. But she was learning more and more about thinking outside the box as she contemplated blending her life with Kyle's. "*We're* her security. And as you said before, we have options. We can hire an entourage of help so we never have to worry about finding sitters. We can afford to rent an entire house wherever we travel. Think outside the box for us, the way you do in your career."

"Your plan is definitely worth discussion." His face creased into a one-sided smile, his hands sliding intimately low down her waist. "We could always talk about it more on a long drive up the coast, since I decided to keep the Aston."

Possibilities flamed to life inside her, for now and all the years ahead. "Top down?"

She could already imagine the sea spray against her face, Kyle pulling over on a deserted stretch of beach...

"Whatever you want, my love," he promised. "I'll make it happen."

Epilogue

Nine months later

Ocean breeze caressing her bare shoulders, Phoebe draped her arms around Kyle's neck, her fingers toying with the hair at the nape of his neck. He wore it slightly longer now that he was no longer in the air force.

But they led a more spontaneous life overall these days as they traveled the world in his job as head of Landis International. Their latest stop? Lisbon, Portugal. They had renewed their marriage vows this afternoon with all the family gathered around the veranda at their rented waterside villa.

Her frothy off-white wedding dress twining around her legs, she tipped her face into the wind on this side of the Atlantic. "So we're really, *really* married now."

"I sure hope so." His hand slid between them to caress her stomach, which would soon start to swell with the baby they'd made two months ago.

Ashley and Matthew had a daughter now, baby Claire, who adored her older cousin Nina. Ginger and Hank Renshaw's grandparent nursery had just about expanded to a wing of cribs and toddler beds. They'd even added an in-ground baby pool and playground. But then, Ginger had openly admitted she was thrilled to entice her grandbabies over to spend time at Grandma's house whenever possible. Phoebe couldn't help but admire her mother-in-law's efforts when they always made her feel so very welcome.

Phoebe rested her hand on top of Kyle's, over their child growing inside her. "We should retrieve our daughter from her grandparents before they spoil her too rotten."

"It is her bedtime, isn't it?" He slipped his arm around her waist and steered her up the steps leading into the peach-colored stucco villa. Castle ruins nestled scenically on a mountainside in the distance. "I packed a new bedtime storybook for her, one about panda bears."

"She'll love it." Her grandparents weren't the only ones who enjoyed spoiling Nina. "Next time we're in D.C. we'll have to take her to the National Zoo to see the giant pandas."

Phoebe found she enjoyed traveling with Kyle, and realized it wasn't a sacrifice after all with unlimited accommodations and a nanny. She continued to teach a class online, the perfect flexible career for a wife and mother on the go around the world. She was finally *seeing* the historical sites she taught her students about.

And she wasn't the only one enjoying her career. Bianca had actually struck it big as an actress after all—in Bollywood. She was totally enjoying her big-screen family in India. The Bollywood film industry had increased English-speaking productions and the viewers loved her. And of course Bianca loved being loved.

The money wasn't too shabby, either.

From all indications, she was very happy being a long-distance mother. She hadn't uttered a peep about the child-custody agreement and didn't even ask to see Nina half as much as she was allotted. They'd never even needed to roll out the incriminating images of Bianca, although they'd made sure she knew they had them. Since the nanny stayed with Nina during the few times Bianca came to the States to see her daughter, they knew the little girl was safe.

Nina seemed to see Bianca as more of an indulgent aunt who sent lavish gifts but rarely made an appearance. With that first sweet word, "Ma-Ma," uttered just for Phoebe, Nina had made it clear who she viewed in that role.

Phoebe paused in the wide-open double doors leading into the villa, inviting a cross-breeze. She turned her new ring around and around on her finger, the diamond-and-sapphire ring nestled alongside her diamond-studded band. "Do you know what I'm looking forward to most today?"

"What would that be?" He skimmed her loose hair back from her face, his gold band glinting in the setting sun. "I'll do my best to make it happen even better than planned."

She tucked against him suggestively, already envisioning exactly how all the pieces would go together once they were behind closed doors. "I can't wait for our wedding night. This time, we'll be celebrating on the same day that we said the vows."

"Now, that wish—" he smiled, dipping to graze a kiss at the corner of her mouth "—will be my absolute pleasure to fulfill again…and again."

* * * * *

every spare minute baking cakes and had built up a steady bank of customers in the local area who came to her for wedding and celebration cakes. After Swindon, she'd stayed with Gabriel in Bath before getting her own place and starting her business. It hadn't been a difficult decision to not return to Gloucestershire. Staying away had always been the better choice than going home. Oh, she'd kept in touch of course, but only the bare minimum. A phone call now and then, cards occasionally. Any guilt she might have felt at leaving was assuaged by the fact her father had never once made any proper attempt to contact her himself and make things right. He'd let her know when he'd changed address but he never bothered with birthday or Christmas cards. She'd sometimes wondered if the change of address notices were so the authorities would know who to notify when he eventually drank himself to death. The gap between them had grown over the years until now here they stood, virtual strangers.

'Must be a reason for you to visit,' he said. 'All this time. Why now?'

He could still read her like an open book, she realised. She'd never been able to keep secrets from him. Goosebumps prickled on her arms. He made no move to invite her in and she was glad.

'I'm thinking of getting married,' she blurted out suddenly, before she even knew what she was going to say.

He nodded slowly, holding her gaze the entire time with the sharp eyes, green just like her own, and a sarcastic grin spread across his face. 'You want my blessing?' He gave a dry chuckle.

She took a nervous step backwards. 'No,' she said. 'I don't need your blessing. I just…' She paused and looked at him closely. The grin was gone. The face was lined and old; tiny broken vessels from the heavy drinking reddened his nose and cheeks. The man was a shell of the person he once was. She realised her overwhelming feeling at that moment was pity for him. He certainly couldn't hurt her or scare her any more. 'I just thought you should know,' she finished.

His face softened almost imperceptibly and he nodded. 'I'm pleased for you.' His voice sounded gruff and he rummaged in his shirt pocket with his fingers. Removing his cigarettes, he lit one and, leaning against the door jamb, squinted at her through the smoke. 'What's he like, then, our Lucinda? Is he good enough for you?'

She felt the back of her throat tingle suddenly and tears pricked at her eyes. Despite all that had happened he was still her father. And however he felt about her, however many years had gone by, he'd cared enough to ask. She swallowed hard to make the tears go away.

'Yes, Dad, he's a good man. He makes me happy,' she managed.

He drew hard on his cigarette and nodded firmly. 'You hang onto him, then. Tell him your old man says he'd better look out for you.'

She smiled suddenly at him and a smile touched his lips in return. She was glad she'd come after all. For the first time she felt she had control over a conversation with him. What could he say or do now that would hurt her? She was an adult now, not a scared kid any more. She had her own life, with no need of him in it. The balance of power had shifted while she'd been away and she could choose the terms on which she let him back in, if she did at all.

'How are you, Dad?' she ventured, more confidently. 'How's work?'

'I get by.' He shifted a little awkwardly. 'I'd invite you in, but I only rent a room here. It's difficult…'

She didn't mind. A few minutes was quite enough for today anyway. She had plenty to think about. It had been a big enough step just coming here and speaking to him.

'Maybe next time. I have to get a move on anyway.' She nodded towards the taxi waiting on the opposite side of the road. 'It's only a flying visit.'

He sighed and nodded. 'It's good to see you, Lucinda.' The green eyes were serious this time and she held his gaze. He seemed weaker, somehow. Smaller. The terrifying presence she remembered so vividly from her childhood was gone.

'You, too, Dad. I'll be in touch.' She smiled at him one more time and then made a move towards the taxi. Halfway across the road he called to her and she turned back.

'You couldn't lend me some money, could you, love?'

Exasperated, she walked back towards him, rummaging in her bag for her purse. And it was then that it dawned on her that he hadn't really changed at all. He hadn't moved on. She had.

Gabriel parked the Aston Martin in the square opposite Lucy's bakery and got out. Darkness was falling quickly and the streetlamps were already on, casting a golden glow. Standing hesitantly by the car, he questioned himself for a moment. So she hadn't rung him back since they'd argued—so what? But then when he'd eventually become impatient enough to call Ed, he'd mentioned in passing that she'd gone to Birmingham to visit someone. That had rung alarm bells with Gabriel, although he was initially unable to put his finger on the reason why. Then eventually it had come to him.

Lucy at the dinner table with his parents. 'My father's in Birmingham. A friend offered him a job...'

How well he knew her. Almost well enough to have a stab at reading her thoughts? Perhaps she was still just angry with him and wanted space. Or perhaps she'd been to see her father.

Locking the car, he strode decisively across the square. The shop, with its sign 'Have Your Cake...' depicted retro style in icing-sugar pink on a pistachio green backdrop, was closed, just as he would have expected at this time of day. But he knew her better than anyone.

A couple of passers-by glanced curiously at the tall man pressing his hands against the cold glass of the cake shop window. Gabriel was oblivious to them. Shading his eyes, he could see nothing but the faint outline of the empty display cabinets and the counter. Then, as his eyes became accustomed to the dark, there at the back he saw a chink of light around the door that led to the back of the premises. To the kitchen, where the big ovens were, and the worktops where the cakes and pastries were made. He was right. She was here.

Feeling triumphant at how well he knew her, he left the shop front and felt his way down the narrow alley at the side to the back entrance, his fingertips trailing along the rough sandpapery bricks as he felt his way along in the semi-darkness. Light streamed from the window at the back of the shop and he saw her rusty old Mini car parked up tightly against the wall.

Trying the door, he was surprised when it opened easily, immediately assaulting his senses with the warm delicious smell of baking. He felt a burst of exasperation that she'd left the door unlocked. How many times had he harped on about personal safety to her?

'Lucy!' he shouted as he walked in, so as not to alarm her. There was no reply, so he continued along the short passageway to the kitchen, and then, rounding the corner, he took a deep breath as he saw her.

Her unruly hair was caught up roughly out of her face with a pencil stuck through it; a smudge of flour crossed her cheek. She was adding drops of a bright green liquid to a huge billowing white mound of something cake-looking on the counter in front of her. Her face was paler than ever, no sign of any colour on the high cheekbones. There were dark smudges beneath her eyes. But he didn't miss the fact that her mouth had a determined set to it.

'Lucy,' he said again, loudly enough that she couldn't fail to hear him. There were batches of cakes and pastries on every surface. God knew how long she'd been here.

'I'm busy.' She didn't even bother to look up, simply whisking the green liquid into the white gloop, watching it streak.

He grimaced involuntarily. 'What the hell is that?'

'A bit like a meringue,' she said, looking at it apprais-

ingly. And then, glancing up at him, 'I'm experiment-
ing with some funky macaroons.'

'Looks like you've liquidised a frog.'

A second glance up at him. And the faint glimmer
of a smile touched the corners of her mouth. His heart
twisted as he noticed how tired she looked. He ached to
just grab her and sweep her into a hug and he clenched
his fists in a supreme effort to stop himself doing just
that. He needed to talk to her first. To apologise. To
make it right.

'Lucy, I'm sorry,' he said. When she didn't look up,
he walked over to her. Putting an arm around her, he
firmly removed the spatula from her hand and cast it
onto the worktop next to the ghastly blob of green stuff.
She still didn't speak but she made no move to stop him
as he propelled her over to a chair. Pushing her to sit
down, he knelt down in front of her and took both of
her cold hands in his. They were sticky from the cake
mixture.

He looked deeply into her clear green eyes. 'I had
no right to talk to you like that about your parents.' He
searched her face for some response. 'After everything
they put you through, I don't know what I was thinking.' She simply looked at him as he squeezed her hands.
'Lucy, I'm so sorry.'

'How did you know I'd be here?' she asked, after a
moment.

He smiled gently at her. 'Because I know *you,* Lu.
Almost as well as you know yourself. Remember when
there was that hitch when you were setting up the shop
lease? And that time you crashed your car? You trashed
my kitchen and cooked for England. When normal peo-

ple need time to think they go for a drive, or maybe a walk. You cook. You had to be somewhere with an oven. I tried your flat. I just narrowed it down.'

A wry smile.

'So am I forgiven?' He looked at her hopefully.

She smiled at him properly this time and he felt a surge of relief that made his head swim. 'You are forgiven,' she said. 'But only on condition that you quit stepping outside your remit. I asked you for a few pointers on how to propose. I didn't expect you to try and counsel me about my past like some agony aunt. Agreed?'

He could hear the tiredness in her voice but she sounded absolutely resolute. He was prepared to accept anything at this moment in order to make it all right.

'Agreed,' he said, thankfully. Standing up, he hooked another chair from the corner of the room with one foot and pulled it over, sitting down next to her.

She loosened her unruly curls and caught them back up, forcing the pencil more securely through them. 'Anyway, things didn't turn out so badly after all,' she told him, without meeting his eyes. 'I took your advice and went to see my dad.' And without waiting for any further response from him she stood up and went back to the worktop, picking up the spatula and scooping a blob of the green macaroon mixture onto some baking paper.

'Oh?' He didn't dare venture any comment for fear of saying the wrong thing. She'd only just forgiven his behaviour and there was no way he intended to risk another argument.

She glanced briefly around at him. 'I know,' she said.

'I can't believe it, either. I'm really proud of myself. I was so angry with you for suggesting I let them back into my life. You had no right. But the trouble was, once you'd said it I couldn't stop thinking about it. It drove me mad, until I just had to go and see him to find out how I really feel.'

'And how do you really feel?' He wasn't sure he really wanted to know the answer to that.

'Well, I'm not scared of him any more.' She put the spatula down and turned to face him, leaning back against the worktop. 'You should see him, Gabe. He's just a sad old man now. His drinking doesn't look any better but he seems to be holding down a job, so it can't be that terrible, can it? I feel like maybe I could have a relationship with him now on my own terms. I have my own life now and I can choose how much of a part he plays in that. I'm totally in control.' She smiled at him and his heart felt as if it would liquefy at the relief he saw in her face. 'It's a good feeling. I've been putting him out of my mind for so long. It's so lovely not to have to do that any more.'

It was no good. He had to ask the question that bothered him the most. 'And how's things with Ed?' He kept his voice as neutral as he could, betraying no feelings.

The oven alarm sounded suddenly and they both jumped. Lucy broke their eye contact to cross the room and remove some cupcakes. With her back to him she was mercifully unable to see the agony that crossed Gabriel's face as she said, 'Good, thanks. If anything this has made me more certain than ever.' She put the cakes down on a cooling rack and turned back to him, removing the oven gloves from her hands.

'Really? You're going ahead with the proposal?' His heart felt like lead in his chest. As if someone had wrung it suddenly, or maybe stamped on it.

'Yes.' She took a skewer from the counter and stabbed it into one of the cupcakes. 'You've done me a favour, Gabe. If I wasn't sure before I damn well am now. I can't change my past but I *can* shape my future. What I have with Ed is based on the most important things. All the things that were missing for my parents, why their relationship was such a train wreck. Ed and I don't compare with what they were. I can make my own family now and I know I'll get it right.'

Gabriel's heart constricted in his chest. He forced himself to smile at her. 'Great. That's great. I'm sure it will all be fine.'

She looked really happy. Tired but determined. And she'd been through so much. He dug his nails into his palms so hard that they left a mark. *Because of your selfish desire to keep her to yourself you've put her through hell this last week. Well, no more.* As he stood there in that moment he hated himself more than he'd ever hated anyone. He, who was supposed to care about her, not caring how much he hurt her as long as the outcome was what he wanted. He now admitted to himself that he loved her. That he'd loved her for years. It was pointless denying it. Too late to tell her now and it served him right. How could he turn her life upside down again when she was so happy and settled?

He made a decision on the spot. He would back right off. And with good grace this time. No petulant outbursts like the one he'd had in Smith's. She would get married to Ed. Live a long and happy life with her kids and her business. And he would stick with the role of friend. Embrace it and be grateful for it. This week he'd proved to himself that he was barely worthy of that.

She was moving the cupcakes onto a rack now, her attention totally taken up with them. He needed to get out of here.

'I'll get going now, Lu. I can see you're busy.' He walked steadily across the room and leaned over her shoulder to kiss her cheek. Closing his eyes, he breathed in the scent of her. She smelled sweet, like vanilla, and he felt his body respond instantly, involuntarily. He clenched his fists tightly and stepped away immediately as if burned. She was so engrossed in what she was doing that she didn't even notice.

'OK,' she said without looking up. 'I'll see you tomorrow, then. What time are you picking me up?'

He floundered momentarily. What the hell was she talking about? And then he remembered. His work dinner. That would be some kind of torture now. But maybe he could use it as an opportunity to work on their friendship. Set some new boundaries that might help him to let go of the image of her as something more than a friend. As his lover. Find a way to help him carry on as just her friend.

'I'll pick you up at seven,' he called over his shoulder on the way out. He didn't wait for an answer.

CHAPTER SEVEN

LUCY looked appraisingly at her reflection in the mirror. She couldn't remember the last time she'd worn a cocktail dress. College ball, maybe? Even then she didn't think she'd ever worn anything as lovely as this. Following the success of the personal shopping session, she'd picked a dress outside the scope of what she would normally wear. It was a simple sheath of black silk, ankle length and bias cut so it skimmed her body in all the right places, giving the impression of curves for once despite the fact she hardly had any. The spaghetti straps showed off the creamy skin of her shoulders and the back was daringly low cut. She had bought a soft black wrap to go with it. The whole outfit had cost more than she could remember spending on one shopping trip, ever. But she'd done her best to ignore her frugal instincts. Gabriel would be proud of her progress, she thought. With a lot of work and plenty of hair products she'd even managed to tame her curls for once. She'd pinned the front sections back and the bulk of her hair cascaded over her bare shoulders and down her back. A few tendrils escaped, framing her face.

A normal night out for her was a meal down at the local pub with Ed, for which she barely made the effort to wash the flour out of her hair. She sprayed perfume in a cloud and walked into it, the way the magazines said you should. She had to admit that she was enjoying the evening so far. It was lovely to get dressed up for a change.

She wouldn't let herself think about Gabriel in any other way than as a friend. That had all been some minor head rush, cold feet about settling down, nothing more. The argument about her parents had made it easier to ignore those feelings; she had been so angry with him. She refused to think about the way her heart had raced at the bakery yesterday when Gabriel had apologised and had looked into her eyes and held her hands. Furious anger with him followed by the misplaced heart-thumping desire that she'd spent the last days fighting. Two extremes.

Does Ed ever make you feel that intense? her mind whispered suddenly, and she suppressed the thought. Tonight would be a good opportunity to get her friendship with Gabriel back on track after their argument. And then tomorrow night she was going to take her life in her hands and propose to Ed. It was all going to turn out perfectly. She closed her eyes briefly. So why did she feel more excited, more on edge, more *alive* about tonight than she did about tomorrow?

She stepped into the black high heels. Instantly the hang of the dress was perfected and the girl in the mirror had a proper womanly figure for a change instead of her usual look of an orphan who could do with feeding up. A dab of lip gloss and she was ready. She checked the clock. It was almost seven. She decided to wait through Gabriel's customary late half-hour downstairs. She could put the TV on and take her mind off her nerves bubbling in her stomach.

For once she actually thought he had outdone himself. Just five minutes had passed before the buzzer sounded, and she pressed the button to open the door and then returned to the sitting room to search for her handbag. She heard the door slam and then footsteps entered the room. She dropped lip gloss and keys into her bag without looking up.

'Pretty much on time—makes a change,' she joked, and then turned around with a grin to see not Gabriel, but Ed, dressed in jeans and a T-shirt.

He let out a low whistle. 'Wow.'

She smiled at him uncertainly. 'I wasn't expecting you.'

'I know. I just thought I'd pop in on the way to the pub.' He was looking at her as if he'd never seen her before.

'Do I look OK?' She turned this way and that, trying to appraise the hang of the dress. She felt a little shy, even with Ed, simply because it was so far removed from anything she normally wore. The heels were three inches, so for once she almost matched Ed for height. Gabe was taller than Ed and so would still tower above her, of course, but she was used to that.

'You look stunning,' he said. 'Shame it's going to be wasted on Gabriel.' He looked her up and down. 'Still...' he walked over to her and ran a finger down her bare back '...I could make up for it now.'

She wriggled away before she could think about how that would look. 'Not now, Ed. It's taken for ever to make my hair look like something other than a bird's nest. The last thing I need is to roll around on the sofa.'

Ed retreated across the room as if stung, and guilt stabbed at her as she caught his hurt expression.

'I'm sorry,' she gabbled. 'I'm just nervous, I suppose. Not used to parties like this, and I won't know anyone apart from Gabe.' She gave a little laugh and walked back towards him, intending to compensate for giving him the brush off. But Ed was having none of it.

He pushed her away roughly as she tried to put her arms around his neck. 'If I didn't know better I'd think there was something going on between the two of you. First you start dressing differently and spending more time with him, and now you're done up like a dog's dinner as his escort and you give me the cold shoulder. When the hell do you dress like this for me? That's what I'd like to know.'

Not this, not now. Jittery enough already at the prospect of the evening ahead, she had to take deep breaths to keep herself calm.

'You're not being fair,' she protested. 'Yes, I've changed my clothes a bit, but only because I thought I was looking a bit tired and boring. And you've got a cheek criticising me for seeing Gabe. You've been out with your mates four times this week.' She turned on her heel and left the room, angry and upset. She hated arguments like this. It transported her back to her childhood when she used to sit on the top stair and listen to the raised voices below. She tried her best to always solve problems calmly, whoever she was talking to, but she had to admit that sometimes she didn't find it easy. She had quite a quick temper and it didn't always behave the way she would have liked it to.

'There's an important distinction though, Lucy,' he shouted after her. 'My mates are all men!'

He stormed after her and caught up with her in the kitchen. 'What would you think if I took a woman out for the evening to a work party? I think I've been more than understanding under the circumstances.' He pointed an emphatic finger at her as she turned to face him. 'In fact I think I've been an absolute saint. And it's gone on long enough. You're not going tonight. I forbid it. So you might as well go and get that dress off and put some jeans on.' He had the air of someone who expected his bidding to be done without question.

Lucy felt any control she retained over her anger disappear and she let fly with full force. 'Don't you dare tell me what to do! This has nothing to do with me having a relationship with Gabe. I'm doing a favour for a friend and that's all. It has *everything* to do with your lazy approach to everything about you and me. When do I dress like this for you? When the hell do you take me anywhere that has a dress code other than jeans?' She opened her clutch bag and pawed through its contents in search of her house keys. She would find them and wait outside. Gabriel would be picking her up at any moment and she didn't want him to wander inadvertently into World War Three. Ed could let himself out.

She found the keys as he snarled his answer.

'If you weren't so damn tired from working God-knows-what hours then maybe we'd have a bit more of a social life. But you're the one who can't leave that damn bakery alone for five minutes. And when I ask you to show a bit of interest in *my* business, put some investment my way, there's zero interest. Zilch.'

A horn sounded outside. She couldn't have timed it better herself. Maybe she and Gabe had some psychic link that enabled him to read her mind.

'I can't do this now,' she said. 'I'm going out.' She walked carefully down the hall towards the front door, deliberately placing one foot in front of the other in the unfamiliar high heels. They clicked against the wooden floor.

'Get back here. You're not going anywhere!'

She ignored Ed's shout but as she slammed the door behind her she couldn't stop the tears beginning to burn at the back of her throat. The night was cloudy and she could feel the threat of rain. It perfectly matched the way she felt. She ran without looking back down the steps to the silver Aston Martin and climbed in. Only then did she look back. Only then did she realise that she'd absolutely expected Ed to run after her out of the house. The door remained closed. He hadn't bothered. She wondered for a moment how she felt about that, what it might say about Ed's feelings for her. She didn't like the thought that right now they seemed to be growing apart instead of closer.

'Are you OK?' Gabriel looked like James Bond in his perfectly cut dinner suit. His eyes looked deeper blue-grey than ever against the black jacket combined with his dark hair. His face was full of nothing but concern for her.

'Just drive,' she said. She pulled the visor down in front of her so she could use the mirror. Fishing in her clutch bag for a tissue, she used a corner of it to carefully mop her eyes without smearing the eye make-up that had taken the best part of half an hour to get right. All these small deliberate movements helped her to get her temper back under control. Gabriel did exactly as she asked and as the car purred smoothly away he didn't speak to her for several minutes. Some unobtrusive and soothing classical music drifted from the car stereo. She found herself marvelling at the way he knew exactly the behaviour she needed from him. Not a huge inquest into whether she was OK or not, or twenty questions about why she was upset. Just a calm background, which allowed her to gather her thoughts and fight the tears back into submission. Again she found him instinctively knowing how to act with her in a way Ed never did.

She used the peace to gather her thoughts about Ed. There was a part of her that was a tiny bit pleased by his angry possessiveness, Neanderthal as it was. The idea that she'd been able to make a few changes and make him take stock of what he had. If nothing else his jealousy, the fact he was so aware of the change in her appearance, showed that his regard for her was clear. She watched Gabriel wistfully, fighting the pang of regret that she had never been able to provoke such a reaction in him. He hadn't even bothered to stay until the end of her styling session. If only it were Gabe feeling jealous, but he barely seemed to acknowledge that she was female half the time. She felt a rush of shame at how these thoughts betrayed Ed. She wanted things with Ed to work the way they always had, not be thrown into disarray like this.

Only when Gabriel glanced across and could see she was calm did he venture any comment. 'Ed still alive?'

She gave a bitter laugh and he smiled his gorgeous lopsided smile at her. He'd always teased her about her temper when they were kids, describing it as a hurricane, against her indignant protestations.

'How do you know this is about Ed?'

'Well, I think the whole street probably heard you slam that front door,' he said. 'In fact I'm surprised the building is still standing.' When she didn't laugh this time he looked briefly across at her again. 'Are you OK, Lu?' He took his hand from the steering wheel and placed it over hers. She felt a sparkling rush of electricity start in her wrists and spread slowly up her arms. The softness in his voice made the tears threaten again and she swallowed hard. *Keep it together, Lucy.*

'Do you want to talk about it?' he ventured, concern obvious in his voice.

She shook her head vigorously. 'It's just a stupid row.' Her voice sounded thick through her stuffy nose.

Why does my heart leap like this when he touches me? Why him and not Ed? She didn't want this. Her future with Ed meant so much to her and she wanted to feel passion for him, not Gabriel or anyone else. She wished she could force her body to react to Ed in the way it did to Gabriel, tingling at his touch and melting when he looked at her in a certain way, but it seemed mind control only went so far and her body was working to its own subconscious agenda.

Maybe she should drop this whole proposal thing. All this upheaval had only begun when she started planning it all out. Her heart sank miserably at the thought.

She'd spent so long wanting her happy family it made her throat tighten to think of giving it up. But she wasn't sure she could ignore the growing feeling that she'd be settling for Ed when he just didn't inspire the passion in her that she knew she felt for Gabriel. Was settling for someone really good enough? For Ed or for her?

'Let's just forget about it and concentrate on tonight,' Gabriel said. 'This isn't a social evening, you know, it's practically a career move. Get this wrong and it could set back my senior partnership prospects by a good few years. It's vital to look and play the part in the right way.'

She shook her head at him, exasperated. 'Don't you think you're taking the whole thing a bit seriously? Surely your bosses wouldn't make a business decision based on who you roll up with at some work function.'

'They might,' he said, glancing across at her. 'Sleeping with work colleagues isn't seen as best practice in current legal circles.'

'Well, why do it, then?'

He shrugged. 'It always seems like a good idea at the time. And it's never meant to be anything serious.'

She was relieved to be talking about him rather than dwelling on her own problems.

'That's where you're going wrong. You obviously don't understand women.' She pointed at him with an emphatic finger. 'If a woman sleeps with you, it's an emotional investment, Gabriel. Most women would follow that up by wondering how your surname would sound after their first name.' She got out her lip gloss and, looking in the visor mirror again, reapplied it before adding, 'And you wonder why they get fed up when you ditch them after a month.'

He grinned. 'Actually I found that a month was a bit long. They tend to be far more accepting if you only see them for three weeks max.'

'You're such a pain.' She looked at him wearily.

'You like me that way, though. You'd hate it if I never annoyed you.' He winked quickly across at her before turning his attention back to the road.

She smiled down at her hands. He was right. His lunacy was just what she needed to cheer her up.

When Gabriel parked the car he opened the door for her, and when she stood up next to him her new heels meant the difference in their height was much more balanced than it usually was. She was used to feeling tiny next to him but now she only had to tip her chin up slightly to look at him properly. She was sharply aware of his hand resting in the small of her back as they walked towards the entrance. The dinner was being held in an exclusive hotel in the city centre and she couldn't hide a delighted little gasp as they walked through the huge double doors into the ballroom. The room had typically lovely ornate high ceilings, like so many of the beautiful Georgian buildings in Bath. It was dimly lit and large circular tables framed a gleaming parquet dance floor. The tables were set with impeccable white china and linen and silver cutlery twinkled beside crystal wine goblets in the candlelight. A jazz band was playing background music at one end of the room, something mellow with a lot of piano, and later there would be dancing. Lucy couldn't remember having been in a room that looked lovelier.

Gabriel took two flutes of champagne from the silver tray of a passing waiter and handed one to her.

'Thanks.' She took a sip and surveyed the room. The men looked wonderful in dinner dress but it was the women who really caught her attention. There were dresses in every colour imaginable. She looked down at herself briefly, and wished for a moment that she hadn't chosen black. How predictable. Much as she'd loved her dress, it now felt drab.

As if he could read her mind Gabriel leaned in and whispered in her ear, 'You look beautiful, by the way. I didn't get the chance to tell you in the car.' She felt his breath against her neck and it made her feel suddenly light-headed. A warm tingling sensation made its way slowly down her body. Her legs felt unsteady. She took another, larger, sip of the champagne. What on earth would Gabriel think if he knew she was having to mentally squash the thought of what his hands might feel like if he touched her like a lover instead of a friend? Her face felt overly warm and she was glad the room was dark. She hoped it would hide her blushes.

Gabriel was smiling and nodding as they walked through the room. 'Must introduce you to a few people,' he said. Sliding an arm around her waist, he propelled her further into the room. She was more aware of his hand against her than of anything else going on, as if her senses had been realigned. The music passed her by. The people were irrelevant.

Gabriel was quite proud of the way he was holding it together. Even after an hour in her company he still couldn't believe how stunning Lucy looked in the silk dress. The fabric clung to her so that he almost felt he could see the contours of her body through it. And the heels made her legs seem to go on for ever. He was actually grateful for the diversion provided by her argument with Ed, much as he hated seeing her upset. At least it meant she hadn't noticed that he was struggling to keep calm while his heart was thundering in his chest. He'd kept his eyes firmly on the road for the best part of the journey, giving him a chance to get himself under control. *Just friends,* he kept telling himself. Perhaps if he repeated that mantra throughout the evening he would be OK.

Their table turned out to be one of the ones close to the jazz band and Lucy was secretly pleased. It gave her somewhere other to look than at Gabriel. It seemed she couldn't trust her body to behave itself and so she would have to rely on external diversions to get through the evening without making a fool of herself. Gabriel would surely think it hilarious if he knew she was suddenly finding him attractive. She tried hard to keep her mind on Ed. Loyal Ed, who'd always been enough for her before. He was obviously feeling very insecure in their relationship and she hated herself for stirring up feelings like that. In fact he probably had every reason to jump to the wrong conclusion about her and Gabriel after the clothes thing, and the fact Gabriel had been around so much in the last couple of weeks. Everything he'd said to her at her flat had been rooted in the truth.

Really, Lucy? Is it really such a wrong conclusion? She felt cheated that she didn't seem able to get that depth of connection with Ed that she had with Gabe.

She would be mad to still consider marriage when she had these doubts. Why press ahead when her head was being turned like this? *Because these feelings for Gabriel aren't real, Lucy. No good can come of them.* Ed was real. In the car Gabriel was just so perfect after Ed's outburst at the flat, knowing exactly how to behave as if he could read her mind. He affected her in so many ways that Ed didn't. But things with Ed were surely too good to throw away on something that could never be. She was so confused.

The evening wore on. The food was delicious. A warm duck salad starter, followed by the most impeccably cooked steak in a delicious sauce. Lucy found she had little appetite, though, and when she looked at Gabriel's plate she could see he'd barely touched his food, too.

As coffee was finally being served people began to disperse around the room after sitting at the tables for the duration of the meal. Lucy felt nervous butterflies rise a little in her stomach. It had been easy while the food was served. Each circular table seated ten people and the conversation had flowed freely between them. There was no real opportunity for a private conversation. Gabriel had networked furiously and she was beginning to see why he was such a success at work. The couple sitting on the other side of him were looking for new legal representation and by the end of the final course he had them well and truly in the palm of his hand. She couldn't fail to be impressed. His work was a world away from hers.

Eventually there were just four people left at their table. Another couple on the opposite side were talking quietly and Gabriel turned to Lucy. She picked up her water glass to keep her hand steady, and took a few sips. The champagne had made her feel light-headed and the last thing she wanted was to get drunk.

'You haven't asked me once about Ed,' she said. Talking about Ed would keep her mind where it ought to be.

'I know,' he said. 'But when we last discussed Ed you asked me to stop meddling. I thought I'd overstepped the mark a bit on that one.' He took a sip from his own glass and looked at her over the rim. 'Still going ahead with the proposal, then?' He raised a questioning eyebrow.

She looked at him. 'I know we argued before I left the flat, but it was my fault really. Everyone argues sometimes in a normal healthy relationship.'

He nodded, non-committally.

His silence made her feel compelled to press on. 'Ed is feeling a bit unsettled with me at the moment. I don't think he's sure of where he stands any more.' She looked at Gabriel and shrugged. 'I can't really blame him, can I? Suddenly I start dressing differently. I start hanging out with you more. He thinks there's something going on between us.' She let out a little laugh.

'Would that be so funny?' Gabriel asked. He was smiling, too, but his gaze was very intense. She felt unable to tear her eyes away from his.

'No...yes...of course not.' She struggled to say what she meant without offending him or giving her feelings away. 'I just meant it was a mad conclusion to jump to, that's all. Mad for you and me, I mean. To him it seems a logical explanation.'

Gabriel looked at her a moment longer, then shifted

his gaze over her shoulder towards the band, who were preparing to raise the noise level of the mellow background music they'd played during dinner.

Lucy took a deep breath and tried to direct the conversation at Gabriel, to take the spotlight away from her. She hadn't talked to him about relationships since the night she'd mentioned Alison. 'Did you think any more about settling down yourself, Gabe?' she asked. 'Looking for Miss Right? You can't carry on for ever, you know, the eternal bachelor. One day you'll meet the right person. Settle down, have kids…'

A shadow crossed his face and he still didn't look at her, watching the band playing behind her. 'Maybe I already have met her,' he said, eventually. Then he stood up purposefully. 'Come on. You can't come to a ball and not dance.' He held out his hand.

'You know I can't dance, Gabriel,' she protested. 'Two left feet, that's me.'

'Rubbish! Just hang on and follow me. No one here really knows what they're doing anyway.'

After a moment she smiled and gave in. It was dark after all. She'd had a few drinks and the band were playing 'Moon River'. The perfect tempo for someone like her. All you needed to do was sway a bit and you were there. She took his hand and let him lead her as he picked their way through the couples on the floor. She caught her breath as he slid one arm firmly around her waist and entwined her hand in his.

She picked the conversation back up where they'd left it. After the night when they'd looked after Steven, she knew now he wouldn't bite her head off if she mentioned his past. 'You can't carry on letting what happened with Alison affect you for the rest of your days, Gabe.' He was holding her hand tightly but she still managed to free a finger and point it at him. 'I should know that better than anyone after the last week or so. Who'd have thought I could see a future with my parents back in it? I know it's hard but sometimes you have to let go of the past and move on. For years I thought I had moved on but it turned out I was dragging all that baggage along with me. Ignoring it instead of really sorting it out. I'm actually lighter now. I really am.'

For a moment Gabriel said nothing, and without talk to distract her she became acutely aware of how close he was to her. She could feel the hard muscles of his thighs, strong from all that rugby in his youth and from the gym now, hard against her own through the thin silk of the dress. He let go of her hand and moved it around her to join the other one, pulling her even tighter to him. She rested her hand against his chest, acutely aware of the breadth of his shoulders, the strength of his arms encircling her. His breath was warm against her hair as he spoke.

'When I said I'd already met her, I wasn't talking about Alison,' he said.

He pulled back from her far enough so he could look clearly and deliberately into her face. The words, the way he'd spoken them, full of meaning, resonated in her mind. She felt as if the moment lasted minutes, not seconds. Every nerve ending in her body was totally aware and fine tuned. Every touch of his body against hers sent dizzying sparks to her stomach, her heart, her mind. The touch of his fingers lightly stroked her bare spine, the other hand folded tightly around her waist so as to hold her close against him. His aftershave, woody and spicy, filled her senses and she felt literally weak at the knees, as if she might suddenly fold into a puddle on the floor.

'Gabe…' she tried to say. She wasn't sure herself what words she would follow his name with. His name filled her mind leaving no room for anything else. He leaned slowly forward and his mouth perfectly caught the curve of hers. His grip tightened on her as if he wanted never to let her go. The music filled the room but the band could have been playing anything or nothing at all. She took none of it in. There was nothing but the feel, the smell, the touch, the taste of him. There could have been a million people in the room, but for her there was no one else but them. Nothing else but this kiss.

As they broke gently apart he didn't speak or even look at her, he simply held her close against him and continued to move gently. For Lucy it was as if the music had suddenly been turned back up. With a jolt she became aware of the room again, the people, the sounds. And her mind suddenly had room for everything else. What the hell was she doing? How could she have allowed this to happen? Where was her resolve? She felt a wave of sudden anguished guilt. Ed had been right to be suspicious of her. Poor Ed, how could she behave so badly towards him? The man she was supposed to love. And Gabriel. Their friendship. What damage had they gone and done? The thought smashed into her mind, chasing out all the warmth, all the delight from moments before. She pushed Gabriel away from her, eyes wide, rubbing her hand across her mouth as she did so, as if she could erase what had just happened, go back to the way they were before.

She saw his eyes widen, a worried expression surfacing, but she wouldn't allow herself to stay and see more.

'Gabe, I'm sorry, this isn't right. I…I have to go,' she said finally and turned before she could give him any chance to speak. Whatever he had to say she didn't want to hear. The damage they had just done to their friendship. How could she have let it get this far? She must have been giving him unconscious signals. What would he expect now—a three-week fling? She wasn't about to waste the last twenty-three years on that. There was only one thing to do to try and save the situation and that was get some serious distance between them. Right now. She ran from the ballroom, down the stairs and into the darkness, leaving Gabriel standing alone in the middle of the dance floor.

CHAPTER EIGHT

GABRIEL stood outside the hotel and pushed an exasperated hand through his hair. Where the hell had Lucy gone? He looked left and right but the road in both directions was empty except for parked cars vaguely visible in the streetlights. She must have found a taxi from somewhere. It was beginning to rain but he was oblivious to it as it soaked his hair and dampened his designer suit. What the hell had he gone and done now?

He hadn't meant to kiss her; he truly hadn't. From the moment she'd stepped out of her front door earlier he'd had to keep himself on constant guard to hide his attraction and he'd been doing a pretty good job, if he said so himself. It was the dancing. He should never have asked her to dance but he hadn't liked the way the conversation was going and it had been all he could think of to do to divert her and stop her talking. He'd known the instant her body was against his that he had no hope left. He rubbed his fingers slowly across his lips as if he could still taste her on them. The softness of her skin under his hands and the delicious scent of her hair had removed all the control he'd had in place. The thin fabric of her dress had meant he could feel every contour of her body against his. The kiss had been the most natural, most right and perfect moment of intimacy he could ever remember having. And now he'd screwed it up.

He turned and walked back into the ballroom to make his excuses and leave, walking the perimeter of the room to try and avoid one of his ex-girlfriends, who was making a beeline for him. He needed desperately to think. One thing was certain though. The way he felt right now he wasn't going to let her go. Not without a fight.

Lucy let herself into her flat with shaking fingers. Her curls were damp and beginning to frizz from the rain. For one awful moment she wondered if Ed would be there waiting for her but the place was quiet and in darkness. She heaved a sigh of relief.

She was shaking all over. The combination of the freezing weather and the after effects of that kiss. She'd never felt such an acute physical response to anyone before. She'd been powerless to stop it. She was staggered by just how right it had felt. Especially when her head had been—and still was—telling her constantly that the whole thing was totally wrong.

She turned on the light in the sitting room, kicked off her high heels and went to slump on the couch. And it was then that she saw it. A piece of paper left on the coffee table.

'Sorry. Call me,' she read, in Ed's scrawling handwriting. Her eyes filled with tears that quickly blurred the words. What had she done?

Gabriel tried for what felt like the hundredth time to call her but the landline at the flat simply rang end-lessly and he assumed she must have unplugged it. He'd been pressing redial since he'd walked back through his front door. Her mobile phone informed him that it was switched off and suggested he try later. It was no good, and he had no idea why he had expected anything else. Why would she react differently to this than she did to every other difficult issue or encounter in her life? He'd known her since she was six and her policy in all that time had been the same. Disengage from the rest of the world until you've worked out what to do. Except he was very worried that if he didn't get to talk to her soon her choice of what to do might not include him at all. He picked the phone back up. He'd just have to keep on trying.

Lucy stood under a steaming shower, letting the water pour down over her closed eyes. She struggled to understand what the kiss really meant to her. *He feels the same way as you do,* her mind whispered. And if that was true, it put things in a whole new light. Should she just brush it off as one of those things, a slip-up? Did Gabriel want her as more than a friend? And if he did what did that mean? A short-term fling before he backed off just as he always did? Their friendship might be able to survive a slip-up of a kiss but it could never survive more than that.

Then there was Ed to think of. Her heart twisted when she thought how hurt he would be if he knew what she'd done. She'd been so happy with him for a long time. She had such plans for them. How could she ever make him understand or forgive her? And even if she could, what hope of a future was left for them now?

Crushing her feelings for Gabriel felt like an impossible task; even shoving him out of her mind for a few minutes wasn't achievable at the moment. Her guilt was growing; she felt she was adding to her betrayal just by thinking about him.

She climbed into bed. It was late and she was tired out from the stress of the evening. But sleep was a long time coming. She finally fell into a thin doze at about three and was awake again by six. Throwing on some old jeans and a T-shirt, she went straight to the kitchen and began lining up sugar, eggs and flour on the worktop next to the mixing bowl. She needed to think things through.

Gabriel was up early on a Sunday for the second time in a month. *And both times it's been Lucy's fault,* he thought wryly. He couldn't let things lie. Not the way he felt now, and not the way he'd felt last night. It had gone too far. He climbed into his car and started the engine. Whether she was ready or not, they needed to talk.

Lucy made sponge cake mixture on autopilot. She was barely aware of what she was doing, but as usual with her hands busy she was able to think clearly. Guilt gnawed away deep in her gut. It was all Gabriel's fault. She'd had everything under control and he had to ruin it. She passed a flour-covered hand over her eyes. *Don't lie to yourself, Lucy.* There was nothing to be gained in trying to make herself feel better about what she'd done. *The only person to blame for all this is you. You could have pushed Gabriel away, laughed it off. Instead you played as much of a part as he did.* More, in fact, because Gabriel was a free agent and she was supposedly on the brink of marriage.

She tried to think clearly, work out how she felt. She took the two ends of the spectrum in turn. Ed. Reliable, kind, loving. Clumsy but endearing. Ambitious in his own haphazard way. She'd always know where she was with Ed; he was predictable, and that made him safe. And to someone with a background like hers those things were to be prized, treasured.

Gabriel on the other hand. Incurably, undeniably ambitious. He'd clawed his way up in legal circles. Partner of the leading firm of solicitors in Bath. Now courting senior partnership and still not even thirty-five. Interesting that he'd rejected London after his initial training contract, wanting to work his way to the top of a smaller firm where he could have some major influence from very early on. He thrived on the buck stopping with him. Inescapably unreliable. Fickle, commitment phobic. Best friend anyone could ever want. Better brother than a real one could be. Sparky, inspiring, challenging. She never felt as if she would win hands down with Gabe, whereas with Ed she was always firmly in the driving seat.

She wondered how Gabriel was feeling, what he wanted from her. For all she knew he could be filled with regret right now. Maybe he'd drunk too much champagne and was now cursing the demon drink for getting him into this mess. While she tortured herself about her behaviour he could be embarrassed and wondering how to let her down gently. Her instinct was to call him, find out what he wanted from her, but guilt wouldn't let her do that. Infidelity had played its part in the demise of her parents' happiness and in her eyes it was symptomatic of a ruined relationship. It hurt to think of herself and Ed like that. Whatever Ed's faults were, he didn't deserve to be treated so shabbily. And she felt so low about herself. She who prided herself on her total control of her life and her destiny, acting on impulse like that. She shook her head. She simply didn't *do* impulsive; she did rational.

She knew one thing. She couldn't have Gabriel near her until she'd sorted this out. It was all she could manage right now to stop thinking about him, about how he felt and tasted. To speak to him or meet him would qualify as infidelity in her eyes now, after what had happened between them, and she wouldn't do it. She owed it to Ed to sort things out with him before she did anything else. That could be the only way she had of feeling good about herself again.

She reached across the counter and turned on her mobile. The second it found the network there came beep after beep of text alerts. Just as there always was when she and Gabriel argued. He never could let it lie. She knew him well enough to be certain that before long he would give up on the telephone and come to find her in person. She couldn't have that. She would have to call him and tell him to give her some space. But before she could decide whether to read his texts or go straight to the point and ring him, the phone itself broke suddenly into Elvis singing 'Blue Suede Shoes'. Ed must have reprogrammed her ringtone again. An incoming call. She glanced at it and her pulse increased and not in a pleasant way. Caller ID showed her that it was Ed on the line. She felt absurdly exposed, as if by her picking the call up Ed would by some sixth sense be able to tell that she'd kissed Gabriel. That she'd betrayed him.

She pulled herself together. She just needed to get this conversation out of the way and then she could get her head straight and work out how to make things right. She picked up the phone.

'Ed, hi!' she cried, in an overly bright tone of voice, which belied the guilt that stuck like a bone in her throat.

'Lucy.' He sounded a little confused. 'I wasn't sure you'd pick up after last night.'

Her heart pounded. What did he mean 'last night'? Had he somehow heard what had happened?

'I'm really sorry for everything I said,' he went on, and she suddenly realised he'd just meant that he was expecting a frosty reception. After all, the last time they'd spoken had involved her slamming the door on him and then swiftly leaving in Gabe's car. Any lingering irritation she might have felt about yesterday's argument had since been beaten into submission by her new guilty role in the situation. But Ed didn't know that, of course, and she needed to inject some normality pretty quickly if she was going to avoid him guessing something was up. She wanted to talk to him calmly about this once she'd had time to think it through, not blurt it out over the telephone and end up with another flaming row.

She covered her eyes with one hand. 'Ed, it's fine. Really it is. It was my fault, not yours. I was so preoccupied with getting ready to go out that I never thought how it might make you feel.'

'Don't say anything else. I saw you looking so beautiful and I got jealous. That was all. Jealous that you'd be spending the evening with Gabriel and not with me. I had no right to shout at you. I know Gabriel is just a friend, I should never have implied anything else.'

Her face burned with shame at this. How was she ever meant to make this right?

'How was the night out, anyway? Did Gabriel make senior partner?' He sounded genuinely interested, eager to hear all about her evening and make up for the things he'd said.

'It was rubbish,' she said quickly. 'Boring group of dull career-obsessives.' She tried unsuccessfully to push the image of Gabriel's kiss out of her mind.

He sounded mildly surprised. 'Shame. I know you were looking forward to it. Well, maybe I can make up for it tonight. And it'll give me a chance to say sorry properly for yelling at you.'

She couldn't bear this. Couldn't bear him being so apologetic when she'd betrayed his trust without a second's hesitation. Her eyes filled with tears and she swallowed hard.

'Ed, please. I've told you there's nothing to make up for.' Her discomfort came out in her voice as irritation and it only made him even more persistent.

'There is. I insist.'

She clutched at her hair in frustration. *Stop apologising!*

'Come to The Abbey with me tonight,' he coaxed. 'Have a fun time, talk things through, eh?' The Abbey was the bar they visited most often together.

She leapt on this. Talking properly was exactly what they needed to do. Not some stilted excuse for a heart-to-heart over the phone. She knew she had to tell Ed what had happened. She had known since she'd left the party. The kiss weighed on her conscience like a stone. She could spend today thinking how best to handle it, find some way to try and make things right. And perhaps being on neutral ground instead of in her flat or his place would help.

'OK, that would be good,' she said. 'Can I meet you there, say seven-thirty? I need to drop some things off at the shop on the way and I'll come straight there.'

'Great!' The delight and relief in his voice compounded her sense of discomfort even further. She couldn't bear being in the same room as herself right now. Her mind refused to quit the endless reruns of Gabriel's kiss, which seemed to make her heart race even harder every time she relived it. She had to get things straight. Now she just needed to keep Gabriel away until she'd seen Ed and her mind was clear. As Ed cut the call off she took a deep breath and clicked speed dial for Gabriel.

She didn't get far. As she waited for the line to connect the entry buzzer sounded suddenly in the hall, making her jump. She walked down the hallway as if in a dream, her hands covered in flour, and picked up the intercom.

Gabriel stood outside on the step. His heart pounded as he waited for her to speak.

'Yes?'

'It's me,' he said simply. There was no need to say any more.

Her voice was laced with panic and he longed to give

her a cuddle and tell her everything would be fine. 'I can't do this right now, Gabriel. I need to sort things out with Ed.'

'Just ten minutes. Please. You know we need to talk.'

'I need you to stay away from me…'

He couldn't believe what he was hearing. Sort things out with Ed? He had to get her to talk to him, let her know how he felt before she stormed ahead with the proposal to Ed on some guilty impulse.

'What? Don't be so ridiculous. You can't pretend nothing has happened, Lucy.'

'I'm not pretending!' Her voice took on an angry tone. 'But until I've seen Ed, talked things through, seeing you will just be cheating on him. Even more than I already have. And I won't do that. I won't make things worse than they already are.'

He didn't like the way she was heading with this. The only way to deal with her obstinacy sometimes was just to storm on regardless and so he tried again.

'Lucy, please. I need to talk to you. Ten minutes, that's all.'

'What part of no do you not understand? Please, Gabriel, just go away.'

'I'm going to say what I've come to say, whether you like it or not, Lu. So you can either let me in or the whole street can hear me yell it through the intercom. It's up to you!' He raised his voice to emphasise his point.

A long pause. And then she pressed the entry button.

Lucy opened the flat door and went back to the kitchen without waiting for him to come up the stairs. Her heart was thundering in her chest and she hoped that concentrating on the cake she was making would keep her calm. She heard the door slam as he came into the flat and she turned as he entered the kitchen. She could see by his face that he'd probably had even less sleep than she had. There were dark smudges underneath the grey eyes.

'I wish you'd turn your phone on now and then,' he grumbled. 'I've spent the last six hours trying to call you.'

She glanced across at the phone on the kitchen window sill. 'I know. I only turned it on ten minutes ago and it practically rang itself off the shelf with all your texts. One message would have been enough, you know.' She picked up a wooden spoon and began beating the cake batter although it was all perfectly mixed already. At least it meant she didn't have to look into his eyes and hold that grey gaze. Her stomach did cartwheels every time she did that. It seemed her body knew perfectly well what it wanted. To be carried by Gabe down the hall and straight into her bedroom. But she had to control her body with her mind, and that was telling her to be careful. Be very, very careful. She needed to follow her head, not her heart. She'd built her whole life around doing exactly that. *Don't throw away twenty-three years plus a future with Ed, if you can somehow salvage one, on something that will last five minutes, Lucy.*

Suddenly he was standing very close behind her and she felt weak. If he tried to kiss her now she wasn't sure she had the presence of mind to stop things and talk to him. But he simply reached around her and took away the bowl of cake batter. Hands left with nothing to do, she turned around and leaned back against the counter, folding her arms across her body.

'We need to talk, Lu,' he said simply.

She looked up at him. His eyes held hers. 'I know,' she said.

'I'm really sorry about last night,' he began.

Her heart began to sink, telling her how deep her feelings for him went. It made her feel guiltier than ever. Did he mean it was a mistake? That he regretted it? If so, how should she feel about that?

Anxious not to give away her own feelings—that would make her vulnerable—she gave a neutral answer. 'So am I.'

His face fell a little. 'I'm not sure you understand, Lu. I'm not sorry for kissing you. I'm really not. I'm sorry because I haven't been honest with you and you deserve a lot better than that.'

She rubbed a hand tiredly across her forehead. 'What do you mean you haven't been honest?' she asked him.

'I don't want you to propose to Ed.' She stared at him. The words spun in her mind. 'You're not still thinking about it, are you?' He searched her face.

'To be honest I don't know what to think.' She took a deep breath and looked down at her hands. 'Up until last night it was all clear to me and now I feel like I don't know where I am. It's all your fault. None of this would have happened if you hadn't kissed me.'

Gabriel raised his eyebrows at her sharp tone. 'Quit kidding yourself, Lu. You're just trying to pass the buck because you feel guilty about Ed. I can understand that. I can. I feel bad about Ed, too, but that doesn't change the facts. I might have been the one who started it but you didn't exactly fight me off, did you?'

She felt a hot blush of shame rise in her face. He was right. It made it feel momentarily better if they both shared the blame, but that was just window dressing. She had to take responsibility for her own actions, not dilute the repercussions by using Gabriel. It annoyed her that he knew her well enough to read her mind.

He grabbed her hand, entwining his fingers in hers. 'That kiss meant as much to you as it did to me. Don't deny it, Lucy. Not to me.'

She made the mistake of looking into his eyes and she felt light-headed. She would not let herself lose control again. A repeat of last night was *not* going to happen. Not while Ed was in the picture. She couldn't erase the kiss they'd shared but she could damn well stop things going any further. With a stupendous effort she removed her hand from his grasp and stepped away, putting cooling space between them.

She had to keep a handle on the facts here or she would go under. She felt awful for discussing anything with him before she'd been able to see Ed. Just talking about the possibility of being with him felt like cheating. But the fact was that she needed proper commitment from Gabriel if they were ever to go anywhere. Proper certainty that what had happened between them was different from his usual relationships. She needed to know he was ready to commit again, not get cold feet after a couple of weeks. This had to come from him. He was the one who was incapable of taking a relationship seriously, of giving it his all. If all he was after was a fling then she would stop the whole thing now, however hard that might be. She forced herself to ask the question that frightened her the most. 'What do you want from me, Gabriel?'

He moved towards her again, reclaiming the space she'd put between them, and took her hands in both of his. His huge hands enveloped her small ones easily, her fingers tingling at his touch. Her heart was beating so hard she thought he might be able to hear it.

He looked seriously down into her eyes. 'I want you, Lucy. I want you to drop the proposal with Ed and give things a try with me instead.' He smiled at her, his eyes crinkling at the edges, the lopsided smile she loved so much lighting up his tired face.

She didn't smile. 'What do you mean by "give things a try"?'

'Try being together as a couple. Not just as friends. For starters we could have a proper night out, just the two of us. Nothing heavy, just a relaxing evening. And then I thought we could both do with a break, so maybe we could think about taking a couple of weeks off, going somewhere hot. What do you think?' He looked at her expectantly. He thought she would jump at the chance, didn't he? Why wouldn't he think that? she supposed. Every other woman did.

Her heart was deflating. She could almost feel it in her chest. Disappointment flooded her. He hadn't changed at all, had he? She remembered some of those lines, almost word for word, from the night he'd met Ed's friends and flirted with Joanna. And why on earth did he think a holiday in the sun was the way to go? As if a relationship between them wasn't unreal enough, he was suggesting they take it and put it in an artificial setting with perfect surroundings. When they came home she knew the honeymoon would be over. And so would their friendship. What she needed to hear was that he was prepared to throw one hundred and ten percent into it alongside their everyday lives and challenges. She took her hands away from his and walked into the sitting room.

'What's wrong?' He followed her, sounding genuinely confused. 'What did I say?'

She sat down on the sofa, elbows on knees, and blew a stray tendril of hair out of her eyes. She looked up at him and shrugged. 'It's more what you didn't say, to be honest, Gabe,' she said.

He frowned. 'I've laid my cards on the table, Lucy. This whole proposal thing of yours, spending time with you, looking at you gaining confidence, sorting things out with your dad. I realised the last thing in the world I want to do is help you get married to someone else. I tried not to show it, God knows I did, but last night it just got the better of me. And there's no point me trying to hide it any more. I've fallen for you and I want you to be with me.'

'Gabriel, our friendship means everything to me.' She looked up at him. He was standing with his arms folded indignantly. Still frowning. *He's not used to women knocking him back,* she thought. *I do believe he thought he'd come here and I'd just fall into his arms.* 'So much that I'm just not willing to risk it by having a fling with you.'

'Hang on a minute—'

She held up a hand. 'Let me finish.' She was firm but quiet. For once she had her temper under total control.

He looked at her impatiently. 'OK, go on.'

'Last night, Gabe, when you kissed me.' She dropped her eyes shyly and looked down at her hands. 'No one's ever made me feel like that before.'

He was across the room in three quick strides, kneeling in front of her, his hands on hers again. 'Then let's give it a go,' he said softly, his mouth so close to hers that she could just touch it in a slight movement, take him down the hall to bed right now. 'What have we got to lose?'

She pulled her hands away and forced herself to stand up. 'Everything, Gabriel. And that's exactly the problem. I don't want to lose you as a friend and if we go ahead with this and it doesn't work out I'm scared that's exactly what will happen. Your relationships last five minutes. And then you can't turn back the clock. Things would never be the same. We'd have lost everything. So if this is just about you panicking because I'm settling down, there's no need. Nothing will change for you and me, Gabe. We'll always be best friends, no matter what.'

He stood up next to her and looked intently into her face. 'It's not about that. It's about us being more than just friends. I've changed, Lucy. I can make this work. And I promise you that, no matter what happens between us, we will always be friends. Always. You don't need to worry about ruining that by being with me.'

Could she really believe that? She looked at him and swallowed hard to keep the threat of tears at bay. She wouldn't let him see her cry; she was absolutely determined about that.

'I need time to think, Gabe. I feel terrible for just

talking about this with you while Ed's in the dark about what's happened. I can't think about anything until I've sorted things out with Ed. I have to make things right with him—you must see that. I can't just pretend last night never happened. I'm not the kind of person who can gloss over that and then sleep soundly at night. All this is too sudden. I need to work out what I'm going to do.'

'Well, you can't still be intending to propose to him,' Gabriel said boldly. 'Not now.'

Her temper stirred. 'Why not?' she asked. 'Because you say so?'

'Because of what happened. The way you just said you feel. You can't go ahead with it now.'

'Maybe I can't. But even if things finish with Ed it doesn't automatically follow that diving into a relationship with you is the right move. Try and see it from my point of view, will you? You're suggesting I throw away a good relationship, one that was good enough, by the way, for me to be ready to marry the guy, for you, who has the track record of a rock star for making relationships work. Already you're suggesting we go away on holiday. What I need is to know we could work in the real world before I would ever take a chance on it working out in some unreal holiday environment.' She sighed. 'You mean the world to me, Gabriel, as a friend. I just don't know if I can give that up. How do I know you've really changed? That you're really ready for this—a proper, grown-up, serious relationship?'

This was getting her nowhere. The way things were headed they would end up having a row. She needed to clear her head, decide what to do. 'I need you to leave, Gabe. I'll call you later.'

His face fell. 'No. I'm not leaving. We need to talk this through.' He grabbed one of her hands. 'Please, Lucy.'

'I need to think!' she shouted at him. 'Stop pushing me, Gabriel!' And then her voice broke a little as she lowered it and tried to speak calmly, to make him listen. 'I need you to get out now and give me some space.'

He dropped her hand as if it were suddenly red hot. 'OK, OK.' He held his hands up submissively. 'I'll go now. Give you time to think. But listen…' He moved back towards her a little, as if he couldn't stop himself, and clenched his fists. 'Just promise me you'll think about how it could be between us,' he said. 'We have so much going for us—you can't deny that.'

She only gazed back at him steadily until he left the room and she heard the front door bang shut behind him. He hadn't once mentioned proper long-term plans. Something in Gabriel had been broken all those years ago when Alison died. Could she really believe that one kiss with her had mended it? That he now had the capacity to give her everything she needed? Because she needed security and safety to be happy, she needed to rely on him in the same way she needed air.

Gabriel didn't bother going home again after he left. He felt that the prospect of their relationship was balanced on a knife edge. He felt uneasy. Had he really given it everything he'd got? Had he really opened his heart to her and let her see in? Or had a decade of keeping women at a distance, avoiding any danger of loss, made him hold back? He didn't know. But if he'd got this wrong he would lose her anyway now and he wasn't sure he could stand that. He knew her well enough not to paint her into a corner, knowing that would only make her dig her heels in against him. The only thing to do was to back off and give her time to think. And it had to be her choice at the end of the day. What she wanted. Not something she'd been pushed into, but something she embraced.

He turned the car in the opposite direction to his flat and made for the motorway. For Gloucestershire. He was determined to get this right. Lucy would never settle for anything less than marriage; he knew that. If he had any chance of winning her over he had to be prepared to be with her for always, to put aside all his fears that the past might repeat itself and that he might lose her the way he'd lost Alison. He had to take a leap of faith. He found with surprise that the idea filled him with nothing but hope and delight. He had spent years avoiding even the thought of it. He just hoped that when she was ready to talk, he could make her listen.

Lucy opened the oven and removed the mess inside. She'd put the cakes in before Gabriel arrived and had forgotten about them. They were burnt and rock hard. A total disaster. She hoped that wasn't a reflection on her life. She felt emotionally drained and exhausted. She did her best to try and think clearly but her mind felt groggy and slow. What she needed was fresh air and she longed for a run by the river to clear her mind. She wasn't sure of what she wanted to do, of where to go from here. So Gabriel didn't want her to propose to

Ed. But he didn't seem sure how he wanted things to proceed between them. He seemed afraid to commit to anything more than 'giving it a try'. Was she not worth more than that? Surely gambling their friendship meant more to him than that.

She had no idea whether she and Ed could work things out, but, even if he could forgive her behaviour, would it be right for her to stay with him after this? Could she live with the lack of passion that came so easily to her with Gabriel as long as she had the settled security that Ed had always given her and that was so important to her?

Or did she risk everything, literally everything, on Gabriel? Her stable relationship with Ed, her friendship with Gabriel, which was more like a family tie really, her home because if something went wrong with Gabriel she couldn't live here, not any more. Heart or head? Which way should she jump? When it came right down to it she was scared. Scared of everything she had to lose.

Gabriel sat in silence in his house. He was deep in thought. Ed's message on his answering machine had been blinking away when he'd got back from the swift visit he'd made to his family home. Still unable to shake the sense of unease that had descended on him when Lucy hadn't simply fallen instantly into his arms, he was immediately put on edge at the sound of Ed's voice. Had Lucy spoken to him? Already? He began to frown as he listened to the short message.

'Er, right...Gabriel?' A pause. 'Not there, then?' Gabriel raised exasperated eyes skyward. For all his business aspirations Ed had yet to master the art of the slick answering machine message.

'Ed here. Lucy's Ed.'

The way Ed spoke, as if he somehow belonged to Lucy, made Gabriel bridle with jealousy. He might not hold Ed in particularly high regard but there was no getting away from how much Ed had meant to Lucy for a considerable time. He would be a fool to underestimate that.

'Just wondering if you can make it to The Abbey tonight. Half-seven-ish. Bit of an evening planned and I'm sure Lucy would like you to be there. Bye, then.'

The machine clicked off. What the hell did this mean? She couldn't have told Ed about them, then, as she'd said she was going to. Was she having second thoughts? Or was this some kind of ruse on Ed's part to get him in the same room, have it out with him? Gabriel had no feelings of guilt. In his opinion Ed didn't deserve Lucy; it was as simple as that. If he'd been up to the challenge she would never have been tempted to look at anyone else. It was Ed's own fault if she found what she needed elsewhere. He knew in his bones that he, Gabriel, was what she needed—it was just convincing her of that fact that was the problem. Lucy felt guilty enough for the both of them, it seemed.

He picked up the square velvet box that rested on the table in front of him. It opened with an almost inaudible squeak. Nestled inside was an ornate emerald ring in a Victorian setting. He took it out and twisted it between his finger and thumb, studying it. The green was the colour of Lucy's eyes. It had been his grandmother's. After Lucy's reaction today he had known he had to find a way to convince her that he could offer the lifelong security and love she craved. Maybe this ring, a piece of his family, to which she'd always dreamed of belonging when she was a child, could help him do that. He snapped the box shut. Whatever this evening was, whatever happened, he intended to be there. He intended to fight for her now in any way he could.

The Abbey was a popular bar showing a mixture of live music and televised sport. Somewhere in the course of her relationship with Ed it had come to belong to them in the way bars and pubs sometimes did when you visited them often enough. As she walked down the steps and through the door into the mellow darkness, dotted with flickering hurricane lamps on tables, Lucy's stomach was a knot of nerves. Perhaps by the end of the evening she would have some clarity about her feelings. About what she wanted to do.

She needed to talk things through with Ed. If everything had been right with their relationship she would never have looked to Gabriel for more than friendship. Yet the moment she had begun to think about pushing for commitment from Ed, her long-buried feelings for Gabe had begun to resurface. Slowly at first but gathering momentum until at the dance she had been unable to exert the self control she always believed she had when it came to principles like infidelity. The physical and emotional way Gabe touched her transcended all rational thought.

She was clear about one thing. She had to be totally honest with Ed about what she had done, how she had let him down. She wasn't sure Ed would still want to talk to her, or even look at her after that. She couldn't let herself think about Gabriel until she'd gone through with this.

She glanced automatically towards the table halfway down the room. Years of sitting at it had given it the tag 'our table' whenever they attended together and both of them felt irrationally aggrieved if anyone else dared to sit at it. She stopped and stared. There was no sign of Ed but Yabba, Suzy and Kate were sitting there, drinks in hand. Digger was standing at the bar and raised a hand in her direction as he caught sight of her. And was that Joanna sitting with her back to the door?

She felt a surge of exasperation. So much for an evening of in-depth soul-searching with Ed. After their argument he'd obviously decided that the perfect way to get things back on track was a night out with all their friends. As if on cue she noticed Ed himself striding across the room from the stage area where the live music, a jaunty-looking man with a synthesizer and backing track, was setting up. So not only an evening with their friends but an evening of shouting all conversation over blaring music. She tried not to tense up as Ed swept her into a hug.

'Great, you made it! Come on, let's get you a drink.' He pulled her by the hand towards the bar as the jaunty man kicked off with a loud sixties track. Ed raised his voice to compensate. 'Orange juice?' he shouted.

She nodded. 'Ed.' She tugged at his sleeve to get his attention. 'Ed!'

He looked round.

'I thought we were going to talk,' she half yelled. 'You know. After yesterday. Straighten some things out.' She could see Digger standing behind Ed, very deliberately not listening, and she frowned at him. He looked away.

'We will, we will! No harm in having a good evening out though, eh?'

He gave her waist a squeeze and she felt an odd sense of unease at his enthusiastic manner. Ed was behaving weirdly. She wondered for a moment if she'd got it wrong on the phone and if he really had somehow found out about her kiss with Gabriel. Was he going to make some kind of scene? She dismissed the thought immediately. Ed was a straight-down-the-line kind of guy. He didn't have hidden agendas; they weren't his style. She was just on edge because of the weight of her conscience. And the way the evening was going there was no way she'd be able to do anything about that here.

They made their way to the table and she reluctantly took the vacant seat between Ed and Joanna.

'How's Gabriel?' Joanna asked her at the first opportunity.

Oh, for heaven's sake. 'He's well, as far as I know,' she said shortly. How could she be expected to put Gabriel out of her mind when people kept mentioning him at every turn?

'Ask him yourself, Jo,' Ed said, raising a hand in greeting towards the door. He kept his other arm clamped firmly around Lucy's shoulders in a gesture of possessiveness that didn't escape her notice.

Lucy's heart felt as if it had been jump-started; she felt her pulse begin to race. Not a gradual climb in heart rate but an uncontrollable leap. She turned to look. The bar might as well have been empty. For her there was no one else here. The irritating music faded to a background hum. Her green eyes met his grey ones and she was home.

Why didn't Ed make her feel like this? Not just now, but ever. She couldn't remember a time when she'd looked at Ed and thought that the world could end right there and then and she wouldn't give a damn as long as she was with him. Gabriel crossed the room and sat down opposite her. Every cell in her body was in a heightened sense of awareness. Her desire for him was so acute that she worried the others would guess her innermost thoughts, and she tried hard to avoid looking at him.

As Ed kissed her cheek and stood up to speak to someone her rational mind kicked in with another twist of unease. What was Gabe doing here? This wasn't one of his haunts; he preferred the trendier wine bars and nightclubs closer to the city centre. She felt a sudden prickling of worry that maybe he intended to confront Ed with what had happened between them, force the issue despite all they'd said that afternoon. She couldn't do that to Ed. For heaven's sake, all she wanted was the chance to come clean to Ed, to treat him with the decency he deserved, and yet all people and circumstances seemed to be thwarting that.

As soon as Joanna had finished her effusive greeting of Gabe—did she need to kiss him on *both* cheeks?— Lucy leaned in across the table towards him, fighting the urge to reach out and touch him.

'What the hell are you doing here?' she asked in an awkward stage whisper, trying not to draw attention from the others. Especially Joanna, who looked none too pleased at having Gabriel diverted.

'Ed invited me.'

Her heart felt like a brick in her chest. 'Why would he do that? He never calls you up, invites you anywhere. He leaves all that to me, if we ever see you socially. Which we hardly ever do.' She looked at him urgently. 'What is going on?'

'Well, I did wonder, to be honest. I actually thought you might have told him about us. I was almost ready for a showdown even though he said you'd be here, too.'

'Of course I haven't told him. I can hardly talk things through with him in front of this lot, can I? Not that I can hear myself think anyway!' She sat back in her seat and cast a nasty look at the entertainer, who was continuing with his hideous set of sixties and seventies music, singing along to an awful backing track. Just at that moment Yabba brayed a loud guffaw two seats away from her that wouldn't have sounded amiss on a donkey. The place was bedlam. And then the last straw: the music suddenly changed to the booming introduction of an Elvis Presley number.

'Oh, you can't be serious! This bar has the worst live music in Bath!' she shouted. She grabbed her orange juice angrily. Nothing was going to be resolved tonight and she might as well get used to it.

'Is that Ed?' Joanna said suddenly to no one in particular.

The hand clutching her orange juice froze en route to her lips. The table fell gradually still as one face after another turned towards the stage. Lucy followed Gabriel's shocked gaze to the pool of light in which

Ed stood, holding a microphone attached to a stand. Her eyes took in every detail against her will in glorious sharp colour. Ed was wearing a silver jumpsuit—*a jumpsuit!*—encrusted with coloured plastic gemstones that caught the light. Even as she watched he struck a pose, opened his mouth and burst into a heavily exaggerated Elvis impression. Her lips pulled back from her teeth in an uncomprehending grimace. An enormous Elvis quiff perched on top of his head. He had even blackened his blond sideburns to match the awful wig. Her eyes refused to leave out the slightest grisly detail as he threw himself with gusto into murdering 'The Wonder Of You'.

Gabriel was motionless opposite her, an expression of dumbstruck amazement on his face.

'I didn't know Ed could sing,' Joanna said.

Ed's voice built to a warbling crescendo, his authentically trembling lip visible even from across the room. He seemed to be working on the policy that loudness would counteract lack of tune. As Lucy watched him through stunned eyes he struck another pose to end the first verse, one hand plastered to a jewel-encrusted hip, the other stabbing the air above his head with a pointed finger.

'Well, let's be honest about it. He can't sing, can he?' Yabba said as Ed's voice took on a screechy pitch.

Mercifully one verse seemed to be enough for him. It was certainly enough for everyone else as a stunned silence fell for an excruciating moment before scattered clapping kicked in. Lucy was transfixed as Ed took the microphone from the stand and began to make his way across the room towards her. The spotlight followed him. He spoke into the mike as he walked.

'That was for mah Lucy.'

She realised with horror that he was staying in character.

'I love ya, little lady.'

'I had no idea you were an Elvis fan, Lucy,' Joanna leaned in and said to her as Ed progressed between the tables, the spotlight taking in his every move.

'I'm not,' Lucy heard herself say. Her mind and eyes didn't seem to be engaged with each other properly. Was that really Ed? What the hell was he doing? 'Not really. Ed's a massive fan, though. Always trying to indoctrinate me…'

Her voice trailed into nothing as Ed finally reached her table. Beads of sweat hung on his face. Was he really wearing fake tan? She was vaguely aware that the spotlight was taking her in, too, now and she knew just from the way her face burned that she was a bright tomato red.

She had no time to think, no time to collect herself. Whatever she'd been expecting from the evening it certainly hadn't been this. It was like some surreal dream and she half expected to wake up and find herself in bed at home.

Ed flung himself theatrically onto his knees at her feet. Looking up at her and still in character, he crooned in a deep-voiced southern drawl, 'Will ya marry me, baby?'

Opposite them, in the darkness outside the spotlight, Gabriel was choking on his drink. Joanna stood up and thumped him artlessly on the back. Lucy didn't notice.

Too late, the penny had finally dropped. Silence fell around her. She was suddenly unaware of anything except for the stares of everyone in the room boring into her, taking in the pair of them bathed in the light. Ed gazed up at her, a silly grin plastered across his orange tinted face, an expectant look in his eyes. And before she knew what she was saying, before she even knew what she was thinking, panic and confusion spoke for her and the word was out of her mouth.

'Yes.'

The room exploded in wild applause, whistling and cheering. And she was swept suddenly out of her seat and into Ed's arms. He twirled her around, her feet inches from the floor, in a bear hug. As their friends crowded around them, slapping Ed on the back and kissing Lucy's cheeks, the music relaunched into an horrific funked-up version of the 'Bridal Chorus'. Like a rush of ice water through her veins the realisation of what she had just done swept through her and in alarm she looked around wildly for Gabriel. She was too late. The door swung shut behind him and all that was left was his half-empty drink on the table.

CHAPTER NINE

GABRIEL glanced around the hallway of his house. Somehow he'd managed to get himself home on autopilot. He remembered none of the physical journey from The Abbey whatsoever. Every ounce of his energy had been spent turning what had happened over and over again in his mind. And in trying to stem the sensation that his heart had somehow been crushed, stamped on and kicked into pulp.

He couldn't believe she'd said yes. Not when she'd spoken the word and not now. And without wavering, without hesitation or even a glance in his direction. Weren't women in two minds supposed to go for the neutral answer and say they'd think about it? That was what happened in the movies and he couldn't for the life of him fathom why it hadn't happened tonight. If she'd had anywhere near the feelings for him that he'd thought she had, then, surely yes would have been the last thing she'd say.

He could kick himself now. Her ridiculous proposal idea. He'd contributed to this. Lining up Amanda to give her a makeover, making Ed sit up and take notice. In a surge of desolation he remembered that a couple of weeks ago this had been her dream. Ed proposing to her. The end of her rainbow. Was it such a leap that when her dream came true she would grasp it with both hands? It seemed entirely possible right now that the kiss, everything they shared, might cease to mean anything to Lucy in the face of the future with Ed that she'd so desperately wanted before.

Lucy watched Ed soaking up the attention from friends and strangers alike in the bar. She needed to get him out of here, somewhere quiet where they could talk. Less than a month ago this would have brought her ecstatic happiness. Ed proposing. The beginning of having a proper family of her own at last. How ironic. *That stupid proposal plan, Lucy. Be careful what you wish for.*

She was horrified that she'd agreed to marry Ed. How could she have done that? She'd just gone and made things a million times worse. Yet even if she hadn't panicked, how could she possibly have done anything else? After the flamboyant way he'd proposed could she really have crushed him in front of all their friends? She couldn't help remembering Gabriel's advice to her back at Smith's. It seemed like months ago now but it was only a matter of days. He'd told her not to propose in front of their friends if she didn't want to force a false 'yes'. And he'd been right. If you cared about someone you couldn't humiliate them like that, so you would take the only other option. Say yes at the time and then do your best to undo it later. That was what she'd have to do now, if she could ever disentangle him from his adoring public.

Two hours were long gone before she managed to get him back to her flat. Even then she'd practically had to manhandle him into the Mini. Now he threw himself back onto Lucy's sofa and sprawled there, letting out a noisy sigh. He was still wearing the silver Elvis jumpsuit, had insisted on wearing it for the rest of the evening as their friends applauded his performance and congratulated them both. He had dispensed, though, with the ill-fitting wig, and his fake tan paled to white at his hairline, the blond hair changing to black at the sides of his face. Lucy had eventually managed to persuade him to leave the party and come back to her flat, and now he leaned back comfortably, arms spread wide, grinning at her sitting-room ceiling.

'What a great night, eh, babe? You know, Suzy said we should go to Graceland as part of our honeymoon. Not such a bad idea, is it? Could do the whole tour. Visit the King's grave, everything. What do you think?'

There was silence for a long moment before she finally took the plunge and spoke.

'It's no good, Ed.'

He looked up in surprise at her quiet tone, such a marked contrast to his overexcitement. He saw her looking at him seriously, steadily. He sat up properly.

'What do you mean?'

She took a deep breath. 'It isn't going to work, Ed.'

His eyes widened.

'I really wish it could work. But I've been deceiving us both. And I've been totally, unforgivably unfair to you.'

Her eyes filled with tears at the expression on his face. This was not some easily disposable two-date boyfriend. She had loved Ed. She had. The fact that it had been more with her head than her heart didn't demean him one bit. She blinked hard. She had to get this over with. He deserved someone who loved him with passion, not someone who was just making do.

As he came back into focus she could see in his face that he'd guessed what she meant. But she needed to voice it anyway, say it out loud.

'Ed, when I went to the dance with Gabriel...' she began. She had to try and find a way to explain, to somehow make things between them not *right*, exactly, she could never do that, but at least make them better.

He interrupted her unexpectedly. 'You know, Lucy, tonight was a spur-of-the-moment thing really,' he said. 'After that row we had I tried to come up with something that might cheer you up. But now that it's over with and I've had time to think, well...'

She watched him, waiting for him to carry on.

He was looking at her, his eyes not wavering from hers, his face contemptuous. She wanted to look away from the onslaught of his hurt reaction, ashamed of how she'd made him feel, but she made herself meet his gaze. He deserved to say his piece.

'You know I've always tried to be what you wanted me to be. You've always harped on about marriage and kids but you know I've never really been the marrying kind. Then after that row the other night I thought if it was what you wanted I'd go through with it to keep you happy, that's all.' He made a disgusted face. 'I was wasting my time, wasn't I? What I really think now is that we should scrap the whole thing. And not just the wedding plans. Everything. I should have listened to my instincts the other night about you and Gabriel. I think I knew, even then. You're not what I want or need any more. Maybe we've had our time, run our course.'

'Ed...' She shook her head at him.

'It's OK, Lucy.' He smiled at her. A strong smile. No cracks in his voice. 'We've had some fun, haven't we? Don't be sad. You'll soon get over me.' He grabbed his jacket in one swift movement and turned for the door.

She jolted out of her stupor as he reached the hallway and crossed the room to swing around the corner after him. He was standing at the end of the hall, the door of her flat held open.

'Ed!' she cried in an anguished tone.

He turned back.

'Ed, I'm sorry.' Her voice cracked. She looked at him, trying to show in her face how true that statement really was. That she regretted her treatment of him with her heart and soul.

He smiled at her. Dignified resignation showed in his face. There was no attempt to talk her round. She didn't blame him for that; it was no more than she deserved. She'd betrayed his trust. 'Goodbye, Lucy,' he said. The door clicked shut behind him.

She stood and looked at the closed door for a few minutes, gathering her thoughts. In a way that door had shut on everything she'd taken for granted. The easy option where she'd always have been able to predict life at every turn. As she calmed down she felt no regret, no pang for that mapped-out life. She walked slowly back into the sitting room and automatically checked her phone for texts from Gabriel. She found herself looking at the screen in dismal surprise. Nothing. No calls. No messages. For the first time ever he appeared to be able to cope with them being at odds with each other. Didn't he care? She tried to ignore the sudden fear that this was a knockback too far for Gabriel. An accepted proposal in front of all those people. Maybe he was washing his hands of her.

She refused to believe that. She put the phone down on the table and dismissed the impulse to dash to his house and explain. Instead she would let the dust settle. There was something vaguely disrespectful to Ed in rushing to Gabriel the instant the door had closed behind him. Plus the fact it was late now. Past midnight. She would wait until the morning before doing anything. And, she told herself, Gabriel would have definitely got in touch by then anyway. He couldn't stand tension between them for long.

Gabriel Blake gave up trying to sleep a little after three in the morning. He made his way to the kitchen and brewed coffee he didn't really want, just for something to do that wasn't lying down thinking about her. He wondered how long it would be before he could sleep soundly again and didn't hold out much hope.

His initial shock at Lucy's acceptance had given way now to a gnawing sense of loss. The thought of her planning her wedding in delight, marrying Ed, making a home and then down the line starting a family filled him with utter desolation. How could he bear to watch that? To see her, a happily married woman, all the time wishing she belonged to him. Torturing himself over the question whether he could have done something, anything, differently. Perhaps if he'd been clearer, stronger with her when he'd told her how he felt. He passed a weary hand over his eyes. It was too late for that now. He'd missed his chance.

He realised with a rising sense of despair that he'd lost her. It was a different kind of grief from the way he'd felt when Alison had died but that didn't diminish the magnitude of it. He had lost her not just as a lover, a wife, but also as his best friend. Because he couldn't see a role in her life for him that wouldn't amount to daily agony as he watched her loving someone else.

Lucy woke up early, the shock of everything that had happened blasting into her mind like a hammer blow. She grabbed her mobile from the bedside table. It hadn't disturbed her sleep even though she'd left it switched on and she could immediately see why. No texts. No missed calls. No communication from Gabriel at all. She couldn't believe it. It was so unlike him and the implication that he no longer cared what she did brought tears springing to her eyes. She rubbed them away angrily with the back of her hand.

She needed to talk to him, to explain. *What if he doesn't want to hear it?* She refused to accept that possibility. Scrolling through her phone list, she called Sophie to tell her she'd be in late and arranged for her to open up the shop. Then, heart thumping in her chest, she dialled Gabriel's number. It took ages for him to pick up. It was so unlike him. She was used to him hounding her after they argued, or when one of them did something to offend the other. It had always infuriated her, but she would take it a million times now over this desolate silence from him. Maybe he'd decided to cut her from his life completely. Decided that she wasn't worth the effort or the grief. Her heart twisted agonisingly at the thought.

Just as she thought he was going to carry on ignoring her—she had no idea how she would deal with that—he finally picked up.

'Lucy.' How tired he sounded. It pulled at her heart.

'Will you meet me?' she asked him. 'Can we talk?'

There was a long pause. She bit her lip.

'Is there really anything to say, Lu? I'm happy for you. You've got what you wanted, what you planned for, haven't you? I know you're worried about us staying friends but I think maybe it's best if you just get on with things for a while. I'll keep a low profile for a bit.'

Her eyes filled with tears. 'Gabriel, please. I haven't. Got what I wanted, I mean.' She clutched at her hair in frustration. 'This is such a mess! Will you please just meet me? Just for ten minutes? After that I'll leave you alone if you want me to, I promise.'

Silence fell again, but her determination was kicking back in. After all this time, all this anguish, she wasn't going to be put off this easily. If he wouldn't meet her she'd damn well just go round to his house and ring the doorbell until he let her in. If he didn't want anything to do with her he could tell her to her face, after she'd told him how she felt. At least then she'd know she could do nothing more.

A sigh. 'Where?'

She clenched her fist in triumph. 'Pulteney Bridge. Half an hour.'

He hung up without saying goodbye.

* * *

Gabriel put the phone down. Hope tried to infiltrate his desperate heart, but he was too quick for it. He'd thought he'd all but won her last time they'd spoken and then last night had happened. He knew how much their friendship meant to her. And that she must be terrified of losing it. He wished he could tell her what she wanted to hear, that he'd be there for her for the rest of her life, just as he always had been, but he couldn't watch her make a family, grow old with someone else, all the time wishing it were him.

He loved her. When it came right down to it, he loved her. And he couldn't bring himself to refuse to meet her. But he intended to keep it short and make it clear that he needed space. Just how long he would need it for he wasn't sure. A lifetime? He didn't know.

He grabbed his car keys and prepared to leave the house. And then at the last moment he turned back from the door. Before he could stop himself he picked up the ring, still in its box on the counter, ready to be returned to his parents the next time he visited, and pocketed it. He knew he was tempting fate but he didn't care. If he sensed the slightest possibility of convincing her to go back on her marriage plans, he intended to fight for it with every ounce of strength in his body.

CHAPTER TEN

Lucy waited patiently by Pulteney Bridge. She wasn't expecting Gabriel to be on time—why would he break the habit of a lifetime? She looked over the stone railings down at the river. The rush of water on the weir below was soothing.

'Lucy.'

She turned from the water to face him. Who had she ever been trying to kid? All those years since she'd buried her feelings for him when she met Alison. All those years had led up to this moment. She was here with the hope of spending all the days of her life after this one with him. She might have been able to convince herself once that there could be another option. That she could squash her feelings and just keep his friendship. But not any more. The thought of giving him up now caused her such acute pain that it felt physical, not just emotional. As if her body and soul would be crushed alongside one another if she had to forgo him now. Had he felt so let down by seeing her accept Ed's proposal that he'd decided it wasn't worth the risk? No, she couldn't let herself think that way. She had to make him understand.

Two weeks ago and her suggestion that they meet at the bridge would be undisputed shorthand for only one thing: a joint run. Things were different now. Nothing was assumed in their relationship any more. The easiness between them was gone. At the very least they couldn't pick up their friendship where they had left off.

They moved away together from the huge stone railing and she followed him down the steps to the path that ran alongside the river. Her heart pounded in her chest the way it did when she'd gone for a run, as she had done with Gabe so many times down this very path. Just walking next to him, knowing he was close enough to touch her, made her limbs feel like jelly, her skin tingle deliciously.

She looked up at him just as he glanced down at her. Nerves writhed in her belly as if she were on a first date. She was determined to go through with this, no matter what happened. He might reject her out of hand, but if she didn't try she'd never know. Her lifelong craving for security wasn't enough on its own. She couldn't base her life, her relationships, on that need alone. Not now she knew the depth of passion she was capable of feeling.

'How's Ed?' he asked. A heavily loaded question.

She looked down at the path. He believed them to be together of course. But why wouldn't he? He'd witnessed firsthand her unwavering acceptance of Ed's outlandish proposal. In her panic she hadn't even hesitated, had she? The question that bothered her now was how he felt as a result of it. He didn't exactly look as if he was burning with jealousy—not such a good sign.

'He's fine,' she said. 'As far as I know.'

She picked up instantly on his slight change of posture. A sudden sharpening of his attention. He stopped walking and touched her arm. Not a strong hold, just a tap to get her to look at him.

She did. She took in the thick dark hair, the determined set of his strong jaw. The grey eyes, which looked almost blue today in the sunshine that was taking the edge off the cold air. She could see he looked tired and before she could stop herself she raised a hand to touch his face. He immediately covered it with his own and electric shocks crackled in her fingers, her stomach, her thighs.

'As far as you know?' He searched her eyes.

She gazed steadily back at him. 'Ed and I are over, Gabe.'

'But last night…'

'I should never have said yes. You know that, don't you? You were there. You saw the trouble he'd gone to. He thought he was losing me to you and so he decided to stake his claim.' She sighed. 'Making him jealous, changing my clothes. My stupid proposal plan. All of that worked in the end. How could I humiliate him in front of all his friends by saying no? You told me yourself proposing in front of all our friends would be a mistake.'

She searched his face for some reaction but he looked completely neutral, unreadable. 'I talked to him afterwards, came clean about what went on between you and me. I wish I'd been upfront with him before I'd let things get that far between us, but I honestly thought I was in control.' She sighed. 'It's no excuse. But I've done the best I can to put it right.'

'So what do you want to do now?' His expression was cautious, giving little away. Of course he was cautious. She'd told him before that just because it wasn't right with Ed didn't automatically make it right with him. He had listened to her. He was letting her have total control this time.

She looked down at her feet. 'I know things have been complicated since the dance, and I'm sorry about that, Gabe. You have to know that I had no choice but to sort things out with Ed before I could talk to you. Ed's proposal just made things even more difficult. But the thing is…' she glanced up at him shyly '…when I realised I'd rather have a three-week fling with you than a lifetime with Ed, there was no contest really.'

An amused expression appeared on his face and he took her hand in his. 'In what universe do you think three weeks with you would ever be enough?' he asked her gently. 'I'm not even sure a lifetime would be enough for me. I know my track record is rubbish, I know you probably think the odds of me holding down something long term are minuscule, but, Lucy, I can promise you that's what I want. To be with you, build a future. You have to believe me.'

Her stomach was doing flip flops. She tried to keep her voice steady. 'I'm really glad to hear you say that,' she said, allowing herself a nervous smile. 'Because although I mentioned the three-week-fling option, it was never really going to be up for grabs. You know me too well for that. Our friendship means far too much to throw it away for a fling. And anyway, I always aim high.'

Her heart began thumping as she took a small step backwards from him and dropped to one knee on the cold paving. The river flowed by behind him, the sun bouncing off its surface. She looked up at his face. An expression of surprise and sudden understanding rose in his eyes.

'Gabriel,' she said, and his name caught in a snag of emotion in her throat. So much depended on this moment. He could still say no. She cleared her throat with a croaking sound. Oh, great. Just what was needed for the perfect proposal: a Kermit the Frog impression.

'Gabriel,' she tried again. 'Will you mmmmf—?'

He was on his knees next to her, grey eyes level with her own, his hand plastered firmly over her mouth stopping the words mid-sentence. She frowned and grabbed his big hand with both of her small ones, tugging at it until he let her pull it away.

'What are you doing?' she asked in a panic. He was stopping her before she could make a fool of herself. He was letting her down gently. Despite what he'd just said, marriage wasn't what he wanted, then. Would she sacrifice her marriage dream as long as she had him? Her heart tightened a little. Of course she would. In a second. How much she had changed.

He smiled at her. 'It's not February twenty-ninth any more, Lu. We're into March now, in case you didn't notice.'

Was that it? The nervous energy she'd expended on this and he was quibbling about the *date!* She pointed an indignant finger into his face, just inches from her own. 'I've loved you since I was sixteen years old, Gabriel Blake. That's my entire adult life. And I am *not*...' she raised her voice an insistent notch '...waiting another four years just so I can ask you on the correct day!'

His eyes crinkled in amusement as his face broke into the lopsided smile she loved.

'So this is your last chance,' she said. 'Don't blow it.' She took a deep breath. 'Gabriel, will you mmmmmf!'

His hand was back against her lips again. She could smell the faintest trace of his aftershave, spicy and deep, making her stomach feel soft. She was glad she was on her knees already as she wasn't sure they would have held her up much longer.

He smiled as she wrenched at his hand again. And then her eyes widened and she quit tugging instantly as his free hand produced something from his back pocket. A tiny velvet box.

'No, Lucy,' he said. 'Will you?'

At last he took his hand away so he could flip open the box for her. But even with her mouth free, she couldn't find any words. She gazed down at the most exquisite emerald ring she'd ever seen. It sparkled up at her.

'It was my grandmother's,' he said, as if he couldn't bear the silent wait for her answer. 'I thought you'd like it better than something I picked up in a shop.'

'It's beautiful,' she whispered. His face was inches from her own. Warmth began to sweep slowly, deliciously through her. He'd put aside his commitment fears. Made the biggest gesture he possibly could to prove it. For her.

'Of course I'll marry you.'

She was in his arms. She was spinning, light-headed, as his mouth crushed hers and his fingers tangled in her hair. She could feel the muscles of his shoulders beneath her hands and she felt his heart hammering like a drum against her own. She was acutely aware of his hands beginning to wander lower, snaking down her back, and she thought she might actually faint onto the cold paving.

The sudden rush of a bicycle flying past them, almost close enough to knock the pair of them into the river, brought them both back to reality with a jolt and Gabriel helped her to her feet, laughing. They linked hands and walked slowly back up the river path towards the city centre.

'You'd better not backtrack on that acceptance tomorrow,' he teased her, sliding an arm around her.

She elbowed him in the ribs. 'Very funny. You didn't ask me in public, did you? So yes means yes—you needn't worry.'

He gave her waist a squeeze. She was acutely aware of his arm circling her, of his touch. The thought of being alone with him made her quake with anticipation.

'Where to, then—home?' he asked her.

'Where is home exactly? Don't you mean "your place or mine"?'

'No, I mean home.' He squeezed her fingers. 'I want this to be proper, from the outset. And much as I know you love that titchy flat, Lucy, you have to agree my place is bigger and we need the space for all those endless bits and pieces you buy from tat shops.' She made as if to slap him, and he dodged her, laughing.

'Anyway, you rent, I own. Move back in with me. You know you want to.'

Her flat held no strong ties for her now. She realised she associated it very strongly with the past and Ed. Perhaps it would be a good thing to let it go. And it demonstrated again how serious he was about them being together. There was no hedging his bets this time with suggestions of holidays.

She grinned at him. 'Only if you promise to relinquish the remote control once in a while and make sure you put kitchen equipment away in its designated drawer.'

'Agreed,' he said.

They continued for a moment in silence. A comfortable silence. His fingers knitted loosely in hers. Her stomach was a mass of soft knots.

'Do you think I should have asked your dad's permission?' he asked her suddenly.

'Are you joking?' She looked up at him with an incredulous expression. 'We might be back in touch but the only person who makes decisions about *my* life is me.'

'With reference to me? And maybe our kids one day?'

She smiled up at him. 'Deal.'

* * * * *

SINGLE DAD, NURSE BRIDE
LYNNE MARSHALL

Lynne Marshall used to worry she had a serious problem with daydreaming, then she discovered she was supposed to write those stories! A late bloomer, Lynne came to fiction writing after her children were nearly grown. Now she battles the empty nest by writing stories which always include a romance, sometimes medicine, a dose of mirth, or both, but always stories from her heart. She is a Southern California native, a dog lover, a cat admirer, a power walker and an avid reader.